Books by Dave Benbow

DAYTIME DRAMA

Books by Jon Jeffrey

BOYFRIEND MATERIAL

ALL I WANT FOR CHRISTMAS
(with Chris Kenry, William J. Mann and Ben Tyler)

Books by Ben Tyler

TRICKS OF THE TRADE

HUNK HOUSE

GAY BLADES

SUMMER SHARE
(with Chris Kenry, William J. Mann and Andy Schell)

ALL I WANT FOR CHRISTMAS
(with Jon Jeffrey, Chris Kenry and William J. Mann)

Books by Sean Wolfe

MASTERS OF MIDNIGHT
(with Michael Thomas Ford, William J. Mann and Jeff Mann)

Published by Kensington Publishing Corporation

Man of My Dreams

Dave Benbow

Jon Jeffrey

Ben Tyler

Sean Wolfe

KENSINGTON BOOKS
http://www.kensingtonbooks.com

KENSINGTON BOOKS are published by

Kensington Publishing Corp.
850 Third Avenue
New York, NY 10022

All Kensington titles, imprints and distributed lines are available at special quantity discounts for bulk purchases for sales promotion, premiums, fund-raising, educational or institutional use.

Special book excerpts or customized printings can also be created to fit specific needs. For details, write or phone the office of the Kensington Special Sales Manager: Kensington Publishing Corp., 850 Third Avenue, New York, NY 10022. Attn. Special Sales Department. Phone: 1-800-221-2647.

Kensington and the K logo Reg. U.S. Pat. & TM Off.

ISBN 0-7582-0615-1

First Kensington Trade Paperback Printing: February 2004
10 9 8 7 6 5 4 3 2 1

Printed in the United States of America

Contents

OUT OF BOUNDS

Dave Benbow

For Dave Kopay . . .
Being first is never easy.

Before

Wade Smith sighed and rubbed his temples. He now understood completely why he had begun to find stray gray hairs in his dark brown locks at only thirty-two years of age. The stress.

He was scanning through some escrow papers, spotted a couple of typos the lender made, and again silently prayed the deal would go through. He really liked the clients involved, Ted and Jim, a terrific couple trying to buy their first home. They had just adopted a two-year-old Chinese girl, and needed more space and a yard.

Even though they had a few dings on their credit, Wade had done everything in his power to make this one stick. He had called the lender five times massaging the paperwork through, but it was *still* up in the air. He had hoped to be able to call the two men and tell them they got the house today. Those were always the best phone calls.

Funny, he thought as he shut his tired, dark brown eyes. *I always get wrapped up in the deals I make no money on.* He rubbed his eyes gently to relieve the eye strain. When he opened them, he casually took in his surroundings. He pushed his ergonomic chair away a bit from his desk and leaned back. He reached up and clasped his hands behind his head.

He liked his new office.

He'd better. He was still in debt over two hundred thousand dollars because of it.

Wade was considered one of the top rising Realtors in L.A., and had opened his own boutique brokerage a little over a year ago. He had hated working for the large conglomerate real estate company in Beverly Hills that had been his home for six years, and decided to take the plunge and put out his own shingle.

He had found space in a small complex on Robertson Boulevard, near the perennially trendy restaurant, Morton's. Centrally located right between West Hollywood and Beverly Hills, it was also close to his small house a few blocks away.

His new space had a narrow reception room, two agent's offices, and a small conference room that also doubled as the kitchen. A tiny but efficient bathroom was just off the main hallway.

His own office was purposely not any more elaborate than the outer reception area. A clean-lined, glass-topped desk, complete with new iMac computer and all the trappings needed for business, was placed in front of the shuttered window that overlooked the alley. Two comfortable guest chairs were positioned opposite his desk, and a small love seat of contrasting color was against the far wall, flanked by built-in cabinets and shelves that Sam, his contractor, had built.

The other agent's office, next door, was empty until Wade felt he could afford to bring in someone else. He hoped to be able to do that by the end of this year. So right now, it was just him and Susan, his former assistant from the Beverly Hills real estate company, who had agreed to a fifteen percent pay cut to come work for him at his own office.

Wade had closed three houses the week prior, two in Beverly Hills, and one in Nichols Canyon. All three were multimillion dollar sales. The commissions would be great, but seeing the small four hundred thousand dollar home sale go through for Ted and Jim would be so much more satisfying for Wade. He liked helping out the little guys.

The phone on his crowded and uncharacteristically messy desk buzzed. He flicked the switch that allowed the hands-free headset he wore to become active.

"Yes, Susan?"

"Ohmigod! You will *never* believe who is holding for you!"

"No, I can't. Who?"

"Colton Jennings! Line three! He sounds so sexy on the phone!"

Susan was audibly excited by this news. As a single, straight woman working in West Hollywood, she took her thrills where she could get them. And personally talking to Colton Jennings, the good-looking and mega-rich NFL star quarterback was definitely a thrill.

"Colt? Jesus, I haven't talked to him in years."

There was a brief pause on the line. "You *know* Colton Jennings? How? You never told me this!"

"There are many mysteries about me that you haven't figured out yet," Wade said, teasing his pretty and extremely competent assistant.

"Ha! Name one other."

"Later. Let me get this call." Wade took a deep breath and punched the blinking line. "Wade Smith," he said in his best Realtor's voice.

"Wade? Is that you? How are ya, buddy!" came the booming, masculine voice that Wade instantly recognized as Colton Jennings's.

"I'm good, I'm good! What's it been? Six, seven years?"

"Mmm . . . more like ten, I think."

"Wow. Hey, congratulations on your move to L.A. From what I understand, the Quakes definitely need you. They sure sucked last season." Wade silently hoped Colt wouldn't ask him any real questions about the new local NFL team, the Los Angeles Earthquakes. Though Wade always kept up with what Colton Jennings was doing, he didn't really keep up with local sports.

"Yeah, well, we'll see. Don't know if I'm going to like L.A. I'm just a small town boy at heart."

"Are you here now? Where are you staying?" Wade felt his face begin to flush, and he actually began to tremble a little bit as it sunk in that he was actually talking to his boyhood idol.

Susan opened the door to his office and confidently strode in and plopped down onto the guest chair opposite him. She strained to listen to every word coming over the phone. Wade covered the mouthpiece and mouthed the word *Snoop!* to her. She nodded eagerly.

"I'm at the Four Seasons. Look. My mom and your mother still talk, and Mom told me that you're a big deal real estate wizard now."

"Well . . . I do okay."

"I need a house," the famous quarterback stated. "Something private with a yard. And a pool. Why live in L.A. if you don't have a pool?"

"Rent or buy?"

"Buy. The Jennings don't rent anymore." There was a tinge of pride in this statement.

Wade began to scribble the info down. "What do you want to spend?"

"I don't know. I understand that real estate prices here are through the roof. A few mil? Maybe more if I really like the place."

"Hills, or beach?"

"Can I see a few of each?"

"Sure, but beach will cost more, for less square footage, and a long drive, so be forewarned. Any particular features you want? Hot tub? Walk-in closets? Does Cindy cook? A gourmet kitchen? Fifty-car garage? Nursery? What?"

There was a quiet pause on the phone, then Colt cleared his throat. "Um, no. This house will just be for me. Cindy and I are splitting up. She's staying in Dallas." Cindy Canter Jennings was Colt's wife. They had been high school sweethearts and had stayed together all the way through college, and were often touted as the NFL dream couple. They even had several commercial endorsements contracts together.

"Oh, Colt, I'm sorry . . . I didn't know." Wade suddenly felt very awkward. Why was he so nervous talking to this man? He dealt with millions of dollars a day, and with some of the most important people in Los Angeles, but the mere sound of his childhood friend's voice turned him to jelly.

Colt cleared his throat again. "No one does. We just decided about a month ago. She's . . . met someone . . ." There was an odd lilt to the man's voice that revealed his vulnerability about the subject.

"Colt, I'm so sorry. If there's anything I can do . . ."

"Thanks. Just find me a kick-ass house. I'm about to be a bachelor again. I'm gonna start a whole new life."

"When do you want to meet?"

"I'm not doing anything today."

Wade cringed. His day was completely packed. Showings, some paper signings, then he had a spin class at BarBell at seven. "Wow, Colt, I'd like to, but I'm booked solid today."

"Oh." Colt sounded disappointed. "Well, let me take you to dinner, then. I'm sick of hotel food. That's all I ever eat. On the road, in Dallas, here. I'm sick of it. Besides, I'd like to see you. It'd be good to catch up."

"I'd like that, really I would, but I have to teach a spin class tonight at seven. I won't be done until eight, eight-thirty."

"You teach? A spin class? What is that, that thing where you pedal those little bikes for a few minutes?"

Wade laughed. "It's a little more than that. Especially *my* class."

"Is the real estate business so tough you have to work two jobs?"

Wade laughed again. "No. I took the classes for so long, that when one of the instructors called in sick, I led the class, then I started filling in and now I have a regular gig on Mondays, Wednesdays, and Fridays. I mean, I obviously don't do it for the money. It's more of a stress reliever for me. I just like teaching."

"Wow. Wade Smith works out? The times have changed." Wade could feel the mirth coming through the line. "You used to never do anything physical. You used to say it was all stupid. Only for, what was it you said? Oh, yeah. Only for 'thick-headed Neanderthals.'"

Wade blushed. "Yeah, well, like you say, the times have changed. So have I. I teach a great class. My students sweat their guts out."

"Oh . . . Think you could make me sweat?"

Wade was momentarily stunned at the question. His first response was something completely inappropriate, and he forced the thought from his mind. "I bet I could. I doubt you'd make it through the entire hour."

"Sounds like a challenge. And you know I never back down from a challenge."

"So I remember."

"All right. I'll take your little pissant class, then I'll take you to dinner afterwards. We can catch up and you can fill me in on what I'm gonna hafta spend to live the good life here."

Wade shifted in his seat and looked at Susan helplessly. "Um, that'd be great, Colt, but I have to tell you something . . . I mean, um . . ."

"Yeah? What is it?"

"Um . . . Well, you see . . . Oh, nothing." Wade sighed heavily. "Got a pen? I'll give you the gym info." Susan held a hand up to her mouth to stifle her laughter at her boss's sudden unease.

"Yeah, hang on," Colt said. "It's going to be hilarious to see you in action."

Again, words came to Wade's lips that he had to swallow. "Er, good . . ." He then gave his old friend the address and told him what to bring and wear, then they hung up. Wade stared at Susan in shock.

"Well? What? He's going to go?" she asked, almost busting.

"Yeah."

"So what's wrong? You look sick."

Wade looked at his assistant and rolled his eyes. "I should have told him . . ."

"Told him what?"

"That the gym I'm sending him to is pretty much all gay. I tried, but I just couldn't say it. How stupid was that?"

Susan laughed out loud. "I'm sure he'll figure it out pretty quick." She suddenly narrowed her eyes. "You don't think he's . . ." She let the sentence hang.

"Colt? God, no! No. I've known him since we were, like, twelve. He's a man's man, no doubt about that."

Susan look relieved. "Well, I wouldn't miss this for the world! Count me in. I'm coming to your class tonight, too."

Wade's eyebrows shot up. "Oh, sure, *now* you want to take my class. I've been pestering you for months to come."

"You didn't have Colton Jennings in your class before," she sassed back, batting her eyelashes. "Did I hear him say he's getting divorced? That's huge! They're like Mr. and Mrs. All-American."

"I guess so, but Suse, don't tell anyone about that. I got the feeling it wasn't general knowledge yet."

"Set him up with me, and no problem!" Susan put her hand to her chest and breathed in deeply. Colton Jennings! He was just about the hottest quarterback ever. He had just been selected as the "Sexiest Man Alive" by *People* magazine, and was a regular on the covers of *Men's Fitness*, *GQ* and *Esquire*. Colton Jennings was that great combination of physical beauty, rugged strength and raw manliness that made women want to bed him, and men want to be like him.

Yes, Susan's active imagination was already working overtime. She and Colton were ravishing each other in her condo's hot tub, and Colt was just about to part her open and slide in when Wade's voice brought her back to down to planet Earth.

"Clear my schedule for tomorrow. I'm gonna need at least the entire afternoon to show Colt around. Call my dentist and cancel my morning appointment, and see if you can get me a lunch reservation at the Ivy. Mmm, around one, okay? Use his name if mine doesn't get us the table."

"You got it." Susan got up to leave, but stopped. "I can't get over the fact that you know Colt Jennings!"

Wade shrugged. "We grew up together in Texas. I thought I'd told you all this."

"Nope." Susan pointed her finger at him. "You aren't keeping any other secrets from me, are you?"

"Please. You buy my condoms and lube. You end up talking to the guys I date more than me, though I can't even remember the last time I *had* a date. You know as much, if not more, about me as I do." He grinned.

Susan nodded solemnly. "That's true." She winked, and left his office, closing the door quietly behind her.

Wade knew he needed to get back to work, but he couldn't focus on anything other than Colt. It had been a monumental surprise to hear from his boyhood friend.

He had read in the paper that the star quarterback's contract was up with the Dallas Cowboys. He had decided not to renew with them and instead, had become a free agent. The Earthquakes had jumped at the chance to pick him up. His huge, multimillion dollar contract had inspired countless jokes by newspaper columnists and drive-time radio disc jockeys, but the whole Los Angeles sports community was ecstatic that he was going to help bring the Quakes up out of the toilet.

Colton Jennings.

Just thinking about him had the curious effect of getting Wade aroused. Embarrassed by the physical reaction to thoughts of his childhood friend, he reached down and tugged at his carefully pressed slacks to free up his hardening cock.

Oh, hell. Who was he kidding? Wade'd had a crush on Colt since the first day he'd met him, over nineteen years before . . .

*   *   *

"Get him!"

"Faggot!"

"Faggotty faggot!"

Wade hurdled the low hedge with the ease of an Olympian. This actually surprised the charging boy because athletic was not a word usually used to describe Wade. Even more shocking, he landed on both feet, and was able to keep on running. His glasses were starting to fog over from his physical exertion, making it difficult to see. He had been running for more than five minutes, an eternity to the chubby little boy. Puffing, and feeling like his heart would surely burst at any second, he rounded the corner of Woodrow Way and Stoneybrook Drive, and kept going.

"I'm gonna kick your butt!" yelled Billy Hanson. He was in close pursuit, and his henchboys, Stuart Beaver, Tim Benton and Steve Crawford were close on his heels. Arms pumping, and legs straining, they too easily hurdled the low shrubs of the Smithers' front yard. They were gaining on Wade, and were supremely confident in their abilities to catch him.

So was Wade. He knew he was no match for the four stars of the neighborhood Pop Warner football league.

Why hadn't he just given them the money? It was only a dollar, and he had five more. But even to a twelve-year-old, extortion was wrong. That, and he didn't want to part with a sixth of his total financial worth. There was a cool Buick Le Sabre model kit at the 7-Eleven he wanted to get with the six bucks, and if he gave one away, then he wouldn't have enough and he'd have to wait until next week's allowance. A whole week!

His already rosy cheeks were now bright red, and his unruly thick brown hair was plastered to his face by sweat. Dark eyes squinted behind the misty lenses as he tried to figure out the best way to escape his own personal lynch mob.

He cut across the Grangers' lawn, and raced toward Mrs. Stone's vacant place, hoping against hope the back gate was open, as it usually was. He could cut through that backyard, climb over a chain link fence and then be in the safety of his own property.

He rounded the back of the Stone house, and found to his immense dismay that the gate was closed. He would lose valuable time either trying to open it, or running around the front of the house.

"We got him!" hooted Billy, triumphant in his twelve-year-old victory. "He's trapped at the Stone house!"

Wade grabbed the handle of the redwood gate door and pulled hard. It wouldn't open. He shook the door hoping to magically jar it free.

No such luck.

He turned around just as he was surrounded by the other panting boys.

"I'm gonna kick your ass," Billy growled, surprising Wade with his bad language. "Then, I'm gonna take all your money." He walked over to the scared boy, breathing hard in front of him. He knew Wade was no challenge to his greater strength, but his gang was watching so he had to follow through with his threat. Billy pulled back a fist and punched Wade in the gut with a hard right.

"Oouppphhh!" Wade grunted, doubling over.

The other kids began to laugh.

"He's so fat, I can't believe he even felt that," Stuart laughed. "Hit him again."

"Faggot!" Billy yelled as he punched him again. "Fat faggot!"

Hot tears filled Wade's eyes, and he tried to hold them back. He knew he would be forever ruined and called a crybaby if he shed one tear, but he didn't see how he could stop them.

"Give me your money, faggot," Billy demanded, drawing his fist back for a third time.

Sniffling, Wade dug into his pocket and pulled out the crumpled bills. He held them out, shaking.

"What's going on?"

Wade spun around to the new voice behind him.

Standing there was a tall, solidly built boy of about his same age, a questioning look on his face. There was something about his presence that caused all the boys present to instantly respect him.

"Hey." Billy's insincere smile was all teeth. "Nothing." His three henchboys each took a step back.

"Nothing? Doesn't look like nothing to me." The tall boy came all the way out of Mrs. Stone's gated backyard. Apparently, he had been playing there. He was wearing a pair of old cutoff shorts and a ratty-looking T-shirt. He looked tough and scrappy, even for a twelve-year-old. His sun-

bleached blond, almost white, hair was sticking up in all directions from his roughhousing, and his square jaw was clenched.

"Fat faggotty Wade here owes me some money," Billy said, pointing at the tearful, chubby boy.

"I do not! They told me to pay them a dollar or they were gonna beat me up!" Wade protested.

The new boy drew himself up to his full height, which was at least four inches taller than Billy. Not to mention about twenty pounds heavier.

"Is that true?"

Billy suddenly smiled an oily smile and slapped his knee. "Aww, hell, no. We were just joking around. Having some fun. We wasn't really gonna take his money, were we guys?" *He faced the others who all nodded automatically.*

"Uh-huh." *The new boy took a protective step in front of Wade.* "Well, fun's over."

"Sure, sure. What's your name?"

"Colton Jennings. But everyone just calls me Colt." *He looked at each of the boys to see if anyone was going to dare to make fun of his name.*

No one dared.

"You just move in?" *asked Billy.*

"Yep. Today." *He didn't say anything else. He just stared at the boys, who began to grow uncomfortable.*

"Well, let's go guys," *Billy said as he glared at Wade. Wade got the message:* This isn't over, yet!

Ignoring Wade, the four boys said good-bye to the new kid, and slunk away. Only then did Wade see the dilapidated pickup truck parked in the driveway. A tall, burly blond man was unloading various boxes into the house.

Wade wiped the sweat from his brow. "Thanks," *he managed to say.*

"Sure. No problem. They're jerks."

"I didn't know Mrs. Stone had sold this house."

Colt blushed, and looked down at the ground. "She didn't. She's letting us . . . um, rent it," *he said.*

"Oh . . . I'm Wade. Wade Smith. I live over there," *Wade said, pointing to his house, right behind Colt's.*

"Yeah, Gramma said there was a kid my age living there. I'm glad. We used to live in an old apartment complex that didn't have many other *kids. I didn't have anyone to hang out with." Colt gave his neighbor one of the amazing smiles that always dazzled anyone within the vicinity of it. Wade was no exception.*

"Gramma?"

"Mrs. Stone. She's my gramma. We're staying here . . . for a while."

"Oh." Wade found it odd that he couldn't quite catch his breath. And it wasn't just from the near death experience he'd just had. Somewhere in the dim, far reaches of his mind, he knew it was because of his new neighbor. He didn't fully understand it, and he didn't know what it meant, but he felt a strong attraction to the handsome blond boy.

It was very confusing.

"Well, I guess I need to get home," Wade said.

"Okay." Colt shot a lonely glance at his new house.

"You wanna come over to my house and go swimming? We have a pool."

"Sure! Uh . . . can I wear these?" The new boy looked down at his ragged shorts. "I don't have a bathing suit." Embarrassment colored his cheeks red.

"No problem."

Colt flashed a another pearly smile, and followed Wade into his backyard.

Wade leaned back in his office chair and smiled to himself as he recalled the fun they'd had that summer. He hadn't thought about those happy days in years.

He and Colt had become fast friends and did everything together. Both of Colt's parents worked long hours, so he had been alone a lot of the time. The sturdy boy had latched onto Wade and his family like glue. Wade had heard his mother whisper to his father once that Colt's dad "drank," though Wade had no idea at the time what that meant.

Colt had also been very ashamed of the precarious financial status of his family, Wade recalled. The Jennings always seemed to be struggling, and Colt never had new clothes, although the scrappy young boy never said a word about it. None of that had mattered to Wade. He was happy to bathe in the glow that was Colt. To Wade, Colt was a god.

Then the summer ended.

School started back up, and Wade, hardly the most popular kid in school, watched as his friend began to slip away. Colt joined the football team and had practice after school every day. He started to hang out with the cool jock kids and spent less and less time with Wade.

Wade remembered how it hurt when he'd see Colt hanging out in the halls laughing and joking with his new friends. Friends that included all the kids that had chased him the day he first met Colt.

Ah, well, the grownup Wade thought as he sat in his seven hundred dollar designer office chair. *That was a long time ago.*

Wade tried to force himself back into his work mode, but his mind kept drifting back to the star football player. Giving in to an impulse, he pulled open the bottom drawer of his desk and rifled through the real estate catalogs that were stored there. Finding what he was searching for, he pulled the Sexiest Man Alive issue of *People* out, and stared again at his school-age friend.

Colt Jennings, tall, broad and blond, was leaning sexily against a tractor, his red cotton shirt unbuttoned and open, showing off a set of rock hard pecs and a light matting of clipped chest hair that barely covered deeply cut abs. His faded jeans were painted on, his crotch full and mesmorizing. Massive quads and hamstring muscles strained the denim fabric to its design limits. The ball player was staring straight ahead through impossibly blue eyes, giving a patented Colt Jennings sexy grin, a small sprig of hay jutting out from between his even, white teeth. A beat-up straw cowboy hat was jauntily cocked on his golden head.

Wade sighed.

He flipped through the well worn pages of the magazine, and found the accompanying article. There were more pictures of Colt: Colt in his Cowboys uniform on the playing field, Colt in the locker room, Colt doing some network color commentary at last year's Super Bowl, and Colt with his stunningly perfect wife, Cindy. She was thin and blond and as dazzling in her way as Colt was in his. They were sitting in their luxurious Highland Park living room surrounded by beautiful antiques. Colt had certainly come up in the world.

So he and Cindy were getting divorced. That's big news, Wade idly thought.

Susan wasn't wrong when she called the Jennings Mr. & Mrs. All-

American. The Jennings were a golden couple, appeared on countless magazine covers and did commercials for five different products. Those advertising promotions brought the couple millions of dollars per year. Colt's face was as recognizable now as Joe Namath's was at his height of fame.

But then, Colt was always comfortable in front of a camera. . . .

"Look, Wade. Colt's in the paper again." Wade's plump mother tossed the folded back newspaper on the kitchen table, and let him have a look. Sure enough, there was another picture of West Houston High's own in full football gear, helmet off, on the shoulders of his fellow teammates. He had a huge smile plastered on his face, and his blond hair literally was a golden halo around his head.

Colt had led the team to another big win and was being held aloft like the god he was. Wade actually sighed staring at the black and white photograph. The article was about the West Houston Tigers' big game that night. If the Tigers won, and everyone expected Colt to lead them to victory, then they would advance to the state finals, and possibly the state championship. Wade slipped the paper into his backpack for later perusal and staring.

"Bye, Mom," he said, rising to his feet. He kissed his mother on the cheek and dashed out the back door. If he timed it right, he might get to walk to school with his hero.

If not, then he'd have to face the gauntlet by himself.

He ran around the backyard and pulled back the busted piece of chain link that allowed him to pass into the Jennings's backyard. He tapped on the smudged sliding glass door. Colt, sitting alone at the scuffed kitchen table, waved him in.

"Hey," he said, a mouthful of Eggo waffle muffling his voice.

"Hey."

Colt looked to see if his mother was nearby listening. She wasn't. His dad had left at five A.M. for his job at the oil refinery, so he wasn't around, either. "Did you do my paper?" he whispered.

Wade nodded. "Yeah. You'll get an A, no sweat."

Colt rolled his eyes heavenward. "Thanks, man. If I flunk out of Potter's class, I'm off the team!"

Wade snorted. "Yeah. Right. Like they would let that *happen!*"

Colt thought for a moment. "I guess you're right." He shrugged. He crammed another forkful of food into his mouth, and swallowed. "Later, Mom!" he shouted as he grabbed his backpack.

Colt was wearing a pair of faded Wrangler jeans that hugged his young, hard ass perfectly, and a pair of worn K-Swiss sneakers. He had on an old, tight Adidas T-shirt that left nothing to the imagination. His pumped up pecs were tempting mounds of hard muscle, and the indents of his abdominals were clearly seen. His shaggy blond hair was haphazardly combed and looked bed tousled. He was already six feet even, and still growing.

Wade, who, by the time he was fourteen, had figured out what his sexual orientation was, had to force himself not to stare at Colt with lust in his eyes. He hadn't yet told anyone about his "feelings."

Not that the meaner kids at school hadn't figured it out. He was routinely called "faggot" or even worse, "Gaydie Wadie." He would be walking down the school hall, and out of nowhere, from behind a classroom door, he'd hear "Hey, it's Gaydie Wadie." Or he'd be walking home alone from school, and a group of kids would dash past him and knock him down, screaming names at him and laughing.

Sometimes it was all Wade could do just to work up the energy to go to school, knowing he would be ridiculed and harassed at some point before the day was through. He was too ashamed to tell his parents about the taunting at school. His father was often gone on business, and his mother, like Mrs. Jennings, was one of the few in the neighborhood that worked. Wade's parents liked to think their family was perfect. They had no clue that their only child was the joke of his school.

Compounding Wade's social problem was the fact that he had not shed his baby fat as his parents had hopefully predicted. He weighed a hundred and sixty-five pounds and was still only five feet two inches. He prayed nightly that he would have a growth spurt while he slept. So far, it hadn't happened.

His hair had only gotten more bushy as he aged, and now he barely combed it, preferring to let it wig out with a bit of mousse and gel. His glasses were now thick black frames, just like the kind Elvis Costello wore. Wade thought they were cool. The kids at school thought they couldn't be geekier.

He loved to wear his black Converse high-tops with his Wranglers. The Wranglers never looked as good on him as they did on Colt, though, and that was frustrating.

"Say, Colt . . . um . . . can I walk with you to school today?" Wade forlornly asked. If he showed up at school with the football star, he might not be teased so bad today.

Colt looked uncomfortable. He actually liked Wade. Well, sorta liked. He now considered Wade a great summer friend, full of stories, ideas and always willing to do something different and all, but Colt was painfully aware that his friend was not socially acceptable at school.

Both sides of Colt's conscience did battle. Finally, realizing that the paper Wade had done for him would guarantee him a passing grade in history, he decided to throw the fat kid a bone.

"Sure," he said magnanimously. "Let's rock and roll." Colt slid open the glass door and walked outside. He slung his used backpack over his shoulder in a cool way that Wade had actually practiced to copy. Wade scurried after him.

"Is Cindy going to ask you to Sadie Hawkins?" Wade said, when he caught up with the football hero. Cindy Canter was the prettiest girl at West Houston High. She was a cheerleader, freshman and sophomore homecoming queen, and Colt's girlfriend.

Colt shrugged. "Sure. Who else would she ask?"

"We have a pep rally today don't we?"

Colt groaned. "I hate those fuckin' things. Cindy came over yesterday to get more fuckin' baby pictures. You're not gonna believe what they're making us do. I'm sure I'll see my baby face plastered on signs all over the fuckin' hallways. Ugh. I hate having to stand up in the auditorium while all those pep squad girls scream at us to pump us up."

"Really? It looks so cool. . . ." Wade was painfully aware that he'd never be on the school stage being cheered for anything.

Colt was a West Houston High School icon, a hero to almost everyone, teachers and classmates alike. He was the most popular guy at school. His record as captain of the JV football team was unparalleled in the school's history, and he was personally leading the Tigers to the all-state finals. There was no doubt he'd be captain of the varsity squad the next year as well. Quite a feat for an incoming junior.

"Man, I hate walkin' to school," Colt said, changing the subject. "I

asked them last night again about that box boy opening at Safeway, but Pop won't let me take it. He says sports are enough. He says I have to concentrate on football so I can get a scholarship to college."

Colt's sixteenth birthday was only a week away and all he could think about was getting his driver's license. He had badgered his parents for over a year, pleading with them to let him get a part-time job, so he could buy his first car. "Pop says that if I play well in college, then I can turn pro and make all kinds of money."

"I know! You're going to be the best quarterback in the NFL ever, you wait and see!"

Actually, Wade secretly knew Colt was getting exactly what he wanted. Colt's mother had asked him months before what car her son would like and Wade had agonized over making the right suggestion. He finally told them to get a Firebird.

They had found a seven-year-old model with high mileage, but after getting it checked out by a mechanic, Colt's father grudgingly bought it. What Wade didn't know was that Colt's old man had worked double shifts at the refinery for over four months to come up with the extra cash. The car was sitting in Wade's garage now, a big red bow placed on the well-waxed hood.

"Damn, I'm so sick of walking to school," Colt repeated. "I want to drive!" Unconsciously, he picked up the pace.

Wade began to puff, trying to keep up. "I know! It'd be cool to drive wherever we want!"

"Uh, right. . . . Say, I'm gonna run on ahead. I'll see you in English. Oh! My paper!" Colt stopped and waited while Wade dug through his overstuffed backpack, pulling out binders, textbooks, spiral notebooks and various loose papers. Finally finding the report, he yanked it out and handed it to the handsome youth.

Colt glanced it over. "Thanks! See ya later!" He took off running, quickly leaving Wade behind.

Wade looked around hopefully to see if anyone had seen them enter the school property together.

No one had.

He sighed. Just as he entered the front door of the school and was trying to restuff his backpack, Billy Hansen appeared by his side and shot a hand forward. This action knocked Wade's books and backpack to the ground. His papers scattered everywhere, and all the kids in the immediate vicinity laughed. Wade bent down to pick up his schoolwork, and Billy began to laugh louder.

"Look! Gaydie Wadie's so fat, his butt's coming out of his jeans!"

Horrified, Wade jerked up and tried to tuck his shirt back in where it had come out of the back of his pants. He managed to scatter his belongings around a second time.

He gritted his teeth, and barely managed to stifle the hot tears that seemed ready to drop from his dark eyes. This time, he bent at the knees to gather his scattered books and papers. Just as he got the last piece of paper up, he noticed Colt lounging against a wall next to the still laughing Billy. Colt pretended not to see him.

The day passed quickly, and before he knew it, Wade was sitting with some others from the math club at the back of the school auditorium. The pep squad was clapping furiously while the rest of the student body halfheartedly joined in. Soon the lights dimmed, and the floodlights on the stage came up. The cheerleaders all came out dressed like babies. They were sporting large baggy diapers, oversize baby blankets and held huge fake baby bottles.

Each of the slim girls wore a mask made up of an oversize blown-up baby picture of each player. Some of the photos were hilarious, and the audience roared with laughter. Cindy Canter was, of course, wearing a Colt Jennings mask.

The girls waddled around the stage and performed a few cheers as babies. Then the announcer came on and announced each player's name. As each name was called, a burly jock would saunter cockily out of the wings and walk across the stage to much cheering and screaming by the whipped up crowd. Each of these players was also wearing a diaper.

And nothing else.

The girls in the crowd went wild as the half-naked boys strutted their stuff across the dusty stage floor. Each player paired up with his baby-faced cheerleader so the audience could see who belonged to which baby picture.

Even Wade had to laugh, but his stomach began to twist in suspenseful knots. Colt hadn't been called yet, and Wade knew he'd be the last

*player announced. He couldn't wait to see his idol come out and walk
across the stage half-naked. Though Wade saw the ball player all summer long running around the neighborhood clad only in shorts, there was
something extremely erotic about knowing he was going to see Colt shirtless at school. The suspense was killing him. Wade wished he had a better seat so he could see more clearly.*

*At last, the announcer, who was actually the assistant coach, paused
dramatically. "And now . . . He's number three on the field, but he's number one with us . . . Your junior varsity captain . . . COLT JENNINGS!"*

*The thunderous cheer that followed this announcement was almost
ear piercing. Colt swaggered out in his droopy diaper and bowed. He had
to hold up the thickly folded rag so it didn't fall down around his knees.
Sensing the crowd was eating this up, he began to play it up a little. He
waddled around, play sucked his thumb (something that almost caused
Wade to pass out), and generally cut up as only a school god can. His an-
tics brought even greater cheers and finally Cindy came over to show the
audience that he was her baby face. The picture was like that of a Gerber
baby. Perfect and bright eyed, the baby could only have been Colt.*

*Cindy handed Colt a mike, and now it was time for him to say a few
words. The audience quieted down to hear him speak.*

*"Well, thanks, y'all, for coming today! I just want to say we've got the
best dang team in Texas, and we're gonna prove it tonight!" The crowd
cheered at this. "We're gonna kick the Panthers' as—er, butts, and bring
home the championship!" More cheering. "So, come on out tonight and
support us as we win another big game! Yeah!" There was much whoop-
whooping and the audience came to its feet to sing the school song.*

Wade hoped no one noticed the hard-on in his too-tight Wranglers.

*Later that night, Wade climbed the concrete bleachers of the school
football field to man the video camera. One of his duties as a member of
the audio-visual club was to videotape all the Tigers' football games for
posterity. No one else in the club had wanted this task, and Wade had
jumped at the chance to be able to film Colt in action.*

*He fiddled with the camera, making sure all was in order when he was
joined by Twyla Jeeter, another member from the A-V club. They discussed the shots they wanted briefly, then settled in to tape the game.*

Twyla was also one of the school outcasts, a tall, skinny, Gothic figure all in black, with curly ringlets down to her waist, dyed blood red. She also had a major crush on Wade. He pretended he didn't notice.

After much cheering and screaming, the teams came on the field and soon the play started. Colt quickly set a high standard, and expertly led his team up and down the field. His passes were perfect, and were caught three out of four times. He even managed to complete a quarterback sneak in the third quarter, that scored a touchdown.

Colt was on fire. Every play he called was executed with precision, and his strength and team spirit were infectious, His teammates looked up to him and deservedly so. The Tigers easily won. After a cavalcade of photographers snapped countless pictures of the team hero, people started to go home.

After helping Twyla pack up and store the video equipment, Wade hung back so he could congratulate Colt, and see what he was doing after the game.

When the boys finally came out of the locker room, Wade was waiting. Colt was surrounded by his teammates, which included each of the boys that teased Wade mercilessly during the day.

Billy Hanson caught sight of him and scowled. He nudged his best friend Stuart and pointed at Wade.

"Hey, it's Gaydie Wadie," Billy said in a singsong voice. Stuart snickered.

Wade instantly began to feel uncomfortable.

This was a bad idea, *he thought. He started to back up. He just wanted to get away.*

"Yeah, hey, Gaydie Wadie," Stuart mimicked.

"Hey, Gaydie Wadie," said one of the other players.

Wade, face flushed, just froze and didn't know what to do. He was being humiliated in front of Colt, and the shame was more than he could bear.

"Guys. Cut it out." Colt's stern voice silenced the other boys. Now, everyone just stared at Wade.

"What do you want, Wade?" Colt asked him, jamming his hands into his jeans pockets. His letterman jacket was open showing his tight T-shirt, and his hair was still damp from his post-game shower. The quarterback smelled of a heady mixture of Old Spice and Irish Spring. He looked so sexy, Wade forgot to breathe.

"Uh, I . . . uh, just thought maybe . . . you'd like to get some food . . . or something . . ."

Colt looked at his teammates. "Um, we're all going to a party. Sorry, Wade."

"Yeah. Sorry, Gadie." Billy smirked.

The group of boys began to walk away, Colt in the middle. He never looked back at his friend.

"Jesus, Colt! Why do you even talk to that fag?" Billy asked contemptuously, as they moved on.

"I thought he was going to kiss you just now! It sounded like he was asking you on a date! What a fuckin' faggot!" hooted Stuart.

"Why do you hang out with that fag?" Billy pressed.

Colt shot a nervous glance back at Wade, then shrugged. "My mom makes me. She's friendly with his mom. She feels sorry for him."

Wade, who couldn't help but hear this, began to hyperventilate. He literally felt like he had been punched in the gut. His eyes filled up with hot, salty tears, and he slid back into the shadows, out of sight.

Wade returned phone calls as he maneuvered his new Land Rover Discovery II through the early evening traffic. He sometimes felt silly with the headgear of his hands-free cell phone. He wore the earpiece and extended microphone on his right ear, and he knew he must look like a deranged lunatic talking to himself as he drove around town. But, it was a great way to continue business out of the office, and every once in a while he felt a bit like Justin Timberlake performing in a sold-out concert. He'd even do a neck bob if there was a good tune blaring out of the stereo.

He'd had a trying day as one of the deals he thought was set in stone threatened to fall apart at the seams twenty minutes before the end of the business day. Quick work and an agreement by the buyers to up their last offer had saved it, but his clients had not been happy and had berated Wade for over thirty minutes.

Plus, he still hadn't heard on Ted and Jim's escrow. Deciding to check the office voice mail one last time before letting it go for the day, he was happily rewarded with the call informing him that it had indeed gone through.

He quickly punched up Ted and gave him the good news. Ted's shouts of joy to his partner were music to Wade's ears.

Sometimes it was great having this job.

He pulled into the parking lot of BarBell with eighteen minutes to spare before his class was supposed to start. He hadn't even picked out his music for tonight, something he tried to do beforehand at the office on class days. Plus, he was going to meet Colt for the first time in ten years.

Yeah. No pressure at all.

"Hey, Wade! Full class tonight," Carl, the front desk guy at West Hollywood's newest, hippest gym said, as Wade burst through the front doors. "And you won't believe who's here to take your class tonight!" Carl's eyes were shiny with excitement.

"Colt Jennings."

Carl's face fell. "How did you . . ."

"He's a friend of mine. He's a comp, okay?"

"Oh, Scotty already comped him. Gave him a free month's pass, too. Couldn't take his eyes off his ass as he did it, but there you go." Carl winked. Scott Gander was the very proud, very built, and very single, owner of BarBell.

"Where *is* Colt?" Wade asked, quickly scanning through the names on the sign-up sheet for his class.

Thank God, he thought, relieved. *Sharique is here tonight.*

Sharique was the hottest model in town, and used exclusively by the famous fashion designer Cameron Fuller. Her exquisite beauty was on full display in countless magazine ads and television commercials. Wade was so happy that she had come tonight. Colt would have a hot babe to stare at, and he might not notice the thirty gay men in class, drooling over him.

Carl nodded toward the rear of the gym. "Colt's in the men's locker room. You'll know that by the fact that the entire male population of the gym emptied out and managed to find some reason to be in the locker room as well."

"Oh, God," Wade groaned.

"Trust me, if I could get away from this damn desk, I'd be in there as well!" Carl winked again.

"I better go rescue him. Thanks." Wade waved, and crossed the lobby and entered the weight area of the gym. Groaning again to himself, he noticed that the after-work crowd was noticeably thinner tonight.

When he entered the locker room, he saw why.

They were all in here. Repeatedly combing their already perfect hair as they tried to steal glances in the mirrors, or having suddenly indepth conversations with other guys who were also dying to get a look at the famous football star in his skivvies. Or less.

Wade nodded to a few guys as he worked his way through the loitering crowds. He saw the back of Colt's head first, and felt his own heart jump. His pulse quickened and he suddenly felt very dry in the mouth. He paused just a second to gather his wits, when Colt happened to turn around and look right at him. There was a blank look at first, then the recognition came, and the quarterback broke out into a large grin.

"Wade!" He practically shouted. Like Moses parting the Red Sea, the pack of ogling men parted and Wade walked up to his idol.

"Hey, Colt." He held out his hand, and was shocked when Colt threw his massive arms around him and pulled him into a bear hug.

Much to the jealous dismay of every other man watching.

"It's so great to see you!" Colt said happily, after they separated. "Damn! Look at you! You look *amazing*! You lost so much weight!" Colt looked Wade up and down, and then up again.

Wade blushed. "I lost a few . . ."

"A *few*? I can't get over the change!" Colt said, shaking his head in amazement. The ball player had just taken off his shirt and had been removing his slacks when he had spied Wade. "Hey, where are your glasses?"

"Lasik surgery."

"Hell, buddy, you just look great! You should be really proud of yourself!" Colt grinned, and then, after an awkward pause, went back to his locker and continued to undress. Wade's own locker happened to be in the same row, and he dropped his bag and unbuttoned his shirt. He peeled it off trying not to look at Colt's amazingly hot chest.

"So, I told the guy at the sports store to give me what I'd need for this class of yours. I hope I got it all right," he said. He held up a pair of padded black bike shorts. "These scare me," he cracked.

"About twenty minutes in, you'll be so glad you have them." Wade said, smiling. He turned to face the football player.

Colt's eyes widened. "Damn, Wade." He whistled, staring at Wade's hard six pack of abs.

In fact, Wade's entire upper torso was the definition of fit. He had pumped up arms, that were actually more bulky on the tricep side than the biceps side, which had the great effect of making his arms seem larger than they actually were. His broad shoulders were thickly muscled, but not bunchy. His squarish pecs were hard from years spent on a flat bench, lifting. His back flared out in a tapered V-shape. Wade's pride and joy, though, were his abs. He worked them daily, and he always enjoyed the attention they got.

Fat faggotty Wade was only a dim memory. He'd been replaced by a hot, built, handsome man who turned heads every day.

"You could grate cheese on those," Colt commented dryly, studying Wade's midsection again. He then looked away and stripped off his underwear. His big, meaty ass was facing Wade, and Wade couldn't help but sneak a peek. It was *perfect*. He forced himself to look away, but not before he caught Colt glance back at him.

If Colt had been any other man, Wade would have thought he had looked back to see if Wade was checking him out. But that was crazy.

Wade unbuckled his pants and let them fall to the ground. He stepped out of them, and peeled off his Jocko briefs. He glanced up for just a sec, and again could have sworn Colt had just taken a quick glimpse at his package.

Well, I do look different, Wade thought. *He's probably just amazed at how thin I am.*

Wade pulled on his own pair of bike shorts, a white Los Angeles Sporting Club wife beater, and changed his socks. An expertly tied white bandana on his head completed his look.

"Hey, I got these shoes, too." Colt proudly showed Wade some Ricaro biking shoes. They were top of the line models.

Pretty extravagant for one class, Wade mused. "They're great, Colt. Same kind I use." Wade held up his own pair. Colt grinned. "Did you bring a bottle of water? I don't want you to get dehydrated."

The quarterback nodded, and pulled a two-liter bottle of designer water out from his locker.

Colt pulled on a loose tank top and then they shut their lockers and Wade led the big man through the locker room back out onto the gym floor. If Colt noticed the men gawking at him, he didn't show it.

Wade went up a wide central staircase to the upstairs cardio area, where the spin classroom was located, and Colt dutifully followed. Once in the bike room, where people were already claiming their bikes and warming up, Wade shouted out a hearty hello. There was much good-natured shouting back at him in reply.

"Colt," Wade called, finding a bike off to one side, in the second row. "How's this for you?"

Colt shrugged. "Fine."

"I'll set it up for you. Hop on." Wade adjusted the various levers to get a comfortable seat for Colt. The big man found clicking in and out of the stirrups with his new biking shoes great fun.

"This is how you increase the tension," Wade explained as he twisted the knob on the center of the crossbar. "And this is how you lessen it. Got it?"

Colt nodded.

"Okay. Have fun. . . . Go at your own pace. . . . Slow down if it gets too much."

"That'll be the day!" Colt chortled good-naturedly.

Wade got up on the raised platform that the teachers used and adjusted his own bike. He saw Susan enter and stake out a bike one row back and three over from Colt. She had put on what Wade knew was her best workout outfit, a cropped tee from Lisa Kline and tight Juicy Couture velour sweats. Wade winked at her. She waved back.

Now that Colt was settled on his bike, Wade could concentrate on his class. He pulled out his CD case and began flying through the plastic sleeves, pulling out CDs left and right. He loaded them into the stereo and soon had Deborah Cox's latest dance remix pumping out over the deafening sound system.

"Okay, folks," he shouted, to be heard over the music. "Let's rock and roll!"

Colt was slightly startled to hear Wade use his signature line, but he followed the rest of the class and began to pedal fast.

Ten minutes into the class Colt was sweating.

Twenty minutes into the class he was soaking wet and breathing hard.

Twenty-five minutes in, he had emptied half his water bottle, yet was dying for fluids.

Thirty minutes into the class Colt was afraid he'd have a heart attack if he continued to go at the pace Wade was setting.

The pro football player was a superior athlete, but he had never endured anything as rigorous as this. His legs ached from the abuse he was heaping on them. His ass was killing him from the constant up and down on the thinly padded seat, and his triceps were sorer than hell, because God only knew why.

Wade was a machine. His feet smoothly flew around and around in a blur that Colt couldn't believe. Wade's thickly muscled thighs and calves were completely fat free, it seemed to Colt, the musculature and veins clearly visible.

But the most remarkable thing Colt saw was the total command Wade had over this group of people. They were looking up to him with unabashed adoration on their faces. Wade was consoling when he knew the pace was hard, and congratulatory when the class achieved it. Wade had all the leadership qualities that Colt recognized as his own. He got these people inspired and excited to do what he wanted them to do.

Colt was a little taken aback by this new Wade. He was confident, earthy, and in control, not at all the somewhat sheepish nerd he had remembered him to be.

After the class was over, and Colt gratefully stopped the infernal peddling, he watched in surprise as half the students went up to Wade to thank him personally and tell him what a great class it had been. It reminded Colt of all the times, after a big game back in high school or college, that fans did the same thing to him. He smiled. It was nice to see Wade get a little recognition.

After speaking to each person, Wade worked his way over to Colt. As the popular spin teacher was talking to his students, he saw a couple of people go up to the burly football player and undoubtedly praise him for his gridiron triumphs. He witnessed Susan going up and introducing herself. Wade had to smile at that.

"Well?" he asked the sweating ball player, after kissing Susan good-bye. He held arms wide in a questioning pose.

"Hell, I've had harder Sunday strolls," Colt bragged with masculine bravado.

"Oh, really," Wade replied.

Colt grimaced as he bent over to pick up his sneakers, which he had tossed next to the bike after putting on his bike shoes. He then groaned. "*Fuck*, man. You kicked my ass, but good! I may never walk again."

Wade laughed at the proud man's admission. "Told ya. Tell you what; for being a good sport about it, I'll buy dinner tonight. You in the mood for anything particular?"

"I don't care what we eat, but, damn, I need more water." Colt held up his empty water bottle.

Wade tossed him his half full one. "Drink up."

The two men quickly showered, though Colt moved a little slower than Wade, and left the gym. Surprisingly, Colt didn't have a car because he'd had the hotel limo drop him off at the gym. So they both piled into Wade's Discovery II.

"Nice car. My wife has one of these," Colt said, buckling his seat belt.

"It's the official gay man's luxury SUV. So, what can I say? I'm a gay man who likes luxury." The flippant response just flew out of Wade's mouth before he thought about what he was saying. He just had outed himself to the football player.

Colt stared straight ahead, and didn't say anything.

Wade looked at him, a little nervous. "Sorry, I meant to tell you later at dinner."

Colt shook his head, and gulped. "Don't sweat it. . . . I actually already knew."

Wade started up the car and put it into gear. "Oh?"

Colt blushed and looked out the window. "Yeah, um . . . your mother told my mom a while back. Mom told me."

"Ah. There are no secrets from dear old Mom."

"Plus, *come on!* You teach at what has to be the gayest gym I've ever seen!" He laughed. "Hey, it's no big deal. I mean, I don't care or anything. Doesn't matter to me."

Wade exhaled and steered the big truck through the light Sunset

Boulevard traffic. "It's funny," he finally said, "all those years in high school of being called Gaydie Wadie and faggot must have took 'cause I sure am one now." He shot a glance at the burly football player next to him. "A *big* one," he joked.

"So, when did you really know? I mean, how did you find out . . ." Colt fumbled.

"I think I always knew. Ever since I was young." He stopped talking and looked embarrassed.

Colt noticed. "What?"

"Oh, nothing."

"No, what?"

Oh, fuck it, Wade thought. He took a deep breath. "I had the biggest crush on you. Man, I thought you hung the moon. I remember watching every one of your home games in college, and just *idolizing* you. Who didn't, right? Hell, you were the big man on campus."

Colt blinked a few times.

"Sorry. I didn't mean to make you uncomfortable. I mean, I was a horny young man. It was a *long* time ago."

Colt gave a half smirk. "I always knew."

"Well. Like I said. It was a long time ago. . . ."

"Tell me why we're here again? I hate football. These jock types always beat me up in high school," whined Mark as he delicately picked his way up the bleacher steps. "Then they'd come sniffing around my bedroom window at night, shit-faced drunk, wanting me to blow them. Or, even better, wanting to blow me." Mark took a second to scan the cheering crowd. Three rows up, he spied a cute frat boy who was obviously on a date with an overdressed sorority girl. The frat boy noticed Mark staring at him, and shot back a scowling once-over, then looked away.

"We're here because it's my turn to pick an activity. I pick this," Wade said, taking care not to spill his beer as he climbed up the steep, narrow steps.

Mark sighed dramatically. "Fine. But afterwards, I get to pick the restaurant. There's a new Indian place downtown. It's off Sixth Street, I think."

"Curry? I don't think so."

"Hey, if I have to sit through another stupid game featuring your personal dreamboat Colt Jennings, then you eat curry."

"Why do I hang out with you?"

"'Cause I'm the only gay friend you have that will sit through an entire football game."

Wade laughed. Mark wasn't that far off the mark. Ever since the two men had met at freshman orientation two years before, they had become fast friends. Wade saw Mark through countless bad relationships with boyfriends who were always attracted to him, but too afraid to be seen with him. Mark had a thing for straight-acting, frat boy types.

Mark was an interior design major, and flamboyant, to say the least. A huge fan of the Divine Miss M, he was never seen without wearing some sort of Bette Midler T-shirt. He liked to wear baggy painter's pants, which was good, because he was extremely thin and the pants helped to beef him up. His hair was a different color each week, and the leather wristband he sported was years ahead of its time.

Wade, studying the tickets, found their row, and the two young men gratefully found they had two seats on the aisle.

"What's dream lover's number again?" Mark asked, already bored.

"Three. Just like in high school. They did that for him when he took the scholarship here."

"Uh-huh, whatever. Look at that cute frat boy down there. Damn!"

"Sit down, Mark! You'll get us lynched." Wade reached up and pulled Mark down onto his hard metal bench seat.

The game started, and soon Wade was lost in thoughts of Colton Jennings and he watched the All-American throw the ball up and down the field. His arm rarely missed its mark, and by halftime, the Longhorns were up thirty-three to seven.

The University of Texas Marching Band came out and kicked off the halftime show. Mark got bored, and decided to go down and see what was happening outside the stadium. Wade stayed in his seat rifling through his game program, staring at the black and white picture of Colt. He adjusted his new frameless wire glasses to see better.

Colt had put on some serious weight since joining the University of Texas Longhorns. He was probably now around two hundred and thirty pounds, and it was all muscle. His cocky grin leapt off the page and Wade cautiously allowed his mind to wander.

Mark returned about twenty minutes later, a satisfied smirk on his face. "Guess what?" he whispered conspiratorially.

"What?"

"Guess who just hit on me, and wants to see me later tonight?" He crossed his arms triumphantly.

"Oh, no," groaned Wade. "Not that frat guy we passed . . ."

"You mean, Kyle?" Mark batted his eyes.

"Christ. Here we go again."

Ignoring the pained expression on Wade's face, Mark prattled on. "He came up to me outside the men's room. Said he liked my T-shirt. Hello? Dead giveaway! Then I said I liked his jeans, and what was in 'em."

"You didn't!" Wade was shocked.

Mark nodded. "I did. He blushed, then whispered he would like to see me after some frat party he had to go to. I gave him my number. I'll be doing him by two A.M."

"Or vice versa."

"God, I hope! Did you see his bulge? Tasty!" Mark winked.

Wade sighed. "Well at least one of us will be getting laid."

"Well, if you'd just give up your fantasy guy, you could, too."

Wade looked at him. "What are you talking about?"

Mark waved his hands in front of his face. "Oh, please, Mary. You don't even consider dating a guy if he doesn't look like Mr. America, down there." He waved toward where the Longhorns had come back out onto the field. Colt's sweaty blond head was easily visible.

"That's not true!" Wade protested.

"Hello? Ken? Blaine? Jacob? All of them were tall, built, blond boys. Just like you know who. My friend Mike wants to go out with you so bad it's pathetic. And you don't give him the time of day because he's a thin, dark-haired guy."

"I don't go out with Mike because he's a total pothead."

"And you're pure as the driven snow?" Mark said archly. "You have the best shit on campus!"

"You're crazy." Wade turned his attention back to the game. But

Mark's words kept running through his mind. The bitter truth was, Mark was right. Wade was only attracted to built, blond boys.

So what, *he decided to himself.* Everyone has a type. So that's mine. Big deal.

The game ended with another Longhorn victory. Filing out of the stadium Wade and Mark were trying to figure out what to do with the rest of their afternoon, before going downtown for Indian food. As he was suggesting going for a beer at the student union, Mark nudged Wade.

"What?"

"Kyle."

The handsome fraternity man and his date were walking a few paces in front Wade and Mark. Wade had to admit that Kyle's ass was pretty fetching in his faded Wranglers. Kyle happened to glance back and spied Mark. Kyle winked at him and then returned his attention to his date.

"Oh, yeah. I'll be nekkid next to him in just—" *Mark looked at his vintage Mickey Mouse watch*—"six hours."

"I hate to rain on your sex parade, but doesn't your roommate have a guest this weekend?"

"Oh, shit!" *Mark groaned.* "I totally forgot! Patrick's sister is here to check out the campus to see if she wants to come here next fall." *Mark shared a one-bedroom apartment with a fine arts major from Alabama.*

Wade had to giggle.

"Let me use your place," *Mark begged.*

"Oh, no! Last time I let you do that I had to sleep in the hallway 'cause you locked me out!"

"Please? Pretty please? Look at that ass! How can you deny me that ass?"

Sighing heavily, Wade caved in. "Oh, hell. Sure. I guess this one last time . . ."

"Hot damn!"

"Just change the sheets when you finish, okay?"

"Don't I always?"

Wade was bored. It was eleven-thirty at night, and he was wandering around the campus. The frat boy Kyle had called Mark and they had met up at Wade's tiny off-campus studio apartment at ten, and by now were well on their way to a second session.

Wade crossed the street and began to window shop along the main student drag on Guadeloupe Street. He kept glancing at his watch, wondering how long he needed to stay away from his place. He tucked his hands under his arms to keep them warm. It had gotten quite chilly, and he was only wearing a light sweater.

He decided to go see if the student library was still open, and if so, he'd kill another hour there, then go home and kick the two men out. Enough was enough. He waited patiently for the light to change at the main campus entrance intersection when he felt a light tap on his shoulder.

"Wade?"

He turned around and was stunned to see Colton Jennings standing behind him. Colt was dressed in a thick black turtleneck sweater and his trademark pair of tight Wranglers. Scuffed roper cowboy boots completed his look. Wade's heart began to race and he took a step back, breaking the physical contact. "Uh . . . Colt! Hi . . ." he fumbled.

"Hey, buddy. How goes it?" Colt was slightly drunk and in a gregarious mood.

"Good! . . . Good. And you? Great game today, by the way!"

"Oh? You saw it? I thought I did just okay. I nearly fucked up that last play, but, hell, we were so far ahead, it wouldn't have mattered."

Wade found he couldn't talk. Being this close to his idol, his dream guy, was almost too much to process. He tried to keep his breathing normal, and he struggled to think up something clever to say.

"Sure is cold," he finally uttered.

What did I just say? Wade panicked. What a stupid thing to say!

Colt just laughed. "Then you should get inside. Go home."

"I can't. I loaned my apartment to a . . . friend who's . . . entertaining . . ." Wade couldn't believe the stuff that was coming out of his mouth. What if Colt asked for juicy details? What would he say? He quickly began to formulate a complicated lie about a boy and a girl from Eco class.

But Colt didn't press him for details. He just slowly nodded. "I have a roommate like that. Locks me out of my room at least twice a week while he bangs some skank he picked up. Pisses me off. I don't do that shit with Cindy."

"Oh, yeah. How is she?"

Colt shrugged. "The same. She's a Kappa Chi. A bitch."

Wade must have looked shocked, because the athlete grinned shyly and explained. "We had a stupid fight tonight. She didn't want to go to my frat's party. So I told her to stay in her fuckin' uptight prissy sorority house then, and I went without her."

"I see."

"Was a waste, though. So boring."

Wade noticed the light had changed and he and Colt began to walk across the street.

"Tell you what. Why don't you come over to my dorm and hang out there," Colt offered. "I haven't seen you in a while. We'll catch up. You can see the infamous Longhorn jock house."

Wade knew nothing good could come of this. But the chance to extend his time with Colt was a carrot dangling in front of him that he couldn't resist.

"Okay."

"We have to walk it. I totaled my car last month. Dad's not letting me get a new one until next semester. Supposed to teach me respect for things, I think." He smirked a lopsided smile, curling up one lip.

"Wow. I'm sorry. You loved that Firebird."

"Ugh," Colt snorted. "I always hated that car. So high school. Who the fuck drives a Firebird? I wanted a Blazer."

Wade, knowing the Firebird had been his suggestion, blanched.

Colt didn't notice. "Say, how's your mother?"

Twenty minutes later Wade was sitting on Colt's bed while the jock snagged a couple of beers from a mini refrigerator located under one of the two desks in the large room. "Don't tell. We're not supposed to have alcohol in our rooms." Colt giggled, pressing his long index finger to his unbelievably sexy lips.

"I won't."

"I'm glad Brick isn't here tonight. He and his girlfriend are at her parents' house. Her folks went out of town." He winked at Wade. "He's sure gettin' some tonight." He opened the two bottles and handed one to Wade. "I wish I was . . ."

Wade laughed nervously.

"So, who you seeing these days? Anyone?" Colt took a deep swig of his beer. He swayed unsteadily on his feet.

"Uh . . . no . . . no."

"Well, you hang in there, buddy. There's someone for everyone. Even you. You'll find her, you wait and see." He gave Wade a funny sideways glance. "I gotta get out of this turtleneck. Damn thing's too tight. Cindy bought it for me and makes me wear it. She says it makes me look less 'savage,' whatever the fuck that's supposed to mean. I hate the fuckin' thing." He put the beer bottle down on a dresser, then reached his massive arms up and peeled off the sweater.

Wade tried his hardest not to stare, but he found he couldn't help himself. Colt's huge and chiseled body was like that of Zeus or Apollo, and Wade felt a sudden stirring between his legs. He quickly crossed them, Indian style.

Colt threw the sweater in a ball on the floor next to his bed. He stretched, and then took another long sip of beer. He came over to Wade and plopped down on the twin bed, next to him. He leaned back against the wall, his cutup abs bunching together.

Wade focused on a poster of some busty-chested woman in a string bikini reclining against a bright red Porsche.

"So, Wade . . ." Colt slurred, the alcohol starting to affect him. "Tell me about you. . . . We kinda fell out of touch. . . ."

Wade, never taking his eyes off the bikini clad model, gave him the barest of description of his life. He was in business school. He wanted to get into real estate. Wanted to move to California. When he was done talking, the two old friends fell into a sustained silence.

The quarterback was staring down at the beer bottle he held in his hand. "Well, you sure look better than you did in high school. You lost a little weight, I think."

Wade nodded. "I started running last summer. It helps."

Colt grinned lazily. "Well, keep it up. You'll be fightin' 'em off with a stick soon. You should start lifting weights, too, you know."

"Maybe. I always thought the lunkheads that did that were pretty much Neanderthals."

Colt pretended to be shot in the chest by an arrow, and dramatically slumped over, his head resting for a minute on Wade's shoulder. He straight-

ened up and began to stare intently at his bottle of beer again. "You ever feel . . . lonely?" he finally said.

"Lonely?"

Colt nodded. "Yeah. Lonely. I mean, I have all these people that want to hang out with me, but I never feel like they want to hang out with me, Colt Jennings. They want to hang out with the Longhorns' number one quarterback. I get tired of all the bullshit. People are always blowing smoke up my ass about how great I am, how fuckin' bright my future is, all that bullshit. Do you know they're already saying I'll get the Heisman next year? So, if I don't, it'll be, like, this huge disappointment for everyone. But no one, not one person, ever asks me about how I'm doing." He paused. "Not even Cindy. She just wants to get married, have me go pro, buy a big house, and start shooting out children. Fuck!" He brought his beautiful head forward and slammed it back against the wall with a loud thunk.

Wade didn't know what to say.

"That's why it's so great to see you today," Colt half whispered. "You knew me before I became . . . this." He dramatically waved his hand in front of himself. "You can see through all the bullshit." He dropped a hand down on Wade's thigh. "You're probably my only true friend."

"You've got to be kidding! Everyone on campus loves you. You're a hero to everyone," Wade said, his senses overloading from the slight pressure of Colt's large palm on his thigh.

"Yeah, whatever." Colt didn't remove his hand. "You know, I'm really sorry about what a shit I was to you in high school. I didn't mean to be. I should have hung out with you more, made everyone stop giving you such a hard time. It's just . . . I don't know . . . I was afraid they'd pick on me if I did, I guess . . ."

Wade hadn't thought about those high school days in over a year, and just the mention of them by Colt made him feel nervous. Or maybe he was nervous because Colt had yet to remove his hand from his leg. In fact, Wade was surprised to feel Colt move it up his thigh a few millimeters. It was only inches away from his hardened cock, and Wade didn't know what he'd do if Colt happened to graze that. He began to sweat.

"I wish I knew how to make it up to you," Colt said. He took another long sip of his beer.

Start talking, *Wade told himself*, and keep talking. You're imagining things. Colt Jennings is not hitting on you.

"Colt, *I appreciate you saying that. I've always looked up to you. Remember what I said about you being everyone's hero?*"

Colt barely dipped his head.

"Well, *you're my hero, too.*" Wade blushed as he said it.

Colt turned and looked him drowsily in the eye. "Really?"

"Totally. *You're the son my father always wished he'd had. Hell, even I wish I were like you.*"

Colt managed to smile another lazy grin. He moved his head in closer to Wade's. "That's *really nice of you to say, buddy . . .*"

Wade was acutely aware that their faces were now only about eight inches apart. He wanted to close the distance and kiss the ball player so bad it ached. He felt Colt's hand purposely move up his thigh another bit, and he could have sworn he felt a single finger reach out and lightly touch the hard-on constricted by his jeans.

"You're *such a great guy . . . to listen to me blow off steam like this, Wade*," Colt said, *his voice dropping a register or two.*

Wade noticed that Colt's breathing was coming in quick, short breaths and that his beautiful chest was moving up and down rapidly. The big football player pivoted his body a bit so he was facing Wade.

Wade glanced down and saw that Colt's unspeakably sexy happy trail of dark blond hair went seductively into his tight jeans, where a prominent bulge seemed to be growing.

Oh, my God, *Wade thought.* Is that a hard-on? No, it can't be!

Suddenly, it was all too much for Wade to take. Knowing he had to have completely misconstrued the conversation, and the quarterback's intent, he practically jumped off the bed, spinning around so Colt couldn't see his erection. "Well, *I should probably be going. I bet my friend is done by now.*"

Colt fumbled to get up himself. "Are you . . . *are you sure? I mean, you can stay here if you'd like.*" *He got to his unsteady feet.* "My roommate *isn't coming back tonight. You could stay over . . . if you want . . .*" *The bigger man's eyes were downcast. He jammed his hands into his pockets, and pushed them out so Wade couldn't tell if he had actually been aroused or not.*

Wade wanted nothing more than to be taken by the burly football player. His mind just wouldn't accept what he thought was happening was actually happening. He must have made some mistake. Colt wasn't . . . like him. It had all been innocent.

"Uh, no. That's okay, really. I should just get going. Thanks for showing me around your dorm. I've never been in the jock house before."

"Sure."

"Okay, then." Wade walked to the door and opened it. "I'll see you around?"

"Yeah. Sure. I'll . . . uh, see you around."

Wade tried a breezy smile, but it came off as a tight grimace. The second he was out of the room and the door shut behind him, he had to lean against a wall to catch his breath.

"Is this place okay?" Wade asked. They were standing in the entrance area of The Daily Grill, a great restaurant located in a small mall across from the famed Beverly Center in West Hollywood. The Daily Grill had good food at fairly reasonable prices.

Colt looked around. "Sure. Great. Whatever."

"They have an awesome steak here, if you eat that."

"Not as much as I want to. My nutritionist won't let me eat red meat more than three times a month. But, fuck him." Colt grinned.

The hostess led them down a short flight of stairs into the main dining room. Wade noticed that heads turned as the famous football player was recognized. They were led to a secluded booth near the large plate glass windows overlooking La Cienega Boulevard. Before they could even order, two small boys came over and asked for autographs. Colt was kind and friendly while signing the napkins for them.

"No one ever asks me for my autograph," Wade playfully whined, after they had left.

"Come on. I saw the way those people in your class fell all over you. You get the same attention I do, just in a different way."

Wade hadn't considered this before. "Really? I hadn't thought about that."

"Yeah, it was impressive. You sure have changed, Wade."

"Well, I lost some weight, that's all really . . ."

Colt shook his head. "No, it's more than that. You are a confident, take charge kinda guy, now. You were always so . . . meek, no offense intended, mind you."

"None taken." Wade smiled.

"But, you seem to have come into your own. You should be proud of yourself. You're a great guy."

Wade sighed. "Yet still single."

Colt didn't say anything for a moment. "Well, that'll happen when it's supposed to, I guess."

"Yeah, sure, but I'm not getting any younger!"

Colt laughed. "I like how you're so comfortable with yourself, now. Like you've attained some sort of state of grace."

"State of grace? What the hell? Who is this eloquent man in front of me, and what have you done with my jock friend Colt Jennings?"

"I do have deeper thoughts than what the next play is going to be, you know," Colt said, slightly indignant.

"Hey, sorry. Of course you do. Sorry."

"Ah, forget it." The handsome football hero sighed. "I just get tired of people always assuming I'm just a big, dumb jock. I *can* think, you know." He reached for his glass of water and took a sip. "And, believe it or not, I can do other things with my hands besides throw a football."

Wade felt really bad. "Of course you can."

"I bet you'd never guess that I make furniture."

That floored Wade. "Um . . . no, I wouldn't have guessed that."

"Yeah, well, I don't know how good I am, but I like it. I've been doing it for a couple of years, now."

"Really? What kind of furniture? How?" This was surprising. Colt Jennings had an artistic side?

"Mostly Mission style. Chairs, bookcases, that sort of thing. I've always liked Stickley furniture. Cindy hated it. Everything in the damn house was antique, or flowery and silk. I built a small shop in the garage. It's sort of my hobby, now."

"I'd like to see your work sometime, if you'd let me," Wade said sincerely.

Colt turned beet red. "Maybe. They're not very good."

The waiter came over and took their order. Wade recognized him from the gym. His name tag said "Taylor." Wade gave him a knowing

smile, but Taylor ignored him. For some odd reason, he seemed to be
putting on a macho attitude for Colt's benefit. Even his posture was
overly manly, which struck Wade as hilarious since Taylor was one of
the nelliest guys at the gym.

Colt ordered the filet mignon, rare, and a baked potato. Wade got a
baked chicken breast and salad. Taylor left, and Wade had to shake his
head and smirk.

"What did I miss?" Colt asked, curious.

"Oh, nothing. Taylor, our waiter. I know him from the gym. Total
queen. He was acting all butch around you, trying to pass as straight. I
wonder why."

"Really?"

Wade laughed. "Oh, yeah. I'm sitting here thinking 'drop the drag,
sister. No one's buying it.'"

Colt began to snicker. "He stared at my crotch the whole time he
took my order."

"You noticed, too?" Wade giggled.

The laughing eventually petered out. There was quiet for several
minutes after, as both men were lost in their own thoughts.

Wade finally ended the silence. "So, I have some houses lined up for
you to see tomorrow. Three at the beach, two in the Hollywood Hills,
one off Mulholland Drive, and two in Beverly Hills. It'll be a long day.
But, now that I know about your affinity for Mission style, I might
make a change or two in the morning . . ."

"That's fine."

The waiter came back with their drinks, a cosmopolitan for Wade,
and a gin and tonic for Colt. They both took hearty slugs.

"So, I'm going to be single for the first time in my life," Colt finally
ventured. "I've never *been* single. I've always been with Cindy. It's
weird."

Wade nodded in support of his friend.

"I feel like it's finally time for me to live my life the way I want to.
Fuck everyone else. If I want to walk around naked all day, in my own
house, then I'm going to. If I want to fly to Hawaii for no reason, then
I'm going to do that. If I want to get a new car every fuckin' week, then
shit, why not?"

"Sounds great to me," Wade said.

Colt got a faraway look in his eyes. "We were always so poor. Growing up, I used to be just mortified about my cheap, ratty clothes and used textbooks. Now I have all this money, and I never spend any on myself. I think on some level, I've been afraid someone was gonna take it all away. Time to change *that* attitude." He grinned. "Anyway, I've always felt constrained, I guess. I have to live up to this image I have. The All-American jock with the perfect life and the perfect wife. What bullshit! Hell, Cindy and I weren't even sleeping together for the last two years."

Wade blinked.

"I just . . . we . . . I . . ." Colt struggled to find the words. "I don't blame her for finding someone else. It's tough to be in my shadow. I was going through some changes. . . . We weren't getting along, and it happened." He raised his glass. "Well, good for her. I hope they're very happy." He raised the glass higher in imaginary salute, and then took a long sip.

"What about you?" Wade asked. "All that travel. All those women falling all over you. You ever . . . stray?"

Colt shook his head. "Not even once. I *wanted* to . . ." Colt cast his eyes down. "But, I didn't. My marriage wasn't great . . . for a lot of reasons, but, I just couldn't give in to my . . . desires."

"Wow. A monogamous man. How rare."

"Really?"

"Oh, yeah. Most of the guys I know in long-term relationships would easily sleep with another guy if they could get away with it."

Colt looked at his hands. "What about you? You the monogamous type?"

Wade chuckled. "Sadly, yes. I once had a boyfriend who wanted to do a three-way. I couldn't do it. I'm a one-man man. I think that fact helped keep me healthy and HIV negative, when guys I knew who tricked around a lot were turning up positive left and right."

Colt nervously took another drink.

"Does it make you uncomfortable for me to talk about men . . . together? I'll stop if it does."

"No! No . . . I just . . . I don't . . . It's cool. I like you, Wade. I always have. You're my friend. My only friend in L.A. I want to know all about you, and what's happening in your life."

"Well," Wade said, flattered to be thought so highly of by his idol, and feeling a rush of emotion. "Back at you. You can tell me anything, you know. I won't blab it around. I'm great at keeping confidences."

"I can tell you anything?" Colt said almost painfully as he looked deep into Wade's eyes.

"Of course."

Colt nodded. "I think I already knew that. Thanks, Wade. I'm glad you're here." He reached under the table and placed a hand on Wade's hard thigh, and gave him a squeeze.

Wade had a flashback to the night in Colt's dorm room. Same hand, same leg. Colt's hand lingered for just a moment too long before he removed it, and brought it back up to his glass.

Was it possible? Could Colt be . . .

No, it couldn't be. It's just wishful thinking, Wade chastised himself. *Just like how every queer man wants famous movie stars to be gay.*

"Sometimes, I feel like I have this stuff bottled up inside that I need to get out, and I don't know how. I'm afraid everyone will think I'm a freak or something if I do. That I'll lose everything I worked so hard to achieve," Colt said miserably. "I figure, just a few more years playing ball, playing the part of Colt Jennings, then I'll be set, and I can do whatever I want. I can just be . . . *me.*"

"I'm here if you want to talk about it. Honest. No judgments." Wade looked back at Colt's face, and thought he saw the big man's eyes watering up. Wade felt great empathy for his hero. Having a marriage end was an extremely painful expierience, and Colt was obviously having a tough time handling it. "Are you okay?" he finally asked compassionately.

"Yeah." Colt, embarrassed, wiped his eyes with the back of his hand. "So, tell me about this house of yours. Your mother is always raving to my mom about your newest house."

If Wade was taken aback by the sudden change in subject, he didn't let Colt see it. "Well, I keep 'upgrading.'"

"Upgrading?"

Wade nodded. "I'm in the real estate business. I see great deals all the time. I've rolled over three homes so far. I really like the one I have now, though. I'm gonna hate to let it go, when the time comes." In fact, Wade owned not only the house he lived in presently, but also three rental houses in West Hollywood, and two small fourplexes. The rental income paid for the mortgages and upkeep, and it helped build Wade's portfolio. He was actually looking to add a third fourplex or even a larger complex.

"So don't let it go, then."

"Well, I'm always looking for bigger and better. It's my sin." He smiled. "The place I have now is on Norma Avenue, in the golden triangle. That's an area of real estate in West Hollywood, the most desired area. One point seven million. Can you believe it? For a two bedroom bungalow!" Wade shook his head.

"Jesus!"

"But, I got land. It's a double lot. I have a pool and pool house on the extra land."

"Sounds great. Private?"

"Completely. I have a ten foot high hedge all the way around. You can't even see the house from the street. I love it."

Colt took a nervous sip of his cocktail. "Sounds nice. I'd like to see it sometime."

"Sure. Anytime."

"How about tonight?" Colt stared at the tabletop with utmost concentration.

"Um, after dinner, sure. The housekeeper doesn't come until day after tomorrow, so it might be a little messy."

"Don't worry about that. You should see my hotel room."

Dinner passed with relative ease, Wade felt. The two men didn't really touch on any topic of depth. They just kept up a steady stream of "whatever happened to" and "did you hear about . . ." Wade noticed that Colt seemed slightly distracted, but he kept up his end of the conversation, so Wade just let it go.

After dinner was over, Colt insisted on picking up the check, and soon they were both sitting in the Land Rover driving to Wade's house. The real estate agent tried to think of what state he'd left his house in that morning. He knew there were dishes in the sink, and probably some dirty clothes lying on the laundry room floor, but all in all, he thought it would be presentable. Wade hated the thought that someone he had always looked up to would see his living environment in less than perfect condition, but there was not much he could do about it now.

He pulled up to his property and reached up to punch the garage door opener. The large, covered iron gate slide sideways, allowing the big SUV entrance into the short driveway. Wade parked the car, and hopped out.

"Here we are."

Colt got out and looked at the house appreciatively. In one of those odd juxtapositions that is Los Angeles, the house was a complete New England saltbox. Aged and weathered cedar shingles covered the exterior walls, and crisp white paint was used on the trim and windows. The front door was painted blood red. Bougainvillea had taken root and climbed up the entire western side of the house, the windows neatly trimmed out. Creeping ivy crawled up the front of the house, and the window boxes of the dormer windows were bursting with bright flowers.

"It's amazing," Colt whistled. "Looks like a movie set."

"I've been approached, actually. They wanted to shoot an episode of *The Practice* here last year. I said no."

Wade walked to the front door, but stopped to get his mail from the mail basket on the inside of the hedge-covered wall. He quickly scanned through it, saw nothing of value and stepped up onto his porch.

"I can't get over this!" Colt said, still digesting the oddity of the prim house in a neighborhood full of Spanish style homes.

"Well, come on in." Wade unlocked his front door and entered his house. The buzzing of the alarm went off instantly, and he expertly punched in his security code on the alarm panel.

Colt entered the house and looked around. The house was decorated in a relaxed comfortable style that the football great might have picked out himself. Sturdy, worn leather sofas faced each other in the main living room, and a huge stone fireplace anchored the room. Kilim rugs, richly upholstered side chairs, and heavily framed artwork hung in a pleasing arrangement on the pale khaki walls gave off an air of masculine comfort.

"This place is great!" Colt enthused as he wandered from room to room. He particularly liked the large dining room's coved ceiling that Wade had painted a burnished gold duchesse satin. The flickering crystal chandelier that hung under it threw up a warm light that caused the tinted ceiling to glow. The simple plank teak dining table and thickly upholstered dining chairs were the perfect furniture for such a room.

"It's a place to hang my hat," Wade said jovially, joining Colt in the dining room. "Let me show you the rest of it."

They wandered from room to room. They went through the redone kitchen that Wade had agonized over renovating. His choice of celedon-painted cabinetry and stainless steel appliances seemed to be the right one, judging by Colt's raves. Wade showed him the master bedroom with its authentic Shaker four-poster bed and nearly wall-to-wall padded sisal carpeting. The guest room, with its own sitting room, completely done in shades of gray, ivory, and camel. The library, with the cut stone fireplace, had a wall mounted flat screen television and bay windows overlooking the backyard and pool area.

When they ended up back in the entryway, Wade grabbed his keys from the hall console he had thrown them on. "Time to get you back to the hotel. It's late."

Colt looked around the living room some more. Then he stared at the peg and groove floor.

"I . . . Do I have to leave? Can't I stay?"

Wade did an actual double take. "What?"

"It's just so . . . homey. I hate my hotel. It's late. I don't want you to have to haul my ass all the way back into Beverly Hills. I can sleep in the guest room." He looked up at Wade with uncertainty in his big blue eyes.

"Uh, sure. Great. At least I know *those* sheets are clean," Wade joked.

He led the big man back to the guest room. "There's the remote for the TV, there're spare toothbrushes in the bathroom. Make yourself at home."

"Thanks."

"What time do you need to get up tomorrow?"

"Whenever."

"Well, I'm going to go for a run at six, and we need to be on the road for our home tour by nine."

"I'll go run with you."

"Wearing what? Your stuff's at the hotel. And I don't think my running shorts would fit over *one* of your thighs." Wade said, laughing.

"Oh, right. I didn't think about that. Okay. I'll see you in the morning, then." He backed up a few steps and awkwardly shut the bedroom door.

Wade went throughout his house, turning off lights, locking up and trying very hard not to think about the naked giant of a man sleeping under his roof.

There was a gentle knock on Wade's bedroom door. Not quite asleep yet, Wade opened his eyes and glanced at the bedside clock. One fifteen A.M.

What the hell?

"Yes?"

The door slowly opened, and in the half light of the hall, Wade could see the large bulk that was Colt. Colt took a hesitant step into Wade's room.

"Are you up?" he asked softly, a slight catch in his voice.

"I am now." Wade smiled. "What's up? Is everything okay? Is it too hot in the guest room?"

Colt slowly shook his golden head. "No, no. I . . . I couldn't sleep."

Wade digested this. He sat up in bed. "What's the matter?"

Colt took another step into the room. Then another. "I don't know," he said miserably.

"You wanna talk about it?" Wade shot a glance at the clock again. They had a full day of house hunting tomorrow, and he needed some sleep. The last thing he wanted to do was listen to Colt ramble on and on about missing his wife.

"I guess . . . I . . ." Colt took a few more steps closer to Wade's bed. Cloud cover that had been hiding the full moon passed, and more illumination came into the dark bedroom. Wade could now see that Colt was only wearing a pair of tight white briefs. His tanned and thickly ripped body almost glowed in the subtle light and Wade began to breathe a little faster. The quarterback's slow movements made his body constrict and flex with each step forward.

This is not good, Wade thought frantically. *I'm getting hard just looking at him!*

"I really don't know why I'm here botherin' you . . ." the large man said as he got ever closer to Wade. Colt's eyes had adjusted to the hazy darkness and he looked down at his boyhood friend under the blue cotton sheet.

"It's okay, I—" Wade started to say. But he stopped speaking when he caught sight of something. Something large and rock hard and straining to be freed from thin white cotton. Colt had a full blown hard-on, and its impressive size was just what Wade would have imagined Colt to have.

Oh, my God, Wade realized. He looked up at Colt's face and saw the sweet torture the big man was feeling. He now knew, without any question, why NFL hero Colton Jennings was in his bedroom at one-fifteen in the morning.

"I . . . uh . . . I can't stop thinking about you . . ." Colt tried to continue speaking, but found he couldn't. He just looked at the man in the bed below him helplessly. He couldn't take his eyes off the prominent lump at Wade's crotch. His heart was racing and his arms ached to reach out.

He didn't have to. Wade decided that this time, unlike the time in college, he would welcome the big man's fumbled moves.

Without saying a word, he threw back the sheet and revealed his naked body. Colt's eyes bulged and took in every inch of Wade's muscular frame.

"Oh, my God," the quarterback whispered, licking his lips.

Wade, still silent, stood up next to Colt. His jutting erection accidentally brushed against Colt's hardened package, causing the blond man to involuntarily shudder.

Wade reached his right hand out and placed it on Colt's chest. He could feel the racing heart beneath the taut skin. He allowed his fingers to slowly run lightly over his pecs. He looked Colt in the eyes. Colt began trembling and Wade pulled his hand back.

"No! Please . . . Don't stop," Colt barely breathed. "I *want* you to . . . God, I've wanted . . ."

"What?" Wade whispered, bringing his mouth close to Colt's.

"Oh, buddy . . . I've made some . . . discoveries about . . . myself," Colt said sporadically.

"Yeah?" Wade teased, a mere inch away from Colt's thick, pouty lips.

"I want . . . I've never . . . Oh, fuck, Wade! *Kiss me . . . !*"

Wade closed the tiny gap between them and planted his lips on Colt's. Softly at first, then harder as the bigger man allowed his tongue in. He probed the inside of Colt's mouth, and felt the quarterback's trembling fade as his passion began to build. The football player pushed his own tongue forward and Wade let him explore the inside of his warm mouth. Wade reached a hand up and placed it on the side of Colt's face and pulled him closer. Murmurs of pleasure gurgled up from deep inside the quarterback.

Colt couldn't believe how amazing it felt. The feel of hard stubble against his own face. The determined probing of Wade's tongue. Colt felt all control leave his body. All his fears and apprehensions faded as he felt a deep well of emotion burst forth. He gasped aloud when Wade grabbed his crotch. The sensations of having another man touch and squeeze and play with him there broke down the last of his barriers and he committed fully.

"God, Wade," he muttered, and he reached out himself and clamped his hand around Wade's rock hard member. He pulled and tugged hard.

"Hey, hey, easy, not so rough . . ." Wade gently instructed. "That's it . . . Oh, yeah, that feels so good. . . . Yeah, stroke it slowly. . . ."

Hearing Wade speak to him so sensually took Colt's breath away. He was confused that hearing a man say simple words could have such an emotional impact on him. He continued to lightly stroke Wade's cock and loved the way the hot hardness felt in his hand.

Wade now dug his own hand into Colt's shorts, and pulled them down, setting the massive erection finally, gloriously, free. He gently removed Colt's hand from his dick and began to rub the two impressive cocks together.

"Oh, my God . . . Oh, my God . . . Oh, my God . . ." Colt repeated over and over. He shuddered and pulled away from Wade. He just took a long look at the nude man in front of him. "God, Wade. You are so . . . *beautiful*. I can't get over how beautiful you are . . ."

Wade, staring at his boyhood idol, just couldn't believe what he was hearing, not to mention doing. He reached a hand up and gently stroked Colt's face. He saw confusion and delight in his idol's startling blue eyes.

"What's wrong?" Wade asked, suddenly alarmed that he had made some ghastly mistake.

"I'm nervous. I'm sorry," Colt breathed. "I've wanted to do this . . . be with a man, for so long. And for it to be *you* . . . It just feels right, that's all."

Wade pulled the big man close and kissed him repeatedly. He kissed his lips, his nose, his closed eyes, his forehead. He then dipped low and kissed his neck, running his tongue hard against the skin, getting the desired result of loud groaning from Colt. Colt's hands had clamped onto Wade's shoulders and he was squeezing them as the pleasure racked through his body.

Wade let his tongue roam free, and found Colt's erect nipples. Large and rosy against his tanned chest, Wade couldn't resist a playful bite. Colt jerked back and sharply breathed in. Wade did it again. And again. He let his tongue tease the nipple, licking over it several times, then flicking against it. Each time he did that, Colt shivered and groaned loudly. Wade reached his hand up and began to play with the other nipple as he went to town on the one in his mouth.

The double assault was more than the pro football player could stand. He started to groan even louder, a loud sustained moan that was almost feline-like in its intensity.

"Oh, God, Wade! Stop! . . . I'm gonna come! . . . It's too much . . . ! I'm gonna . . . Oh, God . . . !"

Wade, not knowing of the severity of the ecstasy he was giving the built man above him, felt the hot cum splatter hard against his lower stomach. Colt gasped in pleasure and embarrassment as he shot his load.

Wade had never made a man climax without touching himself before. And for the first guy to do that to be Colton Jennings? It was the hottest thing he had ever witnessed.

"I'm so sorry . . . I'm so sorry . . ." the big man gasped, trying to catch his breath. "Let me wipe that up . . . God, I was so turned on . . . That was so intense . . . I'm so sorry!"

"Relax, Colt, relax . . . It's okay . . . I love that you did that! Do you know how fucking hot that was? Damn!"

Colt pulled his briefs down all the way, stepped out of them and used them to rub off Wade's abs. He grinned sheepishly the whole time.

His erection didn't abate.

After he was done, he looked at Wade, and flashed his trademark toothy grin. He reached his two big hands out and placed them on Wade's chest. He pushed Wade backwards with a powerful shove that sent the smaller man flat on his back onto the bed. Colt then stepped over him, his two beefy legs kicking Wade's legs apart and wide.

Wade, slightly dazed by being tossed down, looked up at the hot man hovering above him. Colt's protruding hard-on was gently swaying with his labored breathing and had the odd effect of almost hypnotizing Wade. Colt reached an eager hand out and took hold of Wade's hard dick, and began to gently stroke it again. Wade loved the look of pure joy on his partner's face.

Colt, looking down at Wade, couldn't believe he was doing what he was doing. He absolutely loved feeling his old friend's cock in his hand. And if it felt good there, imagine what it would feel like elsewhere . . .

He suddenly sank to his knees and stretched forward. Never taking his eyes off Wade's face, he slowly forced Wade's big dick into his mouth. He found it was a little awkward to go down on a man at first, but after a few rough slithers, he got the motion down and soon had the slippery pole sliding in and out of his mouth like a pro. Wade began to writhe under him and the satisfied moans he emitted were music to Colt's ears. The quarterback wanted Wade to feel as good as he did, and he suspected he was doing a pretty good job.

"Fuck, Colt! . . . That's good! . . . You sure . . . *Ohhhh!* . . . You've never done this before?"

"Never," Colt uttered between head bobs. "But I plan on becoming an expert . . ."

Remembering how he liked to get head, Colt brought a hand up and used it to stroke Wade's cock as he went down on it. The added friction of the spit-slicked hand gliding up and down, along with Colt's awesome mouth, made Wade begin to cry out.

"Oh, yeah! Fuck . . . Oh, yeah! . . . *Fuuuuuck!*"

Colt loved that he could make Wade feel such pleasure. And truth be told, he felt his own arousal continue to build, despite shooting a heavy load mere minutes before.

Getting more and more comfortable at giving head, Colt allowed himself to begin some explorations. He slipped away from the throbbing cock and licked at Wade's shaved balls. His tongue cradled the tender sacks, and then he sucked them in. Wade whimpered his approval.

Emboldened by this reaction, Colt continued his new erotic explorations. He began to lick and suck the areas next to Wade's crotch, letting his tongue slide up the inside of his meaty thighs. He let his hot tongue creep down under Wade's balls and lick the sensitive area between his testicles and his pucker. Getting a hearty reaction to that, as Wade bucked up and grabbed at the bedding beside him, Colt made a quick decision and dove in. He let his tongue probe and tease the pulsating circle, and felt it expand and constrict.

"Oh, my God, Colt!" Wade shouted as he bucked up again.

Colt began to press harder, and let his spit provide a lubricant that allowed him to slide back and forth like a drill press.

"Oh, *fuuuuck!*" Wade cried out, clutching at Colt's head and pulling it in deeper.

Colt began to murmur his approval of Wade's pleasure.

The grunting from Colt only turned Wade on more. The constant, delicious lapping of the ball player's hot tongue was causing Wade to hyperventilate. He felt like he was on the verge of passing out, but he knew he needed to feel one thing more before giving completely over to sublime sweetness.

"God, Colt! I want you inside me! Fuck me! Please!" he begged, shutting his eyes and arching his head back as another wave of delight jolted through his tense body.

Colt stopped what he was doing. Breathing heavily, he looked up at Wade. "Are you sure? I've never . . ."

"Oh, God, baby, I'll show you!" Wade struggled to slide back on the bed. He reached under the bed frame and pulled up a half full bottle of lube. He squirted a handful into his hand.

"Come here," he commanded.

Colt, transfixed, eagerly clambered up on the bed and crawled up between Wade's spread legs. Wade reached down and took Colt's hard cock in his hands and slathered the lube all over it. Colt groaned with this new exciting torture, and hoped he wouldn't come again.

Wade clamped a hand behind the quarterback's head, holding onto his thick neck. He then repositioned himself and smeared some lube on his ass. Then he retook ahold of Colt, and guided him in.

Colt was about to jump out of his skin. He felt the hot tightness clamp around his slick cock and he pressed carefully in.

"It's okay," Wade whispered, looking him in the eye. "I can take it . . . I *want* it . . ."

"God, Wade . . . This feels so . . ."

Wade nodded. "I know."

Soon, Colt was all the way in. He had sunk his huge cock up inside Wade until there was nothing left to push in. Wade's ass was pressed up against Colt's balls.

"Oh, Wade . . . It's so . . . tight and hot . . . and . . ." Colt said in absolute wonderment, every one of his senses heightened tenfold.

"I know . . . *Ohhhh!* Yeah . . . Move it around . . . *Ohhhh!* Yeah . . . Like that . . . *Ohhhh,* damn, baby! . . . *Ohhhh!*"

Colt let his hips pulsate back and forth and he watched in fascination as Wade's face contorted with his growing pleasure. Colt could see the sexual sensations Wade was feeling and it made his heart fill with pure happiness. That he could do this to a man whom he'd thought about for so long was a reward that few men got to have. He felt like he was the luckiest guy on the face of the earth.

"Oh, my God, Colt . . . I wanted this . . . ! *Ohhhh!* . . . I wanted this from the second I saw you today . . ." Wade gasped, one hand lightly stroking himself, the other still clamped tight around Colt's head.

"Me, too . . . !" Colt began to pump a little harder, a little faster.

The tight, slippery sensations his cock was feeling were sending him to a place he had never been before. He felt a connection with the moaning, squirming man beneath him like he'd never felt with anyone before. He now knew what making love was really all about. He'd certainly never felt anything remotely close to this with his soon-to-be ex-wife.

"Oh, my God, Colt . . . *Ohhhh!*" Wade sputtered as he felt a tremendous pressure building deep in his body.

"Wade, I think I'm . . . God, I'm gonna come again . . . !"

Just hearing Colt say that, did it. Wade couldn't even respond. His balls tightened, and the hot, thick cum began to pump out of his overly excited cock. He shot a stream all the way over his shoulder, hitting the pillow behind his head. The cum also spattered all over his chest, and even in his hair. He couldn't believe the amount of fluid that came out of his body. His mouth fell open in ecstasy and wonder.

Wade saw Colt's face scrunch up as he quickly pulled himself out and ejaculated all over Wade in a fury that equaled the climax he'd had not fifteen minutes before.

The big man stayed hovering over Wade while they both tried to regain some semblance of normal breathing. Wade finally reached up and pulled the famous ball player down on him. Colt's massive weight was like a heavy blanket. Wade loved the way it felt to have this man on top of him.

Colt, for his part, was just trying to come back to earth. He had never experienced anything like this, and the onrush of bubbling emotions shocked him into silence. He didn't know what to say to express how he felt. So he said nothing for the time being.

"Are you okay?" Wade finally asked, fearing a negative answer.

Colt barely nodded his head. His heart rate was coming down, now, and he could begin to think clearly. "Am I crushing you?" he asked softly.

"I like it."

"Me, too."

The two men fell back into silence. Wade began to gently stroke Colt's back, his fingertips lightly caressing the broad v-shaped lats. Colt murmured happy moans and snuggled his head into Wade's chest.

"Wade?" he said, his voice barely above a whisper.

"Yeah?"

"I love you."

Wade's heart stopped. "What?"

Colt pulled his head up and looked Wade in the eye. "I know it sounds crazy. I'm in love with you. I think I always have been. Ever since we were kids."

"Colt . . . it's just that you've had a very emotional experience. You're feeling all mixed up inside. Don't confuse that with . . . *love*." Even as Wade said the words, he found his heart racing. His brain was saying no, but his heart was screaming *yes!*

Colt sensed this. He grinned slightly and shook his head. "Nope. I know what I feel. I've always felt it. That night? In college? I wanted to . . . to . . . to do what we just did so badly, I cried when you left my dorm. You've always been the one guy who really knew me, and still cared about me, faults and all." As he spoke, Colt's voice got stronger. He was truly speaking from his heart and it felt so freeing, so natural. "I love you, Wade. I know it as sure as I'm lying here."

"Colt . . . I don't know what to say . . ."

Colt sighed. "You don't have to say anything." His face looked crestfallen.

Wade gulped. "I have been hopelessly, completely and totally in love with you since the time I was twelve years old and you saved my ass from getting whipped by Billy Hanson."

"Really?"

"Duh, *yeah*."

Colt smirked. "I *knew* it."

"You ass." Wade playfully frowned. Colt leaned in and kissed the man he loved. He didn't stop kissing him for thirty-six minutes.

The next day turned out to be rainy. Something very rare in Southern California, but not unheard of. The soothing sound of rain tapping the windows and dripping down the roof gutter drainpipes made it too difficult for Wade to rise out of bed and go for his usual morning run.

Well, that and the two hundred-twenty-pound man snuggled up next to him.

Wade awoke at his normal time, six A.M., but now, forty-five minutes later, he was still nestled in the arms of the sleeping Colt. Wade didn't really want to wake him. He was afraid of what Colt would do when he realized what had happened between them during the night.

Would he freak out and run from the room?

Would he blame Wade for seducing him?

Would he still feel the things he said he did right after he came?

Wade just wasn't ready to find out which answer it would be. He wanted to stay cradled in Colt's arms forever. It felt so warm, so safe. He moved slightly to nervously check the clock one more time. He tried to move carefully so as not to rouse the football player.

"It's okay, Wade. I'm awake."

Wade sucked in his breath. "Sorry. I need to get up."

"No. Not yet." Colt flexed his big arms, and pulled Wade even closer to his warm body. "I don't want to let you go."

Wade thought he would cry. Colt felt the same. Thank God, because Wade sure did.

The relieved real estate agent spun in Colt's arms so they were now face to face. Colt looked so content, so happy. Like a huge weight had been taken away. The quarterback grinned broadly.

"I love you," he whispered, leaning forward.

The two men pressed lips together and soon were headlong into another erotic makeout session. Wade allowed his body to be pulled and placed carefully under the bigger man. He could feel Colt's arousal pressing against his own.

In a matter of mere moments Wade was again filled by Colt and the football hero gently pushed in and out, this time with slow desire. He took his time, relishing the carnal pleasure of being inside Wade's body. With each slow, deep press inward, Colt watched in delighted awe as Wade uttered a low-toned growl that reflected his own rapture. Colt reached a tender hand up and stroked Wade's face as he continued his slowly paced fucking.

"Oh, my God, Colt . . . It feels so good! . . . Give it to me, baby . . . Oh, God . . . Oh, God . . . !" Wade arched his head back and closed his eyes. Colt felt the hot fluid that Wade shot out hit against his lower abs.

"That's what I wanted to make happen . . . Yeah . . . God, Wade, I love you so fuckin' much. . . ." Colt slipped out, and quickly climaxed himself.

"Can we do this every morning?" Wade murmured as Colt relaxed and lay back down on top of him.

"Deal."

"We really do have to get up. I need to get you back to the hotel so you can change your clothes and see houses with me."

Colt sighed. "Okay." He gave Wade a deeply felt kiss, then rolled off him and rose from the bed.

Wade almost gasped. Colt was so unbelievably handsome, so hot and sexy that Wade couldn't believe this was his life.

"Sorry, buddy, but I hated that one! And what was up with that basement?" Colt buckled his seat belt and pulled out his sunglasses and placed them over his clear blue eyes. The rain had finally stopped, and the sun was peeking out in all its harsh brightness.

Wade put the SUV into drive, and pulled away from the house. It had been the fourth one they had seen, and so far, Colt hadn't really liked any of them. "I believe that basement was, at one time, a dungeon. Minus the sex toys." He giggled.

"Jesus! People really do that shit?"

"You'd be surprised at what turns people on."

Colt thought about this for a moment. "Do you like that? Is that what guys do together? I mean, do you want me to tie you up sometime? Or, would you like to tie me up?"

Wade was aghast. "What!"

"Look, this is all new to me. I want to try everything. I'd do that for you. If you want to tie me up and fuck me silly, I'd let you."

Wade looked at the L.A. Quakes newest star. His face was completely open and honest. It was clear he meant what he said. "Colt, that's . . . *sweet* . . . but I'm not into that. Whips and chains, I mean. I'd *love* to fuck you silly, though," he said, winking. He then thought for a moment. "I guess being tied up and teased doesn't sound *so* bad."

Colt grinned slyly. "Oh, yeah?"

"Well, I guess . . . I never really thought about it. Is that what *you* want? You brought it up!"

"Buddy, I just want to make you happy."

It was just after seven, and the two men finally staggered into Colt's welcoming house, Chinese take-out bags in hand. While they were both exhausted from running around town all day looking at property, they had ultimately found a great house for Colt.

Positioned just below Mulholland Drive, on top of the Hollywood Hills, the house wasn't huge, but the grounds included a large yard, pool and Jacuzzi, a regulation tennis court and a separate guesthouse. At three point four million dollars, it was a little more than Colt had wanted to spend, but he had fallen in love with its Mission-style architecture and open floor plan. They had put a lower bid in, and had already gotten a counter offer. It had been too late to counter the counter, so Wade would fax that over first thing in the morning.

Now, they just wanted to eat, maybe sit in Wade's hot tub for a few minutes, ease the tension of the day away, and then tumble into bed. Wade pulled out plates and opened up the food containers. They sat at the teak dining table and devoured the food. They talked about the new house and laughed and got to know each other even better. It was a little surprising to Wade how comfortable it all felt. But he'd known Colt almost his whole life, so of course they felt right with each other.

They had spent an entire day together, and found they complemented each other perfectly. Wade's calm reasoning was a great match for Colt's more impulsive decision making process. But Wade learned that when Colt made a decision, he stuck with it.

After dinner, they shed their confining clothes and carefully lowered their nude bodies into the bubbling hot water. They soaked for a half hour in the Jacuzzi, and began another scorching makeout session. Colt eventually pulled himself away from Wade's tempting lips, and climbed out of the hot tub, his raging hard-on proof of his excitement.

He casually wrapped a towel around himself, then turned to face Wade.

"I'm gonna go to the bedroom . . . and get ready for you. Give me a minute, okay?" He had a mischievous look about him.

"Okay." Wade was curious as to what he was up to, but he let it go. He sank back into the swirling water and let the pressures of the day slip away while he thought about the night ahead.

After about five minutes, he got out, dried off, and shut down the Jacuzzi. He padded through the house and saw that Colt had dimmed the lights. There was soft music coming from his bedroom stereo, and the flickering light of candles. Wade gently pushed open the door, and what he saw almost took his breath away.

Colt was spread-eagle on the bed, both ankles tied with ripped fabric strips to the lower posts of the Shaker bed. He was propped up on pillows and looked seductively at his new lover. He had two other pieces of fabric in his left hand, and his right was gently stroking his very erect cock. A bottle of lube was lying next to him.

Wade walked slowly toward the bed, transfixed.

"Tie up my hands," Colt ordered.

Wade gulped and did it. He discovered the fabric strips had been torn from the thin cotton shirt Colt had been wearing that day. Wade made sure that the restraints were loose enough to be comfortable, but tight enough to inhibit the beefy pro ball player. Then he dropped his towel and straddled the big man. Colt was looking at him with pure lust.

The soft lighting made both men's skin glow and their hot, hard bodies were intoxicating to each other. Wade reached back and grabbed Colt's cock and began to let his hand slide up and down. Colt began to squirm against his restraints and groaned loudly.

Wade dropped his body down and began to lick, taste, and touch every square inch of the famous quarterback. Since Colt couldn't really move, Wade realized he was in complete control. He began to get more aggressive in his tastings and quickly had Colt crying out with husky encouragement.

The Realtor slid down Colt's body and took his engorged cock into his mouth. His moist pressure and rapid slurping had Colt twitching in spasms of ecstasy.

"Fuck! Oh, God . . . Oh, God . . . I'm close . . . I'm so close . . . !" Colt ultimately panted.

Wade backed off. "Not yet," he whispered. He sat up and again grabbed Colt's hard cock.

Colt thought he would go out of his mind. The sensual tinglings he felt all over his body were sweet agony. He wanted to reach up and touch his lover, but couldn't. He had given up control to the hot man who was now untying his feet from the bedposts.

Sliding back on the the bed, Wade gently lifted Colt's legs up and positioned himself between them. Wade looked at the man he loved and checked to see if what he was about to do was welcome. Colt nodded vigorously, mentally bracing himself to experience something he'd only dreamt about.

Wade took the bottle of lube and liberally covered his hand. After smearing Colt's ass and his own dick, he reached down and glided his hand up and down Colt's achingly hard cock. As he did this, he also slowly entered the quarterback. Colt grimaced for only a brief second but soon was urging Wade on.

Wade was gentle and considerate, and soon was sliding back and forth with slow, deep thrusts that felt so good they were sinful. Colt couldn't move his upper body, so the only way to release his pent up pleasure and desire was to shout out in elation when he felt the squeezing, slippery tightness of his ass take Wade all the way in and out.

Sensing Colt was ready, Wade began to pump himself faster, burying his hot, steel rod in his lover's willing ass. Colt's mouth fell open as he couldn't even verbalize what he was feeling. It was the most fulfilling sensation he had ever had. Until this moment, he'd had no idea the sexual heights a human being could reach.

The big jock could only murmur incoherently as he watched the man he was hopelessly in love with stroke him, fuck him, and clench and unclench his teeth in extreme gratification. Wade's ripped and lean body now had a slight sheen of sweat on it that made him glisten in the candlelight.

It was the most beautiful sight Colt had ever seen.

He started to climax before he even realized it. He looked on in wonder as fluid began to erupt from his cock, Wade still expertly stroking. When the actual physical sensations of ejaculation hit him, the ball player bucked up and down, joyously shouting so loud that Wade almost got concerned.

Colt just kept coming. Squirt after squirt continued to spout up. Close to passing out from the absolute pleasure of it, he could only grunt with each thrust from his body. When he finally had nothing left to release, Wade quickly pulled out and noisily added his own seed to the huge quantity puddled all over Colt's chest.

"That was the most unbelievable thing I have ever felt," Colt gushed, after a minute. "We're doing *that* again!"

"You were so fuckin' hot when you came. The look on your face! Oh, my God," breathed Wade.

After a few minutes, Wade untied Colt's hands and they both trotted off to take a hot shower together. In under an hour they were in bed, under the covers, holding each other in the darkness.

"Colt? I want you to stay with me until your house is ready," Wade whispered.

"Are you sure?"

"I have never been more sure of anything in my life."

Colt didn't respond right away.

Wade turned around and faced him. The soft light of the waning moon allowed him to see the indecision on his face. "You don't want to?"

"No! I mean, *of course* I do! Don't be stupid. It's just . . . if anyone from the team . . . should find out . . ."

"Oh. I see."

Colt could tell that Wade was disappointed. "Wade, I just have to be careful. I love you, but I also have a job that requires me to have a . . . certain image."

"And being gay doesn't fit that image. I understand." Wade broke eye contact and stared off into space. "It's cool."

Colt took a deep breath. "Wade, look at me." Wade continued to stare away. "*Look* at me," Colt pleaded softly. Wade faced him again. "You *know* me, so you know how hard this is for me to say. Me, Colt Jennings, Mr. Fucking All-American, I'm in love with a *man*. My life has completely changed, now. Completely. I'm trying to absorb it all. I know that I love you. I have never felt such joy in my heart, ever, so I guess I am . . . *gay*." He whispered the word "gay." "I just need to not blow what I have going here in L.A. I just want a few good years, then I can retire. Then I can show them all the finger and be who I guess I really am."

"And what do I do while you're playing this part, the straight football hero?"

"You'll love me, as I love you. We'll make this work, I promise. It won't be easy, but we'll make it work. I swear it to you."

Wade had a bad feeling.

"How about," Colt added, "I keep the suite at the hotel, but really I stay here? That way, they'll all think I'm there, alone, when really I'll be with you every night."

Wade thought for only a second. "That'd be great."

It wasn't the best solution, but it would have to do, Wade realized. He wasn't going to let Colt get away, and if he had to bend a little, he was willing to do that.

From that day forward, Colt spent every night he was in town in Wade's bed. The ball player was insatiable. Now that he had finally accepted who he was, he wanted to try everything he'd fantasized about for years. Wade was more than willing to help Colt discover himself, though their sexual excesses sometimes made Wade worry he might die a young man.

It was a rare evening that didn't end up in thrashing, frantic lovemaking. As the two men became closer to each other, their worlds started to shrink. They only had eyes for each other, and friends, family, and social obligations began to fall to the wayside.

Wade would dash home from work as soon as possible to get dinner started, and Colt, fresh from a vigorous workout, would soon arrive and they would spend the entire evening alone, together in Wade's comfortable house. Weekends were spent puttering around the house, shopping, or in bed, locked in each other's arms.

Colt's bid for the house on Mulholland was accepted, and soon there was that project to oversee. Wade had some great ideas about

opening up some of the rooms, and eventually Colt let him take over
the entire renovation project.

Unfortunately, as the start of the new football season approached,
Colt had to start spending more and more time with his new teammates. He hated leaving Wade at home while he and his new buddies
went out to dinner, drinking and generally carousing around, but it
had to be done. Colt knew he had to bond with his new team in order
to lead them all the way to the Super Bowl. He gamely pretended to be
into the fun and games with his teammates, but he always came home
to Wade.

Pre-season training took place at a practice facility in Pomona, a
green, leafy suburb forty miles outside L.A. Colt decided not to move
out there for the six weeks of intense training, even though most of his
teammates were staying at the local hotels. The highly paid quarterback drove back into L.A. every night so he could be with Wade.

As the Quakes's hot new player, Colt began to do interviews with
local and national news and sports shows, and soon "Colt Fever" had
gripped the entire town. His picture popped up on T-shirts, posters,
and buttons. He signed a multimillion dollar deal with Nike, to develop his own shoe. He became the hottest thing since Shaq, and
everywhere he went he was besieged by autograph seekers and photographers.

All of this intense attention really put a crimp in his relationship
with Wade.

"I've hardly seen you all week." Wade sighed, and spooned up tight
next to his lover.

It was almost completely dark in the bedroom, the warm, flickering
light of a lone candle providing the only illumination. Wade had just
fucked Colt so hard, he thought he'd hurt the big man, but Colt had
only begged for more before they both nosily climaxed. Now, in the afterglow, they were curled up together on the sweat-soaked sheets.

"I know, buddy. I'm sorry . . . I had practice, then I had to go to Joe's
birthday party, then there was that photo op thing. I'll make it up to
you as soon as the season's over, I swear it." Colt yawned, and stretched

out an arm, pulling Wade closer in to his body. *God, I love this man,* the burly ball player thought contentedly.

"I was thinking . . ." Wade said cautiously.

"Mmmm?"

"Frank and Jack said I could use their cabin in Big Bear for the weekend if we wanted. I know your first game is next week, so I thought maybe we could get away, and just be with each other before the insanity starts."

Colt grunted. "I'd like that, buddy, I really would, but I can't. We have late strategy meetings on Friday, and then I have two appearances with the team on Saturday. One at the Children's Hospital and the other at the cancer center. Sunday, I'm doing that pre-season show for Fox."

Wade sighed again. He'd known it was a long shot, but he thought he'd suggest it anyway. "Okay. It was just an idea . . ."

"Buddy," Colt whispered, as he physically spun Wade around so they were face to face. "I know this ain't fun for you right now. It ain't fun for me, either. Every day I'm in the locker room, and the guys are saying shit about who they fucked the night before, and the problems they're having with their wives, I just want to scream 'Guys, guess what? I've got the best man in the fucking world!'"

Wade smiled at the words.

Colt got a contemplative look on his face. "It's weird. Sometimes I find myself fighting against saying it, actually biting my tongue to keep from speaking, the feeling is that strong. And, Christ, when they start up on the fag jokes, I really want to do some damage." He gently kissed Wade's lips. "I used to be able to just blot that shit out, but, damn! It's so hard to now. I take it all so personally." He sighed. "You wanna know something embarrassing?"

"Always," Wade quipped.

"I've noticed that I check out guys' butts, now." Colt said. "I don't mean to. I love you and I'm certainly not interested in *any* other guy, but I find myself doing it. I *never* allowed myself to do that before you and I got involved, you know? The other day at practice, Dwayne Taggart caught me checking him out. I covered it with some crack about him gaining weight, but still . . . !" He sighed again.

"Well, I would hope you look at men's asses." Wade snickered softly. "You *are* gay, you know. It's what we do. I'd be concerned if you didn't. Just don't make a move on any of them, okay?"

"Please. You've got the only ass I want." The big man reached over and lovingly stroked Wade's face. "But I have to admit," he continued, "I almost don't even know who I am anymore. I feel like I've opened up this bottle and let the genie out, and now it won't go back in. It's like I'm two people, and I always have to remember which Colt Jennings I am."

Wade looked up and studied Colt's open face. "What do you mean?"

"Sometimes, I find myself thinking about you, in the middle of practice, or driving somewhere, or at a meeting, and I'll remember something funny you said or did, or picture you making love to me, and I'll drift away. I get calm and happy and become Colt, the man who is hopelessly in love with Wade, and I can't wait to see you again."

Hearing these heartfelt words caused Wade's heart to fill anew with loving emotion for the gentle giant next to him.

Colt took a deep breath, then continued. "But, then I have to remember I'm also Colt Jennings, star-fucking-quarterback, and I have to put on my game face. My tough guy persona, the guy I become when I kick ass on the field, shoot shit with the guys, tell pussy stories and drink too much beer."

"I know it's difficult. I wish I could make it easier for you."

"The thing is," Colt said, his voice almost a whisper, "I like being Colt, the man in love with Wade, so much more than I like being Colt Jennings, star-fucking-quarterback. I don't know how long I can keep up the charade. Isn't being in love what life is all about? So, how can loving you be wrong? I'm so confused. . . . I know my career would be over if I let everyone know I'm gay, yet it's the one thing I want to do more than anything. Tell everyone."

"I know . . ."

"It just goes against my grain to hide who I am. I've always been proud of myself and what I've accomplished. I hate having this secret. I hate that it hurts you, too."

"Oh, Colt, no . . ."

"Wade, let's be honest. You wish I were out. It's okay. You can say it . . ."

Wade thought for a moment, choosing his words carefully. "I remember when I was in school," he finally said. "And all those kids kept picking on me, making me feel like dirt over something I couldn't control. The only thing that got me through it was that I promised myself one day I would make something of my life, and never again pretend to be something I wasn't." He looked deeply into Colt's eyes. "And I can't say it enough: I know how hard this is for you. But, yeah, since you brought it up, it is difficult not to be able to tell anyone about us."

"I knew it." Colt nodded solemnly.

"It feels like, once again, I have to hide who I am. That I have to hide who I love, when all I wanna do is shout 'I love Colt Jennings!' from the highest rooftop. I'm so fucking proud to be your partner, your lover. It's just so hard for me to go backwards."

Colt stroked Wade's face and smothered him in soft kisses. "But don't you see? That's exactly how I feel! Growing up, I didn't have the things that everyone else did. I promised myself I would have everything important in life—money, position, power. Athletics was my ticket upward, and I used it as much as athletics used me. Please, Wade . . . *please* hang in there with me. I can't do this without you. I can't. I need to know that you're in my corner. I need to know that every time I go out on that field you're right there with me. I need to know that I have you to come home to."

Wade looked Colt straight in the eye. "You don't *ever* have to question that. I'll always be there. I promise you that."

A little over a week later, Wade was picking his way down the stairs of L.A.'s Farrar Stadium, looking for seats. Susan was tagging along behind holding a beer and a hotdog. She was one of the select few Colt had agreed could know about their secret relationship.

"Where are we going?" she asked petulantly.

"Down in front," Wade called back. "I think we got reserved box seats. Colt said he'd take care of it, and it looks like he did." He looked at the seat numbers on the tickets again. Dressed for the day in a pair of worn Levi's, a long sleeve Abercrombie and Fitch T-shirt, new Colt Jennings Nikes, and a faded sun visor shielding his eyes from the late afternoon sun, Wade looked comfortable and sexy.

Colt had instructed him to pick up the comp tickets at the Will Call window. When Wade got to the window a few minutes before, he'd been greeted by a rather bored office clerk. Once Wade mentioned Colt's name, the clerk's surly attitude suddenly evaporated, and she became incredibly efficient, shuffling through papers, stamping this, and having Wade sign that.

"Is Colt as great a guy as he seems on TV?" the clerk had asked as she handed over the envelope continuing the tickets.

"Greater." Wade had smiled.

Now Wade was leading Susan down the steep steps in an attempt to find their places. The stadium was almost filled to capacity, and the crowd was rowdy.

"Dammit!" Susan swore, stopping abruptly. "I wore the wrong shoes for this."

Wade glanced back and looked at the high, expensive stilettos she was sporting and smirked. "You think?"

"Well, I wanted to look good! If we get to meet any of the other players, I wanted to be pretty." She struck an awkward pose for Wade's benefit, showing off her newly purchased tan suede skirt and chunky cropped turtleneck sweater. She was sweating to death in it, but she knew she looked fabulous, so it was worth it.

"You're always pretty," Wade replied, looking her up and down. "But I don't think meeting any of the team is going to happen. And remember, I'm Colt's 'contractor,' okay, in case anyone asks, which they won't because we won't be near anyone who knows him."

Susan continued to step down. "I remember, I remember! I'm not gonna give your tawdry little secret away." She clacked down a few more cement stairs. "Where are the fucking seats?"

"Here." Wade had stopped at a row of box seats near the fifty yard line. The seats were a few in, so they passed by several single women sitting and chatting together. The lavishly overdressed women stopped talking and looked up at them as they passed. Wade got a sinking feeling in his stomach as he located his and Susan's excellant seats.

As Susan settled into her upholstered seat, she looked around.

"Hey, these are pretty good!" She nudged Wade in the ribs. "So glad you're fucking the quarterback!" she merrily whispered into his ear.

"Shhh!" Wade hissed through smiling teeth. "Don't you know where we are?"

Susan looked at him blankly. "At the stadium?"

"No." Wade shook his head.

"Excuse me," interrupted the petite brunette seated next to Susan. Susan turned to face her.

"Yes?"

"We're all trying to figure it out . . . Whose guest are you?" She had a deep southern accent, and far too much makeup on. She looked Susan up and down skeptically.

"I'm sorry?"

"I mean"—the woman blushed—"which player is yours?" She waved airily down at the field indicating the teams.

Without thinking, Susan replied, "His," and pointed at Wade.

The brunette looked over at Wade, questions bubbling up.

Wade quickly leaned in and said in a low voice, "She's Colt Jennings's guest, really."

The brunette's eyes flashed with surprise, then envy. "Oh! So you're his new girlfriend? How exciting! We've all been dying to see who he's dating, he's been so mysterious about it! He told my husband he was seeing someone, but never said who . . ."

Susan looked at Wade with stunned surprise.

". . . I'm Tisha, Dwayne Taggart's wife," prattled on the brunette. "That's Karen, she's with Buck Howard, and that's Joe Miller's wife, Maggie . . ." Tisha then pointed out all the other team wives to Susan. They all leaned in and waved brightly, eager to see who Colt had invited.

Susan waved weakly, and looked back at Wade.

He nudged in close to Susan and whispered into her ear, "I don't know how it happened, but they gave us seats in the wive's section!"

Susan's piercing laugh rang out over the section. All the wives and girlfriends looked at her, each thinking the same thought, *So she's who Colt's banging. And such nice shoes!*

"Smile, ladies!" suddenly boomed out a deep voice. All heads snapped to the left and they spied an overweight photographer holding up a heavy camera with an enormous lens on it. "For the *Post*," he said as he held up the camera and prepared to snap.

Each of the players' wives smiled brightly and showed off her bleached teeth and perfect hair. Wade sank back so he was blocked by Susan.

The photographer snapped off a few shots, and grunted. He turned to leave. His name was Bud Logan, and he had been a popular sports columnist for L.A.'s daily afternoon paper until he'd picked up a woman who turned out to be the nanny of an enormously popular L.A. Laker. In the afterglow of sex, she impulsively told him about the real home life of this famous basketball star. Bud was shocked to hear the player often beat up his wife while in a drug-induced rage.

Bud wrote a scathing column about the man and how bad behavior like his was robbing children of real heroes. The basketball star in question sued the paper for libel, and won, to the tune of three million dollars. As punishment for not getting a second source for his story, Bud was stripped of his column and given the unglamorous task of chasing down human interest sports stories for the Home Style & Living section of the paper.

Snapping pictures of the players' wives for an article he was writing about the home life of the L.A. Earthquakes's team members was as boring a story as he had ever done. Bud hated his life these days.

But he plugged away. He knew he was just one good story away from being back in good graces with his editor. Once that was accomplished, he would get his column back.

As he was walking away, Tisha piped up. "Oh, Bud! This is Colt Jennings's new girlfriend!"

The reporter stopped in his tracks and leaned back, aiming his camera right at Susan. Tisha leaned in next to her and smiled brightly, as if she and Susan were the best of friends. Susan smiled wanly and the reporter snapped off a few shots.

Well, good to know the guy's finally got a girl, he thought, squeezing through the women to get closer to Susan. *I've been watching him for a month and never seen one.*

"He's coming over!" Susan hissed to Wade. "What the fuck do I do?"

"Please, Suse, just fake it, okay?"

"Miss? Miss? Hi. I'm Bud Logan from the *Los Angeles Post*," the puffing reporter grunted. "You the new gal in Colt's life?"

"Um . . . well, I . . ." Susan stammered.

"How long you been seeing him?"

"Isn't she adorable?" Tisha said, interrupting. "I'm just going to have to take her under my little ole wing and show her the ropes up here in the Widow's Pen!"

Bud snickered. "You two pals, then, Mrs. Taggart?"

"Oh, sure." Tisha nodded, fluffing up her hair, getting ready in case he took another picture. "Why just today, Dwayne was saying he wanted to invite them over for a barbecue." She turned to Susan. "Y'all will come, won't you? Next Friday night?"

Flustered, Susan automatically nodded. "Uh . . . yes, of course . . ." She again looked at Wade helplessly.

Bud noticed the look between the hot chick and the good-looking man seated next to her. The guy was well dressed, had a good haircut, was built up and had to be gay. And he looked like he was trying hard not to be noticed. Bud squinted his eyes. He could swear he'd seen this man before, but where?

"And who are you?" Bud finally asked.

"He's Colt's contractor!" Susan blurted out, too quickly.

Wade groaned inwardly, but managed to smile.

Bud missed none of this. "I see." He brought the camera up and snapped off a quick shot of Susan and Wade before they could protest. "Well, thanks for the photos! What's your name, miss?" he asked Susan.

"Susan. Susan Whalley."

"Great," Bud said as he scribbled this down on a small pad. "And your friend here? What's his name?"

"Wade Smith," Susan said blithely.

Wade visibly started, and tried to cover it.

Bud's dark eyes squinted again. "Okay. Great. Well, thanks, you guys." He backed up and left the area.

"Dwayne will be so excited that y'all are coming to dinner on Friday," Tisha chirped.

Susan smiled thinly and nodded. "Of course, I'll have to make sure Colt is free . . ."

"Oh, sure, I understand." Tisha dug into her inappropriately formal

Chanel bag and pulled out an elaborately embossed business card. "Call me tomorrow. We'll set it up."

Bud was halfway to the Quakes' locker room when he suddenly recalled where he'd seen that gay guy who was sitting with Colt's girlfriend before. He was surprised it hadn't occurred to him sooner.

A couple of weeks ago, he had been having a drink at a small restaurant and bar off the beaten path in Santa Monica that his cousin owned. He was waiting at the bar when he happened to glance over and see Colt Jennings sitting in a dark booth at the back of the restaurant, talking animatedly with another man. By the easy smiles, hearty laughter and quick banter between them, Bud had just assumed they were good friends.

That man with Colt, and the gay guy today, were one and the same.

And that fagola is supposed to be Colt's contractor? Bud mused, walking down the ramp way leading to the locker rooms. *If he's a contractor, then I'm a fucking ballerina.*

*   *   *

As the football season progressed, quality time between Wade and Colt became somewhat rare. Wade really only saw his often out-of-town boyfriend at night, when the exhausted player would stumble into his house, coming directly from either a grueling practice, a hard training session or a film shoot for one of the countless products he hawked. Colt would climb into the Jacuzzi, where Wade would join him. They'd fill each other in on their day, make love, and then practically fall into bed.

Wade himself was unusually busy these days as well. His real estate office was hopping, so hopping that he'd finally felt comfortable bringing in another agent, a buddy of his from his old company. And the renovations at Colt's house had become much more complicated than originally planned, so supervising that was like another full time job.

Wade missed seeing his lover more, and occasionally he would gripe to Susan that he felt like a nonentity in Colt's life. But he had to admit that, as difficult as this relationship was, it was also filled with love, humor, commitment, and a sense of belonging to something bigger than himself. Wade was completely besotted with Colt, and he knew that the famed quarterback was equally devoted to him.

He knew in a thousand small ways, even if not many others did. He knew by the unsigned flowers Colt sent to his office twice weekly. He knew by the little notes that Colt left him every time he left for an out-of-town game. He knew by the twice daily phone calls Colt never failed to make, no matter where he was. He knew by the way Colt treated him—with love, respect and attention, things he had never truly gotten from his previous relationships. He had found the real deal, and he knew that they had a shot at beating the odds—being together for the rest of their lives.

After

Six months later, the season was finally over.

Wade was giddy with excitement as he pulled into the restaurant's parking lot. The insanity of the past few months, and particularly the last two weeks, had finally quieted down. Tonight, the two lovers were going to have a quiet dinner out at a place they liked, and plan out the trip they were taking in five days to a private island in Fiji.

He shot a quick glance into the rearview mirror to make sure he looked good. His hair was freshly trimmed, and he was wearing the black turtleneck sweater Colt had given him at Christmas. He returned his attention to the road, and when he spied Colt's black Hummer H2 in the half empty parking lot, he felt his pulse start to race.

Colt had just returned to L.A. this afternoon after being out of town for two solid weeks. Wade had barely had two minutes alone with his lover over the past month to begin with, so it was doubly good to know that he would have Colt all to himself tonight, and then for three weeks in a tropical paradise.

They wouldn't have to pretend for twenty-one whole days. They would be half a world away from America, and a world away from anyone who would know who Colt Jennings was. They could finally be just what they were: two men crazy in love. Wade planned on making love to his partner morning, noon, and night. Outside, even, under the stars!

"Hey, buddy." Colt grinned as Wade slid into the booth. They were in the back of the restaurant, in the booth Colt always got. The handsome player looked as hot as always in a tight, dove gray V-neck cashmere sweater and worn jeans.

As soon as Wade was settled, he felt Colt's hand caress his thigh under the table. "Hey." Wade sighed happily. "God, I've missed you!" He resisted the strong impulse to lean over and kiss his lover passionately.

"I know! I was about half crazy in New Orleans without you . . . I *hated* that you weren't there. I'm so sorry I didn't bring you. The hotel was amazing and you could have stayed there easily. There was no one else from the team on my floor. I fucking hate that I thought it would have been a problem. I wanted to share the experience with you," the bigger man explained forcefully. His eyes blazed with love and passion as he gazed at Wade.

"I saw it all on TV. I liked your Bud Lite commercials, by the way. Very funny."

"I thought I sent you the tapes of them."

"Nope . . . And seeing you play? Damn! You looked so handsome and sweaty that I had to jerk off twice while watching the game." Wade blushed.

"You didn't!"

"I sure did. So you better eat up, and store your strength, 'cause you're going to fuck me all night long." The hand resting on his thigh squeezed tightly in anticipation.

"That's a deal! But only if you do the same to me."

"No problem."

"I love you, buddy."

"I love you, too, Colt."

The two men looked deeply into each other's eyes and each felt the bond and devotion the other felt. It was palpable and real, and seemed to flow from each one of them to wrap gently around the other.

"Well, this is a touching scene."

Wade and Colt jerked their heads up and discovered Bud Logan grinning smarmily at them, beer mug in hand.

Colt pulled his hand off Wade's thigh quickly, but the sudden movement was painfully obvious. He blushed a deep shade of red and forced a lazy, trademark Colt Jennings grin at the photographer-reporter. "Hey, Bud. what's shakin'?"

"From the looks of it, I'd say you were, Colt."

Colt's eyes turned cold. "Huh?"

"Mind if I sit down? Just for a sec?"

Colt glanced at Wade who was white as a sheet. "Uh, sure."

"Thanks." The gruff reporter sank down onto the leather banquette of the booth and stared at Wade.

Colt cleared his throat and attempted to make an introduction. "Uh, Bud . . . this is Wade Smith. He's my—"

Bud cut him off, smirking. "He's your contractor, yeah I know."

"Hello," Wade said.

"Hey," Bud barely acknowledged Wade. "So Colt, great game last week. Congratulations. The Quakes won the Super Bowl because of you, no doubt about it. Should make you really proud."

"Thanks, but everyone on the team won the game, not just me."

"Let's see the ring," Bud requested, looking at Colt's hands. He wanted to see the Super Bowl ring design for this year's winners.

"I don't wear it. It's kinda flashy."

"Huh. So, Colt, tell me. You break up with that looker? I never see her around anymore."

"Um, no. We're still together," Colt grunted, suddenly staring hard at his cocktail.

He and Wade had laughed hysterically when the photos of Susan had appeared in the *Post* touting that she was the new woman in his life. But, soon, they realized, the ruse could work to their advantage. Colt had even taken Susan to a few events, just enough to throw the hounds off the scent.

"Huh. Your first night back in town after your big Super Bowl win and you spend it with your contractor, not your gal. Interesting," Bud said cryptically. "You know, I did a little digging. Turns out your gal works for your, uh, 'contractor' here, who's really a real estate agent." He watched both men begin to squirm in their leather seats.

"What are you trying to say, Bud?" Colt said, vaguely threatening.

"Oh, nothing. Interesting that you still *need* a 'contractor.' Say, how long does it take to redo a fucking house, anyway? You've been under construction for a while now, haven't you?"

Colt felt his anger rise, but he kept it in check. "Yeah, well, you know how it is. One thing leads to another . . ."

"Right, right." Bud nodded. "But, see here's the thing. I've seen you around a lot, and practically never with your so-called 'girlfriend.' No, you're always with your contractor fellow, here. In fact, I know that even though you have a suite at the Four Seasons, the maids there say you never seem to use it. I've followed you, and found out you spend every night you're in town at Wade's house on Norma Avenue in *West Hollywood*. So, my old reporter's nose tells me there's more to this 'contractor' bullshit than you're letting on."

"I don't know what the fuck you're talking about, and I'd like it if you excused us now," Colt growled.

"You know what I think, Colt?" Bud said evenly.

"I don't give a shit what you think, Bud."

"Oh, I think you'll care about this, Colt." The reporter gave him an oily sneer. "I think you're a queer. I think this dude here is your little faggot fuck buddy. And I think you've been hoodwinking the good people of L.A. long enough. Sports hero, my ass!"

"Get the fuck away. Now!" Colt's neck muscles bulged and strained.

Bud retreated a few inches on the banquette, because he knew he was treading on dangerous ground. He had the quarterback nailed, and they both knew it. What Bud didn't know was what Colt would do now that he knew his secret was out.

"Colt, don't," Wade cautioned his lover, while trying to remain calm. "Don't."

"I'd listen to your faggot boyfriend, Colt." Bud now only half sneered.

Colt's nostrils flared at the insult directed to his lover. However, he settled back into his seat and glared at Bud. His fists balled up and then released. Balled up and released.

"What do you want?" he asked, his voice taut.

Bud chuckled. "The story, of course. You give me the exclusive and I'll treat you halfway decent." He then whistled low. "Jesus Christ! Colt Jennings a fucking faggot! I can't believe it. Aren't there any *real* men left? Shit! The fans are gonna freak! Not to mention what your teammates will do to your rump ranger ass!"

"And if I . . . if *we* refuse to cooperate with you?" Colt asked, putting a protective arm around Wade's shoulder.

"Well, you don't have much choice. I'm gonna run this story whether you help or not, you goddamned homo. I'll get the fucking Pulitzer! Either way, you're *finished*."

Colt looked at Wade, then back at the smarmy reporter. "How long? How long do I have before you print this?"

"Oh, I can't wait, this is too good! Tomorrow's paper is already a lock, so it'll have to wait until the Monday edition."

Colt thought for a moment. Then he looked evenly at Bud. "Go fuck yourself, you slimy piece of shit."

"What?" The reporter didn't think he heard right. *I have this homo dead to rights*, he thought, stunned. *This fucking pansy should be treating me with kid gloves right now because I've got him by the balls!*

Colt moved quickly over to Bud and grabbed him by the jacket lapels. He scooted forward and tossed the reporter to the floor as easily as he threw a perfect pass on Sundays.

"You print one word of it, and I'll sue your ass for libel. It won't matter if it's true or not. I'll tie you up in court for *years*, you son of a bitch. So, go ahead, take me on!" Colt seethed. He stood up and towered over the frightened, tubby reporter who was scrambling to get to his feet and away from the enraged quarterback.

"You're through! You'll never play ball again, you . . . you *fucking cocksucker!*" Bud spewed as he backed up, his feet flailing at the carpet to get traction.

Colt followed him, taking small steps to continue to hover over the reporter. "You're an idiot, Bud. I can't fuck *and* suck cock at the same time. While I've gotten really awesome at doing each individually, I'm not that good of a contortionist. Now, my husband here *can* fuck me and suck my cock at the same time. He's *amazing*."

Bud's mouth dropped open and he found he was too stunned to speak.

Colt motioned for Wade to get up and join him. Wade got out of the booth, and both men looked down at Bud. "What I just said," Colt said calmly, "was, of course, off the record, you fucking scumbag."

Colt and Wade were sitting in the H2, driving back to Wade's house. Neither one spoke. Wade would send Susan back tomorrow to get his forgotten SUV.

Finally, unable to stand it any longer, Wade broke the silence. "Is that how you think of me? As your husband? 'Cause that's how I think of you."

"Of course that's what I think!" The big ball player reached out over the H2's massive console and took Wade's hand in his own. "I'm sorry I didn't say it before now."

"Jesus, Colt."

"What?"

"Everything. You just outed yourself. To a reporter!"

"I know. Felt good."

Wade began to giggle, and Colt looked at him quizzically. Then, realizing what an absurd scene had just taken place, he, too, started to laugh. Soon, they were both in hysterics.

"I can't believe you told that man that not only do you suck cock, but that you're *awesome* at it!" Wade hooted.

"Well, you told me I was," Colt said, wiping away tears of laughter from his eyes.

Wade unbuckled his seat belt and leaned over. "And you are, baby. You are!" He kissed Colt gently on the cheek.

"Well, it's gonna be all over the papers now, huh?" Colt said seriously, as the realization of his rash actions hit home.

"Yeah, I think it is. I just hate that that wormy little cockroach is gonna be the one to break the news first," Wade replied, getting back into his seat.

Colt thought for a moment. "Maybe. Maybe not . . ."

"Almost time," Wade said, trying to make small talk. He looked over at his husband and still felt that same warm rush of emotions that he'd felt the first time he'd seen him, so many years before.

Colt took a deep breath, and then exhaled slowly.

Wade knew Colt was tense. He had that rare look he got when he was unsure of himself. The big ball player kept fiddling with his hair, and it was driving the flamboyantly dressed makeup man, Jose, crazy.

"Mr. Jennings?" Jose finally said. "I can't finish if you keep doing that."

"Doing what? Oh, sorry." Colt gave a half smile, then retreated back into his thoughts.

"Mr. Jennings," Jose said softly.

"Yeah?"

"You're going to be fine. It's going to go great, I promise you. Tandra is the best at this sort of interview. You're in good hands." He smiled at the handsome football star and tried not to notice his dreamy blue eyes and rippling muscles bunching up at his shoulders.

Colt's facial features were a blank for a minute, then a trademark Colt Jennings grin came through, and he smiled broadly. "Thanks. Thanks for saying that, Jose."

"Jose," Wade interjected, "can you give us a minute?"

"Oh, sure. I can do a quick puff and fluff right before he goes on set." The thin makeup artist put down his brush and went to the dressing room door. Before opening it, he faced Colt and Wade. "And just for the record, I'm so . . . proud that you're doing this. It's a giant step . . . for all of us." He smiled awkwardly, then left the small room.

Colt left out another big breath of air. "Buddy, I don't feel so good . . ."

Wade crossed to him, and bent over the huge bulk that was his husband. He wrapped his arms around Colt protectively, and squeezed gently. "Oh, babe, you're going to do fine, I know it. I love you so much right now, I can't even tell you."

"Try. I need to hear it," the bigger man said, closing his eyes and relishing the loving touch of his partner.

Wade let go and came around to the front of the chair. He leaned up against the counter of the makeup table and gazed down at Colt. He placed his sweating hands on the well worn denim of his faded jeans. While Colt had dressed up a bit for his appearance on Tandra's show, Wade had dressed comfortably in jeans, Italian running shoes, and a tight LASC T-shirt.

"You remember that first night?" Wade asked. "When we . . . you know . . ."

Colt grinned and blushed slightly. "I remember."

"Do you remember that you were scared and excited and nervous? You *wanted* to cross that line. You knew you could never go back once you did, and you *did* it. You came to me. I love you for that. For taking that chance and putting yourself on the line. You opened up your heart and your mind and you followed your true path."

Colt listened rapturously.

"It's the same thing now. You're following your true path. No more hiding who you are. No more extravagant stories. This is going to make your life . . . our life . . . so much better."

"Then," Colt asked softly, "why am I so nervous?"

"Because you're afraid."

Colt looked at Wade sharply, his eyebrows rising.

"I don't mean it in a bad way." Wade smiled. "You're afraid of what's going to happen with the team, the endorsements, your contracts. And you're right. We've discussed this a thousand times. They might just dry up and go away. But it's not like we're going to starve. You have to do this! You owe it to every other gay athlete out there who thinks he can't be who he really is."

Colt sighed and got up.

"Besides," Wade continued, a sly grin spreading across his face. "It's a little late to rethink it now."

Colt jammed his hands into his pockets, and began to pace around the room. "No shit."

"Colt, you came from nothing and made something amazing out of your life. And you've chosen me to share it with. I couldn't be prouder of you."

Colt looked at him and they locked eyes.

"But, I have something I have to say to you."

Colt mentally braced himself. "Okay . . ."

"If you're doing this for me, don't," Wade said. "It's the wrong reason. You need to do this for *you*. You need to stand up and accept yourself. Be proud of who and what you are. I'll be there for you all the way, but do this to please yourself, not me."

"I love you, Wade. I love you more than I thought it possible to love another human being," Colt said, an odd catch in his voice. "But I'm doing this for *us*. Because without you, I'm not me. And I like who I am when I'm with you." He turned around and faced the door. "And if America can't handle it, screw 'em."

"My God, the man I love is fearless," Wade replied in awe, moving toward him.

"I don't know if it's being fearless or being foolish," Colt said.

"Either way, I'm yours, baby."

There was a sudden knock at the door, and Colt jumped.

"Mr. Jennings? We're ready for you on set," called out a thin, nasally voice from the other side.

"Give us just a minute more, please?" Wade called back.

"I have to pee," Colt said quickly. He dashed into the bathroom and shut the door.

Wade wandered back to the empty makeup chair. Sinking down into it, he sighed and used the few seconds of quiet time to reflect back on the craziness of the past two days.

As soon as they arrived home from the restaurant on Saturday night, Colt was on the phone. He had done several charity events with Tandra Collins, one of the most influential daytime talk show hosts on television, and he had her private phone number.

Tandra Collins had the complete faith of America, and people trusted her implicitly. She didn't do tabloid television, like Jerry Springer or Ricki Lake did. Her shows were about real people doing extraordinary things, or gripping shows about self-realization and improvement.

After speaking with Colt at length about his story and what he wanted to do, she had generously offered Colt an entire hour to discuss his life and address the rumors that would soon start swirling around him. She called him back two times on Saturday night as the details of the show were hastily completed.

He and Wade had flown to New York on Sunday, to be ready for Monday's taping. The special edition show would be shot live for New York audiences, and tape delayed by three hours for L.A. Colt's version of his life would air two hours before the story broke in the afternoon edition of the Los Angeles Post.

Tandra herself had been kind, warm, and understanding. She promised Colt that he would be able to say what he wanted, and she would not embarrass him in any way.

Wade and Colt had discussed the idea all the way across the country on the plane, with Wade agreeing it was a great way to blunt the bad press Bud Logan's story would generate.

Now, in the dressing room, Wade began to rub his temples. What would he do if Colt backed out? He realized he honestly didn't know.

The bathroom door opened and Colt reemerged. He looked slightly pale and his nervousness was clearly apparent.

"Buddy," he said, wiping his hands on his pants. "It's show time."

Wade breathed a sigh of relief. "I'm glad."

"Yeah, I bet you are." Colt finally grinned slightly.

"It's gonna be fine."

Colt gulped. "Nothing's ever going to be the same after this, is it?"

"No. It'll be better."

"I hope so." Colt looked at the mirror and studied his reflection. He knew he looked good. He was in a thin jersey knit shirt that was unbuttoned a few buttons, showing off his impressive chest. Crisply pressed flat front slacks and subtle new Gucci loafers completed his look.

There was another knock at the door. "Mr. Jennings? It's Sandy. I'm the producer? We really need you on set. The audience is in place and we're ready to go . . ."

"I'll be right out," Colt called back. He squared his shoulders and faced his partner. "I love you."

"I know you do. You're making me the proudest man in the world right now, babe."

Colt looked at Wade for a beat. "You know what? *I'm* the proudest man in the world. I have *you*. You stuck by me during the past year and through all this insanity. What the hell am I so afraid of? Fuck 'em if they can't take it! As long as I have you, I can face anything. Let's rock and roll."

Wade thought his heart would burst.

"Ten, nine, eight . . ." counted down the stage manager into her headset.

Wade watched the activity from the wings of the stage. He glanced at the crowd waiting breathlessly for Tandra to come out. He noticed happily that the audience seemed to be filled with gay men, so they would be friendly, and that was a plus.

"... three, two ..."

"Welcome to *The Tandra Collins Show!*" the announcer's voice boomed out over the stage. There was wild applause from the excited audience, and after a few seconds of cheering, the announcer continued. "Tandra's special guest today is the one and only Colton Jennings, star quarterback from the Los Angeles Earthquakes!" The cheering grew fanatical. "And now ... here's our lady, here's Tandra!"

Tandra strolled out from behind a large neon cutout of her name. A tall, whippet thin African-American, Tandra oozed self confidence and honesty. She was wearing a smartly tailored pantsuit of gray shantung silk and had a jaunty yellow Hermes scarf tied casually around her neck. Her trademark hair, a sleek mass of toffee-colored curls, was perfectly in place.

"Hello," she said in her husky voice. "Welcome to the show!" She crossed downstage and approached a pair of cream-colored thickly upholstered chairs. "Today is a very special show. A landmark show. I will only have one guest, and he is the epitome of American 'can do.' He is a Heisman Trophy winner, the Dallas Cowboys' most valuable player three years in a row, and now, some say he personally led the Los Angeles Earthquakes to their Super Bowl victory a week ago. Please welcome a great man, an honorable man, and my friend, Colton Jennings!"

The audience came to its feet, applauding and cheering wildly. Colt ambled out from behind a revolving flat and waved sheepishly at the crowd's adulation.

He went to Tandra and gave her the proper double cheek kiss and light hug, then they both took seats and faced the audience.

"Well," Tandra said. "They certainly love you!"

"It's very flattering to get such a welcome. Thank you."

"First, I have to say, great game at the Super Bowl in New Orleans!" The audience applauded loudly. "Were you confident the Quakes were going to win?" Tandra asked after they stopped.

Colt pondered the question. "Well, I knew the team was ready. We had earned the right to be there. Every man on the Earthquakes team wanted to bring home the championship, so I think we came to the game ready to kick a ... er, to win, and that's just what we did."

"You can say ass on my show," Tandra joshed.

Colt laughed. "I didn't know." He paused. "I'm a little nervous, I guess."

"Well, before we get too far along, I want to roll some tape we put together on you and your many accomplishments over the years. Watch this," Tandra said, turning to a large screen behind them.

A videotape began to play, and Wade, standing behind a shimmering peach-colored curtain, wondered how they had pulled this show together so damn fast. It was amazing.

The tape began with rarely seen footage of Colt playing in high school. Wade was surprised to find he himself had shot most of it.

Then the video segued into Colt's college years, showed him receiving his Heisman Trophy, and then gave a good description of his life with the Dallas Cowboys. There was a section on his marriage to Cindy, and there was even a bit on Colt's many lucrative product endorsements, which had the audience laughing along with him.

Colt's first year with the L.A. Earthquakes rounded out the end of the video, and when it was over there was more thunderous applause from the audience.

"So," Tandra said, after the audience quieted down. "When you watch that, what goes through your mind?"

"Well, it's kind of weird to see me looking so young and handsome, for one thing," Colt cracked. The audience laughed and then Colt grew serious. "Actually, as I watched that, I realized I've had a blessed life. Every goal I ever set out for myself I have been able to achieve, and I think that's a rare thing for a man to be able to say. If it all ends tomorrow, it will be okay, because I'll know I got to live my dream."

Again, the audience applauded.

"But," Colt continued, "It did feel like something was missing."

"Oh? What was that?" Tandra asked.

Colt took a deep breath. "Well, I came here today to talk about my life. Past, present, and future . . ."

Wade found he was holding his breath and clutching the silky curtain with a death grip.

"And while . . . that great video . . . showed my past," Colt said haltingly, "it doesn't represent my present *or* my future. . . . Something, or rather *someone*, important was left out, and I missed seeing that."

Tandra knew Colt was struggling to find the right words. She reached out a calming hand and gently squeezed his arm. "Go on," she said.

Colt looked over to the spot where Wade was standing, and locked eyes with his lover. "What was missing was my partner, my lover, and my husband, Wade. He's the man I love with all my heart, and the man I plan to spend the rest of my life with."

There was a stunned moment of silence in the studio, then murmuring began to build as the audience members began to talk among themselves.

"I came here today to announce that I'm gay, and I guess that makes me the first openly gay player still active in the NFL."

The roar of the audience built to a crescendo. All the gay members of the audience stood up and cheered like they had never cheered before. Colt choked back tears as he watched the crowd scream and yell their approval of his declaration. The waves of love and acceptance flowed over the stage, and even Tandra was moved by the enthusiastic response her guest was getting.

"You're a very brave man, Colt," she said after the audience sat back down. "This announcement could hurt your career, couldn't it?"

Colt shrugged. "Sure. I guess that was my biggest fear, that I wouldn't be able to play ball anymore. But, I have a contract with the Quakes through next season, so there's not much they can do. They don't have to use me, they can make me sit on the sidelines, but they can't fire me."

"How do you feel about that?"

"I think it would be a waste of my talents. Look, I know the team is strong without me, but it's stronger *with* me. I just don't think a player's personal life should have any bearing on his ability to play football."

"What about your endorsement deals?"

Again Colt shrugged. "Only time will tell. I have no idea how this is going to play out. But I can't worry about it anymore."

"So, tell me, Colt," Tandra said soothingly, "why are you coming out now? Why not wait to announce this until after you retire, like others have done?"

Colt grinned. "To be honest? That was my original plan. But certain events have forced me to do this now. A reporter in L.A. is writing a . . . mean-spirited story about me, and I felt like it was my right to discuss my personal life my own way, first." Colt's eyes narrowed and his determination to reclaim his life was all too clear. "And, frankly, it was getting too complicated to pretend I was straight. I have a wonderful guy in my life, someone I am committed to, and I knew I was hurting him by pretending he didn't exist. Well, he does exist, and by coming out, I feel like this enormous weight has been lifted from my shoulders."

"I'd like to meet him. I know he's here, and I'd like to bring him out."

"Only if he wants to," Colt said.

Wade felt his feet moving before he realized he was walking out onto the stage floor. He wasn't even concerned that his attire was less than television worthy, and he was so focused on Colt that he didn't hear the applause that greeted his sudden appearance.

When he reached his lover, Colt stood up, obviously relieved to have Wade by his side, and wrapped his massive arms around him. The two men kissed passionately.

The audience gasped at this display of masculine affection and tenderness, but soon they were happily applauding and cheering. Wade blushed and took a seat next to Colt, in a hastily added extra chair. The quarterback held on to his hand, and didn't let it go.

"Hi, Wade," Tandra said.

"Hi, Tandra," Wade replied, somewhat shy in her presence.

"How do you feel about Colt's decision to come out?"

Wade gulped. "I'm incredibly awed by his courage. But, he's such a strong man that, if *anyone* can handle whatever comes because of this, he can." Colt smiled broadly and squeezed Wade's hand.

"Did it bother you when he was closeted?"

"Well, I'm in love him, so of course I wanted to be able to share that with all of my friends and family, but I knew what I was getting into when we began our relationship. I went into it with my eyes wide open, so while it was really hard at times, I knew if I was patient, one day it would all work out."

"And he was *extremely* patient," Colt joked, before becoming serious. "Wade once said to me what a great world it would be if everyone could just be who they were. 'Drop the drag,' was the phrase he used, I think. I only mention this because I'm kinda ashamed of myself."

"How come?" Wade asked, surprised.

Colt faced his lover. "I'm ashamed that I asked you to compromise your beliefs. I'm ashamed that it was me, who from the time you and I were kids, who was always held up as the standard of what a man should strive to be. It turns out that I'm not half the man that you are. I am, however, willing to try harder."

"Oh, Colt . . ." Wade sighed, deeply touched by the words.

Tandra directed her next question to the ball player. "So, it is true that you've known each other for, like, twenty years?"

Colt nodded and grinned widely. "Yeah. We grew up together in Houston. We drifted apart during college, but I never forgot him. I've been in love with him my whole life. I just didn't know it until this past year."

Speechless, Wade could only beam at him.

"And I've learned so much from him," Colt added.

"Oh?" Tandra cocked an eyebrow. "Such as?"

Colt thought for a moment, wanting to get the words he felt so deeply, right. "He made me realize what being a man is really all about," he finally ventured. "It's not about bluster or acting cool and tough, or making a million dollars a year. Being a man means standing up for your beliefs, even when no one else does. Even if it means being a lone voice." The knowledge that he had a lifetime ahead of him with Wade gave Colt the confidence to continue. "It means never compromising who you are simply to please others. It means being honest and open and making each day count. These are the things I have learned from Wade." His eyes locked with Wade's, and the two men smiled slightly at each other. "He patiently and compassionately helped guide me, kickin' and screamin' all the way," Colt drawled dryly, "on the road to self-discovery, and I love him more than I can adequately express."

Salty tears suddenly threatened to fall from Wade's dark eyes. He blinked them back.

"I think I believed that if I kept my head down, and my mouth shut, I could fool everyone around me into thinking I was something I wasn't," Colt continued, determined to say everything he wanted to. "Wade, here, always saw the absurdity of that, but I didn't. I couldn't allow myself to believe that I needed to stand up and make a difference, so it's easier for the next guy coming along to be who he really is."

When Colt finished speaking, Wade whispered, "I love you so much."

"I love you more," the football hero whispered back.

Tandra, who had seen couples come and go on her show, realized she was witnessing the real thing today. *They're going to make it,* she thought. Clearing her throat, she said, "Colt, have you given any serious thought to what you're going to do after you stop playing?"

"Yeah, actually we have," Colt said, squeezing Wade's hand. "I want to start up a handcrafted furniture company. Maybe open a store."

"You should see the beautiful furniture he's made," Wade said to Tandra. "He's amazing with his hands."

The audience snickered at this, and Wade blushed crimson.

"I'm sure he is," Tandra cracked. Colt, then Wade, began to laugh. "So, Wade. This is the start of a new life for you two, isn't it?" The TV host asked.

"Absolutely! The sky's the limit. I'm always telling Colt that he can do anything he sets his mind to."

Colt leaned over and, nuzzling his husband, sighed happily. "You're right about that. I got the man of my dreams, didn't I?"

Sex and the Single Rock Star

Jon Jeffrey

For Timothy Hedgepeth
aka Tina Peck

A great friend who truly understands my harmless obsessions with the Jackies (Collins and Susann), George Eads, Danny Nucci, Julian Mc-Mahon, Amy from Paradise Hotel, *Kylie Minogue,* Smallville, *gummi bears imported from Spain, and cranberry juice.*

Even better, he gets it when I call him up to say, "I'm worried about Jason Cerbone. He needs new management!"

I used to be snow-white . . . but I drifted.
                                          —Mae West

Chapter One

Grant Browder tore his mouth away from those perfect lips and slowly skated his tongue down the man's neck, closing in on the right nipple . . .

That's when Kirby Rex sighed the sigh of the bored and the frustrated.

Grant froze.

"You know what? Just forget it. I can't do this."

Grant shut his eyes.

Kirby rolled out of bed and began to get dressed. "I should finish packing, anyway."

"Come on," Grant said, hating the desperation in his voice but reaching for Kirby anyway.

His almost-ex twisted out of his grasp. "What's the point? I'm with Jason now. One more time will just make it harder. For you."

Grant felt a flash of anger. "So this latest humiliation is actually a good thing for me. Thanks for looking out." Shoving on his Marc Jacobs jeans and Dartmouth sweatshirt, he watched Kirby pack. "Wait a minute. That Creed cologne is mine."

Kirby spun around. "No, it's not. I bought this."

"No, you bought Green Irish Tweed and left it in the hotel bathroom when we went to Atlanta for your stupid cousin's wedding. That's Silver Mountain Water. A birthday gift from my sister."

Kirby set it back down with a bang.

Instantly, Grant felt a tinge of regret. Being petty at the end was such a sign of weakness. "Never mind. Take it. It smells better on you anyway."

"I don't want your fucking cologne," Kirby snapped, moving into the bathroom.

Grant charged in after him. "What's your problem?" He watched as Kirby stuffed every Kiehl's product within plain sight into his duffel bag.

"You're so goddamn predictable. I knew you'd make an issue out of the cologne. I knew you'd bring up my cousin's wedding. Jesus, you're even predictable in bed."

Grant could feel his face register the hit. First dumped, then branded a lousy fuck. What a week. "Um . . . all of those Kiehl's items are mine, too."

Kirby turned his bag upside down. It hailed Kiehl's, and the clatter was deafening.

"Just for the record, you hated your cousin's wedding more than I did, even though I'm the one who got stuck with your boring uncle for two hours."

Kirby stared back in silent anger. Finally, he spoke. "You don't know boring. Try being me having sex with you. Now *that's* boring."

Grant wanted to disappear through the big cracks in the ugly tile. Sexual confidence was his Achilles' heel, and Kirby, the son of a bitch, knew it. No matter the hurt, Grant managed to just shrug. "I can't compete. Everyone knows that rich guys with great apartments make better lovers."

There was a glint in Kirby's eyes. "Do they say the same thing about delivery boys? Because the guy with the eyebrow piercing from Fat Eddie's Pizza has you beat, too."

Grant knew the shock was all over his face.

Kirby started out. "If I left anything, I'll have Liv drop by and pick it up."

And those were the last words they said to each other.

Instead of looking out the window to watch Kirby get into the cab that would take him to his newer, richer, more sexually exciting boyfriend, Grant plopped onto the couch and stuck in the DVD of *Far From Heaven.*

Just as the hunky black gardener was handing Julianne Moore her scarf, the phone jangled. Deep down, he hoped that it was Kirby calling to apologize.

"Hello?" He tried to keep his voice even, not too upbeat, not too downtrodden.

"Grant?" The voice was female, throaty, and supremely confident. Very Demi Moore. And she didn't waste time on confirmation of who he was. "It's Kate Bobo from *Velocity.*"

He bolted up from his reclining position. Covering film, television, music, and books for the glossier, more successful answer to *Maxim* and *FHM* put him in regular contact with the entertainment editor, but never—until now—the "top bitch in charge," as Kate was so fond of billing herself.

"I hope you're wearing a diaper."

"A diaper?"

"Because you're going to shit when you hear what I'm about to tell you."

Grant hated surprises. He felt his armpits dampen almost immediately.

Kate Bobo could hardly get the words out fast enough. "I need a fresh voice for a very important cover story. Naturally, I tried to find a big name freelancer, but everybody's swamped, and the deadline's too tight. So then I thought of you."

Grant sat there, stunned. He hadn't even realized that Kate was aware of his existence. Now she wanted him for a major feature, the cover no less. "Seriously?"

"Fuck, yeah," Kate remarked easily. "You're a fantastic writer. It's time you got out of DVD reviews and fall TV roundups. That's an intern's job."

Grant couldn't quite believe it. In the last hour he'd been declared a great writer and a lousy lay. But he could live with that. "So what's the piece? You're killing me."

Kate sucked in an excited breath. "Who is the most delicious man in music today?"

"Justin Timberlake?"

Kate sighed. "Only certain women will admit to wanting to fuck Justin. I'm talking about a man who has every woman in America creaming."

Grant halted. "Do you mean—"

"Yes, baby, I'm talking about Ronan."

"No way!"

Kate cackled. "Fuck, I'm dying for a cigarette! Yes, Ronan! Would I lie about something like this? I've been working on it for months. And I've got the battle scars to show for it. His publicist is Sailor Moynihan, and she's an absolute bitch. I think she was born a preemie and instead of the incubator they shoved her in a deep freezer. Anyway, you're cleared to tag along on the promotional tour for his new CD. It's called *Tantric*. Have you heard it?"

"No," Grant said, somewhat breathlessly, his head spinning. "Not yet."

"It's fucking awesome," Kate went on. "Totally rocks. I'll messenger a promo copy over today with a clippings file. Oh, and the tour wraps at the Super Bowl. Ronan just signed to do the halftime show. Poor you."

Grant ran his free hand through his hair and started to pull. Yes, he was feeling that, so yes, this was real.

For all practical comparisons, Ronan was the Colin Farrell of rock— young, Irish, hard partying, a notoriously sexual creature, so crude that every other word required a bleep, and, at the end of the day, still com- pulsively likable. His music was hard charging, hook laden, and in- stantly hummable. Nobody would ever confuse his songs with, say, Bono's, but who didn't love blistering guitars, choruses that stuck in your brain, and a lyric that you had memorized after two spins, three tops?

What added such satisfaction to this excitement was the fact that Kirby loved Ronan. No, it wasn't just love. It was a goddamn obsession. A healthy one, but an obsession just the same. Kirby had paid an out- rageous sum on eBay for a bootleg copy of *Tantric* weeks before its of- ficial release. Then he downloaded to his iPod, and the rest was sheer oblivion.

Grant couldn't wait to break the news. Hmm. Does *Jason* have one-on-one access to Ronan? No, probably not. Ha! God, if ever there was a case of beautiful poetic justice.

"I'm looking for a wild account told in the first person," Kate was saying. "How does it feel to be caught up in the zenith of Ronan's level of fame? What does it smell like? I want this to be sensory driven. Bring the reader onto Ronan's private plane, into his bed, anywhere that—"

Grant hesitated. "Wait a minute. Did you say into his bed?"

"Hopefully," Kate said matter-of-factly. "Everyone knows that Ronan's an equal opportunity slut. The rumor is that he's exceptionally well hung and uncircumcised. At the very least I'll expect a confirmation on that. Okay, so I'll slip the itinerary into this package. You'll have it in a couple of hours. The pay is four bucks a word. Deal?"

Grant had never earned that much for a piece. "Yes, it's fine."

"Just expense whatever you have to. And start packing. They're expecting you in L.A. tomorrow. Listen, I have to fly. Keep me posted on your progress by E-mail. I want a *juicy* cover story. Do you get me?"

"Loud and clear," Grant said quietly.

And then Kate Bobo signed off.

The reality continued to boggle Grant's mind. He screened the rest of *Far From Heaven* in a daze, then fired up his laptop to Google Ronan. The fan-based shrines went on forever. He was engrossed in a particularly ambitious one when three fast knocks rapped the door.

It was a bike messenger with the package from *Velocity*.

Grant ripped it open and shoved the CD into the stereo right away. The first track and first single, "Hard to Resist," blasted throughout the apartment. Before the first guitar solo, Grant was singing along, dancing, too.

Kirby had cheated on him twice, left him for another guy, and dropped an insult that made Grant feel excruciatingly inadequate. But he was feeling pretty damn good right now. His career had just been given a boost, and he was about to embark on a journey that would make Kirby Rex insane with jealousy.

Before he left for the airport the next morning, he called Kirby's cell phone. As expected, it rang straight into voice mail.

"This is Kirby Rex. I'm unavailable at the moment. You know what to do."

The sound of his voice nearly killed Grant. It almost took the fun out of what he was about to do. Almost. But not quite.

Beep. "Hi, Kirby, it's Grant. Listen, if Liv plans to pick up the rest of your things, could you ask her to wait until I get home? I'm off to Los Angeles on assignment but should be back in about a week. I'm going on a promotional tour with Ronan. Can you believe it? Exclusive access, in-depth interview. Should be pretty cool. I'll try to get him to sign a napkin for you, maybe a CD. I know he's one of your favorites. Anyway, I'll be in touch sometime after I get back. Take care."

And then he hung up. There were two words to describe moments like this one: Fucking satisfying.

Chapter Two

"His childhood, his work experiences before stardom, anything related to sex or personal relationships, politics, his opinions about other artists . . ."

Grant sat in the sleek lobby of The Standard Hollywood in Los Angeles, listening as Ronan's publicist, Sailor Moynihan, rattled off an imposing list of off-limits topics.

Sailor's cell phone rang about every three minutes. She answered every call with the same clipped, icy indifference, as if she couldn't be bothered, never once apologizing to Grant for the interruptions.

He sat patiently, observing the rude ninety-pound girl with the bitten nails. Representing Ronan, she had scaled near the top of the Hollywood flack heap. So why did she look so miserable?

"And *nothing* about alcohol or drug use." Sailor beamed a hostile look. "Not a word."

"What about his favorite snack food?"

Sailor didn't crack a smile.

Grant started to laugh. "You're not leaving me with much to pursue here."

"Ronan doesn't *need* the cover of *Velocity*. The tour is already sold out, and the CD has already shipped double platinum. I stand ready to pull the plug on this piece right now. There's a shuttle leaving the hotel for LAX in a half hour. You could be on it."

"I'm just saying—"

"Fine," Sailor cut in. "I'll tell Ronan the interview's off." She pressed a few buttons on her cell phone.

"That won't be necessary," Grant said calmly. "I accept your terms. No questions about anything . . . that you mentioned."

Sailor lowered the cellular and stood up. "Good. Just know that I *will* terminate this story. Anytime. Remember that." She reached into her Lulu Guinness bag and pulled out a pack of Salem Lights. Her hand was shaking. "I've got to leave. There's a crisis situation to manage. Leif will be down in a few minutes. He's Ronan's manager."

A few minutes turned into two hours. When Leif finally showed up, Grant was surprised to be looking into the face of a man younger than he was.

Leif's handshake pumped fast and firm. "You haven't been waiting long, right?"

"Just a few hours," Grant said.

"Oh, great," Leif replied. And there wasn't a hint of sarcasm attached to his answer.

Grant followed Leif to the elevator. "What kind of surprises do you have planned for the Super Bowl show?"

Leif hesitated. "Actually, I'm heading out to Houston to try to save that deal. I want more stage time for Ronan."

"They could always cut the game back to three quarters."

Leif cracked a smile.

The elevator doors opened, and a glorious looking Kim Cattrall walked out, her eyes eclipsed by Christian Dior sunglasses.

Leif watched her ass until it was out of view. "How many guys do you think she's fucked on that show?"

Grant couldn't stand not knowing for one more second. "If you don't mind, I have to ask . . . how old are you?"

"Twenty-five. Why?"

"Because I couldn't make my bed at twenty-five, and you're managing a superstar."

Leif laughed a little. "My dad's in the business. He's managed everyone from Fleetwood Mac to Madonna. That's not to imply that

I'm worthless. I'm fucking great at what I do. But I was blessed with a few shortcuts."

Grant smiled at Leif's honesty.

"I'll introduce you to LaKeisha. She's Ronan's assistant and knows his schedule better than I do." He paused as the elevator journeyed up. "What magazine is this for again?"

"*Velocity.*"

Leif nodded. "Ah, yes. I subscribe. Great shot of Tara Reid's tits on last month's cover."

"I can't take any credit for that, but I'm glad you were pleased."

The elevator stopped on the ninth floor.

Leif exited.

Grant followed him, palms sweating, heart racing a bit. Ronan, after all, was in close proximity.

Leif came to a stop and rapped softly on the door.

A heavy black girl answered. "Why you got to stank up the room with that shit? Eat a goddamn can of Pringles, hell." She frowned at Leif and gave Grant a dismissive glance.

"What's wrong?" Leif asked.

She pointed at a hulking figure on the couch. "That motherfucker's eating hard boiled eggs and making this room smell like somebody's ass."

Leif turned to Grant. "This is . . . what's your name again?"

"Grant Browder." He extended his hand.

The black girl grunted and refused to shake. "I don't need no life insurance."

Grant looked to Leif.

"He's doing a feature on Ronan for *Velocity,*" Leif explained.

"Who?"

"Grant Browder."

She rolled her eyes. "Okay, you're Grant Browder. Get this motherfucker a name tag. Hell. I've never heard of some *Velocity.* What's that?"

"It's a men's lifestyle magazine, similar to *Maxim,* I guess."

She remained unimpressed. "Never heard of that, either. The only thing you'll catch my ass reading is a *Jet* book." A claw of talon-like nails waved through the air. "Whatever."

Leif's face took on a slightly weary expression. "This is LaKeisha Edmonds, Ronan's personal assistant." He pointed to the teamster watching *Ocean's Eleven.* "And that's Jagger, his bodyguard."

LaKeisha scowled at Leif. "I hope Sailor told this man what she don't want him asking, because if she gets all up in my face with that shit, I will force-feed her no eating ass a damn Pop-Tart. And you know I will."

Grant nodded. "I'm clear on the taboo topics."

LaKeisha addressed no one in particular when she announced, "I don't know why she's so damn crazy about that. Knowing Ronan gonna tell all his business anyway."

Leif glanced to the closed door leading to one of the suite's bedrooms. "So, what's our superstar doing now?"

LaKeisha grunted again. "What do you think? Getting his drunk on."

Leif started for the exit. "Help Grant get started. He'll be with us for the rest of the promo tour. I'm off to Houston."

"You better not forget my tickets," LaKeisha warned. "I've got a mama and three brothers worrying the shit out of me about that damn Super Bowl."

Leif left without acknowledgment.

"Come on before this fool falls asleep," LaKeisha said, gesturing for Grant to follow her. She entered the bedroom without knocking.

Ronan was sprawled across a luxurious king-size bed, wearing only tight black Versace bikini underwear.

"This is Grant. He's writing a story for some magazine. How long you want to talk to him?"

Ronan's dark eyes zeroed in on Grant. He stretched lazily, scratching an impressive bulge. "As long as he keeps me interested."

LaKeisha shook her head. "You ain't got no home training." She flipped open a Palm Pilot and played around with it for a moment. "There's a party in the Hollywood Hills tonight. That's it until tomorrow morning. But you've got three radio phoners between seven and nine."

Ronan grinned and winked at Grant. "Fuck that."

LaKeisha shuffled over to replenish Ronan's Vitamin Water. "Fuck your new song if you don't call these damn DJs. You ain't no 50 Cent. He got three songs in the top forty, and you trying to get one up in there."

Ronan winked again. He obviously relished their routine.

"I'm taking me a break. I've been seeing after your ass all day, and now my stomach's growling." She closed the door behind her.

Ronan stared at him. There was mischief in his eyes. "Did Sailor give you the ground rules?"

"Yeah, she did."

"Better write this down, then. I grew up in Castleknock, Ireland. A few years before I signed with Sony, I was in a boy band called Sweat that never got picked up. I choose to be bisexual because that usually ensures my chances of getting laid. I'm not registered to vote and could give a fuck about Democrats, Republicans, or Green Party wackos. Given the chance, I'd beat John Mayer to a bloody pulp with his own guitar. And in my book, a couple of pints, a joint, and a few lines of coke never hurt anybody. There. Have I officially given Sailor good reason to wolf down a box of Krispy Kremes?"

Grant pretended to mull over the question. "Yes, especially if I lead with the John Mayer threat. Unless that was off the record."

"Nothing's off the record, man. That's why I don't give a fuck." He stretched again. "Put it all out there. Let the vultures sort it out. That's what I say."

Grant put his map case down on a chair and began to fish out his notebook. His eyes fell on the voice-activated recorder at the bottom of the bag. "Do you mind if I tape this?"

Suddenly, Ronan bounced from the bed and rushed over to him.

"Audio or video?"

Grant smiled sheepishly, waving the slim silver machine. He was alarmed but also intoxicated by Ronan's invasion of personal space.

At five feet nine, Ronan was shorter than Grant had imagined. Except for a bad highlight job, his dark features ruled—thick black eyebrows, large gypsy eyes, and a scruffy three-day stubble. The body was trainer torture perfect, defined and muscular but not overdone.

Tattoos were inked everywhere, not exactly the Tommy Lee extreme, but he definitely believed in using the body as a canvas.

Ronan reached out and took Grant's head in both hands. "Put the recorder away. We can do the interview later. I want to get to know you better first."

Grant swallowed hard. Generally speaking, a man standing this close in his underwear talking about getting to know you better is probably not that interested in why you chose journalism as a career.

"Jesus Christ, you're so fucking adorable," Ronan said. He squeezed Grant's head and stared into his eyes with a sweet intensity.

Grant averted his gaze. "I'm thirty-three. Technically, I think I'm past being adorable."

"You've got a boyish quality," Ronan argued. He raked Grant up and down with a horny glance. "God, I want to fuck you. Right now. Would you like that?"

"I think I'm the one who's supposed to be asking questions." Grant felt oddly detached, as if he were watching this bizarre scene and not playing a role in it.

"Come on. We'll have some fun." Ronan's breath smelled faintly of beer and tobacco. "Look at what you've done to me . . . Mr. Adorable Boy." He took Grant's right hand and brought it down to his crotch.

Grant tried to get a handle on the insanity. Within five minutes of meeting Ronan, the rock star of the moment, he stood there with a hand on his cock and an open invitation to be his bottom boy for the afternoon.

Ronan's eyes were hooded with lust. What was already big got bigger.

Grant felt himself responding, too. "You know, this is my first major assignment. I probably shouldn't sleep with my subject."

Ronan waved off the concern. "This kind of shit happens all the time, man. How do you think Barbara Walters gets all those interviews?"

Grant laughed.

Ronan's hands worked fast on Grant's belt. In record time, Grant's pants were at his feet, and Ronan's fingers slipped inside his boxers to cup his ass possessively. He slapped the right cheek with a loud pop.

Grant bit down on his lower lip. He was so tempted to just go for it, but Kirby's bad reviews kept playing over and over again in his brain, killing his confidence. "I should be asking you about the new CD."

"Fair enough," Ronan said. "Let's talk about the first single. It's called 'Hard to Resist.' I can tell that's how you feel about me right now."

Grant's growing erection began to press against Ronan's, and he knew, deep down, that there would be no turning back now. "I have a few confessions to make."

Ronan kissed him on the mouth. "Okay, sweet boy. Tell me your sins."

Grant sucked in a breath. "I'm not into anal. In fact, I've never—"

Ronan drew back. "You've never been fucked?"

"No."

"Are you serious?"

Grant nodded.

Ronan stepped behind him and got down on his knees to inspect Grant's ass, gently spreading his cheeks to kiss it. "Oh, man, it's fucking gorgeous."

Grant tensed immediately.

"Never tell an Irishman you're a virgin."

When Ronan stood up, Grant stumbled slightly, bracing himself against the wall.

And Ronan was right there again, pressing against him from behind.

Grant felt pressure on the forbidden opening in question. He tensed up again. "Wait—"

"Relax," Ronan said. "I'd never go in without a condom. I'm just . . . close by." His breath was hot on Grant's ear. "Man, you're so fucking tense. *Relax.*" He started to massage Grant's shoulders. "I've got wine. Do you want some wine?"

Grant didn't answer. He just shut his eyes as images of Kirby flashed into mind. Kirby with Jason. Kirby with the pizza delivery guy. Kirby packed and walking out of his life. And then he thought of Kirby's idol worship of Ronan—the CD collection, the concert tickets purchased at scalper prices, the revolving screen savers on his computer. Kirby had it so bad for Ronan that a typical observer might even think it was sick. So how much would it kill him to know what Grant was about to do?

"I think I will have some wine."

Chapter Three

It took an entire bottle. Only then could Grant relax enough for Ronan to get all the way in. Once there, the rock star alternated between gentle lover and powerhouse fuck machine.

Grant craved it either way. By then he was drunk and enslaved. Sure, there was some pain involved. But the pleasure ameliorated it. His favorite part was Ronan's mouth, clamped down over his during the most urgent thrusting, lips crushed against lips, tongues at war. If there was anything hotter, then Grant had never experienced it.

Now he lay in the same bed, spent from the passion and wasted from the wine. A spinning sensation inside his head threatened his equilibrium. But Grant fought gamely against it, trying to focus instead on the giant leaps in sexual development—first penetration, first famous partner, first time so free of inhibition that he yelled out dirty things.

Ronan was snorting cocaine off the nightstand and gestured for Grant to take a hit, too.

"Maybe later," Grant whispered. "Right now, I think my body's overstimulated enough."

Ronan sniffled, clearing away a faint trace of coke residue with his fingertips. "Where the fuck did you learn to kiss like that?"

Grant felt a moment's pure shame. "What do you mean?"

"You don't kiss like an American boy," Ronan said.

Grant braced himself for another bedroom slam. "Is that bad?"

"No, man, it's fucking great," Ronan assured him. "American guys tend to keep their mouths really tight and use their tongues like a drill bit. Your mouth stays soft, there's give and take, and you really know how to work the tongue."

Grant merely stared. A sexual compliment from a master of the art. There were no words.

Ronan leaned over to kiss him again. "So, who taught you how?"

"Nobody, really. I watched a lot of *General Hospital*."

Ronan laughed. "You suck dick pretty good. Did you learn that from a soap opera, too?"

"I'm serious," Grant said, his tone more earnest now.

Ronan lit a cigarette. A legal one. "You're fucking kidding me, right?"

"No. Believe it or not, I didn't have my first sexual experience until I was twenty-six."

"Were your parents fucking Quakers or something?"

"No, I was just . . . confused."

"I'll say. I got my first blow job when I was twelve. Banged my first girl a year later." Ronan propped himself up on his elbows and looked at Grant with amused curiosity. "So you went through all of high school and college a virgin? That's amazing."

"You make me sound like the Elephant Man."

Ronan paused to take a long drag. He blew smoke rings up to the ceiling in perfect curls. "It is a little freakish, man. I've heard of eighteen- or nineteen-year-olds. But never twenty-six. Except for those cats who dig *Star Wars*. I don't think those wankers ever have sex. And they could have plenty. With each other, at least. Think of all that dead time waiting in line for tickets weeks before the fucking movie comes out."

"Can we change the subject? Please."

Ronan laughed and gently pushed Grant's hair out of his eyes. "I'm just fucking with you. We need some innocence in this world. Shit, I'm so used to banging groupies. This is the first emotional sex I've had in a long time. How's your ass? Is it sore?"

"A little."

"When I come back from the party tonight, I'm going to fuck you again."

Grant felt emboldened by the crude promise. "Sounds like a plan."

Ronan smiled and slipped his cigarette into a near empty bottle of beer. "You liked it, didn't you?"

Grant nodded. "It was intense."

Ronan laughed and rolled Grant over onto his stomach to playfully bite his ass. "I can't believe you never had a boyfriend who talked you into it. If you were my guy, I'd say, 'Either give me that virgin ass, or it's fucking over between us!' "

Grant shook his head and let out an exasperated sigh. "There *are* other ways to be sexual."

"I bet there won't be for you anymore." Ronan winked. "For a first timer, you were hot, man. You couldn't get enough."

"Do you ever talk about anything other than sex?"

"What else is there?"

Grant thought about it. "For a rock star with groupies in every zip code, I guess there isn't much else." He shook his head and started to laugh.

Ronan seemed to sense an internal joke that he wasn't in on. "What's so funny?"

"Nothing . . . it's just . . . my ex-boyfriend—recent ex, as recently as yesterday, in fact—is a huge fan of yours. I mean, he would give up a kidney to be where I am right now."

Ronan stretched to open the nightstand drawer. He pulled out a Polaroid camera. "Come closer." Wrapping one arm around Grant, he fully extended his camera arm. "Say cheese."

There was a flash. Out popped the photo.

Grant watched it develop. This was no Internet cut and paste job. He was in bed. With Ronan. Naked. And it was real.

"Stick that in your ex-boyfriend's Christmas card," Ronan said.

Grant couldn't stop staring at the instant image. Usually, he hated pictures of himself, but this one he liked. The look of his hair, face, and eyes so clearly screamed just-been-fucked.

Ronan lit another cigarette and smiled. "So I guess I'm your rebound guy."

Grant peered up at him. "You came on to me, remember? I just showed up here to ask you things like, 'What musicians have influenced you the most?' "

"Don't play all innocent with me. It only took me about twenty minutes to get your knees back behind your ears. That's called a slut where I come from."

Grant could sense the heat of a raging blush on his cheeks. "I'm not a slut!"

Ronan pointed at him, laughing. "Look at that blush, man. You're as red as a fucking beet. You know you're a slut."

Grant buried his face into a pillow. "I'm . . . not . . . a . . . slut." It was muffled. But the denial could be heard.

"Embrace your inner slut, man. Like me. It's much easier that way."

Grant emerged from the cozy softness of the Frette pillowcase. "How many people have you slept with?"

Ronan shrugged. "I stopped counting after my first tour. It's in the hundreds, though."

A random thought shot into Grant's mind. "Do you think it's true about Mick Jagger and David Bowie?"

Ronan took a quick drag and expelled the smoke with his answer. "Fuck yeah, it's true. If you don't diversify your options with guys, you'll become a real deviant. Some of these groupies will do anything. Man, I mean fucking anything. I was getting so much sex so often that it started to get boring. I kept pushing the envelope to keep it exciting, you know? But I decided I'd rather bang men than have a chick take a dump on me. It was getting to that point. Do you know what I mean?"

"Not really," Grant said. "I'm guessing this is a problem unique to rock stars."

Ronan grinned. "Fuck you." He swung out of bed and stepped over to the window, gazing outside, smoking like a fiend, doing it all in the nude.

There was nothing sexier. Grant felt the urge to bite his fist.

"So what happened with you and the boyfriend?" Ronan asked, a bit distracted.

"He said I was boring and a dud in bed. Then he left me for a rich lawyer with a great apartment in Chelsea." Grant picked up the Polaroid and snapped a full frontal shot of Ronan by the window. "Don't worry. This one's just for me."

"Your ex doesn't know shit. Tell him I said so."

"Believe me. I will eagerly pass that along."

Ronan's face clouded over with a brooding expression. "I don't want to go to this fucking party."

"So don't. You're the star."

"Correction. I'm the commodity." He sighed. "Label people will be there, sponsors of the tour. I'd piss too many people off by pulling a disappearing act."

"Is that your least favorite part of all this?"

Ronan took another drag. "Except for fucking and being on stage, it's all my least favorite part."

Suddenly, Grant remembered what he'd been sent there to do. Officially, that is. He scrambled for his notebook. "That's a great quote. Can I use it?"

"Sailor will lose two fucking pounds over it, but what the hell?"

Grant scribbled the words down and slipped the two Polaroids into the inside back cover. The nude solo shot of Ronan was on top. He picked it up and waved it back and forth. "Do you have any idea how much I could get for this on eBay?"

"If you're going to sell it, give me a minute to get hard and take another one."

Grant laughed. "You really want to kill Sailor, don't you?"

"I just don't understand why anybody goes through the motions of trying to control an image. I'm a young rock star. By law, I'm supposed to drink, take drugs, and fuck everything in sight. Nothing that comes out about me could be worse than what people imagine."

"Gay rumors don't concern you?"

"Why should they? I'm bi."

"But most people don't understand bisexuals. They just assume that they're undecided."

"Well, I guess I fucking change my mind a lot, then, don't I?"

The bedroom door swung open without warning. A tall white man with red hair and a handheld video camera exploded into the room.

Grant moved fast to cover himself with one of the twisted, soiled sheets.

"It's Chuckie Cam!" Ronan sang.

"How goes it?" the intruder asked rhetorically, zeroing in for a Ronan crotch shot. "I need a close up of the most active tool in the business. Second only to Vince Neil's at Motley Crue's peak."

Laughing, Ronan flapped his uncircumcized penis up and down. "Chuckie, this is Grant."

The camera swung around.

Grant tried to block the lens with his hand.

"So tell me, Grant, were you drugged or did you fuck this retard willingly?" Chuckie asked.

Grant suddenly understood the true anxieties of a Sailor Moynihan. "Turn that off."

Ronan was still laughing. "Come on, be a sport, man. Chuckie's my lead guitarist. He's just shooting some behind the scenes stuff for my Web site."

"Your Web site?" Grant was horrified. "I don't want to be naked on the Internet! I have a career!"

Ronan gestured for Chuckie to stop.

The video voyeur shot Grant a pissed look and left.

"Calm down," Ronan said. "We call it *Rock Star Gone Wild*. It's fun. Fans are paying forty bucks a month to download this shit off my site."

"Fine. Let them download you. Not me." His gaze arrowed back to the door. "I want that tape."

Ronan shook his head, walked into the bathroom, stepped inside an enormous glass shower, and turned on the jets full blast. "Come scrub my back!"

For a moment, Grant simply stared. There was room for at least six people in that shower. But right now Ronan only wanted him. Grant let the sheet fall to the floor and walked over.

Ronan pulled him under the water immediately.

Grant screamed. "This is freezing! Turn on the hot!"

"I've got your hot right here," Ronan said. And then he gave Grant the benefit of a wet, bruising kiss.

The cold water was splashing in Grant's eyes, nose, and mouth, but the only thing he concentrated on was Ronan's warm, probing tongue. It reeked of tobacco. And Grant never knew that cigarettes could be so goddamn delicious. On anyone else, they probably wouldn't be.

Ronan drew back and locked his arms around Grant in a vise-tight grip. "Are you going to be waiting for me when I get back from the party?"

"Yes."

"Do you want me to come back here and fuck you all night?"

"Yes."

"Are you going to run and hide the next time Chuckie shows up with the camera?"

Grant didn't have to think about it. He was a goner. "No."

Ronan kissed him again. "Welcome to my world, Mr. Adorable Boy. It fucking rocks."

Chapter Four

Ronan never came back that night.

Grant awoke to this realization the next morning. The sun blazed through the curtains. He turned away from the big, orange, blinding, unforgiving ball and slowly opened his eyes.

Three fast knocks rapped the door.

Before he could answer, LaKeisha stepped inside the room. She frowned. "You all up in his bed, and he's all up in somebody else's bed. Y'all so damn nasty. Why can't you stay in your own motherfucking beds?"

Grant hated to admit it, but LaKeisha presented a very valid question. He gave the room a circular glance and noticed most of his clothes on the floor at the end of the bed. "He told me he was coming back."

LaKeisha grunted. "Yeah, well, that was before some porn star stuck her pussy in his face. The maid's gonna be here any minute, so you need to get your ass up."

"Can I take a shower?"

"I'm sure you can. In *your* motherfucking room."

Grant paused, waiting for LaKeisha to leave.

The sassy girl stood firm.

"A little privacy?"

SEX AND THE SINGLE ROCK STAR

LaKeisha grunted again. "Don't nobody want to see that little white dick, hell."

Fuck it, Grant thought. He flung the sheet off his body and walked bare ass around the room, stopping to pick up his shirt, jeans, underwear, socks, shoes, and notebook, careful not to dislodge the two Polaroids. Within a minute, he was fully dressed.

"Good," LaKeisha said. "Now see if your ass can get through that door as fast as it got into them clothes."

"I'm not finished with the interview. What time will I be able to see Ronan today?"

"If you would interview that man standing up and not flat on your back, you'd probably be done by now. But I'll let *you* know when. I've already had to reschedule the morning's radio interviews, which, technically, ain't my job. That's some Sailor shit. But she put it off on me talking about she's got a 'crisis situation.' I'm like, 'Bitch, the next crisis situation is gonna be my foot up your ass, hell.' "

Grant laughed. "I met her in the lobby yesterday. How can I say this tactfully? Um . . . she doesn't register a lot of warmth."

LaKeisha shook her head. "See, we ain't got time for all that dichotomy where I come from."

"You mean diplomacy," Grant corrected.

"Whatever. You the writer, hell. We just cut to it. That girl's a fucking bitch. There. Case closed."

Grant smiled.

"That's why I haven't told her shit about Chuckie's video. That redheaded motherfucker's running around here taping every damn thing, and he's gonna put it all on the Web site. I can't wait to see how that bitch is gonna crisis manage *that*, hell."

He observed LaKeisha for a moment. She was large, preferred tight-fitting clothes, and spoke in that funny, no nonsense, ghetto girl vernacular. In sum, seemingly not the obvious candidate to be a P.A. for the likes of Ronan.

"Why you looking upside my head like that?" LaKeisha asked.

This broke Grant's trance. "Sorry. I was just wondering how you got this job. You seem an odd fit for Ronan's organization."

"Because I'm black?"

"Because you're you," Grant countered.

"You sound like my damn mama. She's always talking about, 'Why can't you work for R. Kelly?' I'm like, 'Mama, please. What am I gonna do for him? Organize his little video collection?' Uh, no. LaKeisha don't play that. Just because I'm black don't mean I can't work for Ronan. He pays me sixty grand a year. He may be white, I may be black, but money's green, hell. I remember the first day I met that motherfucker. I was working the front desk at a hotel in Atlanta. He came down in the lobby trying to act a fool about his room being too small. I can't remember what was going on that weekend, but every decent hotel was booked solid. I said, 'If you don't get your Lucky Charms sounding ass out of my face and go sit down somewhere! Ain't no rooms in this city. You got a room, you got a bed, you got a pot to shit in, now go on!' Then he tries to get all huffy, talking about, 'Let me see your manager.' I said, 'For what? Let me see *your* manager. You the one who ain't acting right, hell.' Then he just starts falling out laughing and asks me if I'm good at organization. I said, 'I guess I am since I'm cussing you out and thinking about what I'm going to eat for dinner at the same time.' And then he offered me a job. It's crazy, but I like it. I get to travel and stuff." LaKeisha narrowed her gaze. "Why you got me talking so much? I don't want to be in no magazine."

"Don't worry. As charming as you are, I think *Velocity* readers are more interested in your boss."

"Whatever. Boy, just go back to your room. I'll call you whenever I get Ronan's day situated."

Was there anything more lonely than a small hotel room in a strange city when you were alone and had nothing to do? Grant didn't think so. He showered, ordered breakfast from room service, and settled in to wait for LaKeisha's call.

The sudden solitude proved dangerous. It gave Grant time to think about Kirby. And then sadness began to creep in. Shit, he didn't want to do this. But then the tears came . . . in gut-wrenching sobs that burned hot and fast.

What hurt the most was the way Kirby had just replaced him, like an appliance gone bad. "Oh, you're boring. I'm moving in with Jason next week. Bye." And admitting to a tryst with the pizza delivery guy on his way out the door. That was classy.

"Asshole!" Grant shouted, flinging the room service tray off the bed and onto the floor. Seeing the mess made him feel good. It was cathartic. Especially since he didn't have to clean it up. But then he started to feel guilty about making the housekeeper do extra work. So he got down on his knees and started to erase the damage, thinking about how loyal he'd been to Kirby.

"Call me a dog from the animal shelter," Grant murmured, as he retrieved a fork sticky with syrup.

The sick part of it all was that no matter what he told himself otherwise, he would miss Kirby. Desperately. In spite of the fucking bastard act at the end, Kirby was the perfect guy for him. Plus, they had the trump card that all couples long for—a cute story about how they met.

Grant had written a gushing review for the DVD special edition release of Mike Nichols's *Working Girl* with Melanie Griffith, most of his praise heaped on the lavish extras accompanying the release.

Kirby had been the DVD's producer and E-mailed Grant a thank you for his kind words.

Back and forth went the E-mails until Grant finally conjured up the balls to suggest they meet for coffee. As always, a gay couple can do in one date what it takes a straight couple to do in three. Coffee became dinner. Dinner became a movie. The movie became a walk back to Grant's apartment. And the walk back became a sleepover.

Grant had been three quarters in love when Kirby told the story about what a struggle it had been to get Harrison Ford to sit for an interview about his memories of the movie, and how, after it finally happened, the grumpy star had practically nothing to say.

Conversation never lulled between them, at least in the beginning and middle of their relationship, before disenchantment and resentment settled in near the end. They could blather on about movies forever, jumping from one era to another, finishing each other's sentences, or filling in the blanks when one of their memories momentarily faltered.

Physically, Kirby was Grant's ideal. He was masculine, handsome, fit, fashionable but no victim to trends, the kind of man who stirred up interest from both genders wherever he went.

And now Jason Dockett was waking up with him every morning.

Grant checked his voice mail at home. There was one new message. His heart lifted a bit . . . and then sunk. It was Dwight, a pesty friend he tried best to avoid, calling to announce free tickets to *Hairspray*. Grant went through the motions to delete. If it meant seeing Dwight (a wardrobe stylist so tiresome that even therapists dumped him), then the price of free was too high.

Nothing from Kirby. He was either in a mad state of jealousy over Grant's proximity to Ronan or he was so enraptured with Jason that he didn't give a shit. The possibility of the latter began to fuck with Grant's mind as he finished cleaning up the mess from his Neely O'Hara moment.

It was building up inside. The yearning. That obsessive feeling to contact someone you desire, even if it's nothing more than to hang up after you hear their voice or to say something that you know will start an argument. Grant picked up the phone again. He wavered. Better judgment prevailed.

Instead, he called LaKeisha. She answered on the third ring. "Hi, it's Grant."

"Who?"

"Grant Browder, the writer for *Velocity*."

"Boy, you must be crazy. Didn't you just leave up out of here five minutes ago?"

He checked his watch. "Actually, it's been fifty-five minutes. But I've been on the phone and thought you might have tried to call."

"Well, I didn't. And if I had called, I would've left a message, hell."

"Oh, of course." Grant paused, feeling foolish.

LaKeisha had that gift for reducing everyone to a moron. "So . . . do you have plans for lunch?"

Ronan outfitted LaKeisha with a Mercedes G5, the utlility vehicle that looked like an armored tank and drove like a cruise ship on calm water. She took him to the Villa Marina shopping center in Marina Del Rey. Tucked in the corner was Aunt Kizzie's Back Porch.

"Come on," LaKeisha said, turning off the engine and hopping out. "It ain't my mama's cooking, but it's close enough."

The place was down home to the nth degree. Framed portraits of black celebrities and sports heroes lined the walls. Dining chairs were the plastic kind you put out in the yard for an outdoor barbecue. Drinks were served up in old Mason jars.

LaKeisha wasted no time in ordering smothered pork chops, turnip greens, macaroni and cheese, and a basket of biscuits with honey and grape jelly.

Grant speed scanned the menu, trying to factor if there was any possibility of getting a meal that would pass the Atkins Diet test. In the end, he gave up and asked the waitress to bring him what LaKeisha was having.

"Thanks for letting me tag along," Grant said. "I was going crazy in that room."

LaKeisha grunted. "You wouldn't last in my job, hell."

"So what's it like to work for the wildest man in rock?"

"Not as wild as you think. I just do my job. I don't fool with the crazy shit. I ain't pimping for no groupies, and I ain't fucking around with drugs. Leif and Jagger can do that. Here I am working around nothing but white folks, and the black girl gets caught with cocaine? No, baby. Not LaKeisha. My mama didn't raise no fool." She drained her mason jar of sweet tea to the halfway mark. "No, she didn't."

"I suppose the thrill would wear off eventually," Grant reasoned.

"Ain't never been a thrill to me. I don't get excited over famous folks. They need to get excited over my black ass. I keep them in business, hell. I was shopping for Ronan at the Beverly Center not long ago, buying that fool more underwear, because he's such a damn ho. Leaves it everywhere. Anyway, I bump into Denzel Washington. He gives me that look, like, 'I know you want my autograph.' I'm like, 'No, motherfucker, I want my five dollars back for *The Preacher's Wife*,' that weak ass movie he made with Whitney Houston. What I want with somebody's little autograph? Shit, unless you signing a check to pay my bills, you can keep that, hell."

Grant chuckled. "So there's nobody that might make you stop and go, 'Wow.' "

LaKeisha thought about it. "Now I do love me some L.L. Cool J. He might be that one star I'd stop and pay attention to."

"I've met him," Grant said. "It was at a press junket for one of his movies. I think it was his millionth interview of the day, but he was a nice guy. Very gracious."

"You should've told him to take off his shirt. That's all I would've had to say to him."

The waitress swooped in to deposit two steaming plates and a large basket of biscuits.

Grant stared at the food like a *Fear Factor* challenge. He felt as if he'd just eaten, which, basically, he had. Still, he put forth the effort to at least pretend that he was hungry.

LaKeisha sampled the macaroni and cheese first. "It's okay," she said. "Ain't as good as my mama's. That's for damn sure."

"Do you miss your family?"

LaKeisha took an enormous bite of greens. "I see them just enough. Too much family is too much bullshit. You know what I'm saying?"

Grant managed an affirmative nod as he moved the gravy around in search of the pork chop. "So, any idea if Ronan will have some time for me today?"

LaKeisha frowned at Grant's eating habits. "Boy, quit playing with your food and just eat the shit. Damn. And no, that man ain't got time for you today unless you got silicone titties."

Grant looked up. "So he's still with the porn star?"

"No, he's at the Playboy Mansion. That fool blew off those radio interviews, too. I told him, 'Fine. It's your career.' Shit. Ain't nobody gonna look at me crazy when his song don't get no airplay. I just make sure the motherfucker got clean socks, hell."

Grant shrugged. "At least I know not to wait around. Maybe I'll take a tour of the Getty Museum."

"Do whatever," LaKeisha said. "That fool probably won't show up until sometime tomorrow." She laughed a little. "At least you got sense enough to not get all *Fatal Attraction*. Ronan messed around with this other man, and damn, if that motherfucker didn't go straight up crazy. He does dirty movies for funny boys like you."

"What's his name?"

"Nicky Lawrence. You know him?"

Grant couldn't believe it. "*Nicky Lawrence?* The gay porn star?"

LaKeisha grunted. "If you say so. He ain't no star to me. Just a crazy faggot, hell."

Grant's mind jumped into composing mode, possible leads he could use, clever phrases he could employ. Kate Bobo wanted a juicy cover story. She would definitely get one.

Chapter Five

Grant was in that zone, a higher plane of intellectual concentration on work, not thinking about Ronan, not lamenting the loss of Kirby, when the MIA rock star knocked on his hotel room door.

"I heard you were looking for me," Ronan said. He wore a vintage Jack Daniel's T-shirt, dirty jeans, and black motorcycle boots, the rough look helped along by the fact that his nails were a little dirty.

"I was told the Playboy Mansion had you in lockdown until sometime tomorrow."

Ronan smirked and stepped inside uninvited. "Fred Durst showed up. It was either bail or drown that cunt." He went straight for the minibar, opened a bottle of beer, and drank it to the halfway mark.

"You told me that you were coming back last night."

"I thought you were a writer."

"I am."

"So why do you sound like a jealous wife?"

Grant laughed to himself. "Did you come here to finish the interview?"

Ronan approached him, his eyes locked onto Grant's. "Is that what you want to do?"

Grant tried to will his desire away. There was something so decadent about ending up in bed with Ronan again. He didn't want to do it. "How was the porn star last night?"

Ronan was so close that Grant could breathe his breath now. "What can I say? She's in the right line of work."

"And the playmates at Hef's house?"

He lewdly flickered his tongue. "Miss January in the hot tub."

"You know, it's highly probable that you're a sex addict. You should get some help."

Ronan's practiced fingers worked on the snap and zipper of Grant's khakis. "Lucky for you I'm not going to." He started to push the pants down.

Grant stopped him. "I mean it."

"You know what would be good for you? Since we're passing out doctor's notes here, give me a fucking crack at it. You need to get drunk, have a little blow, and let me do all the things to you that you were thinking about last night while you waited for me to come back."

Grant swallowed hard. It was a war between desire and disgust. "You're a pig."

Ronan smiled and pushed Grant's pants down to the floor. He offered him the remaining half of his beer. "Drink up."

Grant guzzled every drop.

Ronan dipped into his front pocket and pulled out a small vial of white powder. He tipped a little into the cap. "Take a hit of this."

Grant started to back away.

"You'll fucking love it," Ronan promised. "Come on. Take a hit."

Reluctantly, Grant obeyed. It felt like micro shards of glass going up into his nostrils. About ten seconds later, the euphoria kicked in.

Ronan kissed him passionately. "A tight ass can be a bad thing . . . and a good thing." Then he peeled off his shirt and started to undo his own pants.

After a half hour, the coke high faded. Grant lay there, completely fucked out, the sex god feeling down for the count. He put a hand on Ronan's impressive six-pack. "Look what you've done to me."

Ronan smiled. "It's about time someone fucked you properly. That mind of yours is clear now. You'll probably write The Great American Novel. If you do, promise me you'll dedicate it to my cock."

Grant laughed.

Ronan stretched to reach his cigarettes and lit one right away. "That would be fucking cool. A book dedicated to my dick. Maybe I should save that idea for my memoir."

"Not so original. Mark Wahlberg already did that in his Marky Mark autobiography."

"Fucking punk."

Grant rolled over onto his stomach. "I heard a rumor. About you and Nicky Lawrence. Care to elaborate?"

"Me and Vicki Lawrence? The old bitch from *The Carol Burnett Show*? How'd you find out? I didn't think anyone knew that I did her from behind in her Mama costume."

"*Nicky* Lawrence," Grant corrected, rolling his eyes.

"Oh, I fucked him, too. Once. Now he wants to pick out fucking china patterns. He's a psycho."

"Maybe he just wants to settle down and retire. You know, bottoms don't make a lot in the business, and let's face it, starring in *Sucking Private Ryan* isn't the fastest way to a SAG card."

Ronan shrugged. "Life's a bitch. I just had to change my travel name. He found out what it was, and the wanker was showing up at every hotel. I fucking loved that name, too. Johnny Wadd. Two Ds."

"Brilliant. Is there a lesson here?"

"Not to go fucking Glenn Close on me. Can I count on you for that?"

"Do you ever stop to analyze your own behavior?" Grant asked.

"Now you sound like a fucking shrink."

"Have you ever been to one?"

"Once. She stopped seeing me after we ended up in bed."

"You don't have to be Dr. Joyce Brothers to see a pattern here."

Ronan dragged deep, mulling the thought. "I make a fucking obscene amount of money, okay? My hobbies are banging chicks and banging guys. My vices are booze, coke, and cigarettes. The nose candy I keep in check. I'm not fucking Keith Richards. See, I've still got my original septum." He touched it for emphasis. "I don't drive when I'm wasted, so you won't catch me wrapping my sports car around a tree like that dick brain from Motley Crue. No wife. No kids. There's not even a bitter girlfriend wondering where I am at night. And you'll never catch me whining about a lost fortune on *Behind the Music.* Who am I hurting?"

"Maybe yourself."

"What is this? The fucking *Prince of Tides*? You want me to feel the pain?"

"That was a Barbra Streisand reference. Now I'm thinking the porn star from last night might be a beard."

"Ha! Fuck you."

"Answer this. Honestly. Are you happy?"

"Haven't you figured it out yet? I'm not that fucking complicated. You're not looking at a tortured artist. I'm a performer. I don't even write my own songs. This whole ride is a party for me. Why turn off the lights if I'm having a good time?"

"I guess you're right," Grant observed.

"About what?"

"Being uncomplicated."

"More people should try that on for size. It's a good thing."

"For you, I suppose so. I mean, you're never going to be Bono."

"Never wanted to be."

Grant experienced a flash of frustration. He could dig, dig, dig but never make it beyond the shallow end. Suddenly, another angle came to him. "Speaking of Bono, what about his place in rock history? People regard him as a thoughtful, serious musician. You've never longed for that?"

"What? A bunch of music critics jerking off to my CDs? No. I could give a fuck. Look at Bon Jovi. Their songs are dumb as shit, and they've been around for two decades. 'You Give Love a Bad Name?' Come on! But they can still fill arenas."

"In twenty years, do you still see yourself doing this?"

"Maybe. If the fans still want it. I'd have to be doing it on a certain level, though. You won't catch me touring the loser circuit for fucking ten thousand a gig like those eighties metal bands do today. But sometimes I look at Mick Jagger and Aerosmith and think, 'That could be me one day.' And I'd be cool with that." He stubbed out his cigarette and rolled over to face Grant. "Have I disappointed you?"

"What do you mean?"

"You wanted to get beyond the surface rock attitude to the deeper man inside. Sorry. There isn't one."

Grant smiled. "I hate to be the one to break it to you, but that level of self-awareness signifies real intelligence. You do have some depth, after all."

Ronan playfully smacked himself on the forehead. "Fuck me. But I just want to be an idiot rock star!"

"Don't worry. You're that, too."

"Good. You had me worried there for a minute." Ronan craned his neck to check the clock. "Shit, I better jet. I've got some radio stations to make up to for bailing on interviews."

"Does that mean this interview's over?"

Ronan swung out of bed. "Party with me tonight. We'll continue it then. Chuckie's having a blow out at his house. It'll give you a chance to meet my band. Justice, Kaleel, Maxwell, Natalia, Angus—they'll all be there."

Grant had a vague premonition of personal Waterloo if he agreed. "Thanks, but I think I'll pass. The last two days have been a pretty big party on their own."

Ronan jumped back into bed and straddled Grant, pinning his arms over his head. "When are you going to stop being such a fucking pussy?"

Grant knew that his eyes were wide. "I'm not . . . it's just . . . give me a break . . . I didn't go to Headbangers University."

"I want you to party with me tonight. It's time we cracked open that uptight college boy shell. You're going to get drunk. You're going to get loaded. You're going to fuck a complete stranger. Hell, it might even turn out to be a woman. And if Chuckie shows up with his video camera, you're going to scream like a Viking and not run and hide like some seventeen-year-old bitch who's scared daddy's going to see her on *Wild Spring Break Girls*. You want to write a kick-ass piece about a rock star? Then live like one for one night. Just one fucking night. I dare you."

Chapter Six

Grant woke up in a strange bed. His arm hurt like hell, and his mouth throbbed. He had no idea where he was or what was going on.

Lying next to him was a marginally attractive woman with a botched implant job, one breast obviously larger than the other. She had bad skin and kinky blonde hair in need of a good conditioner. The girl was no reason to suddenly become a heterosexual.

His eyes glanced at the area of pain on his upper arm. A medium-size tattoo of a skull screamed back at him. He could tell by the rawness of his skin that it was real.

Grant left the bed and made a beeline for the bathroom. It was filthy. The mirror was smudged, but he could see. No! A front tooth was chipped. Almost half of it simply gone.

He buried his face in his hands, wanting to forget but trying desperately to remember.

The sound of a television in one of the outer rooms captured his attention. He went in search of another person, hopefully a conscious one. The place looked trashed. And deserted. MTV blared from a high-tech plasma screen. An ugly rapper was showing off his collection of expensive cars.

Grant explored the three bedroom ranch style house. Ikea furniture and Pier One furnishings dominated the decor. In the kitchen, he found a stack of mail addressed to a Charles Tyler. And then he remembered.

Chuckie's party.

The big throw down before everyone left for New York. Apparently, everyone already had. Except Grant. He glanced at the clock. It was way past noon, going on one. He sought out a phone to call LaKeisha's cellular.

Ronan and company could be anywhere—back at the hotel, on their way to the private plane, or cruising in the sky at thirty thousand feet. Shit. He didn't know the itinerary in New York, where they were staying, or even Ronan's new travel name. After all, *Johnny Wadd* had perished in that terrible stalking incident.

The call went straight into LaKeisha's voice mail.

Grant set the receiver back into the cradle with a bang.

"Hey, not so loud," a female voice croaked.

Grant turned to see his bed companion massaging her temples. She was naked except for her thin pink cotton panties.

"Is there any coffee in this place?" She poked around in the kitchen, then stopped to inspect his arm. "Hey, I like your tattoo. It's cool." The smile that followed revealed teeth that could've used braces fifteen years ago.

"Who are you?"

She sighed. "How quickly they forget! I'm Ashley. Chuckie's a regular at the club where I dance. He said I could crash here while he's gone. I got in a fight with the bitch I was rooming with, and she kicked me out." She shrugged. "What can you do? Her name was on the lease." Ashley squinted her eyes. "Aren't you the guy who broke his tooth last night? How's your mouth?"

Grant covered it with his hand. "It's been better. Do you remember how it happened?"

"Justice got drunk and threw a spoon. It hit you in the face."

Grant stared at her blankly.

"He's Ronan's bass player."

"God, I can't remember anything."

Ashley nodded knowingly. "Chuckie's Red Death Punch. Getting wasted on it the first time is always pretty wild. You know, he won't tell anyone what he puts in it."

As the shock of Grant's circumstances began to wear off, the strength of his hangover began to catch on. A wave of nausea threatened to topple him. He steadied himself against the counter.

"Are you okay?" Ashley asked.

"I'm fine. I just . . ."

"Sometimes it's better to keep on drinking when you wake up like this," Ashley said.

Grant gave her an annoyed look. "That's called alcoholism." He picked up a piece of Chuckie's mail and inspected the address. "We're in *Chatsworth?*"

Ashley nodded. "It's in the San Fernando Valley."

A mild panic began to set in. He needed to get to the hotel. Back to his belongings. Anything remotely familiar. "How can I get into the city? I'm staying at The Standard Hollywood."

"I'll drive you," Ashley offered agreeably. "Just let me get a cup of coffee first."

"Let's just stop on the way. *Please*. I need to get back. As soon as possible."

"Okay," Ashley said. "At least give me a second to get a top on."

He waited for her in the kitchen, drawing up a mental ledger of everything that he needed. A dentist for the hillbilly mouth. A blood test for possible STDs. A brain scan for getting into this situation in the first place.

Ashley reemerged wearing a Ronan Master-Slave Tour 2000 T-shirt. She led him out to a red Toyota Corolla that had seen better days. Apparently, deformed strippers didn't do that well in Los Angeles.

They stopped at the first gas station on the way. She still wanted coffee, and the tank was below E. Grant paid for both and tried deep breathing to relax as they set off toward the hotel.

"Are you sure you're okay?" Ashley asked. "Do you need an inhaler or something?"

"I'm fine," Grant assured her.

She turned on a pop radio station, and Michelle Branch screamed "Are You Happy Now?" from the cheap speakers.

Grant realized that the answer was no. Contrary to popular fantasy, sex with a rock star did not make one *happy*. His gaze veered over to Ashley.

She cut a glance to him and smiled secretly.

"Did we . . ."

"How much Red Death Punch did you drink?"

Grant gestured to his new tattoo and his freshly chipped tooth. "Entirely too much. Obviously."

"We had a three-way with Ronan! You don't remember any of it? That's why I love Chuckie's parties. They're always crazy."

Grant merely shut his eyes and rode the rest of the way in silence. When he got out of the car, he thanked Ashley for the ride and for the sex he couldn't remember.

The moment he stepped into his room, Grant noticed the message waiting light blinking ominously. He snatched his cellular from the bedside table. Two missed calls. Both from *Velocity*. Checking the room calls first, he fought for calm.

"Grant, where the fuck are you?" It was Kate Bobo. "Sailor Moynihan just called to tell me that you're *not* on Ronan's private plane, which is heading here to New York as we speak. Call me!"

"Goddammit!" Grant screamed. Kate was pissed, *and* he had to buy a same-day ticket back home. Add to that a trip to the dentist and laser treatment to arena the tattoo. Whatever money he stood to make on the Ronan piece was being pissed away.

He took a few deep breaths and called *Velocity*.

"Kate Bobo's office." It was Jeremy, her bitchy assistant. He was impossibly slim, wore regulation Prada, ate at his desk every day, and packed a meticulously prepared Martha Stewart–worthy meal in a Hello Kitty lunch box. His lips were always curled into a perpetual, you're-not-worthy sneer that often provoked thoughts of random violence. But the worst part of all—he had a dedicated, long-term, *gorgeous* boyfriend, Kris Keith, who was a regular on *All My Children*, was constantly taking his shirt off on screen, and, if *Soap Opera Digest* could be believed, was a dream to work with and always a gracious fan favorite at personal appearances like Wal-Mart openings and special soap days at Disney World. And here Grant was . . . a sudden slut and just out of a relationship meltdown with a jerk. Plus, he ate out practically every meal. Ugh! To be Jeremy for a day.

"Hi, Jeremy, it's Grant Browder returning Kate's call."

"And this is regarding?"

"The cover story on Ronan." Grant tried to sound smug. Because he could. Finally. That sounded so much better than, "I'm writing a review for the DVD of *My Boss's Daughter* starring Ashton Kutcher."

"I'll see if she's available. Please hold."

He waited for long portentous seconds.

Jeremy was back. "Transferring."

"Where the fuck are you?" Kate demanded without preamble the nanosecond she picked up the line.

"I'm still in Los Angeles," Grant admitted.

"This better be good."

"It's a long story."

"I catch on quick. Condense it," Kate snapped.

Grant didn't have the energy or the fortitude to deliver a believable lie, so he just cut open a truth vein and let it bleed. "Ronan took me to a party in the Valley, the punch was spiked with an indeterminant substance, and I woke up with no memory, a hideous tattoo, a chipped front tooth, and a stripper in my bed."

"Oh, my God!" Kate screamed. "This is fucking unbelievable. You have to write about it! You partied with Ronan but lived to tell. Rock on!"

Grant glanced down at his notebook on the nightstand, fingering the Polaroids. "It gets better, Kate. I slept with him, too. And I have the pictures to prove it."

"Fuck me running!" Kate shouted. "I swear, if you're lying to me right now, you are so fired."

A plot began to percolate in Grant's mind. He hoped Ronan had a good laugh at his expense. Because payback was going to be a bitch. "As sure as I have a new skull tattoo on my arm, I'm telling you the truth."

"*This . . . is . . . awesome.*" All of a sudden, Kate got quiet. Perhaps that cover copy brain was recharging? Her snazzy headlines alone had helped put *Velocity* on the map in a crowded field. "Don't tell me any-thing else. I want to read it. Shit, I want to read it *now*. Does Sailor have any idea what's coming down the chute?"

"Not a clue."

Kate cackled. "That bitch is going to freak! One hundred bucks says she'll start eating Taco Bell until she gets really fat. God, I am so psy-ched! Listen, I have to sprint. The art department has a million things for me to approve. Jeremy will make arrangements for your return flight and call you back with the details. *Great* work. I never figured you for a slut! But I would've screwed him, too. So I guess we both are." Kate giggled at her own joke. "Bye!"

Grant hung up. When he caught his reflection in the bathroom's unforgiving light, he gasped. Oh, God, he looked awful! The bags under his eyes. The tattoo. The chipped tooth. Right now he could easily pass for one of Ronan's roadies. He stripped and hit the shower.

Officious as ever, Jeremy buzzed back with the flight arrangements. There was just enough time to pack and make it to LAX for the two hour security window. Once ensconced at the departure gate, he dug in for the wait to begin boarding. But Grant used the time for pre-evil plot-planning worthy of the most delicious soap vixen. Say, Donna Mills as Abby Ewing in one of her schemes to take over Lotus Point. Sufficiently inspired, he rifled through his address book, dug out a contact from yesteryear at Cream Fix Films, and dialed.

"Publicity, Jeff White."

Bingo. "Hi, Jeff, it's Grant Browder. I know it's been a million years. Do you remember me?"

"Of course! How are you?"

"Good. Doing real good. I'm writing for *Velocity* now."

"Let me guess. They're adding a gay porn section to please the straight but curious reader."

Grant laughed. "We're not there yet. But there is a new column from the *Queer Eye for the Straight Guy* group. So it won't be long. I took a chance that you'd still be there. I wasn't sure."

Jeff sighed. "Who's going to steal me away? Miramax? Please. I'm stuck in gay porn just like the actors."

There was a levity to his self-deprecation that allowed Grant to laugh with him. "It could be worse. I know a guy who's worked in the same position for twelve years with Hi Ten Entertainment. They produce Barney. You know, the big purple dinosaur."

"I know, I know." Jeff sighed. "Thank you for that. Sometimes you just have to hear about the less fortunate to realize how good you have it. So, what's the reason behind this blast from the past? Are you tired of paying for your porn and want to start doing freelance reviews again?"

"Never," Grant said lightly. "My last review was the original *Frat Hazing*. It doesn't get any better than that. To go back would be a letdown."

"That's our best-selling series now. We're already up to *Frat Hazing 9: The Dungeon*. I just finished catalog copy for it."

"I need a favor, Jeff."

"Sure. What is it?"

"Can you get me a contact number for Nicky Lawrence?"

"Have you tried to reach him through his Web site?"

"I'd rather talk to him. I mean, the Web site is for people who want to buy his sweaty jockstrap, right?"

Jeff laughed. "I suppose so. Hold on. I should have his cell phone in my database. You're not playing spy for a rival studio, are you? Nicky's a nutcase, but he's our most popular bottom boy."

"It's nothing like that. I promise."

Jeff's voice went down an octave. "Just between us, he says his overnight rate is fifteen hundred, but you can get him for a thousand and a meal in a good restaurant."

"Don't even go there," Grant warned playfully. "All the sex I've had in my life I've paid for emotionally. Don't make me start paying financially, too."

Jeff laughed. "Just an FYI . . . okay, here we go." He called out a number with a 310 area code. "By the way, we never had this conversation. I could get fired for giving out talent's personal info."

Grant jotted down the ten digits and underlined them twice. "What conversation? I haven't spoken to you in years."

"I feel better already. Stay in touch, Grant. And good luck with everything."

"You, too. Thanks." He hung up, glancing around at the people waiting to board. His mind began to wander. It was too soon to call Nicky. That trump card would be played later.

First things first. The necessary prep work . . .

Chapter Seven

Another message from Dwight about those stupid free tickets to *Hairspray*. That's all. Not a word from Kirby. Or even Liv, the straight girl at his production office who, curiously, could only sustain friendships with gay men.

Grant considered packing all of Kirby's shit into a big trash bag and leaving it outside the building, then dismissed the thought. The truth was, right now he really wasn't that mad at Kirby.

But Ronan. That son of a bitch was another story altogether. Grant could visualize the hedonistic rocker laughing at him with his band buddies. And he could just hear that Irish brogue . . .

I fucked him within an inch of his life.

I got the tight-ass high on coke.

I got him blind-ass drunk.

I tattooed his arm.

My bass player fucked up his Pepsodent smile.

I left him stranded in the Valley.

Grant didn't need to sign the guest check-in book at Promises Malibu to know that he had, in fact, hit bottom. Waking up in Chatsworth, California, with no memory had clued him in to the fact, thank you. And the clarity of that moment parted the curtain. To how dangerous it could be to totally let down your guard the way he had. To how cruel the bored and the reckless could be.

Throughout the years Grant had heard all the stories. What Led Zeppelin did to this girl. What Pink Floyd did to that one. Motley Crue's never-ending appetites. How Def Leppard decided which groupies could go backstage.

There was something almost sinister about the power charismatic stars could wield, Grant thought, their ability to intoxicate practically lethal. Ronan had definitely sucked him in. What else was there to say? In that moment, when desire kicks in, the probability of stupidity is ninety percent. And someone famous kicks that other ten percent chance out the door.

Not to say that Grant wasn't accepting any responsibility. He fully admitted to the fact that he was a complete idiot. But that was yesterday. Today he was wise to the game, mad as hell, and determined to give back to Ronan just a little bit of what the son of a bitch had dished out.

He rang LaKeisha's cellular again.

"Hello?" The sound of her lazy drawl was sweeter music than any of Ronan's hits.

"Hi, it's Grant."

"Boy, where are you at?"

"I'm back in New York. Where are you?"

"At The Mark."

Grant nodded knowingly. The five-star Upper East Side hotel was a favorite among the music elite.

"He did Conan O'Brien tonight." LaKeisha hesitated. "Look, Grant, what they did to you was wrong. It ain't right to be marking up somebody's body with a permanent tattoo of anything, much less a damn skeleton, hell. I told them, 'Y'all keep laughing. One day y'all gonna mess with the wrong motherfucker, and the shit ain't going to be pretty.' They just kept on laughing. I said, 'Okay, just you wait.' "

"It's fine. I think I can have it lasered off."

"*Lasered off?* That sounds like some painful shit."

"Not any more painful than keeping this skull on my arm. Listen, I'd like to see Ronan again. There are a few blanks in the interview I'd like to fill in."

"Damn, are you dedicated to your work, or what? I'd never want to see that motherfucker again."

"At the end of the day, I'm the dumb ass. Nobody put a gun to my head."

"You right about that," LaKeisha said. "But that Red Death Punch will fuck you up, and those fools know it. Might as well be a gun, hell."

"So what time would be good to head over?"

"Now, if you want to. The band is just partying in the hotel."

"I forgot his new alias," Grant said. "It's not Johnny Wadd . . . it's—"

"Richie Rotten," LaKeisha finished. "If that ain't a perfect fit."

Grant scribbled it down and signed off. Before he left, there was just one more call to make. He dialed Nicky Lawrence's cell number.

The gay porn king-alleged psychopath answered on the third ring. "Hello?"

"Hi, Nicky, this is Peter Sammler. I work with Ronan's management office. How are you?"

A cagey silence. "Fine."

Grant laughed a little. "You know, unfortunately, I've done this enough. It should be getting easier, but it's always a little awkward. Uh . . . Ronan would like to spend some time with you. *Privately.* How soon could you be in New York?"

Nicky didn't wait for so much as a beat to drop. "I can be on the next plane."

"Perfect. He's staying at The Mark on Madison and East 77th. Call my room once you arrive. I'll give you the rest of the details then. I'm registered as Peter Sammler."

Nicky hesitated. "It'll be in the middle of the night."

"That's okay. Ronan's usually not a morning person, but in your case, he's assured me that he will be."

"This is awesome. I thought he was avoiding me."

"Not at all. He's just been extremely busy. Have a good flight."

"Okay," Nicky said, still sounding a bit stunned. "Thanks."

Grant hung up and immediately called The Mark to reserve a standard room under *his* new alias. He started to feel guilty for pulling Nicky into his plot, but then, he reasoned, better a porn star than a Boy Scout. Bitchy, yes. But these were bitchy times. Heart and self-esteem stomped on by Kirby. Made a fool of by Ronan. Grant felt a mean streak coming on strong, and whoever got caught up in the current . . . well, too fucking bad.

He called LaKeisha from the cab. By now it was after midnight. Grant should've been exhausted, but he was running on pure adrenaline. "I'm on my way. Where should I go?"

She gave him the Tower Suite number, muffled something about trying to get to sleep, and hung up.

When he arrived outside the room, Grant could hear the party going strong. He knocked loud enough for the rehab dodgers to hear.

Jagger answered the door.

Grant smiled.

The bodyguard remained stone-faced.

"I'm here to finish my interview with Ronan."

Jagger pushed the door closed. "Wait here."

And Grant did. Anxiously. Until Ronan himself turned in an appearance. His dark eyebrows shot up immediately. "This is a fucking surprise."

"Why?" Grant asked, keeping his face relaxed and his voice tone light as he stepped into the suite's darkened foyer. "Did you leave me for dead or something? I guess that would explain the art choice for the tattoo." He raised the sleeve on his T-shirt to display the damage. "I would've preferred a less permanent prank. I don't know. Maybe gum in the hair?"

There was no apology in Ronan's eyes. "It suits you, man. Toughens you up." He got too close too soon, as was his way. "You're almost rough trade."

Grant could feel himself slipping already. God, this man was radioactive with sexual energy. So he tried thinking of gross things. Like what Joe Rogan tells people to eat on *Fear Factor*. An old person with terrible osteoporosis. Pat Sajak. It almost worked. "Don't get too excited. I plan on having the tooth fixed."

Ronan gave him a long, smoldering stare. "You're a surprising little fucker. I'll give you that." He moved toward the suite's living area. "Hey, guys! Look what the fucking cat dragged in!"

Grant followed him in to find most of the band—Justice, Kaleel, Maxwell, Angus, and Chuckie. All of them close to passing out. Oddly, for as much as Ronan professed a hatred for Fred Durst, Limp Bizkit's *Results May Vary* CD was going full blast.

There was a chorus of half-assed waves and greetings.

"How's that tooth, man?" Justice asked, laughing.

The rest of the guys joined in.

Ronan's eyelids looked heavy as his gaze darted around. "Where's the fucking clock?"

"Don't strain yourself," Grant said. "It's a few minutes after one."

"After one?" Ronan said, practically slurring. "It's still fucking early."

Grant smiled invitingly. "On the West Coast, maybe. You're pretty well lit."

"I'm always better when I'm drunk," Ronan promised, slyly pulling Grant into the master bedroom and shutting the door without generating much notice from his rapidly fading band mates. He started in on Grant's jeans button and zipper right away. "I thought you'd be so fucking pissed off that you'd go crying home to write a nasty article about me. And here you are. Back for more. It's that good, isn't it? You can't get enough." Mouth open and tongue ready, Ronan moved in to kiss him.

Grant was tempted, so very, very tempted, to just capture one more taste, but a sudden impulse of resolve hit him at the last millisecond. And he drew back. "Look at you," he admonished Ronan. "You can hardly keep your eyes open."

Ronan pretended not to hear and pressed on.

Grant took another step back. "I've got a better idea," he trilled, dangling his room key between thumb and index finger. "Take this. Get some sleep. Sneak into my room tomorrow morning, slip into the bed, and show me what you're made of then. Don't warn me. Don't even wake me up."

Ronan nodded to the beat of the fantasy. "By the time you realize what's going on, I'll already be inside you. That's fucking hot." He reached out and grabbed the key. "Sleep in the nude."

"I'm way ahead of you." Grant left him there to anticipate. As he was passing through the living room, Chuckie held up the camcorder with an unsteady hand.

"You should check the Web site, man," Chuckie said. "You're a star."

Grant couldn't get out of there fast enough. He speed walked to his room, and hooked up his laptop to the hotel's high speed Internet access. Typing like a demon, he keyed in RONAN.COM only to get an electronic circuitry company. And then he remembered from his marathon Google session. RONANMUSIC.COM.

The site downloaded to life, an impressive flash intro of music and hyper speed Ronan images. Grant hovered the cursor on the button bar, clicking RONAN TV the moment he saw it.

Son of a bitch. He had to pay the first month fee of forty dollars and swear that he was twenty-one before he could see so much as the first clip. With increasing fury, he clacked in his credit card number. It took a moment to authorize.

Grant could feel the tension in his shoulders. He just had a dreadful feeling that this was going to be bad.

There was a NEW VIDEO option and an ARCHIVES choice. Grant selected the former. QuickTime did its work, and a grainy image started moving in a small window. Grant leaned in closer.

It was Chuckie's party! He recognized the house. Unable to sit still for the striptease by Ashley and her friends, Grant zipped through clip after clip, fast forwarding to the frightening footage he hoped would never materialize.

But those hopes died fast. He watched himself in a Red Death Punch shot glass duel with Ronan. He watched Justice throw the spoon that took out part of his front tooth. He watched a morbidly obese tattoo artist they called Needle Dick deface his arm with the skull image. Amazingly, Grant was concious for this, and seemingly in full support of it. But he couldn't remember a thing. Viewing the video was like seeing it happen outside of his own body.

The worst of all was the Ashley footage. Very explicit. X-rated, in fact. Ronan and Grant kissing each other as Ronan took her from behind, and she fellated Grant. Again, it was like watching someone else. Even this shocking footage didn't jar so much as a minute of memory.

It sickened Grant to know that this was lurking in cyberspace outside of his control. The only mollifying factor was the poor quality of the resolution. *He* knew that it was him. And those closest to him could probably determine the same. Beyond that, it only served to join the millions of amateur sex videos that filled up the Net like so much garbarge.

He waited anxiously for Nicky Lawrence to call. About four o'clock in the morning, he finally did. A car service was bringing him to The

Mark. Grant played his new role of Peter Sammler, outlining the fantasy for Nicky precisely the way he had outlined it for Ronan. Nicky could barely contain himself. For him, it was so clearly an erotic dream come true.

Grant certainly hoped so. The room was setting him back over five hundred dollars. But the payoff would be worth every penny. If only Chuckie could be there with his video voyeur act, capturing Ronan's reaction when he realized that he wasn't back in bed with Grant but with a crazy porn star suffering from serious fixation issues.

Chapter Eight

Grant waited patiently in the lobby for the sex bomb to detonate. His watch had just ticked past six o'clock, and everything was quiet. Nothing but a single guest at the front desk checking out, presumably to catch an early flight.

And then came a near-frantic staffer from the back.

A hotel security guard appeared next and made a beeline straight for the elevator. But just as he went up in one car, another car came down.

The doors opened. Out marched Jagger, manhandling a half dressed, completely maniacal Nicky Lawrence.

"The police are on the way, sir," one of the harried clerks assured Jagger.

"Get your goddamn hands off me!" Nicky screamed. "He asked me to come! He asked me!" His gaze swept the lobby up and down, looking for anyone who might believe. It zeroed in on Grant. And what was confusion morphed into burning hatred. Nicky pointed. Suddenly, he wrestled free from Jagger's grip and charged after Grant. "You're in that video!"

Helplessly, Grant stood there, frozen, silently imploring Jagger to help.

But Ronan was no longer in danger. So Jagger made no move to intercede.

It happened so fast. Nicky was on top of him, beating Grant with both of his fists, screaming, "Who the fuck are you? Ronan's mine! I'm the one he wants to be with!"

Grant managed to get a punch in, then a violent shove that sent Nicky off of him and against a piece of lobby furniture. Glass shattered.

And then another pair of hands, stronger ones this time, were on Grant, shoving him face first onto the floor. He heard something about NYPD, then the clink of metal as the cuffs cut into his wrists.

Fuck! He was being arrested. Oh, God, this wasn't the plan! This wasn't the plan at all!

Before seven in the morning, the holding cell in the Upper East Side precinct was chockablock full of unfortunate incidents from the night before. The drunk who refused to be cut off at the neighborhood bar. The hothead who got physical when a B-list actor put the moves on his girlfriend. The homeless man who exposed himself outside a restaurant window.

And then there was Grant Browder, who only a few days ago had led arguably one of the most nonconfrontational, benignly sexual, absent of water cooler chatter worthy lives on the East Coast.

He'd tried to explain this to the arresting officer. Of course, if tender innocence was your schtick, it helped, as a general rule, *to* have all of your front teeth, *not* to have a skull tattoo on your arm, and to be *nowhere* around a gay porn star screaming that he saw you involved in a three-way sex act on the Internet.

When it was time for his phone call, Grant dialed Kirby's cellular. He was probably still sleeping, but he used the device as an alarm, too.

"Hello?"

"Hey . . . it's Grant." Right away his voice started to break.

Kirby picked up on this right away. "What's wrong? Where are you?"

The instant concern in Kirby's voice touched Grant to the point of breakdown. He choked back a sob. "I'm in jail. I need bail money."

*   *   *

Coming up with cash was never a problem for Kirby Rex. The guy could easily have been the love child of Heloise and Dave Ramsey. Frugality ruled. And because he believed in the concept of always being prepared for an emergency, he had immediate access to money. So, at a moment's notice, plopping down a grand in cash for Grant's ten thousand dollar bail was not a problem.

Kirby arrived and quietly made arrangements for Grant's release.

Neither of them murmured a word until they reached the sidewalk. And then it was Kirby who spoke.

"I thought you were supposed to be in Los Angeles with Ronan. How did you end up in jail with *Nicky Lawrence?* What happened to your tooth? And since when did you ever want a tattoo?"

"I'm so tired, Kirby. I just want to go back to The Mark, get my computer, take a shower *in my apartment*, and sleep for three days. I'll pay you back for the bail. And, thank you—I mean that—for saving my ass from that place. I didn't know who else to call, and I'm sure Jason thinks I'm some kind of—"

"Forget about Jason."

Grant halted, a question in his eyes. There was an odd finality to Kirby's tone.

"I never unpacked," Kirby explained. "We had a huge falling out on the first night. I've been staying with Liv."

"Where do you sleep? She's got that tiny little apartment and two roommates."

"The couch."

"It's a love seat. You must curl up in the fetal position."

"It's temporary. I'm looking for my own—"

"Oh, please. Just move back in with me." Grant blurted out the offer without thinking.

Kirby flashed a cornered animal look.

"Until you find your own place," Grant finished quickly. "Most of your things are still at my apartment. I think we can coexist without killing each other. We're both adults."

"Oh, really? So why do I feel like I'm picking up a teenager at juvenile hall?" Kirby asked, smirking. "Thanks, but I don't think that's such a good idea."

"Why? Are you worried about me wanting to get back together

again or something? Because you shouldn't. The offer on the table is just a friendly and platonic one. Get over yourself."

Kirby, instantly pissed now, uttered an incredulous little laugh. "*Get over myself?*"

"Yeah," Grant continued hotly. In spite of the ridiculous circumstances, he felt indignant about this. "Like I would want to get back together, anyway. You cheated on me. *Twice.*"

Kirby opened his mouth to speak.

Grant cut him off before the first syllable could drop. "And don't stand there and try to tell me that it's because I'm a dud in the sack. I have it on very good authority that what you think is absolute bullshit. Maybe you're just not wordly enough to realize. You see, I don't kiss like American boys. Oh, and by the way, I'm an insatiable bottom boy now. Ronan broke me in. And he says it's *fabulous.*"

Kirby's expression was apoplectic. "You fucked Ronan."

Grant nodded, as if getting it on with Ronan were as possible an event as making it with the delivery guy from Fat Eddie's Pizza. "Uh, *yeah.*"

Kirby stared back at Grant as if seeing him for the first time. Suddenly, his face clouded over with skepticism. "Are you—"

"Joking? No. I've got the pictures to prove it. There's also some video footage on the Internet. I'll explain later. Long story. But it includes the origin on the broken tooth and the tattoo."

"You fucked Ronan."

"Yes. We need to accept that as reality and move on." Grant pretended to be annoyed by Kirby's shell-shocked reaction, but the truth was, he loved every second of it. "It's not as if I performed some incredible feat. Like single-handedly convinced the film industry to stop rappers from ever acting again."

Kirby looked at his watch. He was actually smiling now. "Are you hungry? Do you want to get some breakfast? My treat. But you have to tell me *everything.*"

They took a cab to Bubby's in Tribeca. Grant loved the omelets there, and it'd been months since he'd indulged. The ride over was surprisingly easy. Kirby's brother-in-law had a dental practice on the Upper West Side, and he promised to get Grant in right away.

When they arrived at the restaurant, a muscular, tough-looking lesbian with multiple piercings and more tattoos than Angelina Jolie seated them.

Grant was grateful for the coffee that came right away. God, he felt so dirty and grimy. Instead of a shower, he should just go somehwere and get pressure washed.

Kirby's eyes were locked on him expectantly.

Grant made a show out of adding one more sugar to his coffee.

"Come on. You're driving me crazy. *Tell!*"

Grant took a long, thoughtful sip. "Ah, Ronan." The sigh that came next was informed. It was the sigh of someone who *knew* what they were sighing about. "He's everything that you want him to be. Initially, at least. He's not shorter than you imagine, which is always a big letdown when you meet famous people. Remember when we met Tom Cruise, and he was, like, not any taller than Judge Judy? Anyway, he's got this amazing sexual energy in person. Within twenty minutes of meeting him for the first time, he had me naked, in bed, and ready to do things that I'd never done with anyone before."

Kirby laughed and shook his head. "You lucky son of a bitch. I hate you."

"And sex with him is amazing," Grant went on. "But that's all there is. I mean it. That's practically all he talks about. I wondered aloud whether he needed to seek treatment for sex addiction. It was fun, but at the end of the day, he's really kind of boring. And he's not that nice of a person. You see this ugly ass tattoo on my arm? It was done without my consent. At least consciously. His guitar player made some kind of punch that was spiked with something so potent that I had a complete blackout."

Kirby leaned in, his expression serious. "Do you think it was GHB?"

Grant had vaguely heard of the club drug. "I don't know. Maybe. There was more in there than just alcohol. That's for sure. But this guy left me stranded in the Valley, passed out in a strange bed with a B-list stripper and a broken tooth."

"There's an A, B, and C list for strippers, now?"

Grant nodded. "This girl couldn't get a job at Scores. Trust me. But she was sweet. She drove me back to the hotel in her old Toyota that shook like it was about to fall apart every time the speedometer went past sixty. You know, I should send her a card."

"You're off point," Kirby said. "Let's stick to Ronan."

Grant took another long sip of coffee. "Okay, I'll tell you, but then we have to diversify topics. I've got to write a story about him, and this man is basically the reason I got arrested. So in addition to a fierce deadline, I've got a trial date in my future."

"But the officer remanded it down to simple disorderly conduct," Kirby pointed out. "Any decent lawyer can get that dismissed."

"Will Jason take my case?"

Kirby gave him a half smile. "Jason does entertainment law."

Grant felt a bitchy sense of confidence. "This case is entertaining. It involves me, a psychotic porn star, and Ronan."

Kirby nodded quickly, clearly anxious to shelve the subject of Jason. "Donnie will help you out. He's competent."

Grant shrugged his approval. Donnie was a mutual friend who advertised in the Yellow Pages.

Kirby was still waiting to hear more.

"Okay, listen good, because I'm only going to say this once. First things first—he's uncut and bigger than any man has a right to be. Slight curve to the left, too. His body is incredible. For all the drinking, smoking, and drugs, he smells great. Even his breath. Plus, he's very demanding and quite the dirty talker. Sexually, he's amazing. I mean, the experience is practically out of body. At first, you think you're there emotionally, too, because physically it was just so . . . *great*. But then he opens his mouth to start talking and you come back down to earth. I know you're mildly obsessed with this man, and I don't want to sound like some millionaire who says money can't buy happiness, but take it from me, there's a big difference between the man of your dreams and the man of your wet dreams. Still, I wouldn't give up the chance to sleep with Brad Pitt. At least he's into architecture. There'd be more to talk about." Grant let out a deep sigh. "Now. Can I please eat?" He looked around. "Where the hell is our action hero lesbian waitress?"

Epilogue

On the cover of *Velocity* was a smoldering shot of Ronan in a wet, ribbed cotton sleeveless undershirt. The headline screamed, "IF THIS MAN WANTED TO F*#% YOU, WHAT WOULD YOU SAY?" Underneath that, in a smaller font, read, "GRANT BROWDER SAID YES. AND HE'S TELLING ALL INSIDE."

Kate Bobo could hardly contain herself. "You do realize that we have *never* received this much advance press for an issue before! It's fucking amazing. But now I'm starting to get depressed, because there's no way I'm going to be able to top this. This is it. This is our peak." She sighed heavily. "So sad."

The last month had been a nonstop whirlwind. Grant had closed his eyes and jumped into the deep end on the feature, spilling every detail in first person, no matter how embarrassing or revealing. A gut thing told him that the more uncomfortable he felt, the better the piece would turn out to be.

His instinct had paid off. Kate Bobo had flipped and passed it on to a few of her media mover colleagues. A few days later, Miramax bought the film rights and hired Grant to write the script. Just when he thought the chaos had started to die down, the magazine hit newsstands, and it whipped up all over again.

No official word had come down from Ronan's camp. Sailor Moynihan had quit after the first press leak. But the controversy had ultimately only done Ronan good. Bad publicity swirled around him when the NFL pulled the plug on his Super Bowl halftime performance, citing creative differences. His new CD *Tantric* and its first single, "Hard to Resist," had started out weaker than expected. But the torrent of attention on his backstage moves had been accompanied by new attention to his music. Both the CD and the single subsquently stormed into the top ten.

The revelations of Ronan's bisexuality stirred up cultural waves as well. Morning news programs and talk shows were yakking it up with pundits here and pundits there, screaming for and against the new generation's open and accepting attitude toward swinging both ways.

The story had become much bigger than Grant's own experience, and he had been quite thankful for that, as it allowed him to recede into the background. Unlike Nicky Lawrence, who had pushed hard to sell his own story about his night with Ronan. At the end of the day, the porn star got little attention, even when one of the tabloids eventually picked it up.

Grant broke from his reverie and came back to the present.

Kate Bobo was on a roll about trying to quit smoking, hating Bonnie Fuller, and scoring a reservation at Sixty-Six for that night. "Do you want to come?" she asked.

"No, but thanks," Grant said easily. "I've got plans with my boyfriend." That felt great to say, to mean it and know that the relationship was happy and solid, not toxic with insecurity and ready to fall apart at any moment.

Kirby had moved in and never moved out. In fact, he hadn't so much as given a casual glance to the apartment notices. At first, it had been a platonic courtship—watching classic DVDs, going to new movies at their favorite cinema, long dinners at their regular haunts. Until one night it'd changed on a dime. Instead of sleeping on the couch, Kirby had come to Grant's bed. They'd put it all back together, and it felt fabulous.

Still, Grant hadn't jumped back in the deep end unaware. Kirby had cheated on him before—twice, in fact—and he had the propensity to be a real asshole. But Grant had the emotional maturity to forgive, and for now, things were great.

And it helped to have LaKeisha on speed dial. She was always ready with relationship advice. "I get so damn tired of my sister girls carrying on about some raggedy ass man," she'd told him recently. "I'm like, 'Bitch, you need to pull yourself together. You don't need no man to put gas in your car and buy you a Wendy's combo meal, hell.' Shit, especially a sorry man. They ain't good but for a minute anyway. That's when they try to be all attentive and hot in the bed and get you to be like, 'Ooh, girl, my man put it to me last night.' Yeah, that shit's good for about two weeks. After that, the motherfucker just wants to sit up and look at TV with a beer in his damn hand. LaKeisha don't play that. My fat ass better be the show you watching, hell."

Grant beamed back to the present.

Kate was snickering at him. "What is the happy couple going to do? Watch another movie at home? You guys are like an old married couple. It's hilarious. So what are you screening tonight?"

Grant thought of Kirby and smiled. *"Almost Famous."*

Spanish Eyes

Ben Tyler

For William Relling Jr.

Chapter One

Don't get your meat where you get your bread. Brad could hear the echo of his best friend Garreth's advice reverberating in his head. His increasingly dizzy head. The head that held two glazed-over eyeballs, ears that couldn't believe the words that were bursting from his lunatic boss, and a brain that should have been lobotomized before allowing Brad to have sex in the first place with his butterball turkey employer, Gill Truitt.

Gill Truitt, producer of the Saturday morning sitcom *Enough is Enough!*, was a bark beetle in the chip off the block that was his Emmy Award-winning old man—minus his dad's genius, good looks, and sixth sense for recognizing and attracting talented writers to his television projects. Gill would never be able to fill his old man's legendary shoes. And that sucked. As did the fact that his show attracted an audience that was lower on the intelligence-quotient curve than *Saved By the Bell* and *Lizzie McGuire*. Combined.

"And, by the way, babe," Gill added, salting the wound of Brad's lashed ego, "the season's almost over, and we're not renewing your contract. Ratings, you know. But hey, you look hunky in that T-shirt."

Brad was incredulous. Dumped by a mercy fuck and fired from his staff writing job in the same breath. It happened to other people, like secretaries and ambitious actors who bartered sex for financial security or a shortcut up the fame and fortune ladder. Brad wondered: *Could I,*

subconsciously, have slept with this jerk just to further my career? He realized that even though he hadn't considered Gill as anything resem-
bling a gravy train, nonetheless, he had just been pushed onto the
third rail.

"Bastard prick," Brad said almost inaudibly.

Gill had hamster-size ears, but Dobermanlike hearing. "Don't make
this personal. Not everything is about you." He pushed a button on
the intercom. "I want Bochco!" he snapped. Gill picked up a video-
cassette, swiveled around in his chair and pushed the tape through the
mailbox slot of his office VCR. He divided his attention between Brad
and an unedited episode of *Enough is Enough!* "I've gotta spend more
time on this shitty show," he said as if to further explain the demise of
their semi-weekly circle jerk sessions.

Translation, Brad thought to himself. *A new stud is in the wings.
Someone with aspirations to write for a barely breathing sitcom starring
a ditzy teenage blonde with incestuous desires for her hunky but vapid
high school football star stepbrother.*

"Catch you later, man," Gill said as the credits rolled on the television monitor. Then he smiled at seeing his own name.

His dismissive tone was meant to usher Brad out the office. "Beverly
keeps my calendar. Schedule drinks in a week or so." Gill turned
around and picked up his telephone headset, laying it over where his
hair used to be. He then pushed a series of numbers on the instru-
ment's keypad with his index finger. He was oblivious to Brad's nearly
inert body, which had just had its life force vacuumed out.

Gill hissed impatiently to someone on the opposite end of the optic
fiber cable.

Jolted by the sibilant vibration in the room, Brad sputtered,
"Drinks? A week or so? No can do. I'm leaving for London first thing in
the A.M." He was speaking on automatic, without thinking about what
he was saying.

Gill stopped mid-rant at a voice on the other end of the line. He
stared at Brad. Stupefaction halted his neurotransmitters. "Get serious," he finally said, his brain synapses clicking back from freeze
frame. He punched the release key on the telephone.

"I was canceling your insipid show from my life anyway," Brad said.

"News flash. You have a contract." Gill smirked.

Parroting Gill's accusing tone, Brad smiled back and said, "Dateline, Hollywood. You just said you're not renewing." He waited a beat. "Anyway, my enormously wealthy and super hung *new* boyfriend, a man who puts Toby and Ben and Colin to shame in the physique section of the looks department, the guy who taught Harry and Wills to play croquet at Balmoral, insists that we get married straightaway. In Hampshire. In the formal gardens of his fantastic ancestral home . . . er, estate . . . er, castle. Butlers and upstairs-downstairs maids and cooks and equestrian types all lined up in the great room eager to greet the master when he comes home. Very Merchant-Ivory. His ancient mother's a doll. Even has her own crown. Swans on his private lake, too. Ever see *Brideshead Revisited?* Yeah, that's like my rich, very hung *new* boyfriend's house. Er, palace. Only smaller."

"Like you're serious or something." Gill waved a dismissive hand. "No one's that rich these days. Plus, you were too satisfied having sex with me to have a boyfriend on the side. Not to mention I kept you too busy with the show. You haven't left the studio lot for six months."

True, Brad thought. Gill's last comment caused a surge of resentment at the months of lost time. He rose regally from his chair. He hated to be told that he was lying, even if he was.

"Satisfied is not a word I would use to describe how I felt about having sex with you." Brad pointed two fingers down his throat. "I'll forward a JPEG of Rupert—that's my super hung, rich new boyfriend—and me, romping through his topiary."

Gill snort-laughed. "You've been writing way too many dream sequences, babe. Cinderella, you're not."

"You can reach me through the American embassy if you want a rewrite on that last script," Brad said.

"No fucking way you're leaving this town, let alone getting married." Gill snorted in Brad's poker face. "A royal. Ha! Lifetime wouldn't even buy *that* tall story."

"You're addressing a soon-to-be monarch." Brad arched an eyebrow in an attempted display of threat. "Careful, or I'll command, 'Off with his head!' And I don't mean the one on your shoulders." He was reaching for the door handle. "*Enough is Enough!* is enough. It isn't worthy of my talents."

"Talents?" Gill sneered. "You're a sitcom writer."

Brad pulled open the door and stepped into the corridor.

"A lousy sitcom writer!" Gill shouted once again. "That's as low as a Starbucks counter person in the real world!" He retreated to his desk and quickly found Brad's most recent script, then hurried back to the doorway and hurled the pages at Brad. "This episode you wrote is worse than anything from the last season of *Evening Shade!* It's stinking up my office!"

"It's the odor of your dying career," Brad teased.

"Get off the lot, you worthless, ungrateful . . . *writer!*" Gill spat.

"Cheerio, ole sport. Off to ye olde Londontown." Brad used his best mid-Atlantic accent. He then issued Gill the finger, and turned and walked past Beverly who smiled and shrugged her shoulders in silent solidarity.

The adrenaline rush that enveloped Brad during his altercation with Gill soon wafted away, replaced by a haze of melancholy. Brad walked from Gill's office in the John Davidson Building back to his cubicle in the Betty Buckley Tower, on the other side of the studio lot. Preoccupied with thoughts of Gill and what Brad should have said, as well as feelings of failure, both as a writer and as a suck-up to a Pillsbury Doughboy producer, made Brad's journey to his office laborious. When he arrived at his cubbyhole of work space, he found a security guard seated in his black, armless desk chair. The bored guard, legs spread wide apart, monotonously rolled back and forth on the chair's casters over a plastic carpet saver. Brad noticed a square patch of dust on the desk that outlined where his computer had been.

"Sorry, Mr. Quinn," the guard said. "Gotta observe what you pack up."

"Afraid I'll stuff the color copier into my backpack, Fernando? What about my hard drive?" Brad was vaguely concerned, looking at the empty space on his desk.

The guard shrugged. "Orders from that David E. Kelly wanna-be you work for. *Worked* for," he amended.

Brad rolled his eyes at the swarthy, sexy security guy. He'd once furtively watched Fernando taking a shower in the studio gym. In a flash of recall Brad pictured the man's six-foot-two frame, smooth dark

skin, his sculpted body lathered in soap, his long, glistening penis surrounded by a cloud of suds.

Coming out of his reverie Brad sighed. "Intellectual property."
When he signed his *Enough is Enough!* contract, he'd also signed away
all of his creative ideas.

Fernando said, "You must've backed up your files, didn't you?"

Brad smiled. Of course he'd backed up his files. In fact, as the television season ground to a close he'd removed all but his most lame
story ideas, as well as his carefully guarded, top-secret feature film
screenplay, and his collection of nude gay celebrity photos. He then
defragged the computer so that his personal work and bookmarked
porn Web sites were untraceable as *favorites*.

Under the scrutiny of Fernando, who was actually more interested
in the framed poster of *The Bird Cage* hanging on the wall, Brad picked
up a few reference books and his *American Idol* coffee mug stuffed
with pencils, red pens, yellow highlighters, and a pair of scissors. He
placed them in the white cardboard storage box that had been provided by security. He laid several scripts and a *Far Side* desk calendar
on top.

He then looked around his work area. For the past six months Brad
had spent more time here writing, and in story meetings, than in his
own West Hollywood apartment. Gill had been right about one thing.
There was no opportunity to meet a potential boyfriend. *Which is why
I got it on with Gill.* Brad felt an odd relief as he put aside the fear that
he might have subconsciously had sex with his boss just to get his story
ideas accepted. "For that I deserve to be rescued by a real prince!" he
said absently, out loud.

"Charming." Fernando smiled, giving Brad a mischievous and un-
mistakable look of a guy who could be had for less than the price of a
six-pack of Corona.

Brad wondered to himself what lines of dialogue he might write if
Aimee, the sexaholic lead character of the show, were in similar limbo,
between self-restraint and the possibility of a paint-peeling fuck.
"Darn it!" he finally said in a tone that imitated Aimee pretending to
be coy. His eyes locked onto the security guard's, and he summoned
words from a scene he'd written earlier in the season, when Aimee was
suddenly hot for one of her stepbrother's football buddies who was

leaving the playing field on a stretcher. "I should have made the time to get to know you sooner," Brad said.

"Anything more you need before I take away your studio ID?" Fernando asked.

"Er . . . blow you?"

The guard sniggered. "You comedy writers! That piece of crap show needs more jokes like that! You're gonna get an Oscar someday."

"If I had Oscar, I wouldn't need Fernando," Brad said.

Fernando raised an eyebrow. "Now look what you've done!" he whispered a harsh admonishment to Brad. Then he pointed to the boner in his pants.

Brad grinned.

"This is your fault," Fernando continued. "You'll have to take care of it. And I don't have all day." Fernando cocked his head toward the bank of elevators.

Brad picked up his cardboard box.

Rather than wait for the elevator car, Fernando escorted Brad to the stairwell. Walking down six flights, they came to the building's basement. "Under the stairs," Fernando said. He moved into the shadows, leaned against the wall, and unzipped his fly.

"Now I'm really sorry that I didn't get to know you sooner," Brad said as he kneeled onto the cold concrete and reached his hand in through the metal-toothed opening in Fernando's pants. There was no underwear between the fabric of the guard's uniform and the soft dank thicket of pubic hairs. Brad made immediate blind contact with the warm walls of Fernando's tubular flesh and felt the tacky wetness that coated the head with pre-cum. His heart raced. For Brad, when confronted with sex, it was never a simple desire as much as it was an emergency.

Fernando took a bow-legged stance against the wall. He closed his eyes and tilted his head back as Brad wrapped his hand around the lengthy piece and wrestled it out from its lair. Fernando was satisfied with his own sex equipment and half grinned as he recognized that the nano-second of hesitation from Brad was a response of awe. And when Fernando felt the humid wetness of Brad's covetous mouth surrounding his cock, his mind involuntarily shut out all thoughts other than the self-serving urgency to climax.

The dementia-inducing need to accost the shaft with his lips and tongue completely controlled Brad and he deftly unzipped his own pants and dragged out his completely hard dick.

The dense surface of smooth concrete under Brad's knees was a discomfort made numb and distant by the inebriating tactile sensation of owning a mouthful of Fernando's long, thick veined cock, and stroking his own dick. Fernando cupped Brad's head in his large hands and forced him to swallow the length of his shaft. Brad gladly gagged as its head passed his tonsils. The pungent aroma he inhaled when his face plunged forth into Fernando's heavy, hair-covered balls sack only made his desperate need stronger.

Delirious with lust, Brad, divided his concentration between the exotic sex cylinder in his mouth, and the familiar one in his hand. He reached up with his other hand to pull out Fernando's shirttails from his pant's waist.

Simultaneously, Fernando hastily unbuttoned his blue, regulation work shirt, and exposed his tapered torso tufted with straight dark hair in the cleft between his pumped pecs. He unconsciously explored his own perspiration soaked chest and harshly pinched his nipples between his thumbs and forefingers.

Brad placed the palm of one hand on Fernando's rippled and mossy stomach, and caressed his skin. He raised his eyes in order to commit to memory what he knew would be the in-the-flesh equivalent of his fantasy man. He was not disappointed and felt himself ready to come at will.

Brad focused all of his concentration on enjoying the length and girth of Fernando's dick plumping in his mouth. He slathered it with his warm tongue and saliva. When he could hear Fernando's breathing became labored, and he gripped tightly to tufts of Brad's hair, Brad braced himself for the thick load of cum that he knew was about to be emptied into his eager oriface.

The possibility that they could be caught at any moment was not nearly as important to either of them as was completing the encounter. Still, with the echo of doors to the stairwell opening and closing above them, as well as the reverberation of shoes ascending or descending the stairs, Fernando was quickly ready to get off. His throat constricted as he fought to mute the rush of air that was being forced up from his diaphragm in perfect synchronization to the waves of his oncoming orgasm. Then, with his face contorted and his eyes clamped shut, Fernando, wishing that he also had Brad's tongue in his mouth to battle with, discharged his load. Brad greedily accepted the pungent sperm and savored the flavor as it passed over his tongue.

Brad, too, was unable to hold back. Withdrawing his lips from Fernando's still dripping piece, he spat what was left in his mouth of his partner's cum onto his own cock. He worked his shaft into a heart pounding ejaculation, which puddled on the floor.

Afterward, still clearing his throat and picking the hairs off his tongue, Brad was walking toward the Natalie Wood parking structure in lock step with Fernando, who was still adjusting the swollen tool in his regulation security guard uniform pants. Finally, at Brad's silver BMW, they popped open the trunk and placed the storage box inside. The two men shook hands, then Brad opened the driver's side door and slipped into the bucket seat. He turned the ignition, and pushed a button to roll down the window.

"If you want some freakish fun, make your security rounds to Gill Truitt's office at about midnight, after his Monday night story meeting," Brad called. "That's when he usually bangs someone from the writing staff. Bring a video camera."

It was winter in southern California. The evening temperature was seventy-two degrees. The aphrodisiacal scent of night blooming jasmine perfumed the air. Brad and his best friend Garreth relaxed in the bubbling hot tub on the patio deck of Garreth's Hollywood Hills home. They shared a bottle of Merlot, a wedge of Brie, and the bitter pill that made them lament Brad's employment termination, lack of interest in his screenplay and the dearth of eligible mate material in WeHo.

With his current favorite CD, *Essential Michael, the Black Years*, playing in the background, Garreth spoke with the enthusiasm of one who needs to be needed. "Number one, you're not to worry about money. If you need anything, there's always plenty left over from my monthly allowance."

"The Writers Guild minimum was decent," Brad said. "And I didn't have time to spend much of it."

"Never fear. My third ex-lover, the shit before the real shit, is now a producer on *The Arnold and Maria Show*. Owes me big time. I already have a call in to him."

"Proactive is your middle name," Brad said, sincerity floating from his lips as warm as the steam rising from the foaming blue water.

"As for marriage, you now have plenty of time for shopping around." Garreth quickly outlined what in his mind was the most pressing issue of Brad's life. "I'll host a coming out dinner party! Reverend Sally says if you're looking for a mate, that mate is looking for you, too!"

Reverend Sally was the New Age philosophy guru of the moment. Garreth could always be counted on to offer, verbatim, advice that Reverend Sally espoused during her fifteen-hundred-dollar-weekend therapy retreats. Garreth had all of Reverend Sally's classes on his resume, and he played her CDs on a continuous loop in his car stereo. He was a self-professed authority on what Reverend Sally would say on practically every subject, from morality to tithing to her organization.

"It isn't enough to bag a ton of guys until you find one who you're altogether groovy about, or who isn't a complete and utter fuck-up," Garreth recited from Reverend Sally's "Love Consciousness" seminar. "You must bag yourself first."

"I do that morning, noon, and night," Brad said, beginning to feel exasperated.

"What Reverend Sally is saying, I'm sure, is that what you're looking for is right where you are," Garreth said. "I think."

"The Dorothy Gale speech again?" Brad rolled his eyes, then reached for the wine bottle. "In story and song, Mr. Right is only two doors down the hall. But cosmically, we can't recognize him until after we've circumnavigated the globe and explored some deep philosophic self-evaluation that makes us feel worthy of true love. Only then can we understand that the guy we see every week at the dry cleaners is our one and only." Brad sighed. "Why should Mr. Right be so close in the first place? Why do we tend to pair up with the locals, so to speak? There's a whole universe out there."

Garreth replied, "Reverend Sally says most people don't think they deserve Joe Millionaire, so they stay out of Beverly Hills. That doesn't apply to you and *moi*, but you get her idea."

Brad was still ruminating over his thesis about casting a wider love net. "I lied today," he said.

"Non sequitur." Garreth wagged a wet chlorine finger. "Evading an issue. That's number two on Reverend Sally's *Get Over It* list. It comes just after blaming your parents for everything from your fucked-up social skills to your pathetic dick size. Oh, not you personally, dear."

"I told some untruths to Gill. But I think I was actually lying to myself."

"You agree with Reverend Sally!" Garreth trumpeted. " 'Liars are not deceiving anyone but themselves,' she says."

Garreth noticed that the music had ended. "Some Milli Vanilli?" He stood up, naked, wineglass in hand, and stepped out of the water. Exiting the hot tub, Garreth opened the French doors leading to the living room of his art deco style home, leaving Brad in the darkness of the evening, with only a citronella candle and the hot tub lights for illumination.

Despite the temporary lack of obstreperous recorded music tracks issuing through the Bose, it was never completely silent in the Hollywood Hills. Here, just above Sunset, in this residential area of steep, serpentine streets and even steeper mortgages, the steady, unvarying drone of perpetual traffic and police helicopters melted into white noise. Although it became hardly noticeable, like the sound of a steady rain, there was no escaping the cacophony of Los Angeles. However, without the further intrusion of Garreth recycling expensive theories on life, love, and masturbation, Brad momentarily slipped into contented woolgathering.

"England," he said aloud, picturing London pubs, sheep grazing on green hillsides, a thatched-roof cottage, his last visit abroad, the bobby who had redeemed a traffic ticket in exchange for sex in a South Kensington bed-and-breakfast.

The memory of that tryst was suddenly obliterated when Ethel

Merman cleft the air and dismembered his thoughts. "I had a dream! A wonderful dream, baby!"

Recovering from the jarring sound, Brad sang in a louder voice, "It's time to move on, baby." Just as Garreth opened the patio door and stepped back into the tub.

"The Merm was handier," he said, explaining the change in music selection. "Move on? Where?" Garreth looked at his friend, who was in deep thought, staring past the eucalyptus trees that surrounded the patio. Brad's arms stretched out like a span of wings over the back of the spa. "Why so pensive? More vino?"

Brad collected his thoughts enough to focus on his empty wine-glass. "I was just thinking about getting the heave-ho today. And about lying that I was going to the U.K. to get married. Maybe it wasn't a lie after all."

"You don't need the fuss of a marriage when you can do as I do. Just get a friend . . . with benefits."

"I've just made a huge decision," Brad stated abruptly.

Words between Brad and Garreth weren't always necessary. They could read each other's thoughts simply by the look in the other's eyes, when an exceptional specimen of masculinity walked by. "Doll face, I hate to break the news, but you're unemployed," Garreth said. "I'm thinking that you should start sending out resumes instead of postcards."

Brad looked down for a moment into the bubbling water. "Not vacation," he explained. "Research. Looking for Mr. Goodwrench. So to speak." He leaned over and picked up the wine bottle, then poured the dregs of the Merlot into his glass and took a sip. "I can always scrounge up a crummy job," he said. "I may not always have the opportunity to cut a swath across the continent to explore the mating rituals of the European homosexual. I'm off to see the Wizard about a heart."

"Just make sure it comes packaged with a dick," Garreth said.

Chapter Two

*A*ll gaydar and electronic devices must be switched to their off and locked positions until the aircraft has arrived at the gate.

Brad never actually heard that exact announcement. Regardless of FAA rules, his genetic GPS was having zero success navigating toward any man on the plane with whom he could dish the latest episode of *Designing for the Sexes*.

The journey to Europe had begun with a promising stare from across the aisle. Brad returned the compliment with a lascivious smile, until the man flashed his undercover sky marshal badge. Brad quickly moved on to the distracted and harried but adorable flight attendant who he thought might have boyfriend possibilities. However, after personally aiding Brad with his seat belt and generously dropping an extra packet of complimentary honey roasted peanuts onto Brad's fold-down tray, the young man was summoned to another cabin of the plane, and he disappeared for the remainder of the flight.

Modern jet travel being the cramped, time-consuming bummer that it is, Brad tried other means of amusing himself during the almost unendurable long flight from LAX to Heathrow. He opened the *TV Guide* edition of *Crossword Challenge*. *Laugh-In's Johnson? Too easy*, Brad said to himself as he inked in *Arte*. *Raines or Fitzgerald?* Who other than *Ella* fits that one, he answered. Before crossing over Denver, he had completed every puzzle in the magazine.

For a while, the new David Sedaris book was a chortle-out-loud page-turner. But that lasted only across the Plains states as several passengers around him pushed their flight attendant call buttons and begged to be reseated next to the crying baby several rows back. When a glass of wine, a flat pillow, and a stereo headset arrived, *gratis*, from a snippy stewardess, Brad assumed they were bribes to be exchanged for him going to sleep. Although he accepted the offerings, Brad was so amped up with the anticipation of his new search to find a mate that he could not recline his seat and doze. Besides, he loved to fly. Perversely, he thought it was very pleasant to be strapped into a cramped, narrow, uncomfortable seat, hurtling through the sky at an impossibly fast speed, in a metal cylinder crammed with three hundred strangers, all of whom were silently praying, "Dear sweet Jesus," and imagining heat-seeking, shoulder-launched missiles shadowing the aircraft.

It took the old man strapped in beside him to begin babbling about his dead wife—but she was getting better—for Brad to close Sedaris, control his involuntary laughter, slide the window shade down, and pretend to sleep. This feigned inactivity eventually brought on genuine slumber.

Many hours later, the wafting scent of instant coffee issuing from the galley, and the crinkle throughout the cabin of passengers unwrapping soggy bacon, egg, and cheese biscuits from cellophane, wrested Brad into consciousness. He yawned and stretched and looked at his wristwatch. He calculated the time in Los Angeles and London, and how much longer before landing. When the captain announced their final approach to the U.K., Brad let a surge of excitement wash over him.

Brad cleared customs at Heathrow. With passport in hand—and eyes ricocheting from a platoon of ruggedly handsome, square-jawed royal military security guards in green camouflage fatigues, holding AK-49 semiautomatics positioned across their strong chests—Brad wheeled his suitcase-laden trolley past a bank of immigration officials. He moved through a mass migration of saris, tunics, grand boubous, and wrapped skirts.

As if joining a mass exodus of refugees, Brad found himself in a stream of humanity that was represented by every conceivable nationality and culture. Together, they flowed through a long corridor to the building's exit. *The forest for the trees,* Brad thought as he plastered a smile on his face and searched among a sea of faces behind a cordoned area. Garreth had promised to arrange for a friend of a friend to be on hand to serve as an international welcome wagon, and Brad searched for that anonymous someone among the throngs of people meeting arriving passengers. Aside from an assurance that the greeter would be "utterly adorable," Garreth couldn't be more specific about who might accept the task of fetching Brad.

"You must be the wayward Yank." A male voice with a thick cockney accent spoke loudly enough for Brad to hear over the din of a dozen foreign languages chattering simultaneously. "I'm s'posed to drag you up to London."

Brad looked in the direction of the voice, and he discovered the brooding face of what he could only think of as a throwback to Sid Vicious. With a bed head hairstyle of green, burgundy, and cobalt blue spikes, and silver body piercings that Brad imagined did not stop at the ears, nose, and tongue, the young man made an immediate impression. Brad's smile faded slightly as he tentatively acknowledged that indeed, he was probably the guy in question. "Garreth sent you?" Brad asked, extending his hand in greeting.

"Me mate told me to collect an American bloke. 'Bring 'em back alive' was all he said. I'm Basher." The guy ignored Brad's extended hand in greeting. "We're off this way." Basher cocked his head, indicating that Brad should keep in tow.

Basher. Sounds like a name you'd give an infomercial kitchen gadget, Brad thought. He pushed his luggage trolley behind his punk-rocker escort, asking himself, *Who is this kid? Am I the guy he was sent to meet? I was hoping for Prince William.*

"You the new boy?" Basher asked without turning around.

"Excuse me?"

"You're not exactly like the other Yanks that Gusher's had."

"You're talking about what?" Brad had come to a stop, deciding that it would be better to take a cab into London. "I think you've picked up the wrong guy."

Basher himself stopped and turned around to face Brad. Raising an eyebrow pierced with a silver safety pin, Basher hooked his thumbs in the pockets of his ripped jeans and rested his weight on one hip. "Listen. I never pick up the wrong pissin' guy."

Defiant, Brad stared back at Basher. Although he was filled with trepidation, he also admitted to himself that Basher, in his denim jacket, seductively unbuttoned to reveal that he wasn't wearing a shirt underneath, was a bit of a turn-on. From what Brad could see, Basher's creamy, white skin was smooth and flawless, stretched over a lean swimmer's frame. He was adorned with a string of nuts and bolts around his neck. Brad suddenly found himself thinking that if a genie in a bottle had given him a wish, he'd wind up as the metal against this guy's bare flesh.

"You're the bloody unemployed chap from Hollywood, who got himself dumped by a bloke, and now you're on a needle in a haystack mission to find another fool to settle down with and have a brood of sniveling tykes. Ain't ya?"

"I wouldn't exactly state my case in so many words," Brad said self-consciously.

"All the same. And you're buyin' the petrol, and McDonald's for me trouble." Basher turned on his thick-heeled boots and exited through the sliding glass doors. Brad stood still for a moment, tired from the long flight, trying to mentally digest his first encounter with Basher. After inhaling a deep breath, he decided that he was on an adventure, and that this unexpected path was part of the journey. He took another lung full of air and pushed his trolley, following his escort.

Outside the airport terminal, Brad momentarily forgot that his chaperon made him, in equal measure, ill at ease and sexually excited. *I'm in England!* He wanted to shout his enthusiasm. Instead, he consciously inhaled the crisp, damp air, looked into the slate gray sky, smiled with a sense of utter fulfillment, and pursued Basher who had picked up the pace considerably, en route to the car.

Against the red light of a crosswalk, and the shrill warning whistle from a bobby directing traffic, the two men arrived at the parking structure. "It's the silver one," Basher said, ambling toward a row of vehicles in parking slots.

Brad looked toward the bank of cars, pushing his trolley. He stopped behind a rusted old BMW and waited for a moment.

"Over here." Basher sneered from several cars farther on.

Brad looked over, then saw Basher opening the trunk of a Rolls Royce Silver Cloud. "Stuff your crap in the boot," he called. Brad was too perplexed to move. He looked at the Rolls. Then at Basher. Then at the BMW. And then at the Rolls again. *Grand theft auto in my first hour in the U.K.!* Brad screamed to himself in a panic.

Basher read the expression on Brad's face, and for the first time that afternoon, he laughed. "Either you've never been riding in a Rolls and you're frightfully impressed, or you're scared shitless that the rightful owner will be along at any moment to haul away your American ass and dump it at the Tower of London." He smiled, obviously taking enormous enjoyment from Brad's look of anxiety. "Figure it out on the way to town. Get in. But not in the back!" Basher scolded. "I ain't no bloody chauffeur!"

Brad tentatively wheeled his trolley up to the car, then carefully placed each piece of luggage in the plush interior of the trunk. Basher opened the driver's side of the car and slipped in behind the wheel, onto the burgundy leather seat. He started the engine before Brad could close the trunk. Brad pushed his cart to where several others were abandoned, then he started to move to the right side of the vehicle. Seeing Basher seated there, he quickly remembered that the driver and passenger sides were opposite American cars. He opened the door on the left and got in.

A palpable barrier of silence divided the two men. It was a thick, invisible barricade drawn down the center of the vehicle. The lack of interaction was making Brad nuts. Two cute guys from opposite sides of the Atlantic should have tons to discuss, he thought. However, Brad couldn't begin to think of what he might say that wouldn't have Basher either ignoring him or taunting him. He knew that the longer they existed in this void of communication, the harder it would be to break the silence. It was the same way that putting off writing a thank-you note eventually renders the deed pointless. He had to say something or risk never saying anything at all.

He must be with a band. He looks like he's with a band. We could talk about MTV, Brad thought. *No, ask about the weather, that's always a safe topic. Stupid. There's only one weather here. Rain, followed by ex-*

tended periods of rain. Gay clubs! Ask him about the trendy nightspots. No, bring him out with something completely innocuous.

"What's it like having the queen of England practically in your own backyard?" Brad said. Immediately he wanted to pound his forehead against the dashboard. *Christ, you're such an idiot!* Brad berated himself.

"She's just there. Don't think much about her, really," Basher said. "Probably the way you feel 'bout movie stars."

Brad nodded in agreement. *Good analogy,* he thought. But rather than spin the cylinder of a pistol and risk possibly blowing away the thin rapport they had just established, he decided that he would offer something more sure-fire as a follow-up comment. "Hey, man. Really great of you to take time to pick me up."

Basher shrugged.

"I'd like to show my gratitude with more than a McDonald's hamburger and fries."

"Pissin' Christ, I hope so!" Basher cried out. "I said McDonald's, but I didn't mean no toxic sludge dump burger take-away, for Christ sake. I meant the pub in South Ken. Jeez, Lord A'mighty. You wanna give me mad cow disease, for God's sake?"

Brad figuratively threw up his hands. He obviously couldn't read this man. As for his fantasy of burying his face in Basher's ball sack, *that* would never happen, as long as Basher thought of him as a made-in-the-U.S.A. fool.

"Whatever," Brad said, turning away to take in the sight of Big Ben in the distance. Brad went for one last play. "So, who's this Gusher you mentioned?"

Surprisingly, for the second time, Basher smiled. "Gusher is . . ." He paused. "Didn't your Yank friend tell you about us? He'll fancy you. I've got that right."

It was Brad's turn to smile. Once again, at least for the moment, he was feeling less intimidated, which made Basher more attractive. "What makes you say that?"

"Sixth sense. Gusher and me 'ave similar tastes."

"What's he do?" Brad asked.

"Nothin'," Basher said.

"He must do something," Brad pushed.

"Specializes."

"In what?"

"What's it matter?" Basher said.

Brad retreated into silence as the car passed more sights that he remembered from a previous journey to London. Earl's Court Road, King's Circle, Admiralty Arch, Buckingham Palace, Leicester Square. Basher eventually made a left-hand turn and followed a narrow side street bordered by centuries-old horse stalls that had been converted to small but expensive apartments. Finally, the car drove through a stone archway and into an open park anchored by a grand, three-story residence.

"I done my part," said Basher. "Got ya safe and sound to Horseferry Hall. You can pay up for me services after Gusher gets hold of ya."

Brad was nervous. He still had little in the way of a clue who Gusher was. From the looks of the house, though, Brad thought his host could be a lord or an earl.

"I'm poppin' the boot," Basher said, with obviously no intention of lifting a finger to help retrieve Brad's bags.

The men opened their respective doors and stepped into the blustery day. Brad's hair quickly became a mess of tangles. From the trunk he lifted out the four suitcases and placed them on the gravel driveway. Taking his shoulder bag, he followed Basher up the granite steps of the portico to a pair of massive carved wood entry doors. Basher didn't bother to knock. He inserted a key into the lock and pushed open the right-side door.

Brad tentatively peered in and his jaw dropped. The only reference to which he could compare the interior of the house was something he'd drooled over in *Architectural Digest*.

He entered the foyer. "Park it," Basher said, his voice echoing in the large hall. He indicated that Brad should place his bag on the black-and-white marble floor, beside an alabaster statue of two naked men embracing each other. "I'll tell the master that his project has arrived."

Basher disappeared down the hall, his boots scraping the marble tile and reverberating in the vast room. He stepped onto the plush runner on the carved staircase and ascended out of sight.

Brad looked around. He studied the details of the foyer: a French tapestry, a portrait of George I, Gothic sitting chairs, paisley wall coverings. The room reeked of hereditary aristocracy.

Brad was absorbed in the detail of a satin brocade dress depicted in a large oil canvas, when he was startled by Basher's voice. " 'Asn't been too sociable, this one," Basher spoke. Brad whirled around to find himself facing the effulgent smile of a man whose bright white teeth, aquamarine eyes, and dimples rendered him weak and speechless. "Told you," Basher spoke again, this time to Brad. "Ain't got no manners, either."

"So sorry!" Brad extended his hand in greeting and apology. "Are you Gusher? Basher's told me so much."

"Not a word!" Basher bellowed.

"Can't escape the nickname," Gusher said, accepting Brad's handshake. "Basher can't bear to call me Poindexter, and he thinks that Dex is too bourgeois. You be the judge."

Basher made a grunt sound of impatience. "A rose by any other . . . ?" Brad shrugged, trying to dodge being caught in the middle of what seemed a long-standing domestic disagreement.

"A diplomat, eh?" Gusher said. "You'll be an easy one to place."

Before Brad could counter with a query about being considered *easy*, Gusher pressed on. "You're California Garreth's unemployed chum who's running away from a lover, and you're now on the prowl to snag a mate. And I'm the social worker with a file on all the open cases in the U.K."

Brad made a face. "He wasn't a lover, thank God. The guy, I mean. And I'm hardly a charity case."

"I don't do charity. Introductions only. Courting is up to you. Paid for in advance by our dear sweet Garreth." Gusher looked Brad up and down with an obvious hunger. "Bash," he said without taking his eyes away from Brad, "have Mrs. Peel serve in the Hunting Hall."

"*Please?*" Basher snipped. Then he huffed out of the room.

Gusher chuckled. "Ignore Basher. Loves to throw a tantrum in public." Gusher smiled warmly. "You must be exhausted. Let's run along and get you drunk . . . er, a drink. Follow me."

Soon, Brad and Gusher were seated in an impeccably decorated drawing room. The walls were aubergine. There were porcelain flowerpots on gilt pedestals, chintz draperies, and a crystal chandelier. A painting over the fireplace mantel depicted a pack of hounds playing tug-of-war with a fox. "I confess, I'm responsible for all of Garreth's past lovers, and quite a few one-night stands, as well," Gusher boasted.

"He doesn't have a very good track record. For stability, I mean," Brad said. "Garreth can hardly keep a date, let alone a man."

Gusher pondered the comment. "But at least they've all remained loyal friends!" he declared. "Except the shit. And the other shit. Twice I've erred," he conceded. "This bit of an assignment—meaning you—should be a piece of cake." Gusher took Brad's hand into his own. "Of course, you'll want Mr. Prospective to be titled. Won't have you wanking with just any ole bloke on my watch. Perhaps an MP? I've got dozens of 'em."

Brad was about to explain the shape and content of the man of his dreams, when the door to the drawing room opened. Entering with a serving cart on which a full high tea service was laid, along with a bottle of La Grande Dame ninety-nine, was a middle-aged brunette woman wearing a knee-length wool skirt, knee-high white stockings, and flat shoes. She curtsied, first to Gusher then to Brad.

"Thank you, Mrs. Peel. That will be all." Gusher smiled at the woman. She curtsied again and then backed away toward the door. Just before she reached the exit, she stopped. "I'm runnin' to the chemist. Bash says you're low on willy warmers. 'Ave to restock."

"Awesome. And get the ribbed ones he likes," Gusher said, completely jettisoning his pretense of Victorian civility.

"The usual, eh? Ta." She closed the door behind her.

Gusher smiled at Brad. "Never mind us. We're all affection in this house," he said, referring to his sudden metamorphosis from pretentious lord of the manor with an obsequious servant girl to a *Billy Elliott* commoner. "I confess, this is all relatively new to Bash and me," Gusher explained. "We played make-believe for so long, and now we've really got the goods." He gestured for Brad to look around and take in the exquisite surroundings. "Call us *nouveu*. Inga does. That's our serving girl . . . er, woman. She indulges us. Of course, we pay her plenty. So whether it's Mrs. Peel today, or Hazel or Ann B. Davis tomorrow, she still curtsies. Isn't that cool?"

Brad looked puzzled. Gusher continued. "It's what the royal seal and dozens of commissions from the Windsors will buy. You must have thought it was terribly fun having Basher Braithwaite pick you up and take you to his manor."

Brad was still confused. "Basher is . . . ?" He didn't know what to say next. "What? He's a rock star or something?"

"Rock . . . ?" Gusher laughed loudly. "Hardly! He's just now passing through his Bing Crosby phase and starting to have an affair with everything that Dinah Shore ever sang. Hardly a rock star, dear. He's an authority on Elizabethan and Victorian restorations. He decorates all the royal apartments."

Braithwaite. Architectural Digest. Hampton Court. Brad now remembered the interior design he'd loved having been created by someone who he now recalled from a photograph, seemed inordinately young for the job, and way out of context with the designs he created. "God! Basher Braithwaite!" Brad exclaimed. "We were in the car for nearly an hour, and all he said was that everybody knows who *you* are! He made me feel as though I was an idiot for not knowing Gusher No Last Name!"

"It's Finch. And you *should* have heard of me, since I practically invented your Garreth! Didn't have a clue what to do with that trust fund until he met me! Champies, dear?"

Gusher poured from the bottle of La Grand Dame. "Get over your jet lag, and tomorrow we'll start the rounds of potential mate material."

Chapter Three

Within a week, Brad was affecting a British accent. When offered a telephone number and a shag, he said, "brilliant," to express satisfaction. He muttered, "bollocks," to exhibit exasperation when Gusher informed him that some man in question was affirmatively domesticated or inferior to their station. He used the word "lift" for elevator, "wank" for jack off, "fortnight" for two weeks, and the initials "O.A.P." for senior citizens. Brad softened the harsh "r" consonant in his speech, which transformed "Martin" to *Mah-tin.* As in, *"Mah-tin* Sackville has invited me up to his mother's house in Northamptonshire, for the weekend." Brad made that cheerful announcement after their final dinner guest departed the house late one evening during his second week.

"Sickie Sackie?" Gusher roared with incredulity as he closed the front entryway door, then turned on his heels to face Brad in the foyer. "You want to kip down with the likes of him?"

"He hasn't got a bean!" Basher added snidely.

"We only invited that *swisher* 'cause he's so pathetic and we wanted everyone else to shine a little brighter!" Gusher continued.

"Their luster must have rubbed off on him, because I thought he was a bit of all right," Brad said.

Basher leaned against the sculpture of the male nudes and studied

Brad. "You've quaffed too much bubbly t'night, my friend," he said in reproach. "You couldn't possibly find *him* winning!"

Brad felt defensive now. "Pinstripes. Neatly combed hair. Soft-spoken. Genteel."

"Frayed cuffs. Floobie. Socially inept. Tedious," Basher countered.

Gusher interrupted. "He's not on the schedule. You're going to Northumberland. A week in the country with Nigel, the duke of Waddesdon. It was all arranged when you were in the loo."

"Not that life-sapping old poop with the gin nose!" Brad rolled his eyes. "You're supposed to find someone smashing for me."

"Old?" Gusher backtracked. "Thirty-five. Tops!"

"In AOL years," Brad countered.

"He is a bit ropey, now that you mention it." Basher wrinkled his nose. "But his overdraft is stuffed."

"He never stopped yammering about his alleged affair with Prince What's His Face, or droning on about what it's like inside St. James Palace," Brad parried. "I tuned him out right after he tallied how many crossings he'd made on the QEII."

"Nigel wasn't boasting," Gusher corrected.

"Just providing highlights from his c.v.?" Brad sneered.

"All you need to know is that Farringdon Hall has been in his family for over three hundred years," Gusher said. He turned out the lights in the foyer and walked down the hall toward the drawing room. Brad fell into step with Basher, faltering behind in an inebriated brume.

"And he's a Tory, for Christ sake," Brad continued. "A gay Tory! Probably wears garters, too! What's so unacceptable about Martin, anyway?"

Entering the drawing room, with its yellow silk wall covering, tapestries, and portraits of long-dead nobles painted by John Singer Sargent, Basher plopped onto a deep chintz-covered sofa and folded his arms across his chest. "He works in a *shop*, for God's sake!"

"That *shop* is *Van Cleef & Arpels*," Brad said. "He supervises the London, Paris, Geneva, and Moscow branches." He reached into his pocket and presented an engraved business card.

"We're well aware of his employment status," Gusher said as he flopped onto the sofa next to Basher. "We met him while selecting this." Gusher extended his right ring finger on which he wore a band with multiple diamonds and sapphires. "He was so helpful in the vault that we were mislead into believing that he might be a bit of trade to pick up."

Sour grapes, Brad realized, interpreting that Basher and Gusher must have failed in their attempted conquest.

Gusher said to Brad, "Tell us what could you possibly have found the least bit interesting about ole Sackie, for Christ sake?"

Brad made a face of uncertainty. "Let me start the dishes for Mrs. Peel," he said.

"Don't evade the question," Basher said, throwing a brocade pillow and missing Brad by a foot. The champagne, chased with marijuana, had made him sloppy—in speech, dress, and aim. His white dress shirt was untucked from his black jeans, unbuttoned to reveal enough flesh to become a focus of Brad's attention.

"He's not an heir," Gusher stated. "He's not a member of any of the clubs—Brook's, White's, or Boodle's. I don't think he has any prospects."

"Toting up Martin's shortcomings?" Brad sniffed. "Granted, he's not as cute as, say, your pal Malcolm. And physically he's probably not as pumped as Duncan or Jon, whom you seated on either side of him this evening. Still, he looked like a bit of a taster, to me."

"And that's all that he would be," Gusher declared. "Trust us. When you get back from Northumberland you'll be a happily married man. Like me. I practically guarantee it." He rolled over on top of Basher and gave him a deep, satisfying kiss. Soon they were ignoring Brad, as if he had evaporated from the planet.

Brad got up and left the display of alcohol-induced lust. He moved to the grand piano on which a half-full bottle of champagne was set on a silver tray. He poured three flutes. "I did rather fancy that Simon Dials, from the British Museum."

Silence filled the room. Basher and Gusher stopped kissing. They looked at each other, then at Brad. "Copping off with Simon was tolerable, wasn't it?" Basher said to Gusher. "Remember that three-way tryst we enjoyed at Holland Park Sauna?"

"A bum-numbing bloke, but okay," Gusher agreed. "He's on my list of post-Nigel candidates. Although I never figured we'd have to sift down that far. He was inked-in only on the off chance you were turfed out by all the others. I'll ring up ole Simon at first light, if you like."

Brad sighed with satisfaction.

"But I'm not canceling your invitation to Northumberland," Gusher continued. "You're simply having a night out with Simon. Covering all bases, so to speak."

Sipping from his flute, Brad admitted to himself that his hosts probably were in a far better position than he was to make a determination on his behalf about the dating suitability of their coterie. He placed two champagne flutes on the table next to the sofa and said, "I'm wrecked. We'll chat more in the A.M."

His departure went unnoticed as Gusher unbuttoned his partner's shirt the remainder of the way and began slathering his tongue over Basher's smooth chest.

"No tan lines," Brad said with a smile. He was responding to a question from Simon Dials as they nursed cosmos in the upstairs chatting space of a popular East End club, The Spike. "That's the principle difference I've discovered between Brits and Yanks," he continued. He was trying to ignore the swelling wave of men washing around them, as well as the music from the sing-along conducted downstairs at the club's piano bar.

Simon returned the smile. "So little sun here," he explained. "Any other surprises since coming to the U.K.? I mean, other than the homo alternative scene with whom you're bunking."

Brad took another sip of his drink as he pondered the query. "I suppose I'm surprised at how sturdily put together the blokes are here."

"You expected emaciation, coal dust-embedded fingernails, and bad teeth? That's Wales." Simon laughed.

"Hardly. But surely, more than a few gyms must have opened up since I was here last." Brad took in the shape that Simon's pecs and biceps gave to his Abercombie and Fitch short-sleeve, button-down shirt. "The last time I was in London, it seems there were only tarty boys to shag. They've grown into real men."

"Speaking of tarty . . ." Simon reached out and touched Brad's hand. "Time's passing tickety-boo. If we're going to have a go at each other, I suggest we taxi over to my flat, pronto."

"Brilliant," Brad said.

Both men drained their martini glasses, placed them on the bar counter, gathered their jackets, and walked hand-in-hand to the stairs. They descended to the club level, passing through the piano bar as crocked choristers completed a spirited rendition of "The Man That Got Away." "My theme song," Brad quipped as he followed Simon outside to be enveloped into the cold night air.

Their exit allowed another couple in a long queue to enter The Spike. Walking along the sidewalk, past a diverse clique of men, several of whom cast them a prurient gaze, Brad and Simon found a black hackney for hire just as a group of four passengers had stepped out and were paying their driver.

"Bloomsbury, please," Simon said before he and Brad had closed the door and settled into the backseat.

"A theme song of your own, eh?" Simon was recalling Brad's comment of a few moments earlier. "Generally speaking, in American gay culture, does everyone have a theme song?"

Brad laughed. "Only the likes of Carol Burnett or Tracey Ullman. I was being facetious. That was just a song that I like a lot."

Simon nodded in understanding as they rode down Shoreditch High Street, passing the Tube station. He leaned over and tenderly let his lips touch Brad's. "I'd like a theme song," he whispered playfully. " 'My Foolish Heart.' "

"That's mine, too," Brad teased, returning the kiss.

"Can't have *two* theme songs, can we?" Simon whispered as he nibbled Brad's earlobe.

"One for every occasion." Brad turned his face to find Simon's lips again. "*Take me Home* seems appropriate at the moment."

Simon smiled, then called to the driver to take Stepney Green Road. "Number eighty-one, please."

Presently, Brad was being led by Simon up the dimly-lighted stairs of his duplex apartment. When they reached the second floor landing, Simon pushed a switch to illuminate the hallway. He inserted his key into the door lock. "Don't mind the mess," he apologized in advance. "I'm doing research for an exhibition of Greek antiquities." Stepping into the apartment, Simon flipped another light switch. Brad looked around. His first impression was that the apartment was astoundingly small. There wasn't much more than a narrow living room, a kitchenette, bathroom and one bedroom. *But then only Buckingham Palace could compare with where I'm staying*, he reminded himself. *And you're not judging guys on their toys and material possessions anymore.*

"Heya, sexy Yank," Simon said. He faced Brad and began to casually unbutton his guest's shirt. Simon leaned his body into Brad and began hungrily feasting on his mouth and tongue, while sliding his hand down to Brad's crotch and kneading his already fully erect penis. Brad reciprocated, and simultaneously stripped off Simon's shirt. He let his hands wander over his playmate's wide shoulders and smooth strong chest.

"Christ, I've wanted to fuck you ever since Basher's dinner party," Simon panted as he embraced Brad and drew him tightly against his bare skin.

"That saves me having to beg," Brad groaned as he buried his face in Simon's chest and dragged his tongue over the flesh that seemed barely able to contain his muscles. Brad slipped to his knees and placed his hot mouth on the fabric of Simon's slacks, homing in on the precise location where the head of his cock was straining against the right pants leg.

Simon heaved a sigh and in a moment he roughly urged Brad to his feet and shoved him toward the bedroom. "Get your ass in my bed and your legs in the air," he growled and led Brad down a short hallway. En route, they each removed what remained of their respective clothes and then fell onto the bed together. Brad, on his back, welcomed Simon lying on top of him. He whispered in a horse voice, "Hope you've got the condoms and a lot of lube, 'cause I've come all the way from the New World for a long, hard, British fuck."

Simon grinned as he leaned over the side of the bed and felt around the floor. He righted himself, and seductively wiggled a wrapped condom before Brad's face. He simultaneously handed him a bottle of *Intimate Action*. "Roll over on your side," Simon commanded.

"No way. I want to see what I'm getting," Brad said, as he emptied a dollop of lube onto his four fingers and brought his hand around to his asshole, where he massaged his pink puckered orifice. He handed the lube bottle back to Simon who had removed the condom from its wrapping and now dripped the lube into the well of the rubber. Adjusting the condom at the head of his throbbing penis, Simon expertly rolled the latex down his long, thick shaft. "God save the Queen," he said, as he adjusted Brad's legs over his shoulders, wrapped his fingers around his own piece and began to slowly maneuver himself into the warm tight space in Brad's body.

Brad was delirious with satisfaction. As his body easily opened up to receive Simon, Brad rearranged his legs, wrapping them around Simon's waist. He was hypnotized by the sight of the male body that was accosting his own. The pumped shape of Simon's chest, and his ribbed abdominal muscles sent Brad into a state of rapture from which he never wanted to return.

As Simon thrust and retracted his tool to an internal rhythm, Brad became drunk with the ecstasy of being taken by a man who knew how to deliver a mind altering fuck, and there was nowhere else in the universe that he wanted to be. This was what sex with a man was all about, he thought, and he savored every moment of holding back his own aching need to climax. Both men were covered in perspiration and soon, it was impossible for either of them to control their own oncoming orgasms.

"Tell me when you're ready," Simon said as he pushed harder and deeper into Brad.

"I can't hold off much longer," Brad confessed. "If I touch myself I'm gonna lose it all over the place."

"That's what I want," Simon said, contorting his face in agony. "Christ, I can't . . ." He suddenly removed himself from Brad's ass and ripped off his condom.

Brad grabbed his own dick and as if synchronized, he cried out and shot his load at precisely the same moment that Simon whimpered in gear grinding strain, and he, too, came. Brad ran a hand over his stomach and chest, collecting his sperm and Simon's into a warm sticky paste. "God, I love the feel of fresh cum," he said, holding back his desire to suck his fingers.

Simon flopped onto his back beside Brad and continued to sigh and breathe heavily for a minute. "Fuck," he said with a raspy voice. "Fuck," he said again, and reached blindly beside the bed for his jack-off towel, which he picked up and draped over Brad's stomach. He made the sound of a slight chuckle, which Brad interpreted to be Simon's way of expressing his complete satisfaction. "Let me catch a few winks and I'll be ready to go again," he said as he rolled onto his side and spooned with Brad.

For a long moment the drawing room was stone silent. Gusher exhaled heavily, making the room vibrate with tension. He looked over at Basher.

"What's done is done," Basher responded. He noisily propped his booted feet up onto the marble-top coffee table. "Can't say that I personally give a rat's ass. Although I have a hunch ol' Nigel won't feel the same way."

"A promise is a promise," Gusher said.

Brad leaned against the fireplace. "Look," he began, "I didn't come to England to be just a novelty shag for anyone. If I accepted Nigel's offer to come to Northumberland it would mean that as a houseguest I would have to be charming and scintillating. He's the type to come to one conclusion—that I was there because I fancied him. He'd be encouraged by my irresistible charisma, and I'd have to pretend that he was equally tempting. It wouldn't be fair to him. After the week was over and I avoided him afterward, he'd go insane wondering what was wrong."

"What isn't fair is that you've placed us in a very awkward social position." Gusher sighed. "Nigel's rung me up every day asking if I was positive you'd finally accepted his invitation. I've continued to reassure him that you've simply been inordinately busy, but that you were enthusiastic about seeing him. Now, I'll have to make up another lie."

"I never agreed to go in the first place," Brad said. "If Nigel was so damned keen on me, why does he only speak to you?"

"He's shy."

"Bollocks!"

"I'll simply tell him that you've been summoned to Milan. Which is sort of the truth."

"This devil you invited into our home shouldn't have been allowed to date Simon first," Basher said, looking at the now sullen Gusher. "It just reinforced the reality that Nigel's not exactly top of the crop. Unless one is blinded by his personal treasury."

"Which, alas, is his primary attribute," Gusher agreed.

Basher gave Brad a thumbs-up, which Brad assumed was meant to convey that Basher was satisfied that Brad wasn't a gold-digger. "But why are you leaving now? You and Simon appear to be getting on."

Brad wandered over and seated himself in a chintz-covered chair that anchored the two sofas where Gusher and Basher were seated. "He's dumping me. But he doesn't think I realize it," Brad said. "Too bad. He's sexy. Bright. Tells me he's going away on business. An archiving expedition to Greece. He'll be away for three months."

"Good riddance." Gusher harrumphed. "You haven't begun to tap the trove of beaux right here in London. So why should *you* leave the country, too? Haven't we been everything that you expected?"

"Oh, much more," Brad said genuinely. "The fact of the matter is just that none of your friends are exactly Mr. Right For Me. I thought Simon came close. However, I promised myself not to stop searching until I'm absolutely certain."

He stood up again and moved over to a tall, multipaned window that overlooked the back garden. "Chances are that I'll be back, and you can walk me down the aisle with Nigel," Brad said. "Then you can boast to Garreth that you're still ninety-eight percent successful when it comes to making a match."

Gusher smiled. Basher rolled his eyes and stated, "You still owe me for the petrol that I used fetching you from the airport."

Brad smiled. "Take me to Heathrow in the morning, and I'll throw in the cost of a new tattoo."

Chapter Four

W*hoa. Baciami, you fool!*
Brad had thrown himself into a spontaneous sex fantasy as he boarded the Alitalia airbus to Florence and took in the sight of the dark Mediterranean male flight attendant standing sentry at the cabin door. Brad flashed his ticket and an enticing smile. *Mr. Right For Me is in Italy. I can feel it,* he thought as he pictured the flight attendant modeling for the swimsuit edition of *The Mile High Club* monthly newsletter.

Brad entered the aircraft behind two barely in motion relics. By degrees he proceeded down the narrow aisle so he had plenty of time to glance around at other passengers. *La dolce vita, indeed!* he thought as he spied one heart-stopping man after another, all of whom, Brad decided, had been planted by the Italian Ministry of Tourism to sucker up business.

As he looked down the aisle he was pulled up short by what he decided was physical evidence that God was the true devil behind temptation. He spotted another passenger: olive skin, short-cropped black hair, deep dimple in his square chin, a face that was definitely assembled by a focus group for a marketing team promoting indiscriminate sex. Brad sighed. *Never mind the flight attendant.*

Brad prayed his seat assignment was the winning lottery number.

"Yes!" He almost did a bunny hop as he approached and realized that they would be seated side by side.

For a moment Brad held up traffic as he stood beside the man. He couldn't stop himself from staring, imagining what the guy looked like naked. In bed. In a shower. On a beach blanket. He was tall and slender, even sitting down. Tufts of dark underarm hair that had never been defiled by antiperspirants and that would welcome the warm, wet tongue of an admirer. Brad knew this man intimately. He had fantasized about him for years.

"*Scusi,*" he finally spoke tentatively, his Berlitz dissolving into muddle. He gestured that the seat by the window was his.

The man glanced up. Long, silky lashes fluttered like a plume of black ostrich feathers. A warm smile spread across his face. His dark eyes actually sparkled. "*Si! Si!*" he said as he unbuckled his safety belt and stepped into the aisle.

Brad smiled back. "*Grazie,*" he said as he slipped into his assigned space. He stashed his carry-on shoulder bag on the floor under the seat in front.

"*Americano?*" the man said to Brad as he refastened his seat belt.

"Yes. I mean, *si.*" Brad wondered if perhaps he should have said that he was Canadian. He turned to the man and allowed his eyes to continue the grand tour. "*Non parlo molto Italiano.*" Brad forced out the one phrase he had actually learned. "Do you speak English?"

"*Si.* Yes. A little. *Michaino* Paolo."

"Brad."

Paolo extended his hand toward Brad's. "*Piacere.* A pleasure."

The V of Paolo's open collar shirt revealed more strands of dark hair. He had tiny but attractive crows feet next to his eyes.

"My pleasure. *Entirely.*" Brad smiled again.

Their fellow passengers continued to board the plane, sucking the space out of the cabin. They crammed the overhead compartments with everything from duffel bags to skateboards to shopping bags from Harrods. Brad tried to ignore them, pretending to read his *GayPlay* tour book. However, he was on the libidinous equivalent of orange alert, a heightened awareness of every move and glance from Paolo. With an in-flight magazine open on his lap, Paolo, too, seemed to pretend to read.

Eventually, the plane rolled away from the gate. A woman's voice came over the PA speaker system. *"Buona sera."* Although the language was Italian, Brad knew it was the beginning of the safety drill. Another flight attendant took the spotlight and began pantomiming the instructions that her colleague was relating.

Brad feigned attention as the flight attendant went through her routine of pointing to emergency exits, holding up a sample seat belt and demonstrating its use, as if the one person in the universe who did not know how to operate a seat belt might be on this very flight. Other passengers read their newspapers or griped about the flight's delay, but the stewardess paid no attention. She moved on to the oxygen mask portion of her routine, simulating the cup dropping from a compartment above each seat. Brad imagined himself giving his own breath to Paolo should there be a drop in cabin pressure.

Brad wondered how many times the flight attendant had performed this routine during her career, and why she even bothered with the water landing. Rather than think about using seat cushions for flotation, Brad paid attention to the musky scent wafting from Paolo's hot body. Brad began fantasizing about kneeling down in the cramped space on the floor in front of Paolo and pulling down this gorgeous man's pants. Blowing his seat mate, rather than plastic tubes to inflate life vests, seemed a far more enjoyable way to spend the last few moments of life.

Soon the aircraft was in a queue to take off. As the plane began to taxi down the runway, Paolo genuflected and turned to Brad. "Air travel," he said. "It is for birds only. *Si?*"

"You're not a fan of flying?" Brad asked.

"Tom Hanks made me not so easy. *Castaway.*"

Brad wanted to agree with Paolo, if only so that they would appear to have something in common, but the truth was that Brad loved to fly. "Take-off and landing are the best," he teased. "Only the in-between is boring."

The airplane picked up speed. "According to statistics, these are the most dangerous times," Paolo said, white knuckling his armrests. "One is never safe until one is in the airport bar."

Brad laughed. He leaned over and whispered, "I've got good flying karma. Trust me."

"Then I am certain to fly safe." Paolo smiled. "*Grazie.*" But his voice sounded tense as he stared straight ahead.

"Umm. Allow me to take your mind off the flight," Brad suggested. "I've never been to Italy. Maybe you can tell me the best places to visit. What are the sights in Florence that I absolutely must see. I know about the typical tourist stuff. Michelangelo's *David*, the Duomo, all those palaces built by the Medici."

"Your first time?" Paolo seemed to be waiting to feel the plane lift off. "Why so far from home?"

Brad shrugged. "I'm on a mission."

"CIA?" Paolo asked, now with a hint of suspicion.

Brad shook his head. "A search to find my soul mate."

"*Si!*" Paolo said, nodding. "*Amore!*" He laughed, just as the plane left the planet. "The best place in the world to search."

"Italy?" Brad said.

"We Italians are very sexy hot. No?"

Brad took a deep breath. "*Si!* Sophia Loren. Puccini. Joey Tribbiani. Tell me about the best gay bars."

Paolo gave Brad a quizzical look. "Do I appear as though I would know about such things?"

Brad immediately turned red. "It's simply that . . . er . . . you, ah . . . seem to be an intelligent guy . . . a man of the world, who would know a little about everything."

Paolo smiled. He waited a beat. "Good save, Brad. As a matter of fact, I can take you on a personal tour."

Brad broke into a wide smile of relief.

Paolo continued. "First, you have to understand that Italy is a very Catholic country. Religion dominates our life. Although the church is a very sexually charged institution, it is still archaic and intolerant."

"But Italy is supposed to be so romantic," Brad countered. "You've got all those nude statues." He frowned. "Don't tell me that Italians are as rigid about sex as Americans. Am I doomed to remain a virgin during my entire visit?"

Paolo shook his head. "No."

"What about the Vatican?" Brad asked. "Surely, all those priests . . ."

Paolo shook his head again. "I would not recommend you visit the Vatican. Everybody who works there is a bitter . . . how you say . . . 'old queen'? Nothing but defrocked clergy. Unpleasant celibates. It's like they have contempt for tourists. Especially gay tourists. The place is garish and grotesque."

Brad noticed that the Fasten Seatbelt sign was no longer illuminated. He gestured. Paolo looked at the sign, then sagged with relief. "*Grazie.*"

"It's the least I can do for someone who's offered to be my tour guide," Brad said. "Although if the Pope still has the country so repressed, you probably don't even have a gay bar."

"There's a saying." Paolo faced Brad. "Every bar in Italy is gay . . . if you know which corner to look in."

Paolo nudged Brad conspiratorially with his elbow, as a flight attendant pushed her snack cart down the aisle. She handed Brad and Paolo clear plastic cups and single serving bottles of red wine.

"Can you suggest a decent place to meet other guys?" Brad no longer cared if passengers around them could overhear their conversation.

Paolo was thoughtful for a moment as he unscrewed the cap from his bottle. "Florence and Venice. They are not like Paris or London, which are very open to gays. Italy doesn't have a nightclub culture. I don't know so many popular discos. It's very much a café society. You can't even get a coffee to take away. You must sit down and enjoy your beverage at a leisurely pace. The bars, they come and go so quickly. One cannot keep up. Chances are that your guidebook is out of date before it is printed."

Brad was beginning to have doubts about leaving London. "Tell me, Paolo," he said, "how do people meet each other in Italy if gays are so closeted?"

Paolo considered the question. "The way you and I have met. Fate. But I think you mean for sex dates. Yes? I have friends. We will find a place for you to dance and get drunk."

"No," Brad countered. "I can do that in America. I want . . ." he stopped mid-sentence.

Paolo completed Brad's thought. "The perfect *machismo?*"

Brad shrugged, as if apologizing for considering such a ludicrous idea. "It's my natural inclination."

Paolo inhaled deeply. "There are special women . . ." he said, as if trying to select the right English words. "I think you call them . . . and I don't intend disrespect . . . 'fag hags'? Beautiful women of means who love gay men. They are very adept at pairing the boys with the boys. Do you follow me?"

Brad sipped from his cup of red wine. "A matchmaker. One who seats eligible men together at dinner."

"*Si!*" Paolo exclaimed. "Gina, the countess! She will have a dinner for you!"

The flight attendant offered another round of drinks, and both men accepted. Their conversation was so engaging, that the flight time evaporated. Presently, Brad could feel the plane begin to descend. The Fasten Seatbelt sign came on with a chime, and the captain made an announcement that Brad supposed were instructions about approaching the airport and pleading with the passengers to stay seated until the aircraft reached the gate.

"Say something clever to me," Paolo said with anxiety in his voice. "To take my mind away from the landing."

Brad thought for a moment. "Hmmm. Okay. Name an American celebrity you like, and I'll burst your bubble with some unthinkable gossip about them. You'll be too overwhelmed with grief to care about the landing."

"Please don't tell anything naughty about Miss Delta Burke."

"Who?" Brad asked.

"The large lady on that home decorating show."

"I don't watch much HGTV. Try again," Brad said.

Paolo thought for a moment and said, "David Hasselhoff."

"Strike two," Brad said. "He's too nice. No scandal there. Ask me about Faye Dunaway, Kate Beckensale, or Martha Stewart."

At that moment, the plane touched down at Amerigo Vespucci Airport. The impact of tires meeting tarmac gave the aircraft an abrupt wrench, which clearly obliterated any thoughts in Paolo's mind about celebrities as he gripped the armrests of his seat.

At last, the plane slowed to a crawl. "Did you ever doubt my extraordinary powers?" Brad said.

"Certainly." Paolo smiled. "To trust in a stranger is as dangerous as trusting that the pilot did not get his wings with low test scores."

As the aircraft rolled along, Brad reached for his shoulder bag and withdrew a pen with which to fill out his immigration card. As he was writing down the information required by the Italian government, Paolo glanced over at the line on which he had written where he was staying while in Italy. "Not *Abiènte!*"

Brad looked up. "*GayPlay* gave it three penises. They listed it as 'surprising and affordable.' "

"Code for 'You'll shit when you see the size of the roaches and the amount you will forfeit to get *out.*' You cannot stay at that pigsty."

Brad was chagrined. "What should I do?" He sighed. Silently he begged, *Please suggest that I go home with you! I won't be any bother! I'll make you espresso every morning! Please . . .*

Paolo said firmly, "Gina. The countess. She has a very large *appartamento* with many rooms. Perhaps you could stay with she?"

"With her."

"*Si.*"

"I couldn't impose," Brad said. "I don't even know the countess. I hardly know you."

Either Brad's disappointment at being abandoned in a strange country was obvious, or Paolo hadn't had the nerve to propose anything more intimate. He tentatively suggested, "If you like, you could . . . what is the American phrase . . . *camp out?*"

"With you?" Brad said. "Yes. 'Camp out' is a good phrase. And yes, I'd be delighted to accept your offer. You're too kind."

"Alas, I am outside the city," Paolo said. "Still, my house, it is only about three kilometers from Piazzale Michelangelo. The views are quite impressive."

"Sounds divine," Brad said.

"I have plenty of rooms to make you comfortable. And I can guide you around much easier, if we are close."

Guide me! Brad wanted to scream. *I'll be as close to you as the hair on your chest!*

As the airplane finally came to a stop at the gate, Brad was still flying high. He sang to himself: *I've got me a sexy Italian and I haven't even set foot in the country!*

The Fasten Seatbelt sign went off. The two men unbuckled and rose into the crowded aisle. Brad picked up his shoulder bag, reached into one of the zippered pockets and withdrew his passport. "Customs," he said, an apology for the amount of time he'd have to make Paolo wait.

Paolo shook his head. "I will be with my *autista*. You'll see us parked outside."

"Don't keep the meter running," Brad insisted. "I haven't exchanged my sterling for lira yet."

Brad and Paolo began inching their way toward the front of the plane. At the cabin door, Mr. Mediterranean sex magnet was again standing at attention, the best advertisement for flying Alitalia. *"Arrivederci,"* he said over and over, almost wearing out his paper smile. *"Arrivederci. Arrivederci. Prego. Arrivederci."*

But Brad was with Paolo now, and he barely took notice of anyone else. They were carried along the stream of travelers, and were eventually deposited into the delta of the terminal. They waded through throngs of happy people offering hugs and kisses to arriving family and friends. Others in the waiting area craned their necks to peer down the Jetway tunnel, hoping for a glimpse of a lover or spouse coming in from London.

"Buona sera." Paolo's voice in greeting caused Brad to return the focus of his attention to his host. Paolo was shaking the hand of a tall, thick, bald man in a black suit, white shirt, and black tie. *Where's the funeral?* Brad thought. The man flipped open his cell phone and handed the unit to Paolo, who immediately began an animated conversation. The bald man then turned around and faced Brad. "Follow the immigration signs." He pointed, and Brad watched the two men walk away.

Globetrotters five deep surrounded the luggage carousel. Impatiently, Brad watched the chute from which hundreds of pieces of luggage were birthed. One by one, he collected his four pieces of Samsonite, placing them on a trolley, and proceeded to customs.

The queue to have his passport stamped was long. But because Brad was still reeling from hitting it off so well with Paolo—and being invited to stay with him for at least one night—he was unconcerned about the line. He was occupied with thoughts of being naked with Paolo.

Immigration turned out to be a breeze, and soon Brad was pushing his suitcase trolley through the building to the passenger loading and unloading area outside the terminal. Idle taxicabs stood waiting for patrons. Brad covered his mouth and nose as buses cruised by, hacking out toxic clouds. Car horns startled pedestrians trying to cross from the terminal building to the parking structure.

Brad shaded his eyes with his right hand and looked around for Paolo. He stood beside his trolley, peering to the left and then to the right. Then a familiar-looking man approached. Brad recognized him as the man who had whisked Paolo away at the airline gate. The man was emerging from a black stretch limousine. When he was within a few feet of Brad, the man nodded his head and said *"Buona sera, signore. Allow me."* He took hold of Brad's trolley.

Brad surrendered his luggage. *"Scusi?* Where's Paolo?"

"The car, *signore,"* the man said, pushing the trolley to the limo. *"Per favore,"* he said.

The man opened a rear passenger door. Brad peeked into the back of the car, and he was immediately relieved seeing that Paolo was there. *"Ciao!"* Brad called. Paolo, however, was speaking on the telephone, and he merely acknowledged Brad with a wave of his hand. *Christ, he's sexy* and *rich!* Brad thought, admiring the plush interior of his car. He climbed in.

Brad heard the trunk being closed. Then the driver opened the front door and slipped into his seat. He pulled his door shut, adjusted the rearview mirror, lowered the classical music that was issuing through the limo's speakers, signaled a left-hand turn, and pulled away from the curb.

"Cretino! Stronzo!" Paolo exploded to whomever was on the other end of his cellular transmission. He ended the conversation with a flip of the phone cover. He snapped to no one, "They don't fuck with me!"

Then, after cooling his temper, he smiled at Brad and offered a litany of "*Scusare.*"

Brad held up his hands to protest the apology. "You've got work," he said. "And it looks like you're damn good at your job," he added, indicating the automobile. "I was so busy talking about myself on the plane that I never bothered to ask about your occupation."

"Family business," Paolo said vaguely. "Nothing as interesting as you who writes for American movies."

"Just television," Brad said modestly. "Unless you know someone with lots of money who wants to back a great film project based on my screenplay."

"And you really don't know Miss Delta Burke?" Paolo was disappointed. "Never to mind. I capture her on many videos which I will play for you."

Television wasn't the sort of play that Brad had in mind, but he wanted to be gracious. He smiled and nodded his head as if in happy anticipation.

Paolo's telephone rang out again. "*Scusi,*" he said politely, smiling at Brad. Paolo flipped open the cover of his cell. "*Ciao,*" he announced in an irritated salutation, then began speaking rapidly in Italian. Brad could tell by the tone of Paolo's voice and the sharp gestures he made with his free hand that the call was more unpleasant business.

The obstreperous conversation went on for a few minutes before Paolo made an irate noise that seemed to rise up from his diaphragm. He pushed the cell phone disconnect button and threw it the long distance into the front seat of the car where it hit the windshield and ricocheted to the driver.

Seething for a moment, Paolo then composed himself. He registered the look of confusion and consternation on Brad's face. "*Scusare!* I am so sorry!" he lamented. "Business. You understand." He rolled his eyes. "Too many people to please at once. The pressure is great. Soon I shall have only myself to please." He lowered his voice so that the driver could not hear. "And you, of course. I will be happy once I am with you only."

Paolo's lascivious grin gave Brad an ache from his teeth to his groin.

Brad had begun to wonder if it had been a wise idea accepting a ride and lodgings from a mercurial man whose lack of anger management went from zero to sixty faster than a Fiat.

Paolo continued to apologize as the car drove down the highway and eventually began ascending into the hills above the city. The streets were almost too narrow for the limo, but the driver adeptly maneuvered through the serpentine turns. Soon, they stopped in front of a large, ancient villa with two tall massive wooden doors, each bearing bronze lion's head doorknockers on the center panels.

"*La Casa di Lanzi,*" Paolo announced proudly. He opened his door and stepped out. Brad followed.

The atmosphere was serene and bucolic. Brad could hear birds in the trees and the faint sound of trickling water coming from somewhere beyond the old doors. Paolo said something to the driver, who had already begun removing luggage from the trunk of the car, and placing the bags outside the front step. Paolo inserted a key into the right-side door of the façade and pushed on the door. "Please, watch the step," Paolo advised, indicating a granite lip that separated the house from the street. Brad looked down, then looked up to peer into the light-drenched quadrant.

Worn and uneven flats of stone with grass growing up between each of them made up the floor of a spacious courtyard open to the sky. Brad observed that the source of the sound of babbling water was a moss-covered fountain in a corner of the enclosure. Beyond, under a columned, covered piazza, was the entrance to the main house. "I've been away for two weeks," Paolo said as he unlocked another set of double doors leading to the house, "but it feels like two years. I miss my villa when I am away."

"If I lived in a place like this, I'd never leave," Brad agreed.

"We are here at last!" Paolo moved to unlatch the French doors. Blossom-scented air wafted in and circulated through the room.

Brad was mesmerized at the opulence of the house's interior. The floor was black and white marble set in a classic diamond motif. Frayed and faded tapestries adorned the walls. A white limestone fireplace dominated the great room. Overhead, a fresco of a pergola decorated the vaulted ceiling.

"Of course, some wine!" Paolo said as he removed his sport coat, tossed it on one of the large sofas, and disappeared down a hallway.

Brad wandered to the floor-to-ceiling French doors and stepped out onto a balcony. He leaned over an iron railing and was taken aback by the picture-postcard view. He was astonished that he could see the Duomo not far in the distance. Directly below the house was an exquisite garden.

"From my family's cellar," Paolo boasted as he reentered the room and joined Brad outside. Paolo handed his guest a glass of Casa Balocca Cabernet.

Brad raised his glass in a toast. They clinked their crystal and Brad nearly swallowed his wine in one parched pull.

Paolo then instructed Brad to close his eyes. The Italian removed the wineglass from Brad's hand and set it down. Paolo then took Brad by the hand and escorted him back to into the villa. "Parts of this house date to the Middle Ages," he said along the way. They stopped, and Paolo placed Brad's hand on a cold, hard surface. "Not to look," he instructed. "You must guess what this is."

Brad reached out with both hands. He felt a deep cleft in the center of two convex curves. The planes of each had an outgrowth. As he explored the object, he could feel himself getting an erection, growing harder. His hands continued to travel, to *absorb* the object. He was aroused just being alone with Paolo, but the form he was exploring made him as hard as the surface that his hands were stroking.

"Open," Paolo demanded.

Brad lifted his eyelids. He gasped in pleasant surprise. He took a step back to take in the full beauty. A male nude sculpture in marble.

"You're in *Firenze*," Paolo said, delighted by Brad's response. "Art is everywhere. My family and I, we collect what we can. Often as trade for services rendered." For a moment, the two men stared at each other. "*You* are art," Paolo said, and he took Brad in his arms.

Brad returned the advance and the two men melded into a deep harsh kiss. As their passion became more fervid, each played at overpowering the other. Finally, Paolo anxiously and expertly guided Brad toward a staircase. At the first step, Paolo removed his shirt. Then he raced to the second floor landing. Brad followed in delirious pursuit, unbuttoning his own shirt along the way.

He chased Paolo down a long, art-filled corridor and into a vast room with an enormous canopy bed. By the time Brad caught up with Paolo, the host had shed his clothes and was waiting on the mattress, lying on his stomach grinding himself into the sheets. Brad quickly undressed, and he mounted Paolo's bare body.

Splayed over Paolo's back, Brad licked his neck and kissed his shoulder blades. As his hands massaged the wide plane of skin, he dragged his tongue down Paolo's spine until he found the two plump orbs of his ass cheeks. There, at what was to Brad the most intriguing and fascinating part of a man's body, he began to playfully gnaw at the smooth muscled flesh. As Paolo moaned with satisfaction, Brad continued leaving teeth marks and expanded his exploration to include fingering the deep crack of his lover's ass. A greater cry of satisfaction issued from Paolo, which implied that Paolo was desperate to be fucked.

Shit, Brad thought. *I want this Italian inside of me!* He continued teasing Paolo's ass for a few more minutes and decided he was so horny, it didn't matter if he had to take the dominant role. He forced Paolo to roll over, and for the first time he saw the enormous cock on his host. Brad swallowed hard and automatically leaned his face down to make contact with the exquisite equipment. He flicked his tongue up and down the shaft and then began to make circles over the head. He opened his mouth, but it was no use trying to take more than a couple of inches. Brad quickly realized he could never comfortably take Paolo into his own body—front door or rear. It would be best if he took the initiative and donned a condom. He would give Paolo the fuck that he really wanted for himself.

Working together telepathically, Paolo sat up and swung his legs over the side of the bed. He stood up and quickly padded to a chest of drawers from which he produced a condom and a travel size bottle of lube. He returned to the side of the bed and removed the rubber from its packaging.

Brad ached as Paolo gently pushed him to lie back and then did the work of preparing Brad's cock to wear the condom.

Now, rejoining Brad on the bed, Paolo spoke something in Italian but his body language was easily translated. He wanted Brad inside of him.

Gazing at Paolo, who was already stroking his rock hard member and begging, "Fuck me, Americano," Brad nodded his head and positioned himself to let Paolo guide his shaft to his hole. In a moment, they were connected. Brad was surprised at how much gratification he felt with his cock in the vise of Paolo's tight sphincters. "Christ," he moaned as he methodically pushed and pulled himself along the walls of Paolo's canal. With each piston-like action, Brad could feel himself coming closer to climax.

However, the exhilarating sensation was too great to let go too soon, and he tried to take his mind out of the act by thinking of less enjoyable experiences. With Paolo stroking his massive phython and crying out in staccato whimpers, it was impossible for Brad not to be in the moment overwhelmed with all the audible and physical aspects of great sex. Soon, Paolo was holding his cock in one hand and forcing his middle finger up Brad's ass with the other as they worked in unison to achieve a mutual and simultaneous orgasm.

Then Paolo cried out in English, "Fuck!" as he lost control of his authority over his own climax, and pumped out an ample load of semen commensurate with the size of his penis. The thick fluid first exploded out from the center of his dick and hurled onto his face. Then came a second round which spit onto his chest.

Brad was mesmerized by what he had caused to spew from Paolo's body and in the following seconds he too was in a losing battle against a powerful climax. He pulled out of Paolo's body, peeled off the condom and in the instant that followed, he ejected his own opaque cream, which mixed with Paolo's.

When sleep finally came to them it was overpowering and deep. Brad cradled Paolo in his arms, and they did not stir until shortly after the sun had come up. And then, despite Brad's discovering a life-size crucifix bolted to the wall above the bed, which he did not remember seeing the night before, they began to maul each other all over again.

Chapter Five

Aghast at his reflection in the bathroom mirror, Brad shaved, show-ered, towel-dried and finger-combed his hair. He completed his morning grooming and, reexamining himself, was satisfied that Paolo would approve.

Dressed only in jeans, he walked barefoot down the long hallway to the wide staircase. The scent of coffee saturated the air. Stepping through the French doors that opened onto the tiled veranda, Brad found Paolo clad in tight blue briefs, reclining on a chaise longue. He was speaking with fury and exasperation into his cell phone. Paolo was so engaged in his call that he paid no attention as Brad came into view.

Good morning, to you, too, Brad said to himself, miffed that he wasn't being welcomed with roses. "Guess I know what his priorities are," Brad muttered to himself. "Better start thinking about a hotel."

Picking up a coffee mug from a serving cart on which was laid a con-tinental breakfast for two, Brad poured from a silver carafe. He wan-dered over to the railing of the patio and looked out over the red tile rooftops of the city. It was a perfect late spring day. No clouds intruded on the blue sky. In the distance below was the view of a city so ancient and steeped in history. Brad felt insignificant, and yet at the same time a part of the legacy of the eternal flow of life through Florence. He couldn't help contrasting this panorama with that from the hills above

Sunset Boulevard in Los Angeles. The comparison was futile. Florence was real and permanent. Hollywood was superficial and transient.

Brad's reveries ended when Paolo shouted something into his telephone and abruptly hung up. He huffed angrily. "I'll kill him," he declared in English.

Finally looking up, Paolo noticed Brad—shirtless, holding a coffee mug, leaning against the railing and with all of Florence as a backdrop. Paolo smiled. *"Buon giorno,"* he breathed. "Did I wake you up with my call?"

"I couldn't stay in bed without you." Brad smiled, walking to where Paolo was reclining. He leaned down and placed his swollen lips onto Paolo's. Their tongues began an immediate dance and Brad decided that perhaps his time with Paolo was not quite over. He placed his coffee mug on the patio table beside the chaise and cupped Paolo's head in his hands. Tasting each other's cappuccino, they stayed as one for a long while.

Finally they came up for air. *"Oh, Dio."* Paolo sighed heavily. *"Era incredible."*

"Does that translate to 'Let's go back to bed?' " Brad begged.

Palo smiled. Then: "My driver is coming," Paolo said with disappointment.

"Not into our bed he's not!" Brad feigned indignation.

"Work. A job that I did not expect. I apologize."

Brad nodded his head in mock understanding. He picked up his coffee mug and took another sip. "Sounds as though you were ready to strangle someone," he said, indicating the telephone.

"Perhaps that is an American expression. But you are not so far off," Paolo said.

"Your day isn't starting out so well, is it?" Brad said. "I once had a boss who made me nuts like that. We have a name for such types in Hollywood. 'A scary Shari.' "

Paolo stood up and sighed. "I don't know the time that I will return. Please go about and see *Fierenzie*. We will have dinner together. *Si?*"

"It's a date," Brad said.

*   *   *

Before Paolo departed, he gave Brad a key and wrote the address and telephone number on a slip of paper. "If you become lost, do not ask *poliziotto* the way back. Call me instead." He handed Brad a cell phone. Paolo smiled, then gave Brad a long, passionate, wet kiss.

Brad watched as Paolo stepped into the limo. Now, alone in the villa, Brad turned and walked through the house to retrieve his copy of *GayPlay*. He began planning for the day ahead. To the tune of "My Favorite Things," he started to sing, "Churches and statues and statues and paintings. Fountains and . . . fountains and sexy men mating." He couldn't rhyme fountains or Renaissance architecture, Palazzo Vecchio, Piazza della Signoria, or Piazza Michelangelo, so the song dissipated.

Back in the bathroom, Brad pulled a white T-shirt over his body, slipped into his walking boots, and grabbed his backpack. "Time for an adventure!" he declared as he closed the main doors of the villa and passed through the courtyard. He opened the front entryway door, stepped outside and inhaled the warm, late morning air. He locked the door and headed down the dusty road.

The hike into town was farther and took longer than Brad anticipated. In the meantime, he enjoyed the sights along the way. The morning had become a warm early afternoon. Finally arriving at the Palazzo Vecchio, Brad was hot and hungry.

He wandered into the first trattoria he could find and seated himself at an unoccupied patio table. Apparently, it was presumed that Brad would order wine, so, without his asking, a waiter placed a pitcher of table wine before him with a single glass. Not able to translate the menu, Brad simply pointed to an item on the list.

Soon after he uttered, *"Grazie,"* to the waiter, a voice from behind him asked, "American?"

Brad turned around to meet the eyes and friendly smile of a man whom he couldn't help but presume was another gay tourist. The torso wrapped in the man's tank top was impressive. Brad guessed the guy was a well-maintained fifty-five, although, as he often verbalized, it was hard to tell these days. A band of barbed wire tattooed the circumference of his left biceps. A gold chain choker was a complement to a diamond stud in his left earlobe.

"L.A.," Brad responded with a smile. "And you?"

"Albuquerque. But I'm in your neck of the woods for the White Ball each year. I'm Mike."

Reaching out to shake Mike's extended hand, Brad identified himself. They made superficial small talk. "Having fun so far? Where are you staying? Are you traveling alone? Where the hell is a decent gay club in this ancient city?"

"Let's share a table," Mike suggested. He signaled for the waiter, to whom he spoke perfect Italian.

Soon, Brad and Mike were seated opposite each other, drinking wine, eating pasta, exchanging personal information about their current travel experiences.

A Latin teacher, Mike was in Florence "because the third time's a charm," he said. He winked at Brad, not making any attempt to hide his lust.

Was I this obvious to Paolo on the plane? Brad asked himself, knowing the answer and realizing that one can pretty much get what they want in life if they're willing to take a risk. *It worked with Paolo,* Brad thought. *If Mike wants me, it will work for him, too.*

"My last two lovers were French and Turkish, respectively," Mike said, explaining why he was in Italy. "This time I'm ordering lasagna, so to speak. What about you?"

Brad waved away the questions as if the answer would produce laughter. "I've got a Jack Haley thing going on."

Mike looked a question.

"Tin Man?" said Brad.

Mike made the connection, then chuckled. "You've got a brain, that's obvious. And you've got enough courage to come to Europe alone. Must be that you're searching for a heart?"

Brad smiled.

Mike nodded in understanding. "Husband hunting is my favorite pastime—even when I have one," he said. "Italy's romantic, all right, but I'm discovering that you won't find much in the way of gay nightlife in this country. Although Florence skews a little younger, mostly because of the university, which is why I'm here. But if it's hot action you're looking for, head up to Milan. Those dress designers are

so desperate for a prick. And I'm not referring to their sewing needles."
Mike chuckled. "Of course, there are the Florence Baths. I've checked
out a few bars, too. Be warned—they charge a so-called 'membership
fee' just to get in. And they really screw you when it comes to the price
of a drink. There's only one disco in town that I know of. They show
American porn, so you've probably already seen whatever they've got
on their screens."

"What about the infamous dark rooms I've heard about?" Brad asked.

"Boring!" Mike cried. "A lot of guys you can't even see. Imagine a
room with no lights for gay men? Makes no sense. Must be a
Catholic thing." Mike shrugged. "If they can't see what they'd sin
for, then they don't have to confess to Father Santorum. When it
comes to gay sex, men are as scared and rigid here as John Ashcroft
back home."

Brad decided to keep his own success with an Italian man private.
"From my experience," Mike continued, "guys don't even talk to each
other in the bars here. And nothing goes on in those dark rooms that
you couldn't do on a subway. It's all so . . . chaste. If you do go, I would
suggest that you bring a flashlight." He chuckled again as the bill arrived for their meal. "On me," Mike insisted as he reviewed the check.
He then took out his wallet and handed his American Express card to
the waiter.

As they waited for the return of the card and receipt, Brad was
thinking that he considered Mike a stud and that he could be a very
hot lay. Although Brad also thought that he should have been sated
from a night of mind-numbing sex and multiple orgasms with Paolo,
he was actually hornier than he could ever remember being. *Sex is like
a narcotic*, he recalled Garreth saying more than once. *The more you
get, the more you need.* Brad had always been skeptical of Garreth's pro-
nouncement—until Europe.

Mike wrote in a tip amount, and while signing his name asked,
"What's on your agenda?" He looked up at Brad with eyes that pro-
jected his next question. "Feel like hanging out at my place for a couple of hours?"

Brad nodded. "Why not."

"*Sei tanto sexy*," Mike said as they left the restaurant together.

*   *   *

It was nearly two o'clock as Brad followed Mike to the Hotel Palace
Ponti. There they climbed the stairs to the third floor. Mike unlocked
the door to his room and whispered, "*Benvenuto.*"

He motioned for Brad to enter. It was a sparsely furnished room.
The bare floor was made of old, wide, wooden planks. The room's sole
window was shuttered. A three-drawer bureau stood against a wall,
below a mirror. The bed occupied most of the space.

Mike closed and locked the door. For a moment the two men faced
each other. They were ravenous, but it took Mike pulling his tank over
his head for Brad to know when to react. "You've wanted to see this, I
could tell," Mike said.

Narcissism was usually a turn-off for Brad, but he caught his breath
as he gazed at Mike's gym-pumped, chiseled chest and cut abs that
were lightly covered with filaments of fine silver hair. He reached out,
and unlike the day before when he'd had to close his eyes as he
touched the inanimate marble nude in Paolo's drawing room, he stared
at the living, breathing facsimile of a gladiator. Brad reached out and
touched Mike's flesh, which was stretched over rounded shoulders and
a chest of muscles. *God, please let me look as good when I'm his age,*
Brad thought. He asked himself why, in the past, he hadn't given older
guys a chance.

"*Baciami,*" Mike said.

He drew Brad into his arms, leaning in for a kiss. Brad was panting
with lust. He bruised his lips against Mike's, opening his mouth to rec-
iprocate tongues. Guttural moans issued from Brad's gut as Mike
guided him backward toward the bed. When Brad's legs hit the edge
of the mattress, he tumbled.

Mike was a hunter, standing over his game. He unbuttoned Brad's
501s, then lifted his legs and, one at a time, slipped off his walking
boots. Then, he grabbed Brad's jeans by their cuffs and with the swift
pull of a magician who yanks off a tablecloth without disturbing a
place setting, tugged at his pants. Brad wasn't wearing underwear and
his erect penis glistened at the head. He felt like a fly to Mike's spider.

Mike shed the rest of his own clothes, and joined Brad on the bed.

"Whoa, buddy, slow down. I'm not going anywhere," Brad said as
Mike began aggressively dominating their lovemaking.

For the next hour they devoured each other. Brad and Mike explored every inch, mound, cavity, and surface of the other.

Mike concluded their foreplay by reaching into his nightstand and withdrawing a wrapped condom and a plastic bottle of lube. He went through the process of preparation before hoisting Brad's legs and resting them on his shoulders. "You want it?" Mike teased.

"God, yes," Brad begged.

With that, Mike eased himself into his writhing playmate. For the next twenty minutes, with the room suffocatingly sultry, and their bodies perspiring, both men indulged their fantasies. For one moment, Brad pretended that he was a victim of a serial rapist. Then he was an Italian woman, unable to resist the sensation of her husband's cock despite the fear of producing more children.

Brad was at the point where it was impossible to hold back his orgasm. Mike, realizing this, withdrew his weapon from Brad's tight hole. He slipped off his condom and the two began greedily stroking themselves. They ejaculated simultaneously, creating a meringue on Brad's chest and stomach.

Exhausted, Mike dropped onto Brad's sticky body. The two lay together, their heartbeats racing, their breathing as rapid as a jogger. Almost immediately Brad began thinking about after sex etiquette: *Wait until his breathing gets back to normal. Then you can get up and leave.*

Throughout their lovemaking, up to the moment of climax, Brad thought he'd never be able to disengage himself from Mike's body. Now, wrung out from the marathon, he looked forward to seeing Paolo again. Although Mike was one of the sexiest men by whom he'd ever been fucked, the chemistry stopped at the moment of ejaculation.

From the angle of the sun filtering into the room through the slats in the window shutters, Brad guessed that it was late afternoon. Although Paolo that morning had said that he'd be late, Brad felt a responsibility. Also a strong desire to return to the villa.

Brad rose from the bed. He toweled off in the bathroom, reclaimed his clothes and dressed. Mike continued to lie in bed on his back, his now flaccid penis resting against his thigh and still leaking semen. Brad leaned down to Mike and exchanged a deep but obligatory kiss. Their lust had been sated. Unless either of them wrote of this encounter on a postcard or in their journals, the afternoon would soon be lost to other encounters of similar brief intimacy.

Walking back through the Piazza Michelangelo, heading toward the hill and Paolo's villa, Brad's thoughts turned to the same old subject: *Finding a man with whom I'm as comfortable in bed and out of bed. It can't be impossible.* He considered several gay and lesbian couples whom he knew who, after twenty years together still seemed a perfect match. Although he presumed that even those pairings couldn't be hassle-free twenty-four hours a day, they seemed to be more than just content with each other. They were more like two halves of a whole. Which was what Brad was determined to find for himself.

It was six o'clock when Brad got back to *La Casa di Lanzi.* Anxious to shower and eliminate the scent of sex from his body, he opened the door to the courtyard. He was immediately taken aback when he heard Paolo shouting from within the house. He wanted to furtively steal his way to the second floor bathroom, but to reach the staircase he had to pass through the great room, where Paolo was having his rant.

Suddenly uneasy about encountering his host, Brad didn't enjoy the feelings that were surfacing. Not only was he concerned about the compromising position in which he had placed himself as a result of having sex with another partner, but the Dr. Jekyll and Mr. Hyde na-ture of Paolo was also a dilemma. For a man so passionate and tender when engaged in sex, Paolo's angry volatility was scary.

The storm in Paolo's voice seemed ominous. Brad decided to move with purpose toward the stairs, to simply toss an acknowledging wave to Paolo, should he divide his focus with the telephone conversation.

But just as Brad reached the stairs, Paolo flipped his cell phone shut and cursed loudly. As he looked up and saw Brad, his demeanor changed. He smiled warmly. "I handled my business meetings quickly so I could come back to be with you," he purred.

Regarding the somewhat disheveled Brad with suspicion, Paolo lifted Brad's T-shirt over his head. Paolo looked puzzled. "You're so sweaty and sticky." He ran his hands over Brad's perspiration soaked chest and stomach. Then Paolo bussed his lips against Brad's. "I've been so horny for you all day," he groaned.

Moving his lips from Brad's face to the hollow of his neck and to his chest, Paolo's tongue lingered on the buttons of Brad's nipples. He raised Brad's left arm and pushed his face into the moist, pungent pit. He groaned as he inhaled, lapping at Brad's underarm hairs as if he were a baboon grooming his mate.

Brad soon was only marginally concerned that Paolo was dragging his tongue over areas of his body that had so recently been coated with a confluence of his own semen and Mike's. "Your scent drives me *pazzo*," Paolo said, removing his silk shirt and carefully placing it over the back of a chair. "Crazy," he translated. By now he was unbuttoning Brad's 501s and reaching into the pants for the steaming piece of meat. Withdrawing the prize, weighing it in the palm of his hand, Paolo stared at the blue-veined member for a moment before kneeling down.

"*Ancora?*" he said, guiding the piece into his mouth. He closed his mouth over the length of the shaft and made sounds of satisfaction as he gorged himself.

Just as Brad was about to ease himself out of Paolo's mouth for fear that he would climax too soon, the damn cell phone began to ring from the breast pocket of Paolo's white suit coat in the great room. For a moment, Paolo seemed to try to ignore the incessant melody from *Carmen*. But Brad could tell from the way that Paolo had changed his mauling that he was dividing his attention between his hunger for sex and his need to determine who was calling. Letting Brad's cock slip from his hungry mouth, Paolo stood up. He yelled out "Fuck!" as he stormed into the great room to retrieve the phone.

This time, however, there was no rage in Paolo's voice as he spoke on the phone. He was surprisingly reverential to the caller. "*Si, Papa,*" he said several times. "*Si.*" The conversation was brief, then Paolo returned with his jacket. He retrieved his shirt and slipped his arms into the sleeves, as Brad stood with his legs wide apart, his pants pulled down to his knees. Paolo buttoned his shirt and tucked the tails into his pants, explaining to Brad that urgent family business would prevent them from being together for the rest of the evening, and possibly into the early morning.

Brad pulled up his pants and buttoned the top button. "Please be naked in the bed when I come home," Paolo asked, genuinely disappointed that their lovemaking had ended so abruptly.

Brad smiled, likewise showing disappointment. "But what kind of business is so important it can't wait until the office reopens in the morning?"

"Family business. You know how it is." Paolo did not explain further.

Although baffled, Brad nodded in polite understanding. He'd heard that Italians had the best work schedules of anyone else on the planet. Forty days of paid vacation per year and a couple of hours off for lunch each day, which enabled them to go home for a nooner or visit their devoted mothers. But Brad didn't comprehend the need for Paolo to rush out for a job in the early evening.

"In the meantime," Paolo offered, "I will send dinner home to you."

"Come back as quickly as you can," Brad said.

"*Si*," Paolo said. He finished dressing, then leaned in for a kiss. "*Buona notte.*"

Brad parroted the farewell, and Paolo left the house.

Except for the ticking sound of an ancient grandfather clock somewhere in a distant room, the villa was quiet. Unlike Los Angeles, the city's noises did not filter up into the hills. Brad was still hard from kissing Paolo and wanted to jack off to relieve the pressure. He decided to do so holding a glass of wine in the other hand and his tongue on the balls of the marble nude. He would then take a shower and slip into bed to sleep until Paolo returned.

"*Signore Brad!*" A distant sound penetrated the dark room. "*Signore Brad!*"

The voice slowly wrested Brad into consciousness. "*Signore!*" He heard the insistent call issuing through the open bedroom window. Brad lay on his back, alone in the bed, staring into the blackness of the night. "*Signore Brad!*"

Brad finally got out of bed and went to the window. He looked down and saw a dark form standing in the garden below. Brad pushed the French windows open. "*Si?*" he asked.

"*Signore!* I have important news from Paolo. Please let me in." The man spoke English but with a very thick Italian accent.

Brad was in a quandary. He knew that he shouldn't let a stranger into the house. Yet, the man claimed to have news from Paolo. "Just a minute," Brad called down.

He turned on a light and found his jeans. He quickly dressed and hurried down the stairs. By this time, the man was knocking on the front door, obviously able to let himself into the courtyard. Perhaps he even had a key to the house Brad thought. "Who is it?" Brad asked from behind the door.

"Filippo. Paolo's driver. We met when I picked you and Paolo up at the airport. Let me in."

Brad had never got the name of the driver, but he decided to take a risk. As Filippo entered the house, Brad relaxed a bit when he recognized that, indeed, it was Paolo's driver. Brad looked at his wristwatch. "It's one o'clock in the morning," he said. "Where's Paolo?"

"He has instructed me to take you back to the airport," Filippo said.

"This is a fine way to get dumped," Brad said testily.

"Paolo's been arrested," Filippo explained.

Brad was incredulous. "What?"

"The details are not important," Filippo said.

"The hell they aren't!" Brad shouted. "Is he all right? What can I do to help?"

"His family will have everything taken care of," Filippo said. "But his father and brothers will surely come here first, in anticipation of the *polizia*. If they find a man in his bed they will not be hospitable."

"He's not out to his family?" Brad asked.

Filippo scoffed. "Some things must remain private. *Si?* I am only to protect Paolo. So get your Americano ass in gear and pack up." He shoved Brad back toward the stairs, then escorted him up to the bedroom. "*Fretarre!* Hurry!" Filippo insisted. "I don't want to get Paolo, or myself, in trouble with the family. *Fretarre!*"

Brad found his T-shirt and slipped it over his head. He then donned a pair of athletic socks and shoved his feet into his Nikes. In the meantime, Filippo had opened a bureau drawer and Brad's suitcases. He tossed underwear and jeans and shirts into the bags. Working together, they were ready in less than five minutes.

"The car," Filippo commanded as Brad hustled himself outside. Filippo popped the trunk of the limo for the luggage and Brad got into the backseat of the car. Soon, they were driving down the hill into Florence.

At last Brad leaned forward in his seat and asked, "Why is Paolo in jail?"

"A misunderstanding," Filippo said. "That is all you need to know. His business meeting did not go well."

Brad had been curious about Paolo's business from day one, and he asked the driver of what the family business consisted. "Why is it all so hush-hush?" he added.

Filippo was silent. Brad pressed for details, but Filippo was deaf to the questions.

Then Brad had a revelation. He sat back in his seat and fastened his seat belt. *Is it possible?* he asked himself. He added up the facts, as he knew them: Paolo appeared to be quite rich. He was young, but he lived in an expensive villa. And he had a dubious job, one that apparently was dangerous enough to get him arrested. *Family?* Brad thought. A shudder ran through his body.

At that moment, he said to Filippo, "Alitalia *per favore.*"

Not another word was exchanged until the limo pulled to the curb outside the terminal. Filippo got out and retrieved Brad's luggage from the trunk.

"Paolo said to say, '*Non ti dimenticher mai,*' " Filippo said. "He will never forget you."

Brad smiled. "Nor I, him. Say good-bye for me."

The driver hurried back into the car. Brad called: "Tell him thanks for the adventure." Then in a low, desolate whisper he said to himself, "I really liked Paolo."

It was the middle of the night, and here Brad was, standing alone, enveloped in the harsh fluorescent lighting of the airport signs. He hadn't a clue where to go or what to do. *Should I just go back to London?* he asked himself. *Should I give up my mating quest entirely and go home to the States?* Brad was lost in thought and wondering how he always seemed to end up with guys with whom he was sexually compatible—if only for a toss or two—but never for the long haul. Or, in the case of Paolo, how could he select a closeted Mafia prince who would never be able to commit to a relationship?

Because they're all so cute! Brad answered his own stupid question.

"Jesus Christ," he said aloud. "I thought that American men were the world's biggest shits. It's universal!"

Brad spied a raft of luggage trolleys, and he stepped over to retrieve one. He piled his bags onto the cart and pushed it up to the automatic sliding doors. He entered the terminal without a clue as to what his plan of action was going to be, Brad wheeled his possessions to a bank of arrival-departure monitors. Looking for the next flight to anywhere, he went down the list of cities.

MILAN
FRANKFURT
ATHENS
NEW YORK
SEVILLE

Suddenly, Brad could hear a song in his head. *"Well, I never been to Spain, but I kinda like the music. Say the ladies are insane there, and they sure know how to use it."* Three Dog Night. It was a mystery from where or why the tune or lyrics were suddenly blaring in his head. However, he made an impulsive decision. "Well, I've never been to Spain . . ."

Brad looked at the empty ticket counters, then at his wristwatch. It was three-thirty in the morning. He would probably have to wait at least another hour before the Alitalia employees came on duty. He pushed his trolley toward an illuminated sign in the distance. Starbucks.

Chapter Six

Reminding himself that flirting at thirty-five thousand feet could result in midair collisions of the heart, Brad avoided eye contact with other male passengers en route to Spain. Any turbulence this time, he decided, would *not* be a result of in-flight seduction and his overactive libido. He intentionally focused his attention on *GayPlay* and what the guide had to say about *España*, its history, customs, and tourist attractions.

When the plane set down at Seville International Airport, Brad collected his carry-on shoulder bag from its place under the seat in front of him. He stepped into the aisle. The queue seemed interminable. He patiently stood among the collective body of fellow travelers, waiting to begin the procession aft.

"What a tangled web we weave, eh?"

Brad was only vaguely aware of the voice speaking in English several bodies behind him.

"Where's that king of England you married?" It was an American dialect. The tone had become bolder. "You boys honeymooning in Spain?"

Brad tried to rubberneck for a surreptitious glimpse at the man with the familiar, annoying articulation. He pretended to look at nothing in particular—the open overhead compartments, plastic cups and napkins on the floor, a Rolex watch on the wrist of a man beside him. Then his eyes settled on the unexpected.

"Gill?" Brad said. His mouth dropped open.

"If it isn't my favorite hack writer," Gill Truitt said, looking Brad up and down. "I picked you out when you came aboard."

"You're in Spain?"

"Hell if I know. I've been to so damn many cities during the past two weeks . . . The new show, you know."

Nudged by the couple sandwiched between them, Brad moved forward. "New show?" he called back. "Didn't know. I haven't read the trades since I left Hollywood."

"A network deal," Gill boasted. "They're so pumped about the program that they want an international version. And of course they want it *yesterday*." The forced calm sound of his voice belied his almost uncontainable excitement. "Hell, it hasn't even aired in the States, and now I have to be over here working among all these foreigners."

Brad refused to give Gill the satisfaction of a congratulatory response. Reaching the front of the plane, Brad smiled at the flight attendant who stood by the door. "*Gracias*," Brad said and stepped onto the Jetway.

As Brad continued up the incline of the carpeted ramp toward the terminal, Gill was still talking nonstop in a voice intentionally loud enough for everyone around him to hear. "Awesome concept . . . my new show. Made a killer deal, too. I personally own a good chunk of the rights," he announced.

"How lovely," Brad said mildly, glancing at his wristwatch, trying to appear distracted.

"*Enough is Enough!* is winding down." Gill's words ran together without punctuation or taking a breath or any modulation in his voice. "That smart-ass little wanna-be star thinks she and her mother are running the show. She's already fading." Gill smiled with glee. "I think sweetie cakes and Mom are in for a major reality adjustment when they try to get feature work."

Brad refused to play along with Gill's malice. "Decent writers and scripts are all Aimee requires—or anyone else in Hollywood, for that matter." A good story line, sharp dialogue, and a clever director are the answer. Just think of all the people Woody Allen makes look good."

If Gill was paying attention to Brad, the remarks didn't seem to achieve Brad's objective. "You'll love this," Gill continued. "My new show? It's called *Rehab*." He coughed up a laugh. "Remember that *Hunk House* series from a couple of seasons back? This is exactly like that, only more insidious. Each week we get someone in a twelve-step program to fall off the wagon. Brilliant, eh? Everybody's addicted to something."

Brad had moved over to one of the unattended ticket counters. He listened impatiently as Gill continued his pitch.

"We've got their respective substances of abuse lying around within easy reach," Gill continued. "*Abstinence* makes the heart grow fonder for another drag, another hit, another pill, another snort." Gill sniggered. "Before you know it, there go the AA birthday cakes."

Brad said, "That's the most morally and socially reprehensible program idea I've ever heard."

Gill cracked a wide smile and he began bobbing his head as would a deliriously giddy kid. "Yeah! The network suits are already planning *Celebrity Rehab* for May Sweeps!"

Brad was outraged. "Well, now," he began, "doesn't that just about represent pretty much the full spectrum of what American culture has sunk to?"

"Yeah," Gill agreed. "Think George and Laura would let the twins guest host?"

Brad snorted. "Clearly, this is what every mindless, monosyllabic nothing in their dreary sexless lives, nor a clue in their feeble brains, conservative, NRA card carrying, Jesus fearing, beer-belching, homophobic, right to life, delusional slug needs." Brad sighed. "It's a sad time in America, and in Hollywood," he said. "Whoever the karma-challenged ignorant soul is who conceived such a hateful, mean-spirited idea, you just have to take pity on them and the asinine TV executives who bought the idea. Try not to judge them, because you know for damn sure they're in for a scud missile–size radiation enema when their life energy is suddenly zapped out of their pathetic bodies, and their pure essence is FedExed to wherever electrical energy and the subconscious mind goes when you die."

"Just call me *The Big OD.*" Gill leered. "I tried to come up with an idea that would get lots of ancillary media coverage and not get lost among other non-scripted shows," Gill explained. "Frank Rich has been particularly great about stoking the controversy. He says he hates the concept *and* me. But at least he's writing about *Rehab.* Wait'll I spin this off to *Political Rehab.* I'm thinking three generations of the Bush family; Daddy, Jenna, Barbara, and their cousin from Florida, what's her face, with the stringy hair?"

Brad was nearly apoplectic. Afraid that if he heard another word from Gill he'd scream, he turned and continued toward Customs. He ignored Gill's recap of all that had been going on in America during the time that he had been away. Nothing had changed. The top stories were still about Ben and Matt, Catherine and Michael, Tom, Harrison, Colin, J. Lo. Brad realized how little he had thought about celebrities and the scraps of gossip about them that he had once craved. *There is life beyond the red carpet,* he reminded himself. He did not miss Los Angeles at all, or for that matter, life in the United States.

"It's making me rich," Gill beamed, catching up to Brad. "By the by, where are you staying?"

Brad countered with the same question to Gill. "The Alphonso," Gill said.

Brad didn't have a clue where he was headed, but he would not be subjected to a room in any hotel that accommodated Gill. "The Doña Pegita," he said. Although he'd heard of the hotel, he hadn't had time to actually make a reservation.

"Spending the bucks, eh?" Gill said, nodding approval of Brad's choice for hotels. "Hubby must want to keep his baby pampered. Let's share a cab."

"I'm being met," Brad said, desperate to avoid any more interaction with Gill than was absolutely necessary.

"Your new Prince Consort?" Gill leered again. "Maybe he can give me a lift, too?" Gill was deviously as curious as he was penurious.

"I'm sure that Holden would be tickled to drop you . . ." Brad cooed, "but his flight from Paris isn't due to arrive for . . ." He looked his watch, stalling. "Four more hours. That is, of course, taking into consideration that Air France isn't delayed. He'd feel dreadful if he kept you waiting that long. It's his breeding, you know. I'm just going to stay here and sit on my bags, daydreaming about the reunion we'll have tonight."

Gill looked at Brad with a dubious expression. "I thought you said his name was Rupert?"

"Rupert?" Brad made a face.

"I remember, because you named Amiee's love interest Rupert, on the show," Gill said. "I changed it in the script to Ed."

The two men had filed into the Customs queue. Brad shook his head. "Nope. It's always been Holden. I don't even remember writing that script." He chuckled. "That's how far away from Hollywood I've placed myself—and damned glad of it, too. Anyway, Holden would never have wanted me to continue working in such an odious profession."

Gill seemed to take Brad's comment as a personal affront. He couldn't have been more peeved if Brad had dissed Ted Casablanca, his personal guru of gossip, and the man Gill most wanted to meet. "I'll toddle along by my lonesome, then," Gill said. "But, drinks for sure. That is, if I can find a night off from scouting twelve-step programs."

"Definitely," Brad said, just as he was summoned to the immigration podium to present his papers. "Adios!" he called to Gill. He placed his thumb and small finger to his ear and mouth, making the international sign for "Ring me." Then, he disappeared into the terminal.

The Traveler's Aide kiosk was not easy to find. Security guards didn't speak English, and Brad was forced to wander the terminal in search of the desperately needed service. When he eventually found the door to the room for guest services, an attendant, who despite Brad's cheery smile, seemed less interested in doing her job and more interested in why Brad was in Spain at all, coldly received him. It soon became obvious to Brad that the woman's telephone calls and delays in finding answers to his simple questions were a ruse to detain him until she was comfortable that he was indeed a tourist and not some threat to world peace. "Only basic comfort," she said with an imperious attitude, when she finally provided Brad with the name and address of a hotel in the heart of Seville. "No reservation needed."

Outside the terminal, Brad found a curbside cab. Soon, he was riding to town, taking in the sights and moving toward yet another unknown destination.

As often in his life as Brad had said that he loved adventures, he was growing weary of simply going with the flow. He decided that he wanted some definitive plans. *But if you blueprint your life, you won't be open to the unexpected gems that come along!* He recalled the oft-repeated remarks of Reverend Sally, as transmitted through Garreth, whom Brad decided he was starting to miss.

Brad mentally toted up what had thus far been the treasures of his foray into Europe. Simon, Paolo, and Mike. Each had been unanticipated and exciting. Even if one had used the excuse of a business trip to extricate himself from the relationship, and another was only interested in an afternoon fuck, and the third had his adorable ass hauled into jail, Brad did not regret any of the encounters.

Keep dating long enough and Cupid is bound to realize that you're serious, and smile down on you with the prize of a boyfriend. Thank God for Reverend Sally's affirmation.

The half-star rating that the Hotel Franco had earned in the brochure the Traveler's Aide lady provided was generous. The accommodations were utilitarian at best, suitable for tourists who simply needed a closet to store their suitcases. Or a bed on which to take a siesta. In fact, *"Siesta Rates"* were an option at the registration desk. Brad's first thought was, *Who'd pay to nap in this sleazy joint?* Later, in the middle of the long near-sleepless night on a lumpy mattress, it occurred to him that *siesta* was a euphemism. He suddenly felt creepy, and he decided to seek other lodgings as soon as the sun came up.

The Hotel de Castillo was a vast improvement over the Franco. Once a Moorish palace, Brad felt at much greater ease in the soundings. The place at least had decorative touches—traditional mosaic tile floors in the lobby, a spacious and comfortable room with a balcony that overlooked a garden, and a swimming pool.

After tipping the porter who delivered his luggage, Brad closed the door to his room and took off his clothes. He switched on the air-conditioning and flopped onto the bed. He was exhausted. Lying on his back, listening to the sound of playful voices emanating up from the pool area and the rhythmic sound of the headboard on the bed in the next room hitting the wall, Brad mentally wandered back to his life in America. What, he wondered, had he really expected to find in Europe? *Was I serious in believing that I was limiting myself by not exploring male options abroad?* he thought. *Why would I think that the men would be any different in Europe than the men I meet in Los Angeles?*

As his tired mind tried to wrap itself around those large questions, Brad began to drift into unconsciousness. Although fatigued, his body somehow managed to achieve a hard-on. He vaguely considered jacking off. Then his mind went blank, and sleep ensued. Sometime during the night Brad awoke, just long enough to climb under the covers and return to his dreams of licking Colin Farrell's testicles.

As morning light flooded the room through the sliding glass doors that led to his balcony, ambient noises from hotel chambermaids knocking on guest room doors wrested Brad from sleep. He looked at his watch. *Tuesday or Wednesday?* he wondered. He settled on Wednesday, but then told himself to get over the idea of time and place. Despite the decision that had taken hold during the past forty-eight hours, that he would spend only a few more days in Europe before booking his return to the States, Brad reminded himself that he was still on holiday and was therefore not governed by deadlines. He told himself: *Settle back. Enjoy a wank. Then clean up and head down to breakfast.*

Twenty minutes later Brad rose from the bed, showered, shaved, dressed in his 501s and a T-shirt and went in search of food. The hotel dining room, an original portion of the old palace, was near empty of customers. The host, a college-age guy with dark, short-cropped hair, brown eyes, full lips, ears that were just a tad too big for his head, and a name badge that read *Julio,* smiled as he overtly looked Brad up and down with obvious approval.

Brad smiled back. *"Desayuno?"* he said, having seen the word for breakfast on a menu in his room.

"Si, señor." The young man grinned. He winked at Brad and cocked his head, a gesture for Brad to follow him to a table.

As Brad was seated he suddenly realized that he'd left his wallet up-stairs. "I'm a guest of the hotel," he said. "May I charge this bill to room 212?"

"*Si!* Of course! Room 212. *Gracias señor,*" Julio said. He handed Brad a menu, tarrying a moment longer than necessary in an effort to make certain that Brad caught his vibrations of sexual interest. Then Julio turned away to greet a couple who were standing by the host's lectern.

After placing his breakfast order with a waitress and taking the first eye-opening sip of *café con leche,* Brad picked up *GayPlay.* He was de-termined to fill his final days abroad with a variety of activities. He re-solved to disregard the male portion of the society, and although he now planned on going home without so much as a friendship ring, at least he could gain a little culture and sophistication.

Brad flipped through his guidebook to the index. Under "S" he found the reference to his location. He fanned back fifty pages. SEVILLE IS NOT JUST AN EXPENSIVE CAR, the chapter heading stated. Bold print called attention to *GayPlay's Hot Spots, for Hot Shots: Cathe-dral and La Giralda . . . Christopher Columbus's tomb . . . Reales Alcá-zares . . . Museo de Bellas Artes . . . Torre del Oro.* Brad studied an accompanying map, then decided to begin where the travel experts who wrote the book said most visitors start. At the cathedral.

Brad rushed through his breakfast of toasted bread with olive oil, or-ange juice, and *boecaeillo,* anxious now to return to his room, pick up his backpack, and head out for what he now decided would be the ad-venture of learning about the rich history of Spain, rather than the selfish hedonism that had brought him here in the first place. But as he exited the restaurant, Julio called out, "*Señor!*"

Brad turned wearing his most winning smile, delighted that he might not have to abstain from sex for the rest of the journey after all. "Please sign for room 212," Julio said, handing Brad his bill.

"*Gracias,*" Brad said, happy that Julio remembered his room num-ber.

"*Hasta luego?*" Julio said. The question made Brad wish he knew the Spanish words for *Drop by this evening.*

*   *   *

The cathedral seemed filled with tourists, mostly priests and nuns. The size of the church, the largest in Europe, according to *GayPlay*, was overwhelming. Although Brad would be the first to debate the existence of an omnipotent, monotheistic Christian God who looks down from a cloud stroking his white beard while blessing America and simultaneously sentencing the rest of the planet to famine, malaria, AIDS, and George W. Bush, he was often awed to the point of speechlessness by the magnificent structures and art created to glorify man's immutable trust in and supplication to such a deity. Gazing up at the cathedral's vaulted ceilings, at the sculpted high altar above a golden fountain, Brad was mute with reverence, until he issued an audible sigh of profound astonishment. "Allah be praised!" he said loud enough for a pair of nuns to look at him askance. A cute college-age boy whispered, "Hallelujah."

Presently, Brad wandered out to the Patio de los Naranjos. He meandered through the orange trees and around the fountain. The sky above was clear, and the warm air moved lethargically. The tranquility of the cathedral, mixed with the peace of mind that Brad felt knowing that he'd soon be back home, made him more fully appreciate his time here.

As he would probably never again return to this place, Brad decided that he should not miss any of the treasures and artifacts for which the cathedral was famous. He wandered back through the main church in search of the most popular attraction: Christopher Columbus—or what was left of him. Or, as *GayPlay* referred to the explorer, "That skanky, homophobic symbol of slavery and genocide."

The atmosphere of the sepulcher chamber was, as Brad expected, one of solemnity. Visitors spoke in hushed reverential tones. Their whispers echoed and reverberated off thick stone walls in the dimly lighted room. Brad examined the carved stone coffin, which depicted four pallbearers, representing the kingdoms of Castile, León, Aragón, and Navarra. He took his time in the tomb, thinking about the bullshit that American kids are taught in school about the Italian navigator. *"In fourteen hundred ninety-two, Columbus sailed the ocean blue . . ."*

There really wasn't all that much to see in the tomb after all, Brad decided. He read several plaques, considered the details of the sculpted bone holder, and eyed several guys who wandered about in shorts and

T-shirts. Then he followed an older couple speaking French out of the chamber, wending his way toward the cathedral's exit. Collecting his backpack from a coat-check woman, he stepped into the bright sunlight and donned his sunglasses. *GayPlay* had suggested several cafés in the area, and Brad set out to find the one with the rating of four penises next to the listing.

Given the time of day and high rating, Café de la Asunción was remarkably uncrowded. Brad selected a table under an umbrella and seated himself. *"Ah, Señor!"* an amiable waiter called out, bringing over a bottle of mineral water, which he placed on the table. He offered a menu.

Brad smiled. *"Habla Ingles?"* A response in the affirmative elicited a more relaxed posture from Brad. He ordered a glass of red wine and tapas. *"Por favor,"* he added, hoping that he demonstrated making an effort to speak the local language. The waiter smiled as he walked away, saying something that contained the word American. Brad hoped it was a pleasantry. But he knew the possibilities. Romance languages sounded very pretty, but the restaurant's kitchen staff could at this moment be doubled over in laughter at a miserable joke perpetrated by the waitstaff.

Brad opened his tour book and began skimming sections about the Casa de Pilatos and Seville's bull ring, the Plaza de Toros de la Maestranza. Although he was temperamentally opposed to the sport of bullfighting, he considered that perhaps, as a once-in-a-lifetime experience, he might attend an exhibition.

As he read on about the Basilica de Macarena, Brad felt a presence behind him. A shadow cast over his book. When, after a moment, the shadow remained, Brad became irritated. He turned around, half expecting that Gill had found him.

To Brad's surprise, it was not Gill, nor the waiter. Rather a swarthy young Spaniard stood before him dressed much as Brad was himself, in jeans, T-shirt, trainers, and clutching a tourist guidebook.

The two men looked at each other. *GayPlay* suggested that there was no particularly notorious area of Seville, but it cautioned against reviewing maps in public and generally looking like a tourist, no matter where one visited. Recalling that caveat, and considering the stranger before him, Brad was suddenly aware of the possibility that he

was about to be robbed in broad daylight. He raised his hand to summon his waiter for protection.

"I could tell that you didn't buy all that Christopher Columbus
bullshit." The man's Spanish accent was thick and the tone meant to
indicate that he knew Brad was smart enough not to be easily manipu-
lated into believing the falsehoods of historical propaganda.

Brad squinted against the afternoon sun and gave the man a quizzical look. But before Brad could respond, the stranger took a seat at
Brad's table. "He was a slave trader. Columbus, I mean," the man said.
"To pay for his voyages he captured the natives from the island of
Hispaniola and crammed them—by the thousands—into the holds of
his ships. He sold off the ones that survived. Did you know that he
hunted the Indians for sport? His men raped, tortured, and killed
them, then fed them to the dogs. He enslaved or killed off one third of
the population there. Now, they're extinct." The man practically spat,
"And now you Americans have a holiday to honor him. He wasn't exactly Martin Luther King Jr." The man finally stopped for a moment
and looked into Brad's eyes of aghast trepidation. "My name is Marco.
Marco de la Vega. And your name is . . ."

Brad's mind was racing. *Am I being marked for robbery? How do I get
rid of this anti-American guy?* he thought.

Although he had never been a victim of crime, even in Los Angeles,
a city with the dubious distinction of being the murder capital of the
United States, he was nevertheless always aware of anyone who came
too close to him. Even in West Hollywood, which was the gay Mecca
of southern California, Brad kept up his guard. The man now seated at
his table was not exhibiting threatening body language, but like most
cons he didn't appear altogether harmless, either, especially given his
diatribe.

"What do you want?" Brad asked coldly, ignoring the question of
his name, withholding his usual open smile.

Marco's smile faded. "I was at the cathedral. You were there. You
looked like a guy I might want to take me to lunch."

"Why would I want to take you lunch?" Brad was indignant.

"I'm sorry. I got my English confused," Marco said. "I meant that
you would take lunch with me. I mean . . ."

Brad cut him off. "Here's a five Euro note," he said, reaching into his pocket. "That's all the charity I can afford today. Now, please go away."

"Charity?" Marco spat, ignoring the attempted handout. "I know the meaning of 'Ugly American'. " Marco stood up and moved to another table nearby.

Brad watched from his peripheral vision as Marco ordered a glass of wine and opened a book to read. *Not your typical transient hustler type,* Brad thought. Then his tapas arrived and he divided his attention between sating his hunger and planning the rest of his day of sightseeing.

He made the decision to next visit the Mueseo de Bellas Artes. Immediately following lunch, Brad walked the longer than expected distance to the museum. He paid his admission, and for a few minutes he sat on a marble bench recovering from his walk, reviewing the brochure of featured exhibits.

Commencing his tour of the museum, Brad admired the arched ceiling in the main hall. Soon he was lost in the detail of an oil canvas by Murillo. Entranced by the work, Brad was oblivious to the other visitors at the museum. Even the security guards—who were inordinately attractive in their uniforms and were standing in the archways between exhibit rooms—only slightly distracted Brad from his study of the art on display.

While most of the visitors whispered as they commented about a particular canvas, one male voice speaking in normal conversational volume interrupted Brad's concentration. "Do not leave without seeing the El Greco exhibit," the voice suggested in English.

Brad turned around and his smile quickly faded. It was Marco de la Vega.

"Is this a coincidence, or are you following me?" Brad asked. He was more peeved by the prospect that he was being stalked than frightened.

"I don't believe in coincidences," Marco said. "And you can add arrogance to your list of disagreeable personality traits. Why would anybody pursue you?"

Brad turned away, moving to the next painting.

"If you weren't so pissy, I would have offered to show you the other Murillo." Marco's tone suggested that he had access to something unique that was perhaps not on public display.

Brad looked over his shoulder at Marco, and for the first time he took full notice of the man. Marco's eyes were dark and shaded by long, silky lashes. His eyebrows reminded Brad of bird feathers: luxuriant on the boundary between a sleek nose, and slightly arched and tapered to a quill point near his temples. Although he had probably shaved that morning, Marco was already exhibiting five o'clock shadow. His straight black hair formed a widow's peak in the front. His chest and arms filled out an old, discolored, once-white T-shirt. Through the fibers Brad could see the shadow of a dark mass of chest hair. Brad noticed the deep indentation in Marco's square chin.

"If you've seen one Murillo, you've seen 'em all," Brad scoffed. "So I'm not missing anything." He moved a little farther on toward a large floor-to-ceiling canvas.

Marco sniggered in irritation. "Just a pretty boy from the States, eh? You could use some better knowledge of art, if you ask me," Marco made an assessment.

"Did I ask for a lesson?" Brad retorted. "And why are you harassing me?"

Marco threw up his hands in disgust. "I am not surprised that you have to travel alone," he said, and then walked away.

"I like to travel alone," Brad argued aloud on the way back to his hotel, refuting Marco's cutting words. "I'm my own best friend." But plagued by Marco's curt observation he cursed Marco for being at once caustic and insightful.

Exhausted from sight-seeing—and from wrestling with his feeling of resentment toward Marco—Brad nevertheless was eager to experience the nightlife of Seville. Knowing that the clubs didn't get into full swing until well after midnight, Brad shed his clothes and fell onto the bed for a nap.

Asleep, Brad heard a tapping noise. A dream was unreeling in which a sun-drenched, bare-chested carpenter wearing only a tool belt and a red bandana, straddling the frame of a roof, was hammering nails into two-by-fours. From the ground below, a buff, shirtless Mexican day worker was calling up to the carpenter in a harsh whisper, *"Señor? Señor Brad?"*

Suddenly awake, Brad realized that there was someone at his door. He called out, *"Si?"*

"Julio," the voice from his dream responded.

Who the hell is Julio? Brad asked himself.

Then he remembered. "Right. Hang on." He rose from the bed, turned on the light on his bed stand, and finger-combed his hair. He walked to the door, looked through the peephole, then decided to admit his visitor.

Julio eagerly entered. Before Brad had an opportunity to say *"Hola,"* Julio had removed his own shirt. They stood face to face, then instantly began smothering each other with kisses.

Soon, the two were naked, with Julio straddling Brad on the bed. Although their sex was perfunctory, it seemed to serve the animalistic needs of two men desperate to taste each other's hard body.

When they eventually climaxed, Julio suddenly became paranoid. "You must not tell!" he insisted. "My job."

Brad shook his head. *"Si. Si,"* he said. "Who would I tell?"

"Gracias." Julio sighed relief as he dressed. Before departing he ran his tongue up and down Brad's chest. "Perhaps again?" he said.

Brad smiled as he pulled the top sheet up to his waist. Julio let himself out of the room.

Once again alone, Brad enjoyed the solitude and the post-orgasm sensation of depleted energy. "Sex is so easy," Brad said aloud. "Finding a man to really sleep with is hard."

It was nearly eleven P.M., and Brad decided to shower and dress for an evening of visiting a couple of clubs.

Examining the map in *GayPlay,* Brad set out for the Calle Reina Mercedes. According to the guide, it was a favorite haunt for the city's student population. Although he wasn't specifically looking to connect with someone for sex, Brad was anxious to play the role of cultural anthropologist and watch the way guys interacted in Spain.

The bar was crowded—jammed, in fact. Entering the noisy disco, Brad suddenly wished that he'd found a quieter jazz club instead. He rarely did this kind of bar scene in L.A., and he wondered if he should be wasting his time here. He decided to stay just long enough to drink a beer.

Strobes raked the room, which was packed with countless attractive young guys, many of whom were shirtless, gyrating in pairs to the pulsating beat of the music. Watching sexy men grind their pelvises against other sexy men, grazing on each other's nipples and chest hair, mixing saliva cocktails, made Brad think once again about his resolve to find a mate. Over the past few days he'd started to convince himself that it had been an absurd idea. *Who wants just one when you can have a whole planet of men?* he said to himself.

He found himself wishing that he were on the dance floor, too, rubbing his hands over sweat-soaked, gym-pumped flesh with one of the myriad dudes moving to the harsh dance track. *I don't have to be alone if I don't want to be,* he thought, recalling Marco's parting words at the museum.

Brad's eyes took in the room. Standing in place, moving slightly to the beat, he started to get into the rhythm of the music. Then, as if he were in a fantasy dream, a pair of hands cupped his hips from behind. Someone's body began slowly moving up and down in sync with Brad's, and a man whispered something in Spanish into his ear. Whatever their translation, Brad thought the words sounded seductive. Without turning to view his partner, Brad pressed against the hard body, the hands of which were now exploring his ass and crotch, lifting his T-shirt to stroke his chest and nipples. Lips kissed his back.

The combination of music, alcohol, and caressing from a mysterious debaucher in a public venue aroused Brad tremendously. He was hard, aching to turn around, to be vigorously kissed by the man who held him in such a firm grip. Absorbed as he was in this erotically charged mating dance, Brad could nevertheless hear whistles of approval from other men as they watched. The approbation served to encourage both Brad and his paramour to continue their intimate show.

It was torture for Brad not to look at his Casanova. A tongue flicking the back of his perspiration-soaked neck was almost painful in its excitement. But each time that Brad attempted to wriggle around, he was locked into an inflexible restraint, which merely intensified his excitement.

As the music grew more furious, so did the exuberance by which Brad was held by his enigmatic lover. Finally, above the music's din, his tongue snapping at Brad's ear, a masculine voice whispered, "*Na say asque tuemenda, say?* Pissy American."

Brad immediately stopped moving. The bond between the two bodies became broken, and Brad was finally allowed to turn around.

He was incredulous. It was Marco, dressed in a sweat-soaked tank top tucked into his faded jeans. "Don't you ever give up?" Brad declared above the music.

"You loved it," Marco explained defiantly. "Why must you be hostile to me?"

Brad suddenly realized that from the very beginning he had been exceedingly unfriendly to Marco, and he couldn't explain why. He shrugged his shoulders in a moment of contrition.

Marco shook his head. "Well, I promise not to intrude on you further. Ever." With that, he turned on his heels and walked to the bar.

Brad felt confused. Although he had been irritated with Marco since their first encounter, and he was furious with the Spaniard for insinuating that being alone was some sort of personal character flaw, Brad had to question why he had felt such a conflict in the first place. In a world in which most of Brad's first impressions of men usually turned out to be wrong, at least when it came to the guys who seemed perfect on paper, Brad conceded that perhaps he was wrong again.

Brad headed for the bar, where he found Marco engaged in conversation with another man who was running his fingers up and down Marco's sternum. Brad approached the duo, standing at Marco's back. The man, making a play for Marco, said something in Spanish to Brad. He assumed it was a variation on "Fuck off, this one's mine." With that, Marco turned around. He pursed his lips, not saying a word, but looking at Brad with contempt.

After a long moment, Brad suggested to Marco, "Would you please ask your friend to leave us alone for a moment?"

Marco twisted his face into a look of incredulity. "Why would I do that?" he asked, giving Brad a harsh stare. "He likes me."

Brad nodded. "Forget it. I'm just an 'ugly American.'"

Marco simply stared at Brad for a long moment. Perspiration

beaded on his forehead and his long hair was glistening. His tank top was saturated, clinging to the curves of his torso. Then he turned and said something to his impatient partner.

"Piñejo!" the man spat. He pushed himself past Brad and into the crowd.

Brad turned to the bartender and raised his beer bottle. *"Dos, por favor,"* he called out.

As two cold bottles were placed on the bar counter, Brad reached into his pocket and withdrew a ten Euro note and laid it down. He waved away the change and set aside his now empty bottle. He picked up the two bottles and made what he hoped was a peace offering to Marco, who accepted his bottle with a slight nod.

"It's so loud in here!" Brad called above the bedlam.

Marco cocked his head toward a door, and soon they were outside, on a dimly-lighted brick patio. Several couples were scattered about the intimate area, making out, practically engaging in public sex. Marco set his beer bottle down on a chest-high brick wall and hoisted himself up to sit beside it. Brad leaned against the wall and took a sip of beer.

"I have no excuse for my behavior today," Brad began. "I guess you just frightened me at the café."

"Your insulting attitude is my fault?" Marco scoffed. "I don't frighten people."

"Well, you'll just have to take my word for it," Brad defended himself. "And then you followed me to the museum."

"Now I'm stalking the cute American? You make up such lies," Marco charged. "I'm an art student. I go to museums. It's part of my curriculum."

Cute? Brad said to himself. "Where do you go to school?" he asked, now genuinely interested.

"Universidad de Madrid. I'm on holiday."

"Alone?" Brad said. It was payback time for Marco's impertinence at the museum.

Marco chuckled, then shook his head.

Brad took a moment to collect his thoughts. For a few uncomfortable moments, a restless silence wedged between the two men. They sipped their beers, both seemingly indecisive about what to say to the other.

Then Marco cleared his throat. He hopped down from the wall. "I'm off," he said, shattering Brad's fantasy that perhaps he'd suggest they go for a late supper. "*Gracias*," he said, holding out his beer bottle.

"Sure." Brad wondered why he was so conflicted about his feelings. He tried to stall Marco. "I guess I never actually apologized for the way I treated you today."

"No," Marco agreed. "But you're in a strange country. You have to be wary of people. Especially being an American. I should have understood."

"But I'm usually very nice," Brad said.

"That's why I approached you in the first place," Marco said. "I'm fairly empathic. Or at least I was until today."

Brad smiled. "I promise not to think that you're stalking me again."

"You won't have to," Marco said.

Brad's hopes were being dashed, but he tried to press on. "I'm only here for a few more days anyway. But if I happen to see you at Parque Maria Luisa, say, sometime tomorrow, I promise not to run away." Brad tried to sound at once flirtatious and lackadaisical. "Will you at least shake my hand to let me know that you won't take away a completely negative impression of an American?"

Marco ran his eyes up and down Brad. Grudgingly he reached out. "*Si.*"

When Brad's hand touched Marco's he felt a definite exchange of energy. Their hands remained clasped and they stared into one another's eyes for a long moment. Finally, Marco said, "Adios, Brad," and withdrew his hand. He turned away.

"Adios, Marco," Brad responded.

Chapter Seven

Arriving back at his hotel, Brad opened the door to his second floor room. Piercing the darkness was the pulsating beacon of the message light on his telephone. Brad switched on the lamp beside his bed and pushed the series of numbers on the keypad for voice mail. *"Usted t'em un nueva mensage,"* said the voice of an automaton. A moment of euphoria turned to dejection, and Brad's heart sank when he heard Julio's voice. He listened to the recording, rolling his eyes. "Thank you, no," Brad said as he replaced the telephone receiver.

Brad sighed as he looked around the room. His suitcases were neatly arranged in a corner. On a table were maps, some sight-seeing brochures, a conversational Spanish language book, and several Euro notes. He looked at the unmade bed and was reminded that he'd had sex with Julio only a few hours earlier. *So why do I feel vacant?* he asked himself.

Brad lethargically performed his ablutions, undressed, and slipped naked into bed. Although he was exhausted, his thoughts raced from Julio to Marco and back again. Julio was a hot, sexy top who'd performed in bed as well as any other men with whom Brad had been intimate. But Brad didn't care whether he ever saw Julio again. His mind ricocheted to Marco, with whom he had not so much as shared a kiss. Yet all he wanted was to enfold Marco in his arms. A fully clothed Marco was somehow sexier than a naked Julio.

For a long while, Brad stared into the blackness of the room. *You blew it, man!* He thought back to earlier in the day, at the museum. *You should have asked Marco to show you that Murillo! You should have offered him another beer at the bar! Should have! Would have! Could have! The point is, he's gone! So much for your charm!*

Brad decided that the only way to extricate himself from his distress was to return home. He planned to make flight reservations first thing in the morning. With the plan firmly settled in his head, he drifted to sleep.

The muffled noise from house cleaning trolleys being wheeled down the hotel corridor, followed by knocking on doors and the announcement of maid service were an unintentional wake-up call. Brad lay on his back, clutching a pillow, vaguely aware of his morning erection. It was always there, like a pet waiting anxiously to be taken outside to relieve itself. But this morning, Brad's thoughts weren't on his usual daily ritual. Instead, he was focused on Marco. What would sex with Marco have been like? Brad felt overcome with melancholy. It wasn't raining. And it wasn't Monday. Still, Brad felt an old Carpenters song coming on.

Then the telephone rang.

Brad thought: *Let it please be him!* Although he didn't believe that Marco knew where he was staying, let alone what his phone number was, he answered hopefully.

"I'm taking you out to see the sights." Alas, it was only Julio. Brad was silent with disappointment. "Then we can revisit yesterday's sights, too. *Si?*" Julio made a guttural sound of pleasure. Pick you up in half an hour." *Click, buzz.*

Julio was so commanding that Brad had not had an opportunity to reject the offer. Against the solitary dial tone Brad vaguely said, "*Si.*"

Brad was savvy enough to be waiting in the hotel lobby when his tour guide arrived. Although he could tell that Julio was disappointed at not being able to visit Brad's room, his frustration seemed to abate as he salivated over Brad's attire: hiking boots, shorts that revealed his slightly hairy, muscled legs, and a white T-shirt that showcased his pumped chest and arms. "Hey, stud," Brad greeted Julio with a teasing grin. "Where are we off to?"

Julio smiled mischievously. "Don't you trust Julio? Think of me as your magic carpet."

"A textiles factory?"

The morning passed quickly. Julio and Brad whisked around the city in Julio's old Mercedes. They stopped at various tourist attractions that had not been referenced in *GayPlay*, and yet Brad could nevertheless tell that they were gay friendly if not outright catering to gay tourists. He found himself having an unexpectedly good time. Julio was fun. Their repartee was easy. And they were comfortable enough with each other to hold hands in between Julio's shifting gears on the car's transmission.

"Change of plans," Julio said as he maneuvered his car through traffic. "Instead of another boring museum, let's go to one of my favorite spots. Then lunch. Then . . ." Julio's last word lingered in the space between the two men. "Sies-*ta*," he finally said, emphasizing the last syllable.

Brad was having such a pleasant time that anything Julio suggested was fine by him. Even Brad's self-imposed injunction against sex with Julio had disintegrated. He could not deny that his companion was sexy and smart. Brad got hard thinking about having Julio inside him again.

The car arrived at the perimeter of a vast wooded park in the heart of the city. "Bring your camera," Julio suggested as they stepped out of the vehicle. "*Muy macho hombres* keep up their summer tans lounging by the lake. I may need a souvenir."

Brad's ego chafed at the suggestion that Julio might be interested in looking at other men. He was slightly annoyed by Julio's flippant remark. Although he wasn't interested in Julio for anything other than sex, and Julio was understandably making out with a lot of men, Brad found himself feeling somewhat territorial about the stud. When it came to sex, Brad never liked to believe that he was a mere link in another man's chain of fools. Still, he sidled up to Julio and wandered into the bucolic, landscaped setting, with its lush gardens, tree-shaded avenues, and flowing fountains.

"Over there," Julio pointed beyond the trees, "is Palacio de San Telmo. It's now the Junta's presidential headquarters."

Brad remembered a reference in his guidebook. "So this must be Parque Maria Luisa," he said, aware that he had planned to come to this very location. "You're reading my thoughts."

"Are you reading mine?" Julio asked playfully. He reached out to slip his hand into Brad's back pocket and cupped his ass. Julio let his hand linger and gave Brad's butt a tight squeeze, which made Brad laugh with giddy embarrassment.

Now, self-conscious about drawing attention to himself, Brad furtively looked around to assure himself that no other tourists were paying more than passing attention. However, someone *was* taking notice. When Brad saw him, for one instant, he was excited. In the next, his heart sank. He took Julio's hand away and stopped walking.

Marco was seated on a bench and had witnessed the frolicsome scene. Julio, oblivious to the situation, continued walking as Brad stood looking at Marco. Even as Brad regained his composure and began to move toward Marco, Julio continued on.

Brad tentatively approached Marco. "Looks like I dropped a big enough hint last night. I said I'd be at Parque Maria Luisa and you listened."

Marco forced a smile. "I'm not stalking you. I swear."

"Then, please rescue me," Brad gushed. "I've been kidnapped by a madman. *Loco.*"

"I'd say you were in good *hands*," Marco said, eyeing Julio's backside.

Julio finally realized that Brad was no longer by his side. He looked around, then wandered back to where Brad and Marco were conversing. "Making friends with the locals?" Julio joked to Brad, at the same time clearly sizing up Marco as both a threat and possible conquest. "We'd better go if we're to make the restaurant before it gets crowded," Julio said to Brad.

Brad stood between Marco and Julio, tugged in two directions. Somehow he knew that whatever he did in the next few seconds could impact his life forever after. He stood trapped in the moment. Was Marco really in the park coincidentally, or had he intentionally sought out the place where Brad mentioned he would be today?

He also realized that Julio had been kind enough to spend his day playing tour guide, and that it would be irresponsible and rude to suddenly disregard him. On the other hand, Brad was certain that all Julio really wanted from him was another fuck that would be forgotten as quickly as a meal that simply satisfied a hunger.

Risking everything, Brad made an abrupt announcement. He said, "Julio, meet Marco. I'm spending the rest of my holiday with him."

Julio looked bewildered. "*Que?*" he slipped into Spanish. He gaped at Marco for an instant, then back to Brad. "No. We go off to lunch, now. Come." He grabbed Brad by the arm and tried to lead him away.

Brad dug in his heels. Marco jumped to his feet and slapped Julio's hand off Brad's sleeve. "*No comprende Ingles?*"

Although Brad tried to offer a look of apology to Julio, he only succeeded in infuriating him further. "Americans!" Julio spat. "You think you own the world!" He stood with his hands on his hips, nearly hyperventilating. "You'd better find another hotel, amigo. The Castillo has just booked your room."

"Please don't be angry," Brad pleaded. "I didn't mean for this to happen."

Julio looked at Marco and sneered, "He's not a very hot lay, anyway." With that, Julio stormed out of the park.

Brad looked at Marco and shrugged. "An eviction and a report card," he said, smiling. But his levity was short-lived, as Marco stood up and began to walk away, too.

"Hey!" Brad called, suddenly alarmed. "You're not leaving?"

"I rescued you. What more do you want from me?" Marco continued walking.

"No! Wait!" Brad sauntered after Marco. "You came to the park to meet me, didn't you?"

Marco continued walking without a response. Brad paused. "You've been on my mind constantly since last night. Please let me buy you lunch, or something."

"Your friend knows you are an arrogant American. Wasn't that what I said, too? Why should I have lunch with an arrogant American?"

"Because you know I'm not such a bad guy." Brad sighed. "And you know that I still feel bad about the way I treated you. And you know that I think you're special."

Marco stopped walking. "But why would I be interested in a man who is such a terrible lay?"

Brad, at first stunned, started laughing. Marco began laughing, too. He wagged a finger at Brad. "I can accept one who is not too bright in the head, as long as he tries very hard. You must be assigned much homework."

After a leisurely lunch at a nearby café, during which Brad and Marco talked easily about philosophy, art, politics, movies, and Madonna, they returned to the Hotel de Castillo. Brad's key no longer fit the lock to his room. Julio had indeed spoken with the hotel management. Brad found his suitcases lined up at the front desk.

"You'll hear from American Express about this," Brad stated as he signed his bill. "It's not wise to piss off a writer. Especially one who contributes to *Conde Nast.*" The apathetic hotel manager bobbed his head, certainly unaware that he was bluffing. "Oh, and tell Julio I'm breaking my promise not to tell. He'll know what I mean."

Marco had suggested that there was enough room for both of them at his own location. However, recalling Paolo's generosity and the way things had turned out there, Brad felt it best to maintain some semblance of autonomy. Soon Brad was ensconced in a finer hotel.

"I leave you to rest for a while," Marco said after helping to carry Brad's luggage to his new room.

"Dinner?" Brad was hopeful.

Marco smiled, then nodded.

The two men stood facing each other, both seemingly timid about making a move. Brad finally blinked out of his reverie and stepped in close enough to Marco to feel the heat emanating from his body. "This is to say thank you," he said as he placed his lips against Marco's.

The instant they connected, Brad let out an involuntary moan, as if suddenly zapped by the purple-blue light of an electrical shock. Marco wrapped Brad in his arms. After what seemed many minutes, they cautiously detached from one another.

"*Hasta luego,*" Marco whispered. He reached behind him and fumbled for the doorknob. Then he was gone.

"Adios," Brad whispered, mostly to himself. He was weak from Marco's kiss. His mind whirled with a desire for more.

Brad untied his shoes and lay down, fully clothed, on the bed.

Exhaustion slowly shut off the spigot of his consciousness and he
drifted off to sleep.

In the days that followed, Brad and Marco were inseparable. Brad's
notion of returning to the States became unthinkable. Together they
explored the villages, churches, and monasteries of Spain. They spent
their nights at a network of *paradors* across the country. Marco would
often stop the car at particularly interesting locations and begin
sketching an old Roman bridge, or the ruins of a Moorish castle or a
statue of the Virgin—of which Brad thought there were more than
enough for one country. Brad, too, had begun writing in his journal—
or reworking his screenplay, jotting down quick, declarative yet cryptic
sentences onto picture postcards to tease Garreth or the guys in
England.

Brad could not look at Marco without becoming aroused. He
seemed to be horny all the time they were together. It had never been
unusual for Brad to see an attractive man and feel a jolt of desire and a
wish to know what it would be like to be fucked by a particular stranger
in a tank with tattoos on his beefy arms. But although he had experienced excruciatingly exciting sex with many men, he was invariably
glad when the encounters were completed and he could once again be
alone.

However, with Marco the dynamics were different. The feeling of
fullness that Brad enjoyed when hugging Marco's warm bare skin
against his own made him crazy with lust and a deep desire to want to
hold fast to this man forever. Their sex was playful, but when they
stared into each other's eyes they felt a deep and concentrated connection.

Each night, as soon they paid for lodgings, the door to their room
was barely closed before they stripped off their clothes and fell in unison onto the bed. Their arms and legs became a tangle of predatory
appendages, each containing a gazillion sensory feelers. Their mouths
and tongues roamed every plane and hollow, from their armpits to
their chests to their navels, backs, legs, and toes. Each encounter was
as exciting as the first. And, from their past experiences, they realized

that their versatility with each other was unique. Marco was as eager to satisfy Brad, as Brad was anxious to please Marco.

Every night after Marco had fucked Brad, and the two had drifted into contented sleep for an hour wrapped in each other's arms, they awoke simultaneously, and Brad could not disregard his urge to slide himself into a wildly appreciative Marco. Every night was like this, followed by mornings of equal passion. And, throughout the day they tried to find obscure places in which to indulge in heavy kissing, which invariably led to both of them taking turns at sucking the other into climax. "I know that my breath smells of you," Brad laughed one day as they drove away from the ruins of a castle where they had indulged their needs. "But I don't care."

"I like to feel that you are literally part of me," Marco agreed, licking his lips. "What is it that Americans say? 'You are what you eat?' "

Brad smiled and nodded his head in pure contentment. Often he thought of what might have happened if Marco had accepted his initial rude behavior and not given him several more chances. Brad was struck with profound uneasiness when those thoughts passed through his conscious mind. However, he checked himself with the truth that the important thing was that they were together and completely in love.

But despite their ideal union, after three months in Europe, Brad was nearly out of money. Marco was equally morose as the term break from the university was coming to a close. It occurred to Brad that perhaps he could get a job, while Marco was in class. Together they went over every possible scenario to delay what they feared was inevitable: a return to reality.

"I don't think you would be allowed to work in Spain," Marco said. There were laws preventing foreigners from taking jobs that might be held by nationals.

"Can't I apply for residency?" Brad suggested.

"Without money or a job, immigration is almost impossible," Marco countered.

"How about political asylum?"

"From America?"

"The government's stripping away civil liberties. I pay enormous taxes, and I'm lower than a third-class citizen."

Marco shook his head. "What if you just go home—"

"I can't leave you!" Brad quickly interrupted.

"—and take me with you," Marco said.

For the next hour Brad and Marco discussed their bleak situation. They finally agreed that Marco could not give up his studies to follow Brad back to the States. And without any prospects for a job in Los Angeles, Brad could hardly afford to support himself, let alone two people.

"It'll work out, I promise," Brad said. He choked back a tear.

But a plan that had been germinating in Brad's mind over the past week now seemed the only solution. It was an idea that he was loath to pursue. But now that he was out of alternatives he had to give it serious consideration. "Let me make a phone call," he said.

After they returned to their hotel room, Marco said he'd take a walk and be back in an hour. He wanted Brad to have the privacy he required to make his important telephone call.

It took several attempts, but Brad was finally connected to Hollywood. Gill's assistant, Beverly, suggested that if Brad needed a job, he'd better contact Gill right away because Gill was expected to return to California within the next few days. She also gave him what she called "friendly advice." "Make his dick hard," she said. "That's where his brain is."

Brad nodded knowingly. It was always easy to arouse Gill. But keeping Brad's own dick stiff around his boss took the combined playacting skills of an Olivier and Streep, as well as mental pictures of a naked Hugh Jackman.

Beverly made the arrangements and soon Brad was speaking directly to Gill who was wrapping up his work in Madrid. "Heard your new show is a smash in America," Brad enthused. "My spies back in Hollywood say you're becoming all the rage." Brad could hardly believe that he was once again sucking up to the likes of Gill Truitt.

"*Becoming* all the rage?" Gill brayed. "Michael Eisner is taking *me* to lunch!"

"Thank God for reality TV, eh?" Brad schmoozed. "And they say it only takes a camera and a gimmick. I say, it takes a creative mind. A real visionary. Otherwise you wind up with crap like *I'm a Celebrity, Get Me Out of Here!*" He forced a laugh.

Gill said, "Saves a bundle not having script writers, too!"

The remark infuriated Brad. However, he would save his breath for the superlatives that he lavished in praise of the series idea.

He started to wheedle his way toward the purpose of his call. "How do you get any work done with all the two-hour lunches, and siestas, and all the other dawdling bullshit these people do over here every day?"

"And they're not as cheap as I thought, either," Gill agreed. "Damn unions are everywhere! When we do *Third World Rehab*, I'll be sure to take the show to Afghanistan."

"Don't you long for the days when you had good, old-fashioned American labor?" Brad said wistfully "Back in Hollywood you could just say screw the union. Remember how you used to work us for, like, eighteen hours a day, seven days a week? I never complained. And none of the other staff did, either."

Gill chortled. "That's because you knew that TV writing jobs were damn hard to come by. Not to mention, you had your perks with me."

Brad wanted to scream. *If you think looking at your pathetic, pickle-size prick was a perk . . .* "Well, I always wanted you to be happy with my work," Brad lied. "Always got my rewrites in on time. I miss working with you."

Brad could hear heavy breathing on the other end of the line, but Gill didn't respond to the last statement. "Gill?" Brad finally said.

"I'm thinking. Hold on."

Thinking? I hope that's not a euphemism. Brad cringed as he remembered what Beverly had said about the location of Gill's brain.

Gill came back on the line. "Are you still all lovey-dovey and tied up with the new husband? Prince Charles, or whatever his name is?"

As if Gill was a marlin to be lured, played with, and then slowly reeled in, Brad let his line slack just a bit. "Things haven't exactly worked out as I'd planned." Brad spoke in what he hoped was a dejected tone.

"Poor baby," Gill said without the least bit of sincerity. "Serves you right for jumping in, heart first. I always marked you for the type who confused sex with love."

"You're a lot smarter than I am," Brad said. "You never made the kinds of mistakes that I do." He sighed. "Life goes on." Brad tried to sound brave and optimistic in the midst of a dirty hand he'd been dealt. "Any sage advice for me?"

"The thought occurred to me . . ."

Brad held his breath.

". . . *You* wouldn't be interested, but maybe you know someone . . ."

Me! Me! Brad silently begged.

"My supervising producer needs a hand."

Brad said, "As a matter of fact, I need something to take my mind off all that love sick crap I'm going through." Brad spoke calmly. "Besides, it's time I got back to work."

Gill seemed to contemplate the situation for a moment. Then, sounding somewhat reluctant, he said, "In that case, maybe you won't be such a prima doña this time. Call Beverly and get the details."

Brad hung up the telephone. "Woo-hoo!" He high-fived the air and yelled, "Thankyeah, Jesus!"

At that moment, Marco returned to the room. He smiled at Brad's euphoria. "Must have been a successful call," he said sitting down on the bed next to Brad. "Now, can you tell me what this is all about?"

Brad looked deep into Marco's eyes. "All in good time, señor," he smirked. He seductively pulled his T-shirt over his head and then reached out for Marco who had immediately taken Brad's lead and started undressing himself. "I don't think that I've fucked you enough today," Brad said as he pulled off Marco's shoes and socks. "I don't think I ever fuck you enough," he added as he slipped out of his own pants and laid himself down on top of his lover. "Oh, yeah, never enough," he said as the two began to ardently kiss.

"*Si*, never," Marco gasped as his tongue pursued Brad's tongue, and then trailed down Brad's throat to his muscled chest and nipples, and over to his slick underarms. Probing every square inch of upper body skin, Marco followed his desperate impulse to move down and nurse on Brad's sweet tasting cock.

Brad moved in sync with Marco's affectionate mouthful after mouthful of his solid penis. The day had turned out perfectly and now the lovemaking made him further recognize and appreciate the value and intensity of love. "Hey, enough of the appetizer," Brad joked. "I promised you a fuck, so get ready and open that hole for me." Then in complete seriousness he said, "God, Marco, I love you. I want you. Whatever makes you happy, will make me happy, too."

Marco sat up for a moment and rested on his knees. He stared into Brad's eyes. As he took in the view of the body he had come to know intimately, his cock throbbed and made an involuntary jump. Rearranging himself on the bed, Marco moved to align himself horizontally with Brad. He laid his cheek on Brad's chest and cradled his man in his arms, while entwining their legs. "It makes me happy just to touch you," Marco whispered. "I am happy to be the man that you want to touch in return."

Brad started to comment but Marco hushed him. "Close your eyes," he whispered. "Feel me inside of you. Not my cock. Me. My spirit. My soul. Shhh."

Two hours later, still holding each other as if in post-climax bliss, Marco flicked his tongue over Brad's nipples. Then Marco asked, "When do you start the new job?"

Eyes closed, and eager to fall asleep in this comfortable and safe position, Brad purred. " 'Sposed to call the assistant for details. Just a few more minutes here," he said. "Feels so good."

Brad, using Marco's bicep as a pillow, holding his lover's body close, inhaling the musky scent of perspiration mixed with semen, he drifted into a deep sleep.

They awoke almost simultaneously later in the afternoon in the same positions. Brad's hands began exploring Marco's chest. He caressed the mossy softness of Marco's body hair, then moved down to his penis, which was once again stiff.

Marco whispered, "You must call about the job, musn't you?"

"Why must you be mean to me?" Brad sang in a sleepy voice. "Okay. Okay. I'm going. But don't move. I want to celebrate as soon as I'm off the phone."

"Again?" Marco teased. He rolled on his side and kissed Brad's bare ass. "Then hurry."

Brad sat on the edge of the bed and looked at the pad of paper by the telephone on which he had scribbled Beverly's number. He picked up the phone and pushed the keypad for an outside number, then the country code, area code and finally the digits for Gill's office. "Beverly! It's Brad!" He stopped to listen for a moment. Then: "He's faster than I thought. What did he say?" Brad's face darkened. "No, he never said any such thing," Brad said gravely. "I can't do *that*. No. That's too indefinite! This is where I live. But my life is *here*, Beverly! What's the offer? Hmmm? Okay. Yeah. I can't talk now. I'll have to think about it. Tomorrow? Yeah, by tomorrow."

Brad hung up the phone. Marco was already at his side. "I can't believe it," Brad said.

"You'll find another job." Marco slowly rocked Brad in a soothing sway. "It's not the end of the world."

"The job's still mine," Brad said.

Marco immediately felt relief. "Then, what's the matter?"

Brad leaned over and gave Marco a sweet kiss on his cheek. "Let's get dressed and go have a drink," he said. He got off the bed and headed for the bathroom.

Brad was pouring himself a second glass of wine. He looked sadly at Marco who was still nursing his first. "We'll work something out," he said. "Anyway, you'll be at school. You won't have as much time for me. This crap TV show will be buried in the ratings and off the air in no time. I'm really going to pressure my agent to sell my movie script. I'll be back in a month. Guaranteed."

Marco nodded. But he could not speak. If he opened his mouth, he knew the words would turn to tears, and that he would dissolve into racking sobs.

Brad reached across the table and placed his hand on Marco's. "Look," he said. Marco raised his eyes. "I've found the man I love, and nothing can ever separate us. I swear, I've never really loved anyone before now."

"What if *we* don't work out. That can happen with a forced separation like this." Marco sighed. "Will you be saying these same words to someone else in six months or a year, or however long it takes for your heart to forget me?"

Brad gripped Marco's hand tightly. "Stop," he begged. "The only reason I'm returning to the States is to earn enough money to get back to you. The job means nothing to me. Nothing means anything if you're not in my life. Believe that, please. I'm in love with you, Marco."

Marco's eyes were filled with tears. "I love you, too, Brad. From the moment I saw you at the cathedral, I think I knew we were destined to be together. I have a confession to make. I *was* stalking you."

Brad chuckled. Then the tears that had welled up in his own eyes slipped down his cheeks. "I always hoped that was true," he said. "I was so stupid not to recognize at first sight that you were the man of my dreams. It's my fault that so many moments were wasted. But not another second will pass that you aren't in my life."

Brad and Marco finished off their bottle of wine. "Let's stay in tonight," Marco suggested, as they were about to leave the café. "I'm not hungry."

Chapter Eight

"It's karmic debt, sweetie," Garreth suggested as Brad mixed a batch of green apple martinis. Brad had been lamenting his fate, working for Gill. "Your pink umbilical cord will be tethered to that man until the Second Coming. Or the rapture. It's the law of cause and effect."

"More Reverend Sally?" Brad quipped. He sampled his drink as he took a seat on the sofa in Garreth's professionally appointed media room.

"Where have you been?" Garreth squealed. "Nobody does Sally seminars anymore!"

Brad was taken aback. "What other consciousness altering events did I miss while bumming across the continent?"

"Sally could *never* be as enlightened as Reverend Harrison if she lived a thousand lifetimes." Garreth proceeded to fill Brad in on the latest wave of theology. "Reverend Harrison says that the root of all your problems is all those years of deceiving so-called straight guys into trusting that a blow job from a studley Y chromosome has nothing to do with being queer."

"You're confusing me with yourself," Brad reproached.

"Oh, don't pretend you've never conquered a weekend Little League dad!" Garreth criticized.

"It has never crossed my mind," Brad said.

"Typically, they're not getting much," Garreth explained his success. "Nine out ten of 'em are so desperate for a pair of lips around their dicks that you hit a home run on the spot. It's basically a matter of maintaining one's principles. Honesty being the best policy and all. Once you enlighten those pathetic dunderheads to the fact that oral copulation isn't really sex."

"Enlighten *me* about how that isn't sex," Brad said.

Garreth stuck his tongue into his martini glass. He made a happy face and smacked his lips. "As it's encouraged in the Russian army, nay, in many of the enlightened ancient cultures, fellatio takes on a single, multimillennia, global village kind of synergistic thing. Education, my dear. It opens their minds."

"And 501s, apparently." Brad looked askance at Garreth, hardly able to imagine what common denominator attracted them to friendship in the first place.

"Reverend Harrison says that until you stop cursing Gill and your crappy job on *Rehab,* you'll never fill in this pothole in the road of life." Garreth explained the cosmic process.

Brad was mortified. "You didn't discuss my private business with this Reverend Harrison!"

"Just your issues."

"God, I hate that expression," Brad whined. "What are 'issues' anyway?"

Garreth thought for a moment. "The usual. Boyfriend. Mother. Genital herpes."

"Genital . . . ! I don't have . . .!" Brad stammered. "And my mother's a saint!"

Garreth took another sip of his martini. "You should be on your knees to me. Although you're not a member of The Promised Land Fellowship, I convinced Reverend Harrison to place you on his special E-mail affirmation list. Thousands of disciples will soon be holding healing vigils for you."

"For my genitals," Brad lamented.

"You are what you eat, babe."

Brad took a long, self-medicating swallow of his martini. He'd decided that a few prayers couldn't hurt. Hell, they might help to get him over his current hurdle. His life had hit its high point in Spain, then plummeted once he returned to Hollywood and began working again for Gill Truitt.

Brad asked, "Does the good Reverend Harrison and his on-line prayer circle have any affirmations for winning the state lottery or getting my screenplay to Spielberg? Which is practically the same thing. I'll take rich over famous."

Between rent on his depressing one-room apartment, the cost of auto insurance, vodka, and all the sundry expenses of living in Los Angeles, Brad could hardly save enough out of each week's paycheck to afford his gym membership, let alone foresee a return to Marco anytime in the near future. Still, with the elimination of so many writing jobs in television, Brad felt blessed to have the gig on *Rehab*. A hit show on his resume was more valuable than the B.A. from UCLA for which he had worked so hard.

His current job title was *Needle Wrangler*. In reality television parlance, it meant that Brad was responsible for maintaining an accounting of all the wine and prescription pill bottles, syringes, and other paraphernalia that the set decorator and rehab mole concealed throughout the halfway house complex. "It's like one gigantic Easter egg hunt," Brad wrote of his tasks in an E-mail to Marco. But he assured his lover that such a role was for a limited time only. "Until the show gets the ax from the network or," he joked, "until my screenplay gets made."

As the martini made its way to Brad's brain, he began to feel that both achievements were next to impossible. For weeks prior to the debut of *Rehab*, the network put its marketing muscle into publicizing the program. The international edition of the program rested squarely on the success of the American version. Viewers of sporting events couldn't tune into the Dallas Cowboys or the Anaheim Mighty Ducks without hearing the *Rehab* rap theme music and seeing video footage from the upcoming series. It was becoming the must-see new reality show of the season. And when *Rehab* finally aired, it easily buried *My Wife and Kids*.

Although all of the major TV critics had unanimously dismissed the program, *Daily Variety* grudgingly reported that a stratospheric thirty-one point five million households had tuned in for the first segment. Overnight, the show was a hit.

Brad's workload was commensurate with the success of *Rehab*. His free time dwindled proportionately. The six-times-daily E-mails between him and Marco decreased. Neither could afford trans-Atlantic phone calls more than once a week, and soon those became twice a month. Brad was doing so well on the show that he was promoted to production assistant. And Marco was earning high marks for his university studies. Both men became immersed in their careers. Within six months, their time together in Seville became only a fond memory. When Marco forgot Brad's birthday, Brad resigned himself to concentrating on getting over his broken heart.

The success of *Rehab* in the States gave an immediate green light for the international editions of the series. Soon, junkies in England were becoming more famous than Graham Norton or Hyacinth Bucket. There was a Russian edition of the show and Italian and Spanish versions, as well. Then, in the middle of the first season, Gill began to panic. He realized that he had to quickly come up with contestants for the next series of shows in different countries.

America practically took care of itself. There were plenty of potential candidates even among Gill's own staff—or at least among the studio executives. However, Europe was another story. Gill had a vision for the types of players that he wanted to see on his programs, but his casting directors abroad were less successful in fulfilling his demands. Then Gill remembered Brad.

"I'll be frank." Gill had begun his meeting in the production office with Brad. "Some people around here think you're working out okay. Not that I believe everything I hear."

Brad sat silently, thinking about what a lard ass Gill was.

Gill continued. "Here's the deal," he said, easing forward, his elbows resting on his desk. For the next half hour Gill proposed that Brad head up the casting team in England. Brad countered that he would be more effective as part of the contingent going to Spain.

"You don't know the language," Gill insisted. "Besides, if it's running into that prince who dumped you that has you worried about being in London, you'll be too busy to see anyone outside dozens of

Her Majesty's twelve-step program meetings. Unless your ex has the DTs, there's nothing to worry about."

Brad said, "I spent a lot more time in Spain than England this past year. I just think I can be more useful there."

"Look, do you want a free trip to England or not?" Gill bellowed impatiently. "It's a simple question. And it'll be a fairly quick trip. You know what works here in the States. I just want the same thing over there."

"They're different cultures, Gill," Brad said.

Gill dismissed the idea with a wave of his hand. "Just gimme a coked-up Page Six girl," he said.

Chapter Nine

When Brad arrived at Heathrow, a casting assistant from the BBC met him. As nattily and professionally dressed as Basher had been the opposite, the man was as dull as the gray skies that hung over the city.

For the ensuing week, Brad did as Gill required. Brad visited countless hospitals, and he attended dozens of meetings of Alcoholics Anonymous, Overeaters Anonymous, Gambler's Anonymous, Narcotics Anonymous, and the ones he dreaded the most: Sex Addicts Anonymous. "They remind me of beggars in the streets of Calcutta," Brad complained in an E-mail to Gill. "Instead of begging for a handout, they're handing me scraps of paper with their phone numbers. The men *and* the women."

As quickly as possible, Brad compiled a list of potential contestants for the second British edition of *Rehab*. All were more than happy to slough off their privacy for an opportunity to be on the telly.

During an interval between meetings and observing recently arrested dope dealers behind the two-way mirror of Scotland Yard interrogation rooms, Brad visited Basher and Gusher for tea at Horseferry Hall. Mrs. Peel who, for the day at least was referred to as Lady Marmalade, served as Brad asked about Simon Dials, Martin Sackville, and the duke.

"Ole Simon stayed in Greece only until you were out of the coun-

try." Basher laughed at the deceit that had been used to break up with
Brad. "What did you do to that poor man?"

Brad shrugged. "He was nothing more than a diversion. What an
ego, if he thought I'd be ripped apart by his calling it quits."

"As for Sackie," Basher said, "he's virtually an amoeba, or some such
asexual thing, if you ask me. You're the only one I know who ever
thought he was worth a toss. And, oh yes, Nigel's actually got a boy
toy! Poor judgment, if you ask me. The boy's gorgeous, and all Nordic,
though he may be barely out of nappies. Nigel has to spend gads to
keep him in the manner to which he's quickly become accustomed."

"Both seem happy enough with the arrangement," Gusher added.
"I rather applaud ole Nige for getting what he wants. We have to pay
for everything else on this freakin' planet, why not sex trinkets, too?
Though Lord knows they aren't received anywhere." Snapping his fingers, recalling something, Gusher purred to Basher. "By the by, hon, I
need you to write a check to cover my account at Virgin Megastore."

Gusher turned to Brad. "And what about you, Mr. American Idol?
With all the sexy men in Europe, you didn't find that elusive Prince
Charming you were seeking? I swear, if you'd only given me a few more
weeks, you would probably be sleeping with a title right about now.
Poor baby. Did you at least have gads of good sex while cutting a swath
across Tuscany?"

Brad nodded. "As a matter of fact, I did find a couple of chaps."

"Only a couple?" Basher mocked.

"Let's say several. I had my fair share of sex."

"No Mr. Right, just Mr. Right Now?" Gusher asked.

Brad suddenly looked dejected.

"It wasn't meant to happen," Basher said, sympathetically. "You
can't force these things. You never know where or when the right
chap'll come along. At least you didn't just sit around California doing
nothing."

"As a matter of fact," Brad began, "I did fall in love. And I never
would have if I hadn't come to Europe, and if Simon hadn't gone off
to Greece, and if I hadn't been thrown out of Italy."

"Do tell!" Gusher implored. "Who? Where? What happened?"

As the afternoon wore on, Brad recounted his trysts with the seductive son of an Italian Mafia don, his afternoon with the sexy and mus-

cled Latin teacher in a cheap *pension* near the Trevi Fountain, and in Spain with Julio. Then he came to Marco. "I've even written a screenplay about him," Brad concluded. "But it doesn't have an ending."

Basher arched a pierced eyebrow. "You mean to tell me that you left this Marco dude for a *job?*" His tone was one of disbelief.

Gusher gave a quick tug on the bellpull to summon Lady Marmalade. Before she arrived Gusher asked Brad, "Have you spoken to Marco since you came to England?" Before Brad could reply, the serving woman opened the door. "I'm craving some bubbly and beluga," Gusher said to her. She departed, then he returned his attention to Brad. "Yes?"

"No," Brad responded. "We haven't been in touch in a couple of months. Things just cooled, I guess."

"You talk as if this Marco was just a bit of leftover kippers," Basher said impatiently. "At first you implied he was The One? What changed your mind?"

Brad thought for a long moment. "Nothing changed my mind. He *was* The One. Past tense. I'll never forget him."

"You seem to have made a pretty dashing start at forgetting him," Gusher mocked. "You don't write. You don't call. For Christ sake, you're on the same continent and you haven't made any plans to see him."

"I'm too busy working," Brad said, trying to make excuses.

"Working!" Basher roared.

"It's what some people do in between weekends and vacations," Brad said.

"For pissin' Christ sake," Gusher trumpeted, "if he was really The One, you wouldn't have ever left Spain in the first place."

Brad tried to explain the myriad reasons why he had to leave Marco—including lack of money and immigration laws. He was met with equal hostility from both Basher and Gusher. "If you want something badly enough, there is always a way to get it," Basher said.

"Just tell us one thing you loved about this Marco," Gusher said.

At that moment, Lady Marmalade entered the drawing room with a silver ice bucket, set on a rolling tea cart. There were three champagne flutes and an ice-chilled dish heaped with caviar surrounded by toast points. The snack was placed on the table in front of the sofa where the men were seated. The servant then poured from the bottle.

"One thing?" Brad responded to Gusher's question. "There are innumerable things about Marco that made me fall in love with him."

"I only asked for one," Gusher said in a harsh tone.

Brad picked up his champagne flute and took a long pull. He was thinking back to all the aspects of Marco that he had worshiped. "I really loved Marco," he said. "Good looks, great sense of humor, artistic—he's a painter and sculptor—intelligent, sensitive. Here's a picture." Brad took his wallet out of his back pocket and produced a glossy color print that had been cut down to fit in the slot where his driver's license was supposed to be. He passed the image to Gusher.

"This is the bloke you left for a freakin' paycheck?" Gusher was astonished. "You Americans have your priorities all fucked."

Basher took the picture out of Gusher's hands. He looked at Marco, then directed his gaze at Brad. "What kind of idiot are you? Even if he wasn't all the other crap you said about him, I wouldn't turf out this bloke!"

Gusher reached for the telephone. "This is none of our business, of course," he said to Brad, "but you're a fool if you don't call the guy."

"It's been too long!" Brad explained. "He hasn't even sent me an E-mail since September. It's over. I have to get on without him."

"Have *you* tried sending him an E-mail recently?" Gusher asked.

Brad shrugged.

"The pendulum swings both ways," Gusher added.

"I know all that," Brad countered.

"Obviously not," Basher sniffed.

Brad said, "Some things you just know. And I know that he's no longer interested."

Gusher asked, "How are you so sure?"

"I just am," Brad said.

"Well," Basher concluded, "I hope that your all-important, life-validating, big-money Hollywood career gives good head. I hear that 401Ks and dental insurance keep a person so warm and cozy on a cold California night."

Brad took a cab back to the Prince Edward Hotel where he was lodging. During the ride along Cromwell Road to Brompton, he thought about Marco and how close he really was to Spain. Brad also thought about what he'd said to Basher and Gusher as he ticked off the positive attributes of Marco. Then he thought about the verbal thrashing he'd received from the two Brits when they learned that he'd chosen some pathetic job over the man he loved. Brad was more depressed than he'd been during the days when he had waited breathlessly for contact from Marco.

He rode the elevator to the third floor of his hotel, and slowly walked down the hall to his room. Brad began to wonder if he had made the biggest mistake of his life by leaving Marco in the first place. But the truth was that he had been out of money, and he couldn't have found a job in Spain. Still, in the back of his mind he kept hearing Gusher's words, *There's always a way.*

By the time Brad reached his room, he'd come to a decision. He opened the door, slipped out of his leather jacket, and tossed it onto the bed. He then sat down at the writing desk on which was placed the room's telephone. He picked up the receiver and dialed directory assistance. "Iberia Airlines, please," he said into the phone. Thinking: *There's always a way.*

Chapter Ten

The ticket agent smiled so sweetly that Brad could practically read her mind. *Foreigner. One way ticket. No checked luggage. Passport with entry and departure stamps from several European countries within the past six months. Too cute to be straight.*

"Lovely, sir. This will only take a teensy momento." She swiftly pushed the F7 key on her computer. Moments later, a cadre of airport security personnel responded to her call and swarmed the ticket counter.

"He's all yours." Her honeyed voice changed to pumice. Brad stared at the men with bewilderment and irritation. The one who appeared to be the supervisor of the team asked Brad for permission to speak with him in private. It wasn't a question.

Brad glanced first at his wristwatch, then at the arrival-departure information monitor. "My flight is ready to board." He wasn't in the mood to act like a modern traveler who pretends to understand the need for and agrees with tight airport security procedures. For once he wasn't going to play the good sport. Until now, he had always been vaguely amused when his luggage was randomly opened for inspection. He had always tried to be gracious when a gloved security person gingerly rifled through his personal items. In the past he accepted the inconvenience of having to remove his belts and empty his pockets of keys and loose change. And when his shoes were taken away and tested for possible traces of evidence that might suggest that he may have recently trampled through a warehouse of potassium nitrate and sulfur, he sat like a good little boy, patiently waiting his turn to receive the bathroom pass.

Brad felt that security should know merely by looking at him that he was not carrying anything combustible or vaguely related to pyrotechnics. They should not for a moment consider that he would come to an airport armed with an arsenal of Kalashnikov assault rifles. "Just let me please buy my ticket," he groaned.

Brad looked around for the agent but she was no longer at her station. Burly agents in blue business suits, white shirts, and neckties surrounded Brad. He was discreetly escorted to a private lounge.

The interview lasted just long enough to ensure that Brad missed his flight. He was furious at having been the victim of profiling. "What was it about me that hoisted a red flag?" he asked. "Is my picture on the Ace of Spades in that deck of American government-issued poker cards? Did Al-Jazeera report that my charm and demeanor are atypical of an American tourist?" He held up his hands. "Never mind. I just want to know if I now have your permission to purchase a ticket on the next plane to Madrid?"

"If that is what you wish, sir," the head of the security said in an accent that was part English, and part Pakistani. He made no apology.

As Brad stood up from his seat in the chair opposite the security man's desk he mused, "In America, people get arrested for what's called a *DWB.*" He waited a beat. "*Driving While Black.* I now have an idea of what some ethnicities have to endure routinely." He picked up his shoulder bag, walked to the door, and turned the knob. The door was locked. He pulled at it again, then heard a buzzer from a switch that Brad supposed was under the security guy's desk. The lock was released. Brad left the room.

Hoping what had happened wasn't a harbinger of what was ahead, Brad headed back to the ticket counter. Once again standing in a long queue, he saw the same agent smiling and nodding her head at the patrons she served. As the line progressed, Brad was in no mood to be hassled. If this passive-aggressive employee caused him the slightest further delay, he was determined to make her day as miserable as she'd made his.

When he was finally once again standing before the agent with his passport, driver's license, and credit card in hand, she didn't give the slightest indication that she recalled their encounter an hour earlier. If she sensed his hostile vibrations, she played dumb. She rapidly swiped his credit card, examined his passport, and promptly issued his ticket. "It's a lovely day for flying," she chirped. "We know you have a choice of carriers and are truly pleased that you selected our airline. Have a nice day."

Up yours, Brad thought.

Outside the Madrid international airlines building, Brad hailed a cab. "*Universidad Complutense de Madrid. Por favor,*" he said to the driver.

As they rode through the city, his fears about how appropriate this mission was, and the possible negative response he might receive from Marco, made him almost sick with nervousness. *Turn back! Turn back!* he cried to himself several times. Finally, the car crawled up to the curb in front of the university's administration building. *You should have found a hotel and cleaned up first*, he thought as the driver said something in Spanish which Brad figured was probably the amount of the cab fare.

Since returning to the States, Brad had kept a few Euros in his shoulder bag along with his passport. Their presence had somehow made him feel less distance from Marco. He'd left England early this morning in such a hurry that the need to exchange his pounds sterling had slipped his mind. He handed the driver a fifty Euro note, silently praying that it would be enough to cover the charge. With a wide smile and an exuberant "*Gracias*" from the cabby, Brad decided the tip was more than sufficient.

It was late afternoon. As Brad stepped out of the cab, scenarios from a dozen "movies of the week" flashed through his mind: *A man returns unexpectedly from a business trip and finds his wife screwing his best friend. What couple didn't communicate enough to let the other know where they were or when they'd be home? And if they were that disconnected, why on earth wouldn't the guy think his wife would be pissed off to find that he showed up without warning to snatch away her private time?* Brad mentally adapted the story lines to this very moment, and suddenly he felt moronic for showing up unexpectedly at a huge university, expecting to find one particular student.

He began walking without any specific direction. Students milled about campus. He stopped one, and then another, and another, asking if they knew Marco de la Vega. It was soon evident that he was waging a losing battle. Most simply replied, *"No hablo Ingles."*

Exhausted, confused, and dejected, Brad sat down on a bench under the canopy of several date palms. He looked at the male students who passed by, simultaneously praying that Marco would be one of them, and hoping that Marco hadn't fallen in love with any of them. Brad sat for ten minutes before deciding to try another tack. He rose from the bench and approached a gathering of older adults. Faculty, he hoped. *"Pardone,"* Brad said, interrupting the group. *"Habla Ingles?"*

They turned. *"Si.* Yes," said a short, thick woman, her flaxen hair pulled up in a bun.

Brad beamed relief. "Where is the art department? I'm looking for a friend."

"There," the woman said, as she pointed to a building across campus. "Your lucky day. I am head of the art department. Whom do you wish to see?"

"Marco de la Vega," Brad said.

"Ah, my Marco!" the woman trilled. "Marco is my pet. My star." The woman looked at her wristwatch. "He's often sketching by the fountain after class. However, it's late in the day and the light . . ."

"Where is the fountain?" Brad begged.

"But I think he goes off with friends after his work," the woman said. She pointed her finger. "Go to the opposite side of that building. You can't miss it."

As Brad bolted away, he called back with *"Gracias, señora! Gracias!"* He sprinted across the campus, threading among the students strolling about.

Rounding the corner of the large brick building, he found himself in a tree-shaded park with an ancient water fountain in the center of a quad. Cliques of students were gathered together. Some sat alone, reading. One young man, not wearing a shirt, lay on his back, his T-shirt serving as a pillow, on the wide granite rim of the fountain, soaking up the last of the day's rays of sunshine. A few students sat at easels, but Brad could see that none of those who were sketching was Marco. He circled the fountain, but returned disappointed to his starting place.

Brad was more frightened than he ever remembered being. He realized that he was alone in a strange city, without much money and nowhere to stay for the night. He considered returning to the art department building, trying to locate the woman who had provided directions. *Worst case scenario, I'll have to return tomorrow and wait for him to show up for a class,* Brad thought.

Then it occurred to him that this was a Friday. There would not be classes over the weekend. He couldn't wait until Monday. If Gill tried to reach him and discovered that he had defected to Spain, even for a day, Brad's punishment could be termination from *Rehab*. But that no longer mattered to Brad, who could hear Basher's voice echoing in his head, taunting him about American work ethics and how a paycheck was a poor substitute for a lover.

Brad sat down on the fountain's edge and folded his arms across his chest. He shook his head at the absurdity of trying to reenter Marco's life. Marco was sexy, talented, passionate, and easygoing. By now he had to have been swept up by someone who appreciated all that he had to offer.

In the waning afternoon light, Brad noticed the shirtless body of the young man on the fountain. *It's getting cool, guy.* He directed his judgment at the young man. *And you're certainly no Adonis. Put your shirt on.* He watched the guy for a while, then began scanning the area for the remote possibility that Marco might still wander through the quad.

Looking off toward a distant cluster of trees, Brad could see two young women sitting on the ground with their legs crossed in semi-lotus positions, sketching on large white tablets. Coming out of his reverie he noticed that the shirtless guy at the fountain had disappeared. Brad took that as his own cue to leave. He stood up, collected his shoulder bag, and began to retrace the path that he'd taken from the curb where the cab had dropped him off. A shroud of dejection settled over him like an oppressive cloak.

Still on the lookout for his love, Brad spotted the shirtless guy again.

This time his T-shirt was slung over his left shoulder, and his jeans were hanging down below his hips. An elastic band of white underpants was showing as he seductively leaned against a doorway, under a sign that read *Hombres*. Brad spent a nanosecond wondering if the guy was hustling. He was just virile enough to cause the heads of female and male students alike to turn, if only for an ephemeral moment of desire.

Before the thought of sex dissipated from his brain, a squad of Shirts and Skins playing an impromptu game of soccer came from seemingly out of nowhere and distracted Brad. The Skins team was as breathtaking as athletic, college-age guys were wont to be. Their strong, agile bodies, their naturally pumped arms and chests, glistened with perspiration as they shouted and laughed and passed the ball back and forth. As they dashed past Brad, he momentarily forgot his mission and became lost in the commotion of the game. When he turned back toward the men's room, the shirtless guy was again gone.

"Story of my life," Brad said.

He looked around for the guy who had somehow become an important thread for Brad in the tapestry of the campus. To his surprise Brad caught sight of him. He was now walking with another man a short distance ahead. The man who had joined him was wearing a red T-shirt, a shirt that reminded Brad of one that Marco had worn on so many outings.

At that moment, Brad noticed that a third man had joined the first two. The new arrival seemed to engage the two men in a lively conversation. As Brad continued walking on, the group stood in animated discourse.

Marco used to do that, Brad said to himself as the man in the red T-shirt gesticulated with his arms to emphasize some point. Brad almost sniggered as he remembered that idiosyncrasy of his lover. *Marco used to stand like that too, one foot in the third position, as if he'd studied ballet*. Again, Brad inwardly smiled. He ambled on, keeping the guys in his peripheral vision. But as he got closer to the group, he heard a too-familiar voice. His eyes went to the one in the trio who was talking.

But even in shadow, from a distance, the man in the red T-shirt, whose wide shoulders tapered to a trim waist, made Brad feel a stab of lust. And as he neared, he once again sensed that the voice he heard was familiar. And the laugh. He knew that laugh!

Brad stopped, frozen in place. He involuntarily inhaled. His heart rate increased to a firing squad drum roll. He couldn't move. He didn't realize that he was staring at the man until the other man with his T-shirt dangling over his shoulder looked up and stared back at Brad. The other men in the group looked up, too.

Then a sketch pad and a box of pencils dropped from the grasp of the man in the red T-shirt.

"Marco?" Brad said quietly. Hot tears fell from his eyes. His knees buckled.

"*Qué?*" Marco mumbled in equal wonderment. "Brad?"

He left his friends and came forward toward Brad. The other two men shot each other baffled looks. As Marco drew closer to Brad, he, too, had begun to shed tears.

Face-to-face, they stood for a long moment looking at each other. They simultaneously reached out to embrace. For Brad, the campus disappeared, as did all time and place.

When they finally pried themselves apart, they stood looking deeply into each other's eyes.

Finally Marco found his voice. "Are you stalking me again?" he asked.

Bad Boy Dreams

Sean Wolfe

Very special thanks to my partner and the real Man of My Dreams, Gustavo Paredes-Wolfe, for all of the love and support you gave me in our thirteen years together. Gustavo passed away on September 4, 2003. Though no longer with me physically, Gustavo is still very much with me, and I feel his presence and spirit every day.

This book, and all others that will hopefully follow, is dedicated to you. Te extraño mucho, babies.

Gustavo, you are truly my inspiration for everything that is good and right and filled with love in this world.

Acknowledgments

Thanks to my guardian angel, Jane Nichols, for loving me and supporting me through good times and bad, and for never giving up on me. And thanks for encouraging me to continue my dream of writing . . . even when I write things I won't let you read.

Thanks to the guys in my writers group: Matt Kailey, Chris Kenry, Jerry Wheeler, Peter Clark, Lake Lopez and Drew Wilson. Your insights and suggestions are greatly appreciated and have helped make me a better writer.

And last, but certainly not least, thanks to my editor, John Scognamiglio, for believing in me and supporting my writing career. You're the man, John!

The Drive

Berkeley, California, is a hell of a long drive from Providence, Rhode Island. Precisely the reason I chose Berkeley as my university of preference. Grammy tried desperately to get me to consider Harvard or Yale . . . anything just a little closer to home. She was not, apparently, aware of my intense need to be as far from her as possible. I'd tried as hard as I could not to hurt her feelings any more than I needed to, and to let her feel I needed her and that she'd been the wonderful, loving grandmother that I'm sure she envisioned herself being. But the truth was that we were two very different people who had very different ideas of what life was supposed to be like and what our role in that life really was. We couldn't have seen things in more different ways, but somehow we'd developed a "safe place" for the two of us the last few years while I was in high school. But ignoring or denying who I am and what I feel was not something I wanted to get comfortable with on a long-term basis. I couldn't keep lying about what was happening inside me.

Berkeley, and its proximity to San Francisco, was the perfect choice. I wasn't there a full week before I had my first date. His name was Rodney. Rodney was the epitome of college jock. He was a forward on the university's basketball team and was a Connecticut state champion wrestler from his high school days. His straw-blond hair and deep

blue eyes made him a favorite of all the girls and half the guys on campus, and I was stunned when he asked me to go to dinner with him.

Rodney was a year ahead of me in school. He offered to show me
around campus and get me into all the "in" crowds. Dinner was at a
chic little Mexican restaurant popular among the university crowd,
and dessert was in his bed. He lived in a small studio apartment just
off campus.

Sex with Rodney was incredible. To this day I'm not sure if it was
because he was my first or if he was really that good. Doesn't matter.
Though he was great in bed and we had a lot in common, it just didn't
work out. It would have, if it had been up to Rodney. He was ready to
put a ring on my finger and move into a house in the burbs with a
white picket fence.

But I knew it wasn't right. It didn't feel right. I liked Rodney a lot,
and had a lot of fun with him. But I wasn't in love with him. I didn't
even love him. He was upset at first, and pulled away from me, but
after a couple of weeks we became best friends.

I was never at want for a date or a good lay. There were plenty to
choose from on campus, and choose I did. My freshman year I dated,
in addition to Rodney, Matt the math major, Chris the chemistry freak,
Peter the psych geek, Lee the litigator and Lake the literature king.

They were all good enough in bed, don't get me wrong. And they
were all great guys. We had a lot of fun together. But something just
wasn't right. That little something that just clicks when you're with
the right man just wasn't clicking with any of these guys. We're all still
friends and are civil when we run into one another on campus, but
we've all gone our separate ways.

Except Rodney and me. We're still best friends, and share an apartment now that I'm starting my sophomore year and he's starting his
junior year. I even spent last Christmas with his mom and stepdad and
four brothers and sisters. They love me, of course, and can't understand why Rodney and I don't just bite the bullet and make it official.
Rodney's a good sport about it all, but it makes me a little uncomfortable sometimes.

Especially when I meet a new guy and start getting involved. Take
last month, for instance. One of my professors, who is really hot, finally
asked me out. After dinner and a little dancing, we ended up back at

my place because Rodney had told me earlier that he was going to be spending the evening pulling an all-nighter study session with some friends.

"Are you sure your roommate isn't home?" Professor James asked. "Because I really wouldn't want to get caught with my pants down with one of my students."

"Nah. He's out studying. He won't be back until at least three or four."

"You sure?"

"Positive," I said and leaned in to kiss him. His tongue still tasted like the martini he'd had earlier at the bar, and I sucked on it and traced my tongue across his lips.

That was all it took, really. It almost always is. Professor James leaned me against the wall and tore my clothes off. He shucked his own clothes while he licked his way down my naked and shivering torso. When he reached my hard cock, he knelt on the floor and took it in his mouth. He was a great cocksucker and swallowed the entire length in one slick swallow.

I was just about to shoot when the front door swung open. We hadn't bothered to lock the door or go into the bedroom because we thought we'd be alone. So when Rodney walked in and switched on the light, he saw the whole thing. Professor James, naked as the day he was born, kneeling in front of me and swallowing my hard cock.

"Oops, sorry," Rodney said as he laid his keys on the table and walked over to kiss me on the lips.

Professor James had frozen mid-swallow at the first sound of the door opening, and was still paralyzed in that position, with my cock halfway down his throat. His eyes were unblinkingly wide and his cheeks puffed out with the effort of not breathing.

"Relax," Rodney said as he walked behind Professor James and slapped his naked ass. "It's okay, I won't tell anyone." He walked into our shared room and shut the door.

"I thought you said . . ." Professor James said as he stuffed his hard cock into his jeans and pulled them up his legs.

"Yeah, I thought so, too," I groaned as I realized we were finished and I would not be spraying my load all over Professor James's beautifully sculpted smooth chest.

"That wasn't cool, Vason. Not cool at all."

"I swear I didn't know he was coming home."

"If I get into trouble for this . . ."

"You won't get into trouble for this, I promise. He won't say anything. I won't say anything."

He was hopping out the door as he struggled to get his shoes on and tied before I had a chance to say anything else. I heard his feet hit the hardwood stairs running from all the way across the room.

"Does this mean there won't be a second date?" I laughed as I closed the door and locked it.

"Lucy," I said loudly as I walked toward the bedroom, "you got some splainin' to do."

I reached for the light, but Rodney stopped me.

"Don't turn on the lights," he said softly.

"Why not?"

"I've got something for you. Come here."

I walked over and climbed into the bed next to Rodney. He was naked, and when I reached down between his legs, his hard cock pounded hotly in my hands.

"You shouldn't have done that, Rod," I said as I leaned down to kiss his cock.

"He wasn't right for you."

"Why not?" I asked, letting his cock head slip from my lips.

"He just wasn't."

"And you are, I suppose?"

He flipped me over onto my back and lay on top of me. "Yes," he said quietly as he ground his pelvis against mine.

My legs parted slightly and he slipped his cock between my legs. I closed them around his hardness and squeezed.

Rodney moaned loudly and raised my legs. "Yes," he said again as he slid inside me.

Things have gotten increasingly better between Rodney and me over the last month. Maybe I should just settle down with him. Maybe he is the one, after all. Something keeps holding me back, but I don't know what. It seems almost right with Rodney, but not just exactly. Is it just me? Am I self-prophesizing and preventing it from feeling exactly good because I'm afraid? I'm probably being foolish. Everyone says we are the perfect couple, and maybe we are. Maybe I should just accept . . .

No. That is my Grammy's influence. I cannot listen to that. Settling for something less than I know I deserve, that I need. I laugh as I tell myself I'm having Bad Boy Thoughts. Grammy wouldn't appreciate the way I twisted her words, but I think it's funny. I left Grammy's home, and her influence, far behind me on the East Coast. I am not about to go back and start listening to it all over again.

As I mull my predicament over, the phone rings.

"Hello?"

"Erique? Is that you, Erique?"

"Yes, this is Erique. Who's this?"

"It's your Auntie Hildred."

My heart stops for just a second. A call from my Grammy's twin sister couldn't mean anything good. "Auntie Hildred? Is everything all right?"

"No. No, it's not, Erique. I'm afraid I have a giant favor to ask of you."

"What is it, Auntie?"

"You must come home, Erique. Please."

"Is Grammy okay?"

"No, sweetie, she isn't. I'm afraid she's taking a turn for the worse, and I simply don't know what to do with her anymore. I need help with her."

"What do you mean she's taking a turn for the worse?"

"She's losing her mind, Erique. Dementia."

I thought about reminding Auntie that Grammy had lost her mind years ago, but bit my tongue. "Is she in the hospital?"

"No, no. She refuses to go anywhere. She just sits all day in front of the TV and watches all those nasty talk shows. She won't eat, she won't bathe, she won't get dressed. All day, just sitting in front of the boob tube."

"Auntie, I really don't know what I could do if I were there."

"Oh, but you must come. I can't do this myself. She doesn't talk much, but when she does, she calls out your name. Please, Erique."

"But, Auntie . . ."

"I swear, Erique, I can't do it myself. If I have to, I'll put her into a home."

"A home? Auntie, you can't put Grammy into a seniors' home. She'd shrivel up and die there."

"She's shriveling up and dying anyway. We're eighty-three years old, Erique. Neither of us are spring chickens anymore. I'm too old to have to take care of Mildred as well as myself. I don't want to do it. I can't do it."

"Okay, Auntie. I'll come home. I'll do it."

"Oh, thank you, Erique. Thank you. I just couldn't do this without you."

"It'll take me a few days. I'm going to drive out. I should be able to be there sometime next week."

"Very good. I'll let Mildred know. She'll be so pleased."

Yeah, sure she will. "Okay, Auntie. I have to go now. I have a couple of things I have to wrap up here before I can leave. I'll see you in a few days."

Later that night Rodney called. He'd been visiting his mom and stepdad down in L.A.

"Hey, sweetie. How you holding up without me?" he asked.

"I hardly noticed you were gone."

"Bastard."

"Hey, I have something to tell you," I said before I could get distracted.

"This doesn't sound good."

"I have to go back home for a while."

"Home?"

"Rhode Island. My Grammy is sick and I have to go back and help out a little."

"Is she going to be all right?"

"I don't know. Won't know till I get there. But my Auntie Hildred says she's not holding up real well."

"I'm sorry to hear that, babe. Is there anything I can do?"

"No. Just hold the fort down without me. I'll probably be gone a couple of weeks. I'm gonna be bored as hell driving all the way across the country by myself."

"I'd offer to go with you, but I've got finals next week and I can't take any more time off work."

"Yeah, I know. That's okay, I'll be all right."

"Hey, I've got a great idea. My dad was just saying last week how badly he'd like to visit his sister in Hartford. He hasn't seen her in years. He has an irrational fear of flying, though, and refuses to get on a plane. And the thought of sitting on a Greyhound bus full of strangers is not very appealing to him, either."

"No."

"But you haven't even heard me out yet."

"No."

"I know it's a lot to ask, but come on, Erique, I don't know what else to do. Dad won't fly out there, and this is the perfect solution. His entire side of the family is gonna be out there for a family reunion, and Dad will be the only one not there if he doesn't go. It's been almost ten years since he's been home."

"But I've never even met him, Rodney. You know how awkward I am around new people. Especially straight in-laws."

I held my breath for a moment, the phone pressed against my ear so hard it hurt a little and my knuckles turned white.

"You are not awkward around new people, baby. You're a social butterfly, and you know it. And my family loves you, you know that, too. It's true you've never met my dad, but he knows all about you and us, and he's fine with it. He just wants a ride home so he can be there for the family reunion, and since you're driving out in that direction anyway, it wouldn't be that much more trouble for you to drive down to L.A. and pick him up. Hartford is only an hour and a half from Providence. It wouldn't be out of your way at all."

"It's *way* out of my way," I sulked, already feeling the resolve settling in. "I wasn't planning on taking the southern route via L.A. to pick up a stray."

"I'll make it worth your while when you get back," Rodney whispered, "I promise."

"But . . ."

"Hold on, Mom is right here and wants to say hi."

"No! Rodney, wait, I'll do it. Just don't put your mom on the phone. You know I can't . . ."

"Hello, Erique, this is Mrs. Peterson," came the woman's sweet voice over the receiver. As if she needed an introduction.

"Oh, Erique, you just *have* to take George with you. He'll be great company, and he really hasn't seen his family in almost ten years."

"Yes, so I hear."

"He won't fly and a bus is just so difficult and it takes forever with all those stops. That bitch he calls his second wife is bleeding him dry in this divorce. It's not like I didn't warn him before he ever married her. But I certainly wouldn't wish this upon him. He doesn't deserve this much unhappiness. No one does. He needs some distraction. You will take him with you, won't you? I'll call him myself and tell him you'll pick him up tomorrow. Is that okay with you?"

It was classic Rodney manipulation, and I cursed him as I spoke for nearly fifteen minutes with my mother-in-law. By the end of the conversation, I had assured her I would be taking her ex-husband to Hartford for the family reunion. She was most appreciative. She put Rodney back on the phone.

"Hi, baby."

"That is *so* not fair. You know I can't say no to your mother."

"Yes, I do. So, I'll tell Dad you'll pick him up tomorrow?"

"I'll call him myself. His number's in the book, right?"

"Yeah, but I should call him first and make sure he really wants to do this. I mean, this is really my idea and it was kinda sudden. I'm sure he'll be up for it, but I better check in with him first."

"Okay, you call him and check in, and I'll call him and get directions and set up a time to meet in about half an hour."

"Good. I miss you."

"Me, too," I said, and hung up the phone. "Damn it!"

I really didn't want to pick up Rodney's father and have him accompany me all the way to the East Coast. But that wasn't the real reason I was so upset. Rodney and I had been somewhat monogamous the last few weeks, and I'd really been looking forward to traveling cross-country by myself and getting into a little trouble with the local boys in maybe Phoenix, and possibly Denver and most definitely Chicago.

Now all of that was thrown aside all in the name of being a Good Samaritan.

Damn it all to hell.

I waited half an hour, then called. Rodney's dad picked up on the second ring.

"Hello, Mr. Howard. This is Erique Vason, Rodney's . . . friend. Did Rodney get a chance to call you? He did. Good. No, no, it's not out of the way at all. I'll be happy to have the company. Yes, just give me the address and some directions. I should be there around eight tomorrow morning if that's all right with you. Good."

I wrote down the directions and address, and hung up the phone.

The drive along the Pacific Coast Highway the next morning was beautiful, and the closer I got to Los Angeles, the less I worried about Rodney's dad and the trip to Hartford together. There was certainly something to be said for the calming effect of the ocean.

George Howard was easy to spot as I pulled up to the apartment complex. Of course, I'd seen several pictures of him over the last two years, but even if I hadn't, I'd have been able to pick him out in a crowd. He bore a striking resemblance to Rodney, or more accurately, Rodney bore one to him. The short, blond, wavy hair, crystal blue eyes with lashes that went on for days, irresistible dimples, strong jawbone and clefted chin were dead giveaways.

Besides that, he was the only person sitting on the curb in front of the apartment complex, with a suitcase at his side.

He looked up and smiled when he saw me pull up to the curb.

"Erique?"

"Yes. Hi, Mr. Howard. It's nice to meet you," I said as I got out of the car and walked around to open the trunk. His handshake was strong and firm, and sent a chill up my spine.

In no time at all, we were on the road. I was amazed at how much George and I had in common and how quickly the time passed. Rodney had been right. George wasn't a problem at all. In fact, I couldn't imagine having to make this long trip without his company.

"Your grandmother must be a very special lady. It's not every grandson that would drive all the way across the country to help take care of his sick grandmother. Things like that are usually left to the kids' parents."

"Trust me," I said as I lowered the top on my Mustang convertible and shook my head in the warm wind, "I would love to be able to leave that to my mom. But she died when I was a kid. She was Grammy's only child, and when Mom died, Grammy stepped up to bat and raised me all alone. I'm sure it couldn't have been easy for her."

"Sounds like your whole family is filled with very special people."

"My mother was special. There's no doubt about that. Of all the things I remember of my mother, it's her voice I recall the strongest and with the sweetest memories. She used to rub her belly while she was pregnant with me and speak soothingly and at great lengths to me even way before I was born. I know it's silly to say out loud, but I recall vividly hearing the sound of her voice traveling through her tummy and into my head."

"That's amazing," George said as he unbuttoned the top two buttons of his shirt and leaned back in the seat. "I don't know anyone who can say they remember their mother speaking to them inside the womb."

"Yeah, I know. It is pretty remarkable. But she talked to me like I was right there in front of her and could understand every word she said. It made a really lasting impression on me, and I'm not kidding at all when I say I remember it."

"Mmm," George said as he closed his eyes. The smile on his face let me know he was enjoying the warm breeze on his face.

I kept my eyes on the road and let my mind wander a little. Remembering my mother was always a mixed blessing. I loved remembering her smell and her touch, and more vividly her voice.

"You're gonna be wonderful," she said over and over. "The sky is the limit with you, my beautiful son. Don't listen to all the negative shit you're gonna hear. I'm telling you it just isn't true. You dream big, okay? Dream big like your momma does, and don't let anyone tell you that you can't make those dreams happen. You can. I didn't make mine happen, because I let all the nasty things that people say get me down. But you're

gonna be different. You're gonna make your dreams come true, right? And I'm gonna help make that happen."

I looked at George and my heart fluttered. The first trace of a stubble was growing on his chin and the tiny crow's feet around his eyes made my cock stir inside my jeans.

"After I was born my mother would spend hours rubbing my head. She'd lean in really close to me and whisper in my ear. *'You can grow up to be president if you want. And if you don't want to, that's okay, too. You can be an astronaut or a preacher or a postman. The world is yours, Kiko. I want you to know that I support you in whatever you decide to become. You'll be the best, I just know you will. I can see it in your eyes.'*

"I adored my mother. I can recall that very distinctly. I used to giggle and kick my feet and flail my hands around just to watch her laugh. She lit up every room she was in just by smiling and dancing around."

"And what about your dad?"

"I didn't know him. He wasn't around. Mom never really said what happened to him. She was kinda evasive when I tried to bring him up in conversation. Never said whether he just left, or died, or what. Just that he wasn't there.

"She would tell me on many occasions how proud my dad would be of me. How he wished he could see me and how sorry he was that he couldn't. She used to tell me that she could tell I was going to look just like my dad—that I had his same nose and strong jawline, even as a young child."

"He must have been a fine-looking man, then," George said offhandedly. He looked over and winked at me, then turned to face forward again and bask in the sun.

I smiled and tried to keep my hands on the steering wheel.

"I'd kick my feet some more and gurgle a little every now and then just to let her know I was paying attention."

"So you were a little manipulative back then?"

"Hell, no, I wasn't a *little* manipulative. I was a lot manipulative. I knew it and my mother knew it. And neither of us would have done a thing to change any of it. My world revolved around my mother, as a small child's world tends to do. And hers revolved around me, as mothers' worlds tend to do. We lived with my grandmother Mildred. My mother worked part time at a convenience store near our home, and while she was at work my grandmother alternated her time between ignoring me and trying to conspire to turn me against my mother."

"Surely she wasn't really conspiring against your mother. That was her only daughter, after all."

"Trust me, she was trying to turn me against my mother. *'You're getting to be a big boy, now,'* Grammy whispered to me one day not long after my third birthday. *'You're starting to talk now, and that means you can understand what I'm saying.'*

"I'd been speaking for over a year by then, but had made a concerted effort to keep my speaking abilities a secret from Grammy. She, apparently, was none the wiser."

"I'm sure she knew you could speak a little by then. Don't you think?"

"Maybe. But I doubt it. She at least knew I could understand what she was saying, though. *'So listen carefully to what I tell you, okay,'* she whispered as she tucked the bib under my chin and set a plate of peas and carrots in front of me. Then she'd look around and make sure my mother wasn't within earshot, even though she knew full well my mother was at work. *'Don't you listen to all that nonsense your mother tells you about dreaming big. She's always had her head in the clouds, and look where it got her. Knocked up and alone to raise a kid at the age of twenty-two. That's no kind of life for a young woman. And it's no kind of life for a little boy, either. You listen to Grammy, okay? Keep your feet firmly planted right here on earth and study hard and get a good job. Be responsible. Take care of your family. Those are the things that are important. Do you hear me, Erique? Those are the things that are important.'"*

"Hmm. I'm guessing that's not a consistent message with what your mother was teaching you," George said.

"You're guessing correctly." I looked over at George and couldn't help but notice the curly hairs poking out of the top of his shirt. Some were brown and some were gray. I took a deep swallow, and ventured a look down to his crotch. I could see the distinct outline of his cock pressing against his shorts, and swallowed hard again. I stared straight ahead at the road ahead of me. It was hot outside, and squiggly waves rose from the road and up to the sky.

*   *   *

Even at that young age, I had a lofty mind. And a flare for the dramatics, it seems. With a grandiose sweep of my arm, I flung the plate of peas and carrots into Grammy's lap, and yelped with joy as she screamed and stood from the table, flicking the vegetables off her dress as if they were poisonous insects attacking her.

"You are a very, very bad boy," Grammy said as she picked up the plate from the floor and placed it in the sink, "and you will sit there by yourself until your mother gets home. I've had it with you today." She strutted around the small kitchen, picking up stray peas and carrots from under the table, behind the china cabinet and under the counters. "It's all your mother's fault, filling your head with all sorts of crazy ideas. Telling you to dream for the stars and such nonsense. My God, she couldn't even give you a real name. What kind of shenanigans is naming a kid Erique? Everyone knows you spell Eric E-R-I-C. And giving you that bum's last name. What's wrong with Moore? Why couldn't she be happy giving you our last name? Erique Vason. Like just because you have some fancy sounding French name you're going to grow up to be something special. Well, you're not, okay. Just remember what Grammy tells you. You're not going to be anything special. You're going to grow up and be a responsible citizen who takes care of his family. You sit there and think about that all alone until your mother gets home." And with that she stomped out of the kitchen and up the stairs to change her clothes.

I didn't mind sitting there all alone waiting for my mother to get home. I preferred it, in fact, to Grammy's company. When I heard Mother's footsteps on the front porch steps, I puckered my lips and blinked my eyes a few times, just enough to produce a couple of tears.

"Hi, sweetie," my mother said as she bounded through the kitchen door. She stopped in her tracks when she noticed the sad look on my face and the tears rolling down my sweet innocent face. "Honey, what's the matter?"

I choked back a sob and pushed the single pea and the single carrot I'd hidden from Grammy forward on the kitchen table.

"Oh, no. Not again, sweetie?"

I nodded my head and reached out with both of my hands for my mother's embrace.

Mother laughed and hugged me tightly. "She knows you hate peas and carrots. When will she ever learn? Does she know you can talk yet?"

I shook my head no.

"Was she filling your head with all those crazy ideas of growing up and being a responsible family man again?"

I nodded.

"Well, don't you listen to a word she says, okay?"

"I won't, Mommy."

"Good boy. You always remember that you're Mommy's little boy, and you listen to what Mommy tells you. Right?"

"Right."

"And what does Mommy tell you?"

"To dream big!" I screamed and threw my hands up in the air.

"That's right. Grammy never had any dreams and so she doesn't know what they're like and how important they are. So it's up to you to dream big and to share those dreams with me and Grammy. Even if Grammy doesn't think she wants to know about them. Because if we don't share our dreams with others, we can never make them come true. Do you understand?

"Yes."

"Good. Now, what's your name?"

"Erique Vason," I yelled with a French accent loud enough for Grammy to hear all the way upstairs.

"And what are you going to do?"

"Share my dreams with you and Grammy!"

"Yes, sir, that's my baby. No, sir, don't mean maybe," my mother sang as she swung me around the kitchen by my arms and laughed with me until we both had tears in our eyes and our tummies hurt.

I looked over at George again, and my breath caught short in my throat. He was absolutely beautiful, lying there asleep in the rich glow of the sun. He snored softly and I thought I could smell the sweet breath of his exhalation. I stole another glance down at his crotch. The plump outline was fuller and larger than it had been earlier. I quickly turned my eyes back to the road, and concentrated on driving.

*   *   *

When we finished laughing my mother cooked me pancakes and eggs and bacon, which were my favorite foods anytime of the day. Grammy, of course, frowned on eating breakfast food for dinner, which made it all the sweeter. Then Mother carried me upstairs and tucked me into bed.

"Mommy?"

"Yes, my sugar bear."

"Where's my daddy?"

I noticed that her body stiffened, but only for a short moment. She tucked the blanket tighter under my chin. "He's in heaven."

"Grammy says he's a bum."

Mother bit her lower lip, then smiled. "Grammy's just a little cranky because she's going through the change of life and doesn't have anything good to say about anybody."

I giggled and covered my mouth with my hand so Grammy couldn't hear.

"But your father is not a bum, Erique. Your father is a very good man and he loves you very much. Don't listen to Grammy. She hasn't been happy in over twenty years and she doesn't want anybody else to be, either. But don't pay any attention to her, okay? You be happy, all right?"

I nodded.

"You listen only to Mommy, and believe me when I tell you that your father loves you very much. He is not a bum. He is a great man. And remember that Mommy loves you very much, too, okay?"

"I will, Mommy."

"Good night, sweet pea," she said as she turned off my bedroom light and closed the door.

George was stirring awake now, and I tried very hard not to notice as he reached into his shorts, grabbed his cock and balls and rearranged them. I was kinda sad to see them go, but was also a little glad not to have the distraction as I drove.

I heard her heavy footsteps stomp into Grammy's room and the bedroom door slam shut. Though there'd been fights in the past, this one was the grandmaster of them all. Mother screamed at Grammy to keep her

*goddammed freakish ideas to herself and to stop interfering with her
raising her own kid. Grammy yelled just as loudly that somebody had to
keep the boy's head on straight because his mother sure as hell wasn't
doing it . . . and by the way, don't she ever use the Lord's name in vain in
Grammy's house again, or she'd find herself out on the streets begging
for money and shelter. It went back and forth like that for several minutes.*

*Then I heard it. The slap. I don't know who slapped whom, because
both women were completely silent right after it happened. Then
Grammy's bedroom door flung open, and I heard footsteps running down
the stairs. A moment later I heard the car rev to life outside in the driveway.*

*I cursed Grammy under my breath and hoped she hadn't hurt Mommy
too much. And then I cried myself to sleep.*

"Sorry I dozed off for a little there," George said as he sat up
straighter in the seat next to me. "That sun and the wind on my face
felt a little too good, I guess."

"Don't worry about it," I said as I looked over at him and smiled.
Any trace of the hard-on he'd had earlier was now completely gone.
"We're just about to pull into a little town ahead. I thought we'd stop
and get some gas and a little snack."

"Sounds great. I'm parched."

The town really was nothing more than a gas and refreshment stop,
so we were in and out in no time at all. George resumed the driving.

"From what I've heard, you had a really great relationship with your
mom," George said as he steered the car back onto the highway.

"Yeah. It was short, but really close while it lasted."

George looked at me more intently and rested a hand on my shoulder as he steered with the other. "Your father really missed out on a
very special moment in your life, Erique. Do you ever wonder who he
is or what he's like?"

I concentrated on not allowing the chill I felt when his hand rested
on my shoulder to cause my own cock to stir. "Yeah, I used to. I asked
my mom about him a couple of times. She always told me he was in
heaven."

"Did you believe her?"

"I don't know, really. Sometimes I did, I suppose. But my Grammy always told me he was a bum and had no respect for his family. So I was a little confused."

"No doubt. That's a lot for a little boy to think about."

I was sitting upwind from George now, and could smell the sweet musky scent of his cologne. There was no way I could stop my cock from growing now, and so I dropped my hand to my crotch and re-arranged it so it wasn't so obvious.

"Yeah," I managed to croak.

"So, it's obvious why you had such a great relationship with your mom. But it's not real clear how you got so close to your grandmother. Doesn't sound like the most loving person in the world."

"Who said we are close?" I asked as I shrugged his hand from my shoulder and stiffened in the passenger seat.

"I'm sorry. I didn't mean to upset you. It's just that you're driving all the way across the country to help take care of her while she's sick. I just assumed you were close."

"No, not really. I guess I just feel I owe it to her."

"You never got close, even after your mother died?"

"No. I'm not really comfortable talking about this anymore," I said as I turned in my seat and faced forward, staring straight at the road ahead of me.

As much as I wanted to be open and frank with George, there were some things I was still not ready to talk about. My relationship with Grammy and the circumstances under which the necessity of that re-lationship developed was one of them. I closed my eyes and turned my ahead away from George so that I was looking out the passenger's side at the open prairie surrounding us. Before long I drifted off into a light sleep.

"Erique, wake up."

I heard the voice from far away, as if it were coming from a tunnel, but it was the persistent shaking of my body that I remember the most, and that woke me up. Someone was squeezing my arm tightly and shaking me vigorously. I blinked my eyes open and stared up at Grammy.

"Honey, there's been a terrible accident."

I knew at least that much must be true. Grammy would never call me "Honey" if something weren't horribly, horribly wrong.

"Get up and get dressed, Erique. We must get to the hospital right away."

"Where's Mommy?" I asked as I tried not to cry.

"She's at the hospital, dear, and we have to go see her. So hurry up and get dressed."

"Honey" and "Dear" all in the same evening. This was much worse than I'd imagined, and much, much more than I could handle without advanced warning.

"I want to see my mommy," I cried, this time unsuccessful in stopping the tears.

"Well, that's where we're going. If you ever get out of bed and start getting dressed, that is."

I just lay there in bed, pulling the covers up around my chin and crying.

"Oh, I really do not have time for this," Grammy said, and yanked the blanket from under my chin. "You get out of bed and get dressed right this instant, young man. I will be back in five minutes and I want you dressed and with your coat on. Do you understand me?"

I nodded numbly and watched her leave my room. I cried as I pulled a clean pair of underwear and socks from my drawer and put them on. Then I wiped the tears away as I pulled on my tiny jeans and tied my shoes. By the time I pulled my sweater over my head, I was calm and collected. If Mommy was hurt, I needed to pull myself together and be there for her.

Grammy returned exactly five minutes later. She looked me over once or twice, and shook her head. I don't think she could believe her eyes, could believe that I was able to get dressed and tie my shoes all by myself. Then she grabbed my arm and dragged me down the stairs with her and stuffed me into the old car that hadn't been driven since Grampy died almost ten years ago.

It smelled old inside the car. It was cold and a little damp. Underneath the smell of dust and oil, I detected a trace of cologne. It was musky and sweet. Grammy took a deep breath and leaned her forehead onto the steering wheel. I heard her whispering "Carl, Carl, Carl" as she pumped

the gas pedal a few times before turning the key. The old car started immediately, and rattled the yellow-faded picture of Grammy and Grampy
that was mounted on the dashboard right above the glove compartment.
When Grammy's head pulled away from the steering wheel, there were
tears running down her cheeks.

She shoved the lever into reverse and pulled out of the garage and
down the driveway. I'd never known that Grammy could drive, but a few
seconds later we were speeding down the deserted street and heading toward the hospital.

When we got to the hospital, Grammy thrust me into the arms of the
attending nurse, and rushed toward a hallway filled with rooms. I tried
to wrestle free from the heavyset nurse, but it was useless. I wasn't even
four years old yet, and this stodgy nurse seemed to have years of experience wrestling kids probably much bigger than me. I finally gave in and
sat calmly in the nurse's ample lap.

It seemed like an eternity, but was actually only a few minutes before
Grammy came walking back toward us. I knew instantly that the news
wasn't good. We'd gotten there too late. Grammy's shoulders were
slumped and she looked at her feet as she shuffled toward me. The
nurse's grip tightened on my shoulders.

"Grammy?" I asked, breaking free from the nurse and rushing toward
my grandmother, who looked at least fifty years older than she had when
we'd walked into the hospital.

Grammy fell to her knees in the middle of the hallway and opened her
arms to me. Tears streamed down her face and her entire upper body
heaved as she cried.

I ran into her arms and fell into her lap. I thought I would cry, too, but
found that I could not. Instead, I wrapped my arms as far around
Grammy's soft bosom as I could. Then I stroked her face and told her
everything would be okay. She hugged me tightly and cried until she
slumped against the corridor wall, and then she pulled me closer to her
and covered my face with salty kisses.

I slept for a little over an hour. When I woke, George and I picked
up right where we'd left off. We talked a lot about our relationships.
George had divorced Rodney's mother ten years ago. He remarried his

second wife, Patricia, a year later. They were very happy for a few years, and then things began to turn ugly. Patricia moved out and filed for divorce a little over a year ago. They were still fighting things out in court, and she was trying to take him for everything he had.

I told him I was sorry. George was such a sweet man, and he seemed to have a really good heart. How could anyone mistreat a man such as George? Not to mention the fact that he was quite possibly the most beautiful and virile man I'd ever met.

He asked how Rodney and I met and how we'd gotten together. I was a little taken aback by his direct questions. Answering such intimate questions was not something I was comfortable with. Especially with my boyfriend's father. But after a while it got easier.

"We met on the basketball court, actually," I told him as I took over the driving for a few hours.

"That figures. Almost anything significant in Rodney's life begins or ends on the basketball courts."

"After the game Rodney asked if I was new to Berkeley and I said yes. He offered to take me to dinner and show me around campus, and I took him up on the offer. We became friends very fast."

"And how did you decide to become boyfriends?"

I swallowed hard and took a deep breath. I couldn't help but notice the silky tufts of hair that sprouted above the collar of his T-shirt. They matched the soft brown hairs on his muscular arms. I could see that his chest was powerfully built under the sheer fabric of the T-shirt, and I had to swallow again before I continued.

"We never really made a conscious decision to become boyfriends," I said as I forced myself to look away from him and stare at the road ahead. "We decided to move in together because it was cheaper for us to share rent and we got along well. The rest just kinda happened from there."

"So you're not boyfriends, then?"

I cracked the window a couple of inches and took another deep breath. "No," I said before I could stop myself. "No, we're not boyfriends."

"I'm sorry. I didn't mean to assume anything. I just always thought, from the way Rodney speaks about you, that you were . . . involved."

"Oh, I suppose we're involved. But definitely not boyfriends."

I didn't know why I was saying these things. I mean, Rodney and I had never officially said we *were* a couple, but we also had never officially said we were not a couple. We certainly were comfortable with where we were heading. At least I thought we had been, until then. Now I was lying to Rodney's father and I didn't know why.

"But do you love him?" George asked, without taking his eyes off the road ahead of him.

I looked over at him and stared at his face for a couple of seconds. His strong jawline tensed and relaxed, and his eyes did this cute little twitching thing every few seconds. He didn't say anything for a while and didn't look back at me. I began to fidget with my hands on the wheel.

"Are you in love with him?"

"No, sir. I'm not in love with him." I spit it out before having time to think about what I was saying. "But I like him a lot. I like him a whole lot. I'm just not in love with him."

"Why not?"

I laughed. "You sure don't hold anything back, do you?"

"Nah. Just gets in the way of what you're really trying to find out."

I looked at his face again, and my heart pinched in my chest. I was looking at Rodney twenty-five years from now. And my heart was fluttering like it never had with any of the guys I'd been with, including Rodney.

"I don't know, really," I answered. "I guess I've always, since I was a little kid, dreamed of my ideal man."

"And Rodney isn't him?"

"I want someone who can teach me something I don't already know. Someone who can take me to places I've never been. Someone with some life experience so they can show me things I haven't seen already. I don't know, exactly."

"It sounds like you do know. It sounds like you know very much."

"I guess, but I can't really put my finger on why Rodney can't do all those things for me. It almost feels right with him. But not quite. You know what I mean?"

"Yes, I think I do, son."

We drove for a couple of hours in almost complete silence. As we approached Salt Lake City George began to nod off. I was getting tired as well, and suggested we find a hotel and call it a night.

Finding a hotel was easier said than done. There was a large convention in town, and rooms were scarce. After three tries we finally found a hotel with a vacancy. One vacancy. One room. One bed.

The room did have a hydrojet in the tub, though, and I decided to take advantage of our good fortune. George threw himself on the bed and began channel surfing. The long drive from San Francisco to L.A. and then on to Salt Lake City had worn me out more than I'd realized, and as I sank into the hot bubbly water I became aware of just how tired I really was. I laid my head back on the edge of the tub, and sulked just a little. Even though I was getting along great with George, I'd really been looking forward to hitting the bars and hooking up with a local hunk for a good fuck while I was driving cross-country. Now there was no chance of that happening.

I reached down and stroked my cock for a few minutes, hoping to get a response, but when it just lay limp in the soapy water, I sighed heavily and decided to call it a night and head to bed. I usually sleep in the nude, but with George in the same bed, I reluctantly put on my boxer shorts and slipped into the soft, thick cotton robe that hung on the bathroom door.

"Jeez, I thought you'd fallen asleep in there," George said when I stepped back into the bedroom. He was lying on the bed, hands behind his head, watching television. He was stripped down to only a pair of bright white cotton briefs, and I swallowed hard as I took in the beauty of my boyfriend's father.

George's tall, muscular body was sculpted and well defined, and contained just enough well-placed fat to sufficiently separate him from all the pretty boys I was used to seeing at school. His huge biceps were cut and bulged impressively as they held his hands behind his head. His massive chest was dusted with short, curly blond hair that separated two muscled pecs capped with impossibly tiny brown nipples. A defined eight-pack of hard abs graced his stomach.

The snowy white briefs were a stark contrast to his tanned body, and clung tightly to the bulge that pulled the elastic waist of the shorts down just far enough to reveal a glimpse of blond curly pubic hair. The cock hiding inside looked long and thick, and I found it a little difficult to breathe.

"I almost did," I finally answered, and walked over to my side of the bed. "I'm beat."

On my way around the bed, I couldn't help but steal a glance at the long, muscular legs that stretched out to fill half the king-size bed. Tanned and covered with a light dusting of silky blond hair, they looked very strong, and perfect except for a small scar just below one of the knees.

"You *must* be," George said as I took my robe off, laid it on the chair next to the door, and lay down on my side of the bed. "I know I am, and I've only been on the road half as long as you have."

"Yeah, it's been a long drive all right," I admitted, "but not as bad as I expected."

"Well, let's get some sleep," the older version of Rodney next to me said as he reached up and turned off the lamp on the nightstand next to him and clicked the remote to the television off. "I'll help you drive again tomorrow and see how many miles we can put behind us."

"Sounds good," I said. *Easy for you to say,* I thought to myself as I rolled onto my side to hide the hard-on that was quickly filling out my boxers.

"G'night Erique. And thanks for letting me tag along."

"No problem," I lied as I tried to hide the pulsing cock inside my shorts. "Good night."

I tossed and turned next to George for several minutes, cursing the hard cock between my legs that kept begging for attention. There was no way I could beat off right now. I am not the quietest person in the world when I'm experiencing pleasure, and I would surely wake George up. So instead, I stared at the ceiling through the dark and remembered back to the time my Grammy became my mom.

It sounds horrible to say, but the first month without Mother was actually the best. It was easy. Grammy was overcome with grief and spent most of the time in her room, crying as she flipped through the pages of a library of photo albums. I spent most of my time watching cartoons or videos. Grammy and I really only saw one another a couple of times a day when she came into the kitchen to cook me pancakes and bacon and eggs for breakfast, lunch, and dinner. Then she retreated back into her bed-room and I lay on the couch watching TV until I fell asleep. Sometime during the night I would wake up and go to bed.

I never really cried for my mother. At least not consciously. Sometimes I would wake up and find my face sticky with dried tears, but I never re-membered dreaming of or crying over my mother's death.

I dreamed about lots of other things, though, and it was those dreams that got me through the next few years. Grammy, of course, eventually got over her grief and returned to her normal self, if "normal" could ever be used in describing my grandmother. I tried to share my dreams with her, tried to develop a relationship with her, but it was useless.

"Grammy, I had another dream last night," I said one morning when I was about six years old. I'd hoped sharing my dreams with her might make her feel closer to her daughter, my mother. I distinctly remembered my mother telling me to share my dreams with Grammy.

"I'm sure you did, Erique," she said as she put a bowl of cereal and a saucer of fresh fruit in front of me. "You spend way too much time dreaming and not nearly enough time getting ready for school. You're in kindergarten now. You have to start taking things seriously. You can't go around dreaming all the time. You have to start studying and practicing being a big boy."

"But I just started kindergarten. I'm still a kid."

"Yes, you are. But you're growing so fast, now. You won't be a kid for long. You're going to be a big boy soon, and you must be prepared for that."

"Do you wanna hear about my dream?" I asked as I pushed the bowl of cereal away from me and smiled at Grammy.

"No, I want you to eat your cereal and get ready for school," she said, pushing the bowl back in front of me.

"Not until you listen to my dream."

"Oh, you are so frustrating. I don't want to hear about your dream, Erique. I'm tired and I want you to get ready for school."

"How can you be tired? It's seven-thirty in the morning."

"Exactly, and I didn't sleep well last night."

"Probably because you didn't dream."

"That's right, I didn't. I have my feet on the ground and my head where it's supposed to be. I have responsibilities. Like you, for instance."

"Yeah, but you don't have dreams. You never did. And that's why you can't sleep."

"You're exasperating, child."

"So, you ready to hear it?"

"All right, all right. I'll hear your stupid little dream. But then you have to promise me you'll eat your breakfast and get ready for school."

"Deal."

"Go on, then."

"I dreamed I was in bed and saying my prayers. And then I heard Mommy's voice calling me from outside my window. I went to the window but I couldn't see her. So I stood on the window and jumped. But instead of falling, I started flying! Can you believe that?"

"Flying? That's ridiculous!"

"I was. I was flying all across town. And there were other boys and girls standing at their windows, too. So I reached in my pocket and pulled out some magic dust and I sprinkled it on all the kids. And then they could fly, too! Isn't that exciting? We were all flying all over town and laughing."

"That is a very childish dream, Erique."

"It was fun."

"That is what I call a Childish Dream. It's rubbish. People can't fly and there is no such thing as magic dust."

"It was fun, and I am a kid, so why can't I have childish dreams?"

"You're almost a big boy now. If you insist on dreaming at all, you can at least start dreaming Big Boy Dreams."

"It was fun. And you just don't like it because you don't like fun. Mommy always said you didn't have fun for the last twenty years."

"You leave your mother out of this. It's all her fault you're dreaming like this in the first place. She had a responsibility to teach you right, and what did she do? She taught you to believe in dreams. It's all her fault."

I ate my cereal and fruit and dressed myself for school. But I'd made a promise to my mother that I would share my dreams with Grammy, and I wasn't about to renege on my promise. I kept at it, regardless of the fact that Grammy became increasingly annoyed at listening to them.

She called all of my dreams for the next couple of years Childish Dreams and warned me against the harm that allowing them to continue would bring. Her rantings and ravings must have sunk in at some point, because when I was ten my dreams started changing a little. No more fly-ing and magic dust. Now I was thinking of becoming an astronaut or President of the World.

"Erique, that is nonsense. There is no such thing as president of the world. And why would you want to become an astronaut, anyway? What's up there in space to see?"

"There's a lot up there to see. I could see all the other stars and plan-ets."

"You can see those down here. All you need is a telescope."

"Yeah, but I could see earth, too. From all the way up there. I could even look down and see you waving at me."

"I will not be waving at you. It's nonsense, Erique. These dreams you're having are Nonsense Dreams. And I will not be a part of them, or in encouraging you to continue with them. They will get you nowhere."

"They are not nonsense. I can be president and I can be an astronaut if I want to."

"Nonsense Dreams."

"Dreams aren't supposed to be something logical, Grammy. That's why they're dreams."

"Then if they aren't logical, why bother with them?"

"It gives you something to reach for."

"Yeah, well reach for your books, and get off to school. You don't want to be late."

I got frustrated with Grammy during my Nonsense Dream stage. I was tired of her telling me that nothing would come of me dreaming like I did. When I went to bed and prayed, I prayed to my mom. I asked her if I could stop sharing my dreams with Grammy because she only made fun of them and discouraged me from dreaming at all. I asked my mother to speak to me and let me know what to do.

She never spoke to me directly, but the last thing I thought about be-fore falling asleep every night was the conversation I had with my mom when I was three. The one where my mom told me that Grammy had never had any dreams and didn't know anything about them. She told me I had to share my dreams with Grammy so she'd know how important they are and so my dreams could come true. I took that as a sign, and continued telling Grammy every detail of every dream I had.

The big mistake came when I was in junior high school. I began *dreaming of naked men. Because I'd never thought about not sharing any of my dreams, I didn't think about the consequences of sharing these particular dreams with Grammy.*

"Grammy?"

"What, Erique?" She was watching Matlock *on TV and hated to be disturbed when Andy Griffith was on.*

"What do you think it means if I am dreaming of naked men?"

"What?" Grammy shrieked, and reached for the remote control.

"Lately I've been dreaming of naked men."

"Erique Moore . . ."

"Vason. My last name is Vason."

"Whatever. You are not to be dreaming of naked men. Do you hear me?"

"Grammy, you can't help what you dream about."

"Yes, you can. And you are not to be dreaming of naked men. Those are Bad Boy Dreams."

"They aren't bad, Grammy. The guys aren't doing anything. Usually just swimming or sunbathing."

Grammy stood up and walked over to the antique rolltop desk that greeted visitors when they entered the foyer. She lifted the roller lid and pulled out a ruler, then walked briskly over to me.

"Put out your hand, Erique."

"What?"

"Put out your hand."

I raised my hands and pushed them forward toward her.

She raised the ruler and brought it down hard across my knuckles in one swift move. The blow was hard enough to cause spots to float in front of my eyes and draw blood on my knuckles.

"What the hell are you doing?" I screeched as I withdrew my hands and stared at them in disbelief.

"Put your hands back here."

"No."

"Erique, I am not going to tell you again. Give me your hands."

"Like hell I will."

"Oh, and so now having Bad Boy Dreams isn't enough, huh? Now you're going to start swearing, too."

"They are not Bad Boy Dreams, Grammy. They're innocent. Just naked men."

"I will not tolerate this in my house."

"It's my house, too. And I can't help what I dream about."

"Yes, you can. You can think about good things. Pure things. If you do that then you will dream about those things and not these Bad Boy Dreams."

"Really? And so if I dream about becoming president or an astronaut, then those things can come true as well?"

"Don't try tripping me up on my own words, Erique. I won't stand for that in my own house."

"It's my house, too."

"No, it is not. This is my house, and you will do as I say while you're living here."

"Or what? You'll throw me into the streets like you threatened to do with my mom the night she died?"

Before I saw it coming, Grammy's left hand swung up and struck the side of my face. From the shocked look on her face, she hadn't known it was coming, either.

"Erique, I'm sorry . . ."

"Yeah, I'm sure you are. Sorry like you were that night, right? The night you slapped my mother."

"I never slapped your mother."

"I heard it, and it sounded exactly like the one you just hit me with."

"I never slapped your mother. She slapped me." Grammy dropped the ruler onto the coffee table, and slumped back onto the couch.

I was stunned and didn't know what to say. I massaged my swollen hand and sat back on the chair I'd occupied earlier.

"I'm sorry, Grammy. I didn't know."

"It's okay. I'm sorry I hit you. I didn't mean to. I didn't want to."

"I know."

"But Erique, you cannot have any more Bad Boy Dreams. You simply can't. It's not right. It's unhealthy. It's a sin."

"Okay, Grammy. No more Bad Boy Dreams."

"Promise?"

"Promise."

The dreams didn't go away, of course. In fact, they got much worse. Better, really, but for Grammy's sake I'll say worse. In the dreams the men were no longer simply swimming naked or sunbathing in the nude.

They were kissing and rubbing one another's hard muscled bodies. They
were making love.

The dreams were exquisite, and I was fascinated with them. I wanted
to be a part of them, but never was. All of the men were older. None of
them were men I actually knew. Just distinguished, handsome, older men.
Some of them had gray hair around their temples and white hairs sprinkled among the black forests on their chests. Some of them were smooth
and lean, with crow's feet around their eyes and stubble on their chins.
They were all heavily muscled and brilliantly built. And they were all
more than just well-endowed. Some of them were cut and some were uncircumcised, but they all had very large cocks.

If Grammy thought the nude swimmers were Bad Boy Dreams then
these would just send her way over the edge. I never shared them with her,
of course. Most of the time we just didn't talk about dreams anymore. It
was easier that way. But sometimes she would try to catch me. Out of the
blue she'd ask about what I'd dreamed the night before.

"Nothing," was my most usual reply.

"Nonsense. You can't just stop dreaming after all these years."

"They're just not as exciting anymore," I'd lie. "Mostly I dream about
building a boat and sailing around the world."

"Oh, that's nice," Grammy would say, and snuggle up on the couch to
watch Matlock.

It was just easier that way. And in junior high and high school, I
needed things to be easier. School was tough enough without adding the
extra burden of a grumpy Grammy to it all. I was smart enough to know
when to shut up.

My eyes grew heavy and I began yawning uncontrollably. Less than
a foot away, George was snoring and breathing deeply. I smiled, rolled
over onto my side, and closed my eyes.

Surprisingly, I fell asleep easily enough. I dreamed of skiing at my favorite resort in Colorado, trying desperately and in vain to catch up
with Rodney, who was skiing half a football field's length in front of
me. I was naked in the dream, and using my grossly oversize protruding hard-on to balance myself, rather than the conventional ski poles
everyone else was using.

I smiled to myself in my sleep, knowing that I was dreaming, and telling myself how silly it was to be skiing naked in the freezing snow. But I loved to dream, especially when I knew I was doing it and could go along with it. I stuck my tongue out and licked at the falling snowflakes, reveling in how cold each flake was as I swooshed down the hill and felt the biting cold wind against my naked skin.

In my dream I twisted an ankle, and fell forward into a large snow mogul. I was surprised to feel that the snow was warm and wet. I was even more surprised as I felt the mogul's warmth tighten and massage my hard cock. Something wasn't right here, I thought, and began to count backward from twenty-five, my usual means of bringing myself out of a dream I was no longer comfortable with.

I blinked my eyes open slowly, and was at first disoriented when I realized I wasn't in my own room back in Berkeley. Then I remembered I was in Salt Lake City, on my way to Rhode Island, and I relaxed. But the warm, wet massaging sensation on my cock was still there, and when I looked down the length of the bed, I almost screamed. Tried to scream, actually, but no sound came from my mouth; only large powdery snowflakes that floated in front of my face and slowly faded away.

Beyond the fading snowflakes, George was lying between my legs, sucking on my cock. I shook my head fervently, thinking I must still be dreaming, yet knowing I was not. When I tried to sit up on my elbows, George pulled his mouth from my cock, and pushed me gently back down onto my back with one strong hand.

"Just relax," George said, and I thought I was going insane.

It was definitely George in front of me. I felt the strength and solid skin as I was pushed back down onto the bed. It was George's deep baritone voice that just told me to relax. And I saw George too . . . his face and the same beautiful body I'd admired when I stepped out of the bathroom earlier that night. Yet even as I looked at my lover's father, I was looking through him. I saw the television set and dresser, which should have been hidden by the massive muscular body lying between them and me. I looked at George's face and saw, in perfect detail even in the dark of the room, his dimples and the tiny mole below his left eye. At the same time, I looked straight through George's smiling, transparent face and saw my own legs and feet at the end of the bed.

"What the fuck is going on here?" I asked the strong older man in front of me.

"I'm sucking your dick," George answered. "Don't you like it?"

"Well, yes," I answered, and shook my head again, my eyes transfixed on the apparition in front of me. "But . . ."

"No buts, then, at least not yet," George whispered, and moved forward on the bed, closer to my face. My heart pounded wildly in my chest as I watched George's face get closer to my own and one strong, warm hand wrapped around the throbbing cock that defied my fear.

George leaned forward and pressed his soft, full lips on mine and kissed me. This could not be happening, I thought as I closed my eyes and tried to count my way backward out of what had to be a dream again. The lips pressing against my own remained, however, and I felt a warm tongue lick my lips and gently, yet persistently part them. I tasted a faint trace of the cinnamon gum George had been chewing earlier during the road trip, and wanted to cry. This couldn't be real, couldn't be happening. And yet it was too real not to be. I was frightened and excited at the same time.

I opened my eyes again, and George broke the kiss. He moved backward a few inches, giving me a better look at him. The blond hair, crystal blue eyes, cleft chin . . . even the irresistible dimples were all there. I smelled the sweet cologne I'd noticed when I first met George earlier that afternoon.

"Freaking out, huh?" George asked.

"Well, yeah," I answered, slowly gaining some composure.

"Understandable. But don't. Just accept it and enjoy it, okay?"

"All right."

George leaned forward again, and kissed me, and this time I didn't fight it. I opened my mouth and sucked gently on the warm, cinnamon-tasting tongue that probed it. My cock pulsed hotly in George's hand, and a gentle squeeze brought a moan of delight from my throat. George playfully bit my bottom lip, and smiled as he moved his body so that he was sitting on the edge of the bed, staring at me.

My head spun with a million questions, but before I could ask them,

George stood up and moved to the head of the bed. I looked through the muscular transparent body moving toward me, and noticed the bleached white briefs lying on the floor a few feet directly behind George's see-through chest. My eyes were immediately drawn to the semi-hard cock that was moving closer to my face. When I breathed in, I smelled the sweet mix of cologne and manly sweat, and smiled.

I looked at George's heavy cock, and noticed it looked very similar to Rodney's. Long, thick and uncut, the fat cock swung temptingly a few inches from my mouth. Half expecting to feel nothing but air, I reached out and touched it. It grew fully hard as my fingers tugged and squeezed it, and I licked my lips in anticipation as I slid the soft, silky foreskin up and down the hard, solid, yet transparent rod. I smiled again when I noticed, near the base of George's dick, a tiny black mole, identical to the one Rodney had just below his pubic hair.

"Suck my dick," George said huskily in a voice uniquely his, yet tinged with a supernatural power filled with lust and desire.

I did as I was told, wrapping my lips around the big uncut cock head and savoring the taste and feel of it on my tongue. It grew even harder as my mouth sucked on it lovingly, and I felt the large veins pounding against my tongue and cheeks as they coursed through the foreskin, stretching tightly against the fat, nine-inch cock.

"That's it, man," George whispered. He positioned himself over my body so that, without removing his cock from my hungry mouth, he was able to lie gently on top of my body and began kissing and licking my dick in a sixty-nine position.

The room spun as I looked through George's translucent body and saw the top of the television and wall behind it that should have been blocked by George's skin and muscles and bone. Somewhere deep in the back of my mind I was certainly freaking out, but right then the feel and taste of George's huge cock was very real as it slid deep into my throat, and I was loving every minute of it.

I breathed in slowly, and opened the back of my throat, allowing the hard pole to slide deep inside me. Breathing only through my nose now, I reached up and caressed the smooth skin of George's ass and legs as George swallowed my cock all the way to the base. A low, deep moan escaped both our throats as we began to fuck each other's mouths with mounting intensity.

It didn't take long at all before I felt my balls tingle and shrivel, and the inevitable load started working its way up the length of my cock. I tried to warn George, and to pull the sucking mouth off me, but George only increased the pressure and sucked harder, while forcing his own cock harder against my lips.

My load shot from my cock in a fiery stream, and my eyes widened with amazement as I looked at the back of George's head and saw my own load shoot stream after stream of cum into what seemed thin air and down George's throat at the same time. A second later I felt the cock in my mouth pulse madly, and my throat grew warm as George emptied his load deep inside me. Swallowing hungrily, I was mesmerized as wave after wave of my lover's father's cum filled my gut.

George reluctantly pulled his mouth from my still hard cock, licking the shaft as he did. I figured we were done, but was surprised when George got up on his knees and instead of moving away, inched his smooth, tight ass cheeks closer to my now empty mouth.

"George . . ."

"Shut up and eat me, Erique."

The silky, hard cheeks were against my lips before I could think of anything else to say, and I reached up and massaged them with my hands as my tongue slid between the crack. My head was still spinning with the force of my own orgasm, but the musky, sweet taste of George's ass kept my cock hard and my heart began to race again.

George wiggled his ass in my face for a moment, and when I hesitantly slid my tongue inside the twitching hole, George moaned loudly and grabbed my legs.

"Oh, fuck, yeah," he said, and tightened his hot ass muscles around my probing tongue.

This can't be happening, *I kept thinking. But I knew it was, and I slowly and lovingly slid my tongue in and out of the burning ass.*

"Oh, it's happening all right," George said out loud, reading my thoughts.

He slowly stood up and turned around and straddled my upper body. A beautiful smile spread across his face, showing off his sexy dimples, and his bright eyes sparkled. Amazingly, his huge cock was fully hard again, and throbbing just inches in front of my face. The fat head poked through the sheath of foreskin and a large drop of precum slid

*down the underside of it. I took a deep breath and licked my lips, ready
for another taste of George's hard cock and his sweet load.*

*"Uh-unh," George said, and smiled even more mischievously. "Been
there, done that. Now it's time to move on."*

*He reached behind him and gently took hold of my cock and moved it
to his ass.*

"George . . ." I started to protest.

*"Shhh . . ." George whispered, and leaned down to kiss me again. His
tongue traced its way around my lips, and this time met with no resis-
tance at all as it slid inside.*

*We kissed for a long moment, gently at first and then with more fervor.
My whole body shuddered when my cock head pressed against George's
hot ass hole, and George wrapped his mouth around my tongue and
sucked it gently as he slid himself down onto my big dick.*

*I still tasted the cinnamon gum aftertaste in George's mouth, and the
ass muscles surrounding and massaging my dick seemed even hotter as
George took me completely inside. A loud buzzing sound echoed in my
ears and bright pins of light spun before my closed eyelids, but nothing
had ever felt better in my entire life.*

*I looked up at the ghost-like figure of my lover's father as I fucked him.
Everything about this night was magical, but I was getting more used to
it by the minute. I looked into George's deep blue eyes, still seeing completely through them, yet also catching the ray of light that beamed from
them.*

*I forced myself to look around the room. A million questions flooded
my mind as I thrust myself inside the see-through body of my father-in-
law. Everything around me was solid and perfectly normal. Only George
was magically translucent and at the same time, fully solid and touch-
able.*

*"What the fuck is going on here?" I asked for the second time that
evening.*

*"Stop asking so many fucking questions," George grunted as he slid
his ass down onto my cock. "Just go with it, man."*

*I did, giving in to the fact that none of this made any sense at all, but
not caring. I fucked George with long, slow strokes, and watched as
George's heavy uncut dick bobbed in front of my face. It wasn't until*

then that I glanced just beyond the big dick, right through George's rock hard abdomen, and saw my own cock, very clear and not at all translucent, as it slid into and out of George's ass.

Seeing both dicks as they moved in perfect sync with one another proved too much for me, and I stopped breathing as I felt my fully engorged cock flex, and my cum work its way up my shaft.

"Oh, shit," I said loudly, and watched in amazement as my cock shot out several large streams of cum inside George's see-through body.

"I feel it, man," George said, and stopped sliding up and down so that he could focus on squeezing his ass muscles against my spurting cock inside him. "It's so hot. You ready for mine now?"

Beyond the ability to speak, I just lay still and watched as George's huge uncut dick began shooting its second load of the night. Incredibly, my own cock was still pouring out a large amount of hot, white cum, and I saw the steam rising slightly from the fluid as it spewed out of my cock head and disappeared up inside George's body. George's load shot wildly, landing all over my face, chest, and stomach. It felt like hot lava landing on me, and when I reached out with my tongue to lick at the drops that landed on my lips, I was not at all surprised to find out it tasted like cinnamon.

When we finished coming, we relaxed, and George slumped on top of my quivering body. Our hearts slowed down at the same time as we kissed again and fell asleep hugging each other lovingly, my cock still buried deep inside George's warm body.

The alarm buzzed at eight o'clock the next morning, and I jerked awake. It took me a moment to get my bearings, and I was afraid I was going to find myself still entwined around George's sweat- and cum-drenched body. I was in bed alone, though, and heard George whistling loudly in the shower. I quickly pulled the covers down and saw that I was still wearing the boxer shorts I'd put on the night before. There were no dried cum spots on my face or body, and I breathed a sigh of relief and lay back down on the bed.

So, it was all a dream, after all. But if that were true, then why didn't I wake up with a pounding hard-on like I did every single day of my adult life . . . except the day after having the most incredible sex of my life?

I didn't have much time to think about it, as the shower stopped running and George stepped into the bedroom. He was drying his hair with one towel, another draped casually around his waist. I breathed another sigh of relief as I saw that George was completely solid and nowhere near being transparent. Each bulging biceps and flexed eight-pack muscle on his body dripped shower water, and kept me from seeing what lay behind them.

"Hey, Erique," George said as he walked over to the bed, "you'd better get up and get showered if we wanna get an early start. We've got a lot of miles to put behind us today."

"Right," I answered. "Uh, George, did you sleep okay last night?"

"Hell, yeah, man. Like a baby. I didn't realize I was so tired."

"No weird dreams or anything?"

"No, not a one. I was out like a log. Why?"

"No reason," I said awkwardly, and shook my head as I stood up and walked to the bathroom to take my shower.

As the hot water pelted my body, I wondered why my muscles were so sore, and decided I'd ask George to start the drive that morning. There was so much to think about the rest of the trip . . . first among them being how I was ever going to thank Rodney for suggesting I take his father along on the trip with me. I whistled happily as I soaped up and thought of how much I'd missed having my Bad Boy Dreams.

The rest of the drive to Hartford was fairly uneventful. Except that I couldn't take my eyes off George's chest and his arms and his legs as he drove. I kept remembering the dream and stealing glances at George's crotch, knowing that the thick uncut cock was just below the fabric of his jeans, and wanting it again and again.

We stopped at several rest stops and gas stations to refuel, and every time we did, I had to run into the rest room and beat off.

It was almost midnight when I dropped George off at his sister's home in Hartford. As tempting as his offer to spend the night before driving on to Providence was, I declined. I had a lot to think about, and facing Grammy again after a couple of years was not going to be an easy task.

I drove the rest of the way with my window down, despite the cool breeze that blew inside the car. When I saw the sign that announced that Providence was only ten miles away, I had to pull over and beat off one last time.

Coming home was never easy.

Grammy

So much had changed in the two and a half years since I was last home. As I opened the door, the first thing I noticed was the smell. Grammy's house had always smelled of mothballs, Pine-Sol, and fresh baked breads. Disturbing as that may seem, it had always been comforting. It was constant. As I stepped inside the front door and slowly closed it behind me, I was assaulted with the smell of old. My mind instantly raced back to the day Grammy tossed me into the old Valiant that hadn't been driven since Grampy passed away. It had smelled old. Dusty and musky and old. And that was what Grammy's house now smelled like.

I stood inside the doorway for a moment, getting used to the darkness of the room. The grandfather clock facing me chimed in at two o'clock just as I locked the door and stepped into the living room. I fumbled around in the dark, hoping Grammy hadn't rearranged the furniture, yet knowing that she most certainly had not. Would never. I smiled as I reached the familiar couch and sank into it.

I thought about turning on the television and watching the Game Show network, then remembered Grammy only had basic cable. Besides, I didn't want to wake and startle Grammy. So instead, I kicked off my shoes, lay down on the sofa, and pulled the afghan from across the back of the couch down across my body. I was asleep in less than ten minutes.

*   *   *

"Come here, Erique," he said to me from behind the curtain.

My heart raced as I put one foot in front of the other and walked toward the deep, comforting sound of his voice.

"There's something I want to show you," he spoke again, and I picked up my pace a little as I advanced toward him.

"Here I am," I said as I stopped just short of reaching the curtain.

"Come inside. Follow me."

"I can't," I said, and then looked around to see who had just said that. It cannot have been me who uttered those words. I didn't mean them at all, didn't want to say them. I most certainly could follow him anywhere. Would do almost anything he asked of me.

But when I tried to step forward I found myself paralyzed. My feet and legs wouldn't move at all.

"It's not that I don't want to," I tried to explain. "I want to, George, I really want to. But my feet won't move."

"It's because you don't trust me, Erique," George said with a note of sadness.

"I do. I do trust you."

"Then come with me. Follow me." He beckoned again, this time pulling the curtain aside so I could step through unhindered.

I caught a whiff of fresh air and spring flowers as the curtain parted. A cool breeze whisked by my face. Ahead in the distance, I'm not sure how far, I saw a rainbow and bright sunshine. I heard birds chirping all around me, just beyond the blue curtain.

"What is it you're afraid of?" George asked. I could see just the shadow of his jawline in the dark just beyond the curtain. He was so close.

"I don't know. I don't think I'm afraid of anything."

"Of course you are. Or else you'd be here with me right now."

"I want to, George. I really do want to. Help me."

He reached out his hand, in front of the curtain, and beckoned me to take it. I reached forward with one shaky hand and took his in mine. Instantly the sensations in my legs returned and I could feel the sharp tingles of feeling shoot up my leg again. A moment later I stepped forward and through the open curtain.

Beyond the blue curtain was another world. Everything was so bright *and clear and vivid. The sun was a brilliant orange, the sky bright blue, the grass a deep emerald, and the roses a vibrant red. Birds flew around contentedly and not only chirped but sang out complete songs. Warm sunshine bathed my cool skin and radiated inside me.*

And George was there, too. Or at least I think it was George. But he was younger and taller and had a little more hair than I recalled. It was definitely his voice, though.

"Welcome," he said, and waved his hand over the beautiful scene before us.

"Who are you?" I asked. "Where are we?"

"I am George, and we are Here."

"But this is so perfect. It can't be real."

"Yes, it can be real. It can be perfect. But only if you want it to be. Only if you believe it can be."

"I do. I do want it to be real. I want it to be perfect. What do I have to do? Click my heels three times and chant something?"

"No." George laughed. "Just believe and open your heart to me, and all this can be real."

I jumped awake with a start at the sound of something sliding and snapping and clicking into place. When I opened my eyes, Grammy was standing above me, pointing a rifle directly at my head.

"Who are you and what are you doing in my house?" she asked as she closed one eye to get a better view of me through the scope.

"Grammy, it's me, Erique. What are you doing with a gun?"

"Erique?"

"Yes, Grammy, it's me," I said as I threw the afghan across the back of the sofa. "What the hell are you doing with a rifle in your house?"

Grammy ignored me, but dropped the rifle and pulled me close to her bosom. She started crying and wiping at her eyes, all the while keeping me in a stranglehold at her chest.

"What are you doing home, son?" she asked when she finally released her grip on my head. "Don't you have school?"

"Yes, I still have school. But Auntie Hildred called and said you were sick."

"Oh, Hildred Pildred! She's always sticking her nose in my business. I don't know why that old bitch can't just mind her own business."

I struggled to catch my breath and stumbled backwards, trying to find my way back to the couch. "Grammy, you just swore!"

"What? I did not."

"Yes, you did. You just called Auntie Hildred a bitch."

"Oh!" Grammy's hands flew up to her mouth and her eyes were wide with surprise. She grinned impishly. "Did that slip out? I meant to keep that one private."

"Yes, it slipped out."

"Well, don't go tell Hildred. My God, she'll get her panties all in a wad."

"Grammy! Now you just used the Lord's name in vain. Where did you learn to use such language?"

"Oh, He won't mind. He's got a sense of humor and He knows I'm an old woman. If He chooses to keep me around this long, He's gotta be willing to make a few concessions."

I laughed and hugged Grammy long and tight.

"I'm very happy to see you, Erique. But you shouldn't have played hooky from school. I'm all right."

"I am not playing hooky, Grammy. I just took a couple of weeks off. It's fine."

"Well, I am glad you're here, son. I've missed you so much."

"I've missed you too, Grammy. I'm sorry I haven't come to visit you more often. I've just been really busy at school."

It felt very uncomfortable for me to be speaking so lovingly with Grammy. We'd never bonded much before and our conversations were usually one-sided and strained, at the very most. But this was not the same woman that I left two and a half years ago. That much was certain after just a few seconds of speaking with her. This woman was lively and fun and sassy. This was the Grammy I'd always wanted.

"Are you hungry, honey?" Grammy asked as she snaked her way from between the couch and the coffee table and moved toward the kitchen.

"No, Grammy, I'm fine. Don't go to any trouble for me."

"No trouble at all," she said without looking back. "I'm gonna whip me up some eggs and Rise and Shine and Give God the Glory Biscuits for myself. I may as well double the recipe and make enough for the both of us."

"Some eggs and *what?*"

"Rise and Shine and Give God the Glory Biscuits."

"What the hell is that?"

"Hey. You watch your potty mouth. They're biscuits from my friend Ruby Ann's cookbook."

"Ruby Ann? I don't remember you having a friend named Ruby Ann."

"Oh, I knew her long ago. Way before you were born. Before your mother was born, even."

"Oh, I see. And she wrote a cookbook?"

"Yes," Grammy said as she gathered the ingredients to make the biscuits. "It's right over there." She pointed to the white wicker basket that held all her cookbooks, close to the refrigerator.

I picked up the cookbook and looked at the cover. *"Ruby Ann's Down Home Trailer Park Cookbook."* I laughed to myself.

"Umm, Grammy," I said as I finished reading the back cover, "I don't think this is your friend Ruby Ann."

"Well, of course it is," Grammy said as she turned to face me. "I knew her when we were both attending Clayson College for Women. She was a very, very good friend of mine. She had a different last name back then, of course. And she's gained quite a bit of weight. But other than that, I'd recognize her anywhere. Same cat-eyed glasses that have absolutely no value whatsoever, same beautiful smile. And who could forget those long, curly eyelashes?"

"No, I don't think so, Grammy."

"I'm telling you, it's her."

"This is not the Ruby Ann you once knew. You have to trust me on this one, okay? This is a white trash trailer park cookbook, Grammy. How many people do you even know who live in a trailer park?"

"What's a trailer park?"

"Exactly."

"I don't understand."

"This cookbook is a joke, Grammy. Just look at the ingredients, for Christ's sake."

"Watch your language, Erique. I won't have you using the Lord's name in vain in my house. And the cookbook is not a joke. It has some very good recipes in it. I use it every day."

"Really? Government cheese, Grammy?"

"Yes. In fact, I'll make one of my favorite recipes for dinner tonight."

"Okay, Grammy, that sounds just lovely. I can't wait."

We sat down to eat breakfast, and I had to admit, the Rise and Shine and Give God the Glory Biscuits were incredibly moist and delicious. They were really just plain old homemade biscuits, so I didn't know why they were given such a grandiose name. Still, they were good. Grammy scrambled some eggs and fried a couple of potatoes to accompany the biscuits, and we caught up on what had happened in Providence over the last two years.

"You remember old Mrs. Patterson? The old bitch who lived down the road a few blocks?"

"Grammy! You swore again."

"Oh, I did not. Stop changing the subject. Do you remember her or not?"

"Of course I do. You two used to play bridge together every week."

"Well, she ran off with the high school principal."

"Mr. Wynette?"

"Yes."

"But he's, like, thirty years younger than she is."

"Yes, we all know that. She's a shameless hussy. She has absolutely no morals or self-respect whatsoever."

"But what about Mrs. Wynette?"

"She fell to pieces. Had a nervous breakdown a couple weeks after the lovebirds skipped town."

"Poor thing."

"Yes, it was sad to see. When she got out of the hospital, she packed up and left as well. The old biddy Patterson came back to pack up a few things and then left again a couple days later. The next week there was a For Sale sign in her front lawn."

"Wow. And here I thought Providence never changed a bit."

"Scandalous, it was. Divinely scandalous."

I laughed and patted Grammy's hands, and once again thought how

wonderful it was to see her this way. She was funny and witty and admitted to loving a scandal. It was so different from the Grammy I left
a couple of years ago. Of course, it could only mean one thing. She
must really be sick to have changed this significantly in such a short
time. She must be suffering from dementia. I'd heard on one of those
television news magazine shows that people suffering from Alzheimer's
disease very often adopt exactly the opposite personalities when they
get sick. Nice people become mean and hateful. Mean and hateful
people become nice and sweet and funny. I was convinced Grammy
was suffering from late stage Alzheimer's, and though I hated thinking
of her being sick, I had to admit that I liked this Grammy much better.

Spending the day with her was a joy, and before I knew it, it was
time to start cooking dinner. Grammy wanted to surprise me with her
favorite recipe, but I begged to help her, so she allowed me to.

"Tonight we're having Tipper's Tater Tot Casserole!"

"What the hell is Tipper's Tater Tot Casserole?"

"Watch your mouth, young man. You're not too old for me to bend
over my knee. I won't have that kind of language in my house."

I laughed. "Sorry, Grammy."

"You'll see," she said with a grin, and wrung her hands together mischievously.

Though I'd asked to help, I really just stood back and watched in
awe as Grammy prepared dinner. She cooked a pound of hamburger
with some onion, then mixed half the mixture with a can of cream of
chicken soup. She poured that into a casserole dish and then covered
that mixture with the remaining beef and onion. She topped that with
a can of cheddar cheese soup and then sprinkled some grated cheddar
on top of it. Then she covered the entire dish with frozen tater tots,
sprinkled a little more cheese on top of the potatoes, and popped it
into the oven.

"Ruby Ann says it's Al Gore's favorite dish, so she named it after
Tipper," Grammy said as she cleaned up the dinner prep mess.

This statement alone confused me, because Grammy had been a
staunch Republican all her life. I was surprised she even knew who Al
and Tipper Gore were.

"Grammy, Ruby Ann would never have met Al and Tipper Gore."

"Of course she has. It says so right in the cookbook. Ruby Ann would never lie." Grammy stood up and walked into the living room. It was time for *Jeopardy*, and she never missed the show. "And once you taste the Tipper's Tater Tot Casserole, you'll see I'm right."

I have to admit, the casserole was really good. Grammy was thrilled when I admitted defeat. We ended the evening with a bottle of wine and curled up by the fireplace, cuddling one another. When she dozed off to sleep in the middle of a story, I picked her up, carried her to bed and tucked her in, then went to my own room and fell asleep almost immediately.

It is him again, and this time I recognize him immediately. His muscular, hairy body floats before me and I can see right through it. This is the George I know and have grown to love. I welcome him with open arms, and he floats into them happily.

"I've really missed you," George tells me as he kisses me.

I taste the cinnamon gum again, and smile. "I missed you, too." I hold his transparent face in my hands and look at and through him at the same time.

I fight to catch my breath as I stare into his beautiful face. His light blond hair and deep blue eyes sparkle, and when he smiles at me his teeth glisten. I lean in and kiss him again, and reach down between his legs to squeeze his hard cock. I'd been dreaming about it for so long, and here it is in front of me once again, and I certainly plan on taking advantage of that fact.

It is George who breaks our kiss first, and leans down to take my hardness into his mouth. Again I am amazed as I see through his head and stare at my own cock as his mouth sucks me deep into his throat and milks me. I wanted it to go on like that forever, but know from the tingling that starts at my toes and continues up my legs and through my cock, that it will not. Before I can stop myself, I shoot my load into George's mouth. I look down and see the sticky white fluid spray past his tonsils and splash against the walls of his esophagus and throat.

I want it to go on much longer. I want to lean down and return the favor to George, to take him into my mouth and get him fully hard and wet. I want to lift my legs into the air and offer myself to him.

But as soon as I finish with my own load, George begins to dissipate.

Slowly and without any warning, he floats above me and then disappears. I reach for him and cry out his name. But it is no good. He is gone.

Auntie Hildred came by to visit the next day. I couldn't help but notice the two sisters could barely stand to be in one another's company. Grammy made every excuse to leave the room.

"You see," Auntie Hildred whispered as Grammy found a reason to visit the kitchen, "I told you she'd lost her mind, didn't I?"

"Yes, but you also told me she was senile and did nothing but sit around the house all day watching television and wallowing in her own stench. She isn't doing any of that stuff, Auntie Hildred."

"Oh, that. Well, she is acting strange, you have to admit that. I figured I'd have to stretch the truth just a little bit in order to get you to come home. I knew if you came home she'd perk up a little. She's been so damned depressed lately. I just know that she misses you so much. Thank you for coming home, Erique."

"No problem," I said, leaning my head back to make sure Grammy was in the kitchen and couldn't hear us. "But Auntie Hildred, Grammy still isn't well, is she? I mean, she's perked up and all, but she is sick. I can see that. Does she have Alzheimer's?"

"Alzheimer's? Heavens, no! At least not that I know of. She hasn't been to a doctor in I don't know how long."

"But she's so different now," I said. "She's not the same person at all."

"Yes, I noticed that, too. Not that I'm complaining, mind you. I like this perky old biddy a lot better than I did that nasty old woman who used to live here."

"Me, too. But I don't want to neglect her treatment if she needs to see a doctor."

"Good luck getting her to go to a doctor."

Just then the door to the kitchen swung open and Grammy walked through into the living room.

"Here they are," she said with a smile as wide as the Grand Canyon. "My famous Devil In The Blue Dress Eggs!"

"Dear God in heaven!" Auntie Hildred cried out and clutched her pearls. "What the hell are those?"

Grammy laughed and set the plate of blue foamy eggs in front of us. "Don't be such a prude, Hildy. They're just deviled eggs with a little blue food coloring to make them fun. They're from the appetizers section in my friend Ruby Ann's cookbook. Good God, you'd think we'd just lost the war again."

"Mildred, we did not lose the war. We're not southerners. We have lived in Rhode Island our entire lives."

"Pooh!" Grammy said, and shoved the plate of blue deviled eggs closer to Auntie Hildred's face.

"I am not eating those things," Auntie Hildred said, and picked up her purse from the floor. "I have to be going, anyway."

Grammy laughed again, and walked Auntie Hildred to the door. She was pulling Auntie's sweater from the coat rack next to the door even before Auntie had stepped into the foyer. They kissed hurriedly on the cheeks and Grammy nearly shoved Auntie out the door. She waved to Auntie Hildred as she walked down the sidewalk. Then Grammy walked back to me and sat down.

"I knew those would put a fire under her ass and get her outta here! She was just waiting for a reason to leave, anyway. I know they look a little funny," she said as she picked up one of the deviled eggs and brought it to her mouth. "But they are really very good. The food coloring doesn't taste like anything."

She looked so cute and all proud, so I indulged her and ate a few of the eggs. They were really good, actually. We made small talk for a few moments, and then she surprised me.

"How come you don't talk about your dreams anymore, Erique?"

I spit out a mouthful of blue creamy egg yolks and choked on my own saliva. It took me a couple of minutes to catch my breath so I could speak. "I . . . just . . . don't . . ."

"You do still dream, don't you? Please tell me you do."

"Yes, Grammy, I still dream. I still dream very big."

"Good. I want to hear about your dreams, son."

"I don't think that's a good idea, Grammy. You won't like my dreams, and I just don't have the energy to make up some lie that you might find acceptable like I used to."

"You used to lie to me?"

"Yes, Grammy. When I lived at home, after we had that really bad fight, I stopped telling you the truth about my dreams because you called them the Bad Boy Dreams. So I made up different dreams that I thought you might find more agreeable."

"I always thought you did," Grammy said, and popped another blue deviled egg into her mouth. "But I never said anything back then because I was all uptight. My ass was wound tighter than a really good French braid."

I choked again. When and where had my Grammy learned to talk like this?

"But I want to know now, Erique. I'm not uptight anymore, everyone says so. I want to know what you dream."

"Are you sure, Grammy? I still have a lot of Bad Boy Dreams."

"I want to know. I'm not the same Grammy I used to be. I can't keep my eyes closed or my head buried in the sand forever. I want to know. They aren't all Bad Boy Dreams, are they? They can't all be Bad Boy Dreams."

"No. I still dream about becoming a famous singer or a professional tennis player. And I still dream of becoming president of the U.S. Sometimes I'm still a little kid at heart. But I also dream a lot about naked men, Grammy. And they aren't as innocent as they used to be."

"I want to know," she repeated, and propped her stockinged feet up on the coffee table right next to the blue deviled eggs.

And so I told her. I told her about every dream I could remember. I was much more uncomfortable with the Bad Boy Dreams than she was. In fact, she seemed to enjoy them. The more detailed I got, the more into the story she seemed to be. When I finished telling her about all the dreams I could recall, she smiled.

"I know your momma used to tell you that I never had any dreams, and that that's why I couldn't understand them or hope for them. But she was wrong."

"She was?" I sat up straight and listened.

"Yes. I used to dream all the time. Where do you think your mother got her dreams from? Your Grampy? Heavens, no! I was quite the dreamer myself in my time. And believe it or not, I even used to have some Naughty Girl Dreams."

"What? You used to dream of naked men?"

"Well, yes, that too. But those weren't my Naughty Girl Dreams.

Those were perfectly normal and acceptable for young girls to dream about."

"Then I don't understand."

"I used to dream of me and other young women. In . . . amorous . . . situations."

"What?" I yelled out, and jumped to my feet. "Grammy, you used to have dreams of you and other women?"

"Yes, I did. And when I got to Clayson, I got to act out on my dreams."

"Ewwww! Grammy, I don't want to hear this."

"Well, too bad," she said and pulled me back down to the couch. "I'm gonna tell you, anyway. All these years you made me listen to your dreams, it's about time you listened to mine. Especially since you've always believed that I never had any dreams."

"But, Grammy . . ."

"Her name was Ruby Ann Robinson. She was a beautiful woman, inside and out. She had long flowing black hair, emerald eyes, and long, curly eyelashes. She had perfect vision, but liked the look of cat-eyed glasses, so she wore them. The kind with little fake diamonds on them, just like in the cookbook."

"Grammy, you think the person who wrote that cookbook is your old lesbian lover?"

"We didn't use such words back then," Grammy said, and smoothed out imagined wrinkles in her skirt. "But we were very good friends. We did everything together. We even made love," she whispered into her hands. "But no one else knew about that part of our relationship. We knew enough to know we had to keep that secret."

"So, what happened, then?"

"We were roommates for three years, and fell madly in love with one another. We spent every single day together. More than that . . . every minute of every day together. People at school used to call us inseparable twins. Oh, she was the light of my life, Erique."

"How come no one ever knew about this? I mean, Grampy and Mom never knew, right?"

"Oh, heavens, no!"

"So what happened?"

"One day Ruby Ann met a man. His name was Glenn Mitchell. He was the star quarterback at our neighboring school, Bolton Boys' College. Quite dapper, really, and very much the ladies' man. At first she said they were only friends. But as time went on, Ruby Ann and I spent less and less time together, and eventually we stopped sleeping together. Then one day she came home and said she was getting married. She'd fallen in love with Glenn and they were getting married that summer. She hoped I'd understand and wanted me to be her maid of honor."

"Grammy, that's horrible."

"Yes, it was. It was devastating. I loved Ruby Ann with every fiber of my being, and I couldn't believe she was leaving me. I cried for weeks and locked myself in my dormitory room. I only came out to eat. People at school started to talk, and so eventually I pulled myself together and came out of my room. But I refused to be her maid of honor or even to attend her wedding. I threw myself into my school work and soon after that I met your Grampy."

"You did love Grampy, didn't you?"

"Yes, I did. It took a while, but eventually I fell in love with him, although at first I was just using him as a replacement for Ruby Ann. That, and to stop all the nasty rumors that were beginning to circulate around campus."

"They were gossiping about you?"

"Oh, that they were. It started out as just a couple of sneers in the hallways. Then I started getting nasty anonymous letters in my locker and then outright name calling. So, when your Grampy came along, I grabbed him. He was my only hope. We dated for six months, and when he asked me to marry him, I jumped at the chance. I wanted to put Ruby Ann and Clayson College behind me and start a new life. A life in which I was responsible and smart and did all the right things. A life where I did everything proper women were supposed to do. It took a while, but eventually I did fall in love with your Grampy."

"How did you suppress all of your feelings for Ruby Ann?"

"I just told myself that she'd betrayed me and that I hated her. I told myself that good girls got married and settled down and had children. And that's what I did."

"But you never stopped thinking about her, did you?"

"Of course not. And I never stopped dreaming about her, either."

"Never?"

"Never. All those years your mother accused me of not dreaming, I was having my Naughty Girl Dreams about Ruby Ann. It infuriated me that your mother couldn't see that I was dreaming, even if I couldn't share my dreams with her. When your Grampy died, the dreams increased. I was miserable. Grampy was dead, I was having a lot of Naughty Girl Dreams, usually every night, and your mother was getting wild on me. I didn't know what to do. I know I became a very harsh woman, Erique. Believe me when I tell you it's not what I wanted to become. I wanted to be a nice and perfect Grammy. But I didn't know how else to cope with everything."

"Grammy, I never knew."

"Of course you didn't. No one did, not even Grampy. When your mother got pregnant and you were born, I was so torn. I wanted you to grow up and be happy. Your mother kept talking to you about dreaming big and never giving up, and I was confused. I had been hurt by dreaming big and acting out on my dreams, and so I thought it was my duty to teach you to be realistic and responsible. To do the right thing."

"So that's why you never wanted to hear my dreams."

"Yes, Erique, that's why. It's not that I didn't believe in dreams or the power they have over you. It's just the opposite. I was having my own Naughty Girl Dreams every night back then. Dreaming of me and Ruby Ann together. Dreaming of us making love and raising children together. It hurt me to dream those things, Erique. And so when you started having your Bad Boy Dreams, I got scared. I thought it was my fault you were dreaming of boys instead of girls. And I didn't want you to be hurt like I had been."

"Grammy, why didn't you ever tell me the truth?"

"How can a grandma tell her young grandson a truth like this? It's not right. But you're older now, and I can tell you're happy. You're living with Randy and you're happy. And so I figured I was safe in telling you the truth now."

"His name is Rodney. And how do you know that Rodney and I are a couple?"

"Of course I know. I'm not stupid. And I'm not senile, either, despite what my twin sister might say. I don't care, Erique. I don't care. As long as you're happy, I'm happy."

"I'm not really happy with Rodney, Grammy."

"What?"

"I'm not. I think we're trying really hard to make it work, but maybe we're trying too hard. It shouldn't be this hard. Not if it's really right. And it just doesn't feel right with Rodney. It almost does, but not quite."

"If it doesn't feel right, then it's not. Nothing you can do or say or try will make it right if it isn't. You'll know it when it's right, Erique. Nothing else will feel quite the same again when it's right."

"Yeah, I know. I've done a lot of thinking about it, and I think I finally figured it out. I just think I need someone older than me. Someone with more experience in life. Someone who can show me things I've never seen and take me places I've never been."

"And that's not Rodney?"

"No, it's not. Rodney is a great guy, but he's my age and shares my experiences."

"Then it's not right. You shouldn't go back to him and pretend it is. It's not good for you or for him."

"What should I do, then?"

"You should go back, explain everything to Rodney, agree to be friends, and then start looking for the man of your dreams."

"But you weren't able to be friends with Ruby Ann when you two split up."

"You're right, we weren't. So maybe you just go back and tell him the truth and not remain friends. But still, you need to start looking for the man of your dreams. The one who will make you happy."

"I think I already found him."

"What?"

"It's Rodney's father. He drove with me out here to visit his sister in Hartford. I dropped him off right before I came here. Ever since I picked him up in L.A., I haven't been able to think of anything but him."

"But, Erique . . ."

"I've dreamed about him every single night since then. I have very vivid dreams of him and me together. They're very Bad Boy Dreams,

Grammy. You'd absolutely hate them. But I can't dream of anything or anyone else."

"And does he feel the same way? He's Rodney's father, which means there must be a wife somewhere in the picture and probably more than one kid."

"Divorced, almost twice now. And yeah, a couple more kids, but they're all grown up, pretty much. I don't know if he feels the same way or not."

"You don't know?" Grammy asked, and swiped her wrinkled old hand at me. "Why not?"

"We haven't talked about it."

"Well, you need to. You don't want to get old and wrinkled like me, and then regret not having acted on your dreams, Erique. Trust me on this one."

"So I should talk with him about what I'm feeling?"

"Yes, you should. When do you see him again?"

"I told him I didn't know how long I'd be here with you. He can stay with his sister as long as is necessary. I'll pick him up on the way back to school and we'll ride together the entire way."

"Well, I think you've pretty much worn out your welcome here, then," Grammy said. "Time to give him a call and get on the road again. Time to make those dreams you've been having become a reality."

"But what about you?"

"What about me? I'll be fine. Hildy's just a little worried that she's getting old. All of this really has nothing to do with me. She can't deal with the fact that she's getting old, so she has to project all that worry onto me. I'll be fine. Me and Ruby Ann will do just fine here by ourselves."

"Ruby Ann?"

"My memories," Grammy said and pointed to her head. "And the cookbook. We'll be just fine."

George

George was sitting on the curb outside his sister's house in Hartford, with his jacket wrapped tightly around him, when I turned the corner and pulled up to the house. At 5:00 A.M. we thought it best not to be honking the horn or ringing the doorbell and waking up George's five nieces and nephews.

"Hey, sport," he said as he threw his suitcase into the backseat of the car and stepped inside where the heater had warmed the car up comfortably. "I really appreciate you letting me hitch a ride back to L.A. with you."

"Don't mention it," I said as I put the car into drive and pulled out of the city limits of Hartford. I was having a hard time controlling my breathing. "How was your visit with your sister?"

"It was good. Nice to see the whole family together again. But I must say we're leaving not a moment too soon."

I laughed. "Funny how that happens with families."

"They were great. Just way too many of them to handle all at once. And they're so loud. I'm not used to babies crying and kids screaming and adults yelling to be heard over the kids and babies."

"When we're not around it all the time, it's easy to forget how busy and loud life can be. Makes us appreciate the peace and calm of our own lives, doesn't it?"

"Yes, that it does. So tell me, how was your visit with your grand-mother? Is she doing better now?"

"It was fine. Yes, she's doing better now. She wasn't really that bad to begin with. Seems my senile Auntie is the one who really needs to be put into a home. She's having a difficult time growing old. At eighty-three you'd think she'd be used to it by now, but apparently she isn't. Anyway, Grammy is doing just fine. Old, but she's still got her wits about her and she's developed quite a sense of humor over the last couple of years, which is really nice."

"That's wonderful, Erique," George said and patted my shoulder. "It's nice to see that you got along so well. I know how apprehensive you were about seeing her again."

"Yeah, that was my own silly insecurities showing through. Grammy was great, actually. We really got close these last couple of weeks. I'm going to miss her."

"Well, anytime you wanna come back for a visit, you can count on me to keep you company. I really shouldn't be such a stranger to Katy and the kids, either."

"Really? I'd love the company next time I drive out here."

"Good!"

We made small talk and took turns driving for the next several hundred miles. When we reached Cincinnati, we decided to call it a night. Finding a hotel in Cincinnati was much easier than it was in Salt Lake City on the previous trip, and we took separate rooms. George paid for my room, as a token of his thanks for bringing him along.

The rooms were large and spacious, and I found myself lost in the king-size bed. I watched a little television, then switched it off and tried to get some sleep. It was useless. I tossed and turned for over an hour, and then decided I needed a little sleeping aid.

I reached into my suitcase and pulled out the porn video I'd brought on the trip with me, then walked over to the television and popped it in the VCR that was built into the television set. I walked back and dropped sullenly into bed. In the suitcase was the dildo Rodney and I sometimes used to spice up our sex life, and I pulled it out and laid it next to me on the bed. My cock got hard instantly as my hand wrapped around the thick rubber dick, and I sighed as I watched a scene in the video and lubed up my own fat cock.

I hadn't come in three days, and my body tingled as I slid my hand slowly up and down my throbbing cock. Sometimes I liked to beat off for quite a while before shooting my load, but I knew I wouldn't be able to now, so I grabbed the dildo next to me and lubed it up. On the video, a cop handcuffed a young man and was in the middle of frisking him, pulling the younger man's hard cock out and sucking on it as he did. The boy was helpless, and I sighed deeply as I watched my favorite scene and moved the dildo to my ass. The cop in the video plowed the young man, and I slowly slid the thick rubber cock up my ass as I imagined myself being bound and fucked by the older, sexy policeman.

I shoved all nine inches of the dick up my ass, and shuddered as the rubber balls reached my ass cheeks. I had to remove my hand from my own dick, because my balls tightened and I felt my load start to build already, with just the pleasure of my ass being speared and spread wide open. The volume on the video was a little low, so I grabbed the remote and turned it up a little, allowing me to hear the moans and groans of the cop and the kid who had been stopped for speeding.

Already at the end of the scene, the cop pulled his big dick out of the boy's ass and shot a huge load all across the back of the blond young man's back, whose hands were still handcuffed behind him. I wrapped my hand around my own cock and squeezed as I watched the bound speeder shoot his load all over the cop's car door. The dildo in my ass worked its magic, and it only took a few strokes of my hand on my own cock before I came all over myself.

Once I came, the pleasure of the big dildo inside me quickly turned to pain, and I pulled it out of my ass slowly. I caught my breath for a moment, letting the cum dry on my chest and stomach, and then rolled over and fell asleep.

That night when I dreamed, I dreamed of being a policeman. I didn't have nearly the thrills the cop in the video had, but I was at peace with myself and happy in the dream. Grammy would have been pleased.

The next day we drove through the Midwest. Anyone who has driven through the Midwest knows that it takes six years, four months, and eighteen days to drive through the five or so states between Ohio and Colorado. Okay, so actually it only took somewhere in the neighborhood of sixteen hours. But it seemed a hell of a lot longer than that. By the time we reached Denver, we were exhausted.

I insisted on paying for my own room, and George took the room directly next door from mine. Sleep came much easier that night, and I was out before my head hit the pillow.

I was sound asleep in my own room when I was suddenly awakened by a noise in the kitchen. Sometimes older houses creak a lot, and when Rodney and I first moved into this house, I was constantly spooked by the noises it made. But that was three years ago, and I had long since grown accustomed to those creaks and moans. The noise that startled me from my light sleep was not the house. It sounded like someone stubbing his foot on the kitchen table. A moment later I heard it again, and this time, heard a distinct whispered curse.

"Shit," I said and sat up in bed. Someone was in my house. Ever since I was six years old and my family came home from vacation to find our house robbed, I have been scared to death of burglars. Of course, as a young gay boy, I had always had sexual fantasies about it also, but right now I was scared shitless. I could think of nothing except being killed by an over-adrenalined masked burglar. I looked around the room quickly to see if there was anything I could use as a weapon, but couldn't see anything. And even if I'd found something, I wouldn't have known how to use it.

I heard a noise right outside my bedroom door, and quickly lay back down, pulling the covers over my shoulder as I did. Maybe if I pretended to be asleep, he wouldn't hurt me. I didn't care if he took everything I owned, as long as he didn't hurt me. I heard the bedroom door open slowly and closed my eyes tightly, barely able to breathe.

The intruder worked his way slowly across the room until he was standing directly next to my side of the bed. My heart was racing and I thought I was going to piss myself as he leaned down to see if I was really asleep. I tried to pattern my breathing to what I thought was a normal sleep pattern as his face got within inches of mine. My eyes were too tightly closed, but I couldn't loosen them any, and hoped it was too dark for him to see how tightly shut they were. That would be a dead giveaway.

He seemed to be satisfied, because he stood up and moved over to the dresser, where I heard him shuffling through drawers and putting some of my things into a bag. He was being very careful, but I could hear him putting my watch and some other things into what was most likely a canvas bag. Then I heard shuffling of clothes. I spend a lot of money on my clothes, and tried hard not to grind my teeth as I imagined him shoving my Tommy Hilfiger and Calvin Kleins into his stash of my belongings. It took all I had not to jump up, throw my hands on my hips and demand that he release my Tommys and leave my house immediately. Instead, I just prayed that meant he was almost finished.

I heard a soft thud and realized he had dropped the heavy bag onto the carpeted floor. Why would he drop his stash, I wondered as my heartbeat raced toward the ceiling. Surely he wasn't leaving it behind. He wouldn't have gone through this much trouble of breaking in and searching out my expensive clothes and jewelry and then just leave without a good reason.

I felt, more than heard, him approach my side of the bed again. He pulled something out of his pocket and once again leaned down close to my face. From this close I could smell the bourbon on his breath and feel the warmth of it as it brushed against my cheeks. I was lying on my side and I felt a tear roll down my cheek.

He leaned to within an inch of my left ear and whispered huskily, "Keep your eyes closed until I'm finished and I won't hurt you."

I sobbed openly but quietly, and kept my eyes closed as he tied first a blindfold across my eyes, and then my hands to the headboard posts. As many times as I'd fantasized about being bound and forced to let my aggressor have his way with me, I have to admit this wasn't doing a lot for me at the moment. I heard him undressing himself, and then felt the covers jerked from my body and thrown to the floor. I shivered as the cold air in the bedroom hit my naked body. Being tied and blindfolded was bad enough, but naked and shivering in the cold was worse, especially when I couldn't see anything. Did I look good, or was my dick all shriveled and my muscles weak and wimpy as I lay bound and exposed on the four-poster bed?

I felt the intruder climb onto the bed with me and take my chin in his hand. It was strong and forceful, but not painful. He caressed my chin as he leaned in closer to my face.

"I won't hurt you, as long as you do as I say." I could tell he was disguising his voice. "Is that clear?"

"Yes," I sobbed, and nodded my head.

He leaned down, and with my chin still in his hand, lightly kissed me on the mouth. He licked the tears that were falling onto my lips, and then kissed me fully and tenderly on the lips. His tongue darted slowly in and out of my mouth, his lips pressed tightly against mine.

His hands moved from my face down my chest and directly to my nipples. He pinched them softly and I felt my cock stir despite my fear and the cold air in the room. He moved his mouth from mine and I felt an emptiness on my lips as his kisses trailed down to take the place of his hands on my nipples. His lips encircled my hard nipples and his tongue skated across them, making them cold and warm at the same time.

I moaned softly and felt betrayed as I felt more blood surge into my rapidly engorging dick. My hips gyrated and inched forward on their own will.

"You want more?" the husky voice asked. Again I smelled the faint trace of bourbon, and this time I wanted to drink it in as well.

"Mmm-hmm," I moaned again, and before I could even finish my response, I felt the intruder move his body around until his hips were a few inches above my blindfolded face. I could smell the clean musky scent of his crotch, and knew it was close, but couldn't see it because of my blindfold. My heart was racing still, but from anticipation rather than fear, now.

"Do you want me?"

"Yes," I whispered and strained to raise my head to meet his unseen cock. I felt his body rise, to keep my mouth from reaching his dick.

"What do you want?" that husky, deeply exciting voice asked.

"I want you."

"You want this?" he asked and lowered his hip to my face. I felt his thick cock lie still slightly soft but getting harder by the second, on my lips.

"Yes," I said, and licked the head with my outstretched tongue. It was salty and slick and sticky and sweet, all at the same time.

I opened my mouth and my intruder slid his dick slowly inside. I closed my lips around it and sucked slowly as it got fully hard. It was long, and very thick with throbbing veins running the length of it. The skin felt soft and silky as it slid along my tongue. He began to thrust it deeper into my mouth, and before long, had all nine inches buried deep down my throat. I gagged slightly when it was first buried, but quickly adjusted to the girth, and swallowed it all. I could feel the thick meat throbbing against *my throat muscles as my burglar moaned in delight when my tonsils danced around his big dick.*

I felt him thrusting a little hard and tasted a few big drops of his pre-cum slide down my throat and knew he was getting close to shooting. I was looking forward to a large load of his cum shooting hot down my throat when he began to slowly pull his huge dick from my mouth. I tightened my grip on his cock with my lips, not wanting to let go, but he pulled all the way out and left the heavy weight of his mammoth cock lying on my mouth and nose.

"Don't stop," I pleaded. "I want to taste you."

Just then the phone rang. I woke up and answered it. It was a wrong number. I cursed the caller as I hung up the phone. My cock was fully hard now, and there was no way I was going to fall back asleep until it got taken care of.

I opened the double doors to the balcony and stepped outside.

It was then that I saw him. His patio was a few feet from my own, to the left. It was dark outside, but several candles were set on the ledge of the balcony and cast an orange glow onto the surface. He was sitting in a deck chair, leaning back so that his face was hidden in the shadows but his outstretched body was in plain sight. Completely naked, his smooth copper skin reflected beautifully in the candlelight. His long muscular legs stretched out several feet in front of him. The twin mounds of his pecs were capped with tiny brown nipples, and surrounded by silky blond chest hairs. His washboard abs were hard and defined. His bellybutton bordered on being an "outie" and trapped a few drops of sweat that trickled down from his ripped, hairy torso.

A thick trail of short, blond curly hair trailed from his bellybutton and down to his bushy pubic hair. His long, thick uncut cock laid limp over the top of his huge, shaved balls.

Then I realized that if I could see him so clearly, that he could probably see me just as well. That was all I needed, for him to know that I was secretly spying on him during his private time. I stepped back and hid behind the curtain on the balcony door.

On the balcony next door, George reached down and tugged lightly at his heavy cock. A few seconds later the shaft began to get hard, and the shiny head peeked out from under the thin, silky foreskin. With his other hand he cupped his balls, and rolled them lovingly across his palm. He leaned his head back and rolled it back and forth as he moaned with delight while he tugged on his balls and cock.

I watched the long dark cock grow harder and fatter as the hand with long thick fingers squeezed it and rolled the foreskin up and down the length of the shaft. Huge veins bulged from the big dick, and a clear drop of precum peeked out of the head and slid slowly down the fat shaft.

I craned my neck and tried to get a look at his face. I wanted to see those sparkling blue eyes, that strong chin and jawline, those cavernous dimples. But it was still completely hidden in the shadows of the night. And even the candles were beginning to flicker low. Soon they would be out completely, and I would be denied the beautiful sight before me. I reached over and turned on my balcony light, hoping it wouldn't scare him away.

The glow was dim, but it did light enough of both balconies to see the show even better than before. I could now see that the man on the chair only a few feet from my own balcony was wearing a baseball cap. But he kept his head tilted down so that I couldn't see his face, regardless of how hard I tried.

Then he let go of the hand holding his smooth balls, and motioned for me to move out from behind the curtains.

I stepped out on the patio, and walked over to the short wall that separated our balconies. It was finally time for me to come face-to-face with the man of my dreams, and I was aroused before the first breath of cool wind whispered against my warm skin. My hard cock bounced up and down eagerly several inches in front of me. It was nowhere near as big as George's, but still I was proud of how engorged and ready it looked. I reached down and stroked myself as I watched him do the same. After a couple of minutes, I sucked one of my fingers into my mouth, then slid it down between my ass cheeks. Without hesitation I shoved my finger into my ass while I slid my other hand up and down the length of my cock. I had apparently decided now was not the time to be shy.

He motioned for me to turn around. At first I was hesitant, because if I did, then I wouldn't be able to continue watching him stroke his own huge cock. Instead, I'd be forced to look out at the black night that was on the other side of my balcony. Then the light went on in my head, and I realized why he wanted me to turn around. I quickly did as I removed my finger from my ass.

A moment later I felt his warm, soft breath whisping against my twitching hole. He blew on it for a second or two, and then his tongue licked up and down between the smooth globes of my ass. I sighed loudly as he lapped at my butt, and before I'd had a chance to collect my breath, his tongue slid slowly all the way inside my ass. I moaned even louder, and felt the muscles of my butt devour his tongue.

I wanted it to go on like that forever, but knew it would not. If he kept this up, I would shoot my load all over the stucco siding of the balcony before I had a chance to warn him. I was not ready to let my first session with George end in premature ejaculation.

"Fuck me," I moaned with animal lust.

He pulled his tongue out of my tight hole, and grabbed one hard cheek in each hand as he kneaded and massaged my ass. A moment later I felt the hot head of his thick cock press against my still twitching hole. It felt exactly like I knew it would. I'd dreamed about it so many times, and now it was really happening. I heard him spit, and a second later felt the warm slimy saliva land on my ass and slide between my exposed hole and his fat cock head. Then he pushed forward, and slid all the way into me in one slow but deliberate stroke.

I squealed as I felt inch after inch of his hot thick cock spear my ass, spreading the muscles inside me as it went deeper and deeper. When his pubic hairs tickled my cheeks and his heavy swinging balls bumped my upper leg, I squeezed his cock with my ass muscles and moaned loudly as I felt it grow thicker inside me in response.

I really can't remember whether he started shoving himself in and out of my ass or whether I was the one who slid up and down the huge length of his massive pole. But it didn't matter. In seconds, we were fucking wildly, and our moans mingled with the chirping of the crickets and the sound of the wind brushing against the big trees several feet from us.

"Shit, man," I gasped hoarsely, "I'm gonna come."

"Me, too," George said as he pumped faster and deeper inside me.

"Fuuuuuucccckkk," I grunted as I sprayed my load all over the short wall in front of me. Several shots spewed from my cock, and I was surprised at the force of my orgasm.

Then, without warning, he pulled himself out of my ass in one quick motion, leaving me tingling and empty. A second later I felt the thick, warm jets of his load land all over my back and ass. His load was incredibly thick and hot, and seemed to last forever. The first few shots were already dripping down my ribs and landing on the floor below as he continued shooting more and more of the sticky spunk onto my quivering body.

Suddenly there was a knock at the door. "Erique," I heard George's voice from the other side of the door.

The guy behind me quickly retreated and I heard the sliding glass doors to his room shut and lock.

What was going on here, I asked myself. How could that not have been George who'd just fucked me? Then I realized that George had taken the room directly to my right, not my left.

"Erique, are you all right?"

"Yes," I croaked. "Just a minute." I frantically searched for some clothes to throw on, but George's knocks became more persistent. Finally, I went to the door completely naked, and stood behind it as I inched it open just enough to see George's face. "What is it, George?"

"I heard your phone ring and then some strange noises. It sounded like you were hurt. Are you all right?"

"Yes, I'm fine. I was just . . . dreaming," I said, painfully aware of my throbbing erection bumping against the cold wooden door.

"May I come in, Erique? I'd like to speak with you."

"Right now, George? I don't think this is a great time. It's three o'clock in the morning."

"Yes, I know. But this really can't wait anymore. Please?"

"Well, all right," I said as I stood back and opened the door. "Forgive me, but I sleep in the nude, and I couldn't find my shorts before."

"That's quite all right," George said softly. I noticed he was looking my body over. "Actually, it's very nice."

I blushed, and reached down to retrieve my shorts.

"Please don't," George said. "Stay like that for a few minutes more."

"What?" I asked, dangling my shorts from my fingers.

"I want to look at you naked for a while."

"George, what are you saying?"

"I'm saying that I can't get enough of you. I haven't thought about a single other thing since you dropped me off at my sister's a couple of weeks ago. I know this is completely out of line, and I should be ashamed of myself. But I think I'm in love with you, Erique. I know it's wrong and I should be ashamed of myself and that Rodney would just kill me, but . . ."

"Shh," I dropped my shorts back to the floor and walked over to him. "It's okay, George. I love you, too. I haven't been able to think or dream about anyone but you since the moment I laid eyes on you. And I don't care who knows it."

"But what about Rodney?"

"Rodney's a big boy. He'll get over it. He knows what he and I had wasn't real. It wasn't forever. He'll understand."

"I don't think so. He can have a bad temper, and he really holds a grudge. And even if he doesn't get mad, he will certainly be hurt. He loves you, Erique."

"And I love him too, George. But I'm not *in* love with him. What you and I have is different. I love you, and you love me. And I am in love with you," I said as I leaned against him and kissed him.

"I know, Erique, and I'm in love with you too," he said as he returned my kiss and laid me gently on the bed.

Living the Bad Boy Dreams

It never turns out exactly the way we think it will, does it? Except that in this case, it did. Every since I was a child I'd dreamed of falling in love with an older man. Someone who could teach me things I didn't already know, take me to places I hadn't already been, show me things I hadn't already seen. And George did exactly that.

The drive from Denver to Berkeley went by much faster than the first two thirds of the drive. We took turns driving and cuddled in one another's arms. We drew more than a couple of odd stares from other travelers who shared the highways with us. We told one another our deepest secrets, our hopes and dreams. It was like we were two teenagers on our first date. At every gas station stop we sneaked into the rest room for a little hanky-panky.

Rodney, of course, was livid when I returned to Berkeley and announced that I was transferring to UCLA so that I could live with the man of my dreams. His father.

"You have got to be fucking kidding me!" he yelled at me.

"Come on, Rodney," I said. "You have to know that this hasn't been working out between us for quite some time now."

"No, I don't have to know that. I think it has been working out just fine between us. I should have realized you were into older men when you started fucking all your professors. I just can't believe you're going to leave me for my father."

"I'm not really leaving you for anyone, Rodney. We never officially said we were ever a couple."

"So we never exchanged rings. That doesn't mean shit, Erique, and you know it. We've been together for the last two years. We've shared everything. You can't just throw that all away."

"I really don't understand why all of this is coming as such a surprise to you, Rodney. I've gone out with other guys in the last two years and so have you."

"Yeah," he said as he slumped onto the sofa. "But we've always come back home to each other. We never spent the night with anyone else. If that's not commitment, then I don't know what is."

"I'm sorry, Rodney," I said as I tried to hug him. "But all my life I've dreamed of finding that one special man."

"And I thought you had," Rodney said as he pushed me away from him. "I thought I was him."

"I never said or did anything to give you that impression. I've always told you that I needed and wanted more."

"Yeah, and I thought you were giving me the opportunity to become that person who could give you more. I thought that's what we were doing together. I thought that was the whole point of us being together. I had no idea you'd go behind my back and look for that special man in my father."

"I had no idea, either," I said. "And I didn't go behind your back and do anything. Remember, it was your idea that your father come with me. Yours and your mom's. I didn't even want to do it."

"Exactly. Come *with* you, not come *on* you! I should have known that you, of all people, wouldn't be able to know the difference."

"Stop being childish, Rodney. You're not making any of this any easier."

"Oh, I'm sorry. Was that what I was supposed to be doing? Making all of this just a little bit easier for you and my father?"

"Well . . . yes. We were kind of hoping you would."

"Fuck you, Erique. And fuck my father, too. Oh, yeah, that's right . . . you already have. Fuck you, Erique. Fuck both of you!"

For a couple of years he avoided both of us altogether. He didn't invite me to his graduation, nor did he come to mine the next year. When he eventually started calling to speak with his dad, he was a living deep freeze to me if I answered the phone. Little by little he began to warm up to us, though.

A year after his graduation he fell in love and moved in with the man of his own dreams. Victor was a sophomore at Berkeley and a philosophy major. Eventually he won Rodney's heart, and soon after, Rodney forgave and accepted George and me for doing the same.

Now we laugh at family gatherings when I refer to Rodney as my stepson.

George is as big a dreamer as I am. We dream of traveling the world arm in arm. We dream of growing old together. We dream of loving one another for eternity. We dream of helping raise George's grandkids.

When I got the call last week that Grammy had died, George and Rodney both quickly agreed to come home with me. George even agreed to flying on a plane. He says that if we're really going to travel around the world, like we keep talking about doing, then he'd better get used to flying.

They've been a great support for me, and are quick to know when I need a moment to myself. Right now they are outside bonding on the front porch while I pack the last of Grammy's clothes into the big wooden trunk.

In the back corner of the trunk is a book. I finger the leather cover for a few moments, and then open it and slowly read Grammy's journal from her college days.

She is like a soft rose petal, blowing sweetly through the wind. Her laughter floats all around me like a buoy atop a gently tossed sea. Her smile lights up the air like a beacon guiding a lost ship to shore. Her eyes sparkle when she's around me, and I can't help but smile when she enters the room. I cannot imagine life without her.

Ours is a forbidden love, but that cannot diminish our desire for one another. From the moment I was a baby girl my mother taught me to dream big. Never to let the world tell me what was mine, what I could and could not do. I've always relied on my dreams to get me through each day. And now all my dreams are centered around Ruby Ann. I never dreamed my life would be centered around another woman, but there are some things we cannot control. Together we will make a life filled with love and hope and dreams.

I want to shout it from the rooftops that I love this woman with all my heart and soul and mind. I want everyone to know my love and desire for her are boundless. But she has begged me not to. She has asked me to keep it between ourselves, at least for now. Someday soon we will be together forever, but for now we must keep our forbidden love a secret to the world. She is the sensible, as well as the beautiful, one in this relationship. I love her all the more for that. I will do it for her, but it will not be easy.

There are page after page of passages like that. Passages of my Grammy's proclaimed love for her secret lover. Of her unbridled dreams and hopes for a future filled with love and devotion and acceptance. Two years worth of entries of unrequieted love and adoration.

And then it suddenly stops. Halfway through the bound leather book, the writing simply stops. The pages are now dotted with dried yellowish spots which could not be mistaken for anything but decades-old tears. A couple of times it looks like Grammy tried to write something, but the entries were just scribbles, really. And then more tears.

My own tears fall down my cheeks as I realize that my mother never knew her own. She grew up believing her mother never dreamed of anything at all. Never knew the power and the beauty of dreams. How she must have tormented herself wondering where she had gotten her powerful gift of dreams when her own mother didn't have the capacity to dream at all. How much easier and more fulfilled her life would have been had she been able to share that unique gift with Grammy.

And then I smile as I realize that my mom is finally getting to know her own mother. They are together in heaven, laughing about the good times and forgetting about the bad. They are sharing their dreams with one another. And looking down on me and making sure I'm living mine.

I flip through to the end of the book, just to make sure I don't miss anything, and am surprised to find one final entry on the very last page of the book.

Erique,

Don't ever stop dreaming. Don't let anyone tell you your dreams are childish or silly or stupid. They are all we have, and when we realize this and allow them to become our realities, we truly live for the first time.

I allowed my dreams to die, and I stifled your mother's dreams as well. And I did my damn best to kill your dreams, too. But you never let me. You are a good boy, with Good Boy Dreams. Make them happen for you. Don't let anyone tell you they are wrong.

Live your dreams, Erique. And when those dreams with George are real, dream more dreams. Bigger and better dreams. They will always be there for us as long as we believe in them. Don't ever stop believing in your dreams, Kiko. They are all we have.

—Grammy

I wiped the tears from my eyes and tucked the book under my arms, then walked out and joined George and Rodney on the front porch. I had a lot of dreaming to do, after all, and a lot of living to do. They weren't going to get done by sitting alone in Grammy's bedroom, looking through her memories.

About the Author

Sean Wolfe has been writing since high school. But his professional writing career didn't begin until 1998 when his first erotic short story was published in *Men* magazine. Since then Sean has had over 50 short stories published in *Men, Freshmen, Playguy, Honcho, Inches, Latin Inches,* and *Mandate* magazines. Several of his short stories have been included in the erotic anthologies *Friction (volumes 3, 4, 5, 6), Best of Friction, Twink, My First Time volume 3,* and *Three The Hard Way.* Sean was also the porn video reviewer for Torso magazine.

Despite his extensive sex writing, Sean insists he is not a sex maniac, and spends much of his free time trying to convince others of that fact. So far he has not been very successful.

Sean's first novella, *Bradon's Bite,* was included in *Masters of Midnight,* published by Kensington Publications in 2003. *Bad Boy Dreams* is Sean's second novella, and is included in *Man of My Dreams.* His third novella, *Bloodlines,* is another vampire piece, and is scheduled for release in October 2004.

Sean lives in Denver, Colorado, where he holds down a day job as Volunteer Coordinator for Colorado AIDS Project.